Black Boogiemen

Black Boogiemen

∞

To Jeff Henderson,
(Honor in spirit)
A truly inspirational Brother!

Tallis Piaget

Library of Congress Control Number:		2011910875
ISBN:	Hardcover	978-1-4628-9534-2
	Softcover	978-1-4628-9533-5
	Ebook	978-1-4628-9535-9

To order additional copies of this book, contact:
Xlibris Corporation
1-888-795-4274
www.Xlibris.com
Orders@xlibris.com
98967

Contents

Prologue

"WHO WOULD HAVE ever thought that couples, living in the rich suburb of Ladue County, would fight to get their kids into inner-city schools?" Roy asked Ms. Fox with a smile. The question was more rhetorical than anything.

Ms. Fox continued her work of reviewing student applications. She looked up from her reading and eyed Mr. Roy McCausland then stated, "There are even some of the really wealthy parents trying to offer donations." She said "donations" with an air quote. She continued, "But we know these are old-fashioned bribes. Well, this isn't Yale, Harvard, or any of the other Ivy League schools, and your child isn't guaranteed entrance merely because you can afford a gymnasium."

Ms. Fox looked over more student applications then said to Superintendent Roy, "You know there are even parents threatening to file suit."

"File suit!" Roy shot back. "Why, when . . . What is this about!"

"Calm down," Ms. Fox said with a laugh, "it's absolutely nothing that will stick. We have some parents claiming reverse racism."

"Are you serious?" Roy started. "I can't believe that. Now that is funny. Once again I say, who would have thought wealthy white folks would actually want to fight, literally, to get their kids into the inner-city St. Louis school district? We owe Dr. Branch so much gratitude."

Superintendent Roy McCausland and Principal Peggy Fox were camped in her office. Her office resided on the top floor of a long rectangular three-story building. It was a nice office – lots of floor space, a fine leather seat, and a black oak desk with a couple of matching oak bookshelves. She had her credentials behind her hanging on the wall, all encased in black oak frames. She had portraits of all of her American heroes elaborately placed throughout the office, a few being MLK, Abe Lincoln, and Obama. The picture that was most grand and the only other item within an oak frame was the picture of Dr. Trenton Branch. He sat in a typical CEO pose clad in a fine business suit; the painting was astounding. That was the first thing one saw when entering her office. She also kept numerous commendations and awards around the office. This woman was beyond proud of her school and wasn't ashamed to show it.

Superintendent Roy, which he liked being called, worked from Peggy's office more than his own. He enjoyed this particular school most. No confusion, he was elated and proud of all of his schools, but this was his favorite. The building she resided in was once used as a magnet school by the name of Classical Jr. Academy on the west side of the city. That was the first school to undergo the profound change that affected the entire St. Louis community. The year was 2025 and a lot had changed.

If one remembers the start of the year 2010, the black American reputation was not the best. Though most would like to think that America had evolved by then, that was certainly not the case. Racism wasn't running rampant, yet the negative stereotypes of black America were still pretty consistent. There was one major difference though: white America could no longer be considered the major culprits portraying the wrong ideas of their black neighbors. Black America put a horrible face on itself and continually perpetuated the negative stereotypes.

The country would have its few black individuals that succeeded in rare fashion, a lot coming from extremely meager backgrounds. These were affluent black people, working extremely hard to change the identity crisis of their ethnic group, always to no avail. For every black stockbroker, black doctor, or black executive, there was a sea of black people choosing the wrong path. For every one black kid that graduated from Yale or Harvard, there were hundreds behind bars. For every black man that passed the bar exam, there were many more selling drugs and gangbanging. So no matter how hard one black person fought to succeed, hoping his success would prove to America that, "We all aren't the typical nigga," there were thousands more saying, "Yes, we are, and we love being that typical nigga." In turn, America's idea of black people never changed. Yet far more disturbing, black America's opinion of itself never changed. Even after electing the first black president to the United States, most blacks were still in a rut and blamed everything and everyone for their condition except the man in the mirror. When told to look inward, the messenger would be ostracized and considered an Uncle Tom.

By the year 2025, everything was completely different. No longer was it assumed that blacks were intellectually inferior. No longer were black men seen on cop shows comically running from the police. No longer were inner-city public schools last on the list of academic excellence. Actually, the inner-city public school's scores were higher than most predominately white private schools, and the inner-city private schools were in a league of their own. No school from ninth to twelfth grade could match the curriculum or student academics one received at an inner-city private school. The kids that graduated from these schools were guaranteed a full ride to any college of their choice. With extreme academic illumination and many other changes, the black population viewed themselves in a new light, and it caused a love of self. With that newfound love of self came the admiration and love from all other cultures.

Black America in the year 2025 was a part of mainstream America, and they were considered great leaders and a people anyone would be lucky to have in their corner. There were less than 7 percent of black people incarcerated, extremely rare cases of black teenage pregnancy, and hardcore drugs were unacceptable in black neighborhoods. Education thrived in the black community throughout America. With that education, a surplus of support, and high expectations came opportunity which was followed by success.

One may ask what transpired, what caused this evolution of cultural growth on an exponential level. The answer cannot be summed up simply. There was no evolution. There was a revolution, and what some may call a civil war. So sit back and enjoy the ride. Maybe this story is more prophetic than fiction.

2010

D R. TRENTON BRANCH was an analytical protein biochemist. He earned his undergraduate degree from the University of Missouri at Rolla (UMR) and his graduate degrees from Washington University. He was born and raised in the heart of St. Louis City. His upbringing came from his grandmother like most black youth during the seventies and eighties. He came from extremely meager standings, some nights crying himself to sleep because of an empty stomach. His grandmother being old fashioned never asked anyone for help, even when it was sorely needed – old-fashioned values. He learned at a young age to toil for any and everything one could want in life. Though his childhood was poor, it did not lack the love and encouragement that all children need. His grandmother worked her entire life. She taught him the value of a hard work ethic. She relayed to him the idea of putting God first and all else would fall into place.

During his youth, he was never unhappy about their situation because he was never really aware of people doing better. He was raised on blacksploitation television, *Good Times*, *What's Happening*, *Sanford and Son*, etc., which infused the idea of all black people being poor . . . He accepted his situation as universal.

With the help of his outdated school books and poor teaching, he never believed that all men were equal and capable of many feats. He was only shown the great works of white America, he was only taught about the wowing accomplishments of the Romans, Greeks, and other Europeans. In his mind, they were superior in all aspects. It wasn't until he was accepted to UMR that he began educating himself on true black history. As far as his previous outdated books were concerned, the only black people worthy of acknowledgment were MLK and Frederick Douglass, and even those passages were brief nondescriptive paragraphs. Nothing compared to the pages and pages on George Washington, Abe Lincoln, Alexander the Great, Caesar, and so many other of history's legends. So once Trenton began to open other non-schoolwork-related material, he learned the true history behind his people. He explored African history and their accomplishments as well as their many contributions to the world. Then he learned of great black American heroes. The ideas of Daniel Hale Williams, George Washington Carver, and Garrett Morgan encouraged Trenton to reach for the stars. Those unspoken heroes ignited in Trenton a drive unparalleled. Although he was the only black person in most of his college classes surrounded by wealthy white kids, he excelled without any assistance.

After receiving his PhD, he landed a job at a major pharmaceutical company and began making some good money. He moved out of his one-bedroom apartment in the city and relocated to the suburbs. He chose to live in a neighborhood that was pretty diverse. The ratio seemed to be fifty-fifty (black to white). He realized his mind-set had changed and expanded dramatically, while the rest of his inner-city neighbors remained the same. They lacked interest among other issues, and Trenton wanted to be around those that thought like him, regardless of their race. At age twenty-nine, he found a woman he instantly fell in love with, and they were married by the time he was thirty. He had his first and only child and could not have been happier with his life. He acquired much success with his career and flourished. All the while he was growing, he saw the city degrading. He would visit his grandmother on occasions, seeing the same associates he grew up with in the same spots. He actually lost a number of dear friends to murder, drug overdoses, and outrageous jail sentences. His old chums that were still around hadn't changed to him one bit. Most of them were still living with their mothers, unemployed, or just doing bad. No drive. Trenton pitied no one and accepted no sob stories. He believed that they all came from the same place with the same lack of opportunity. He made it just fine, so anyone could was his belief. One just needed determination, drive and a serious work ethic.

As he neared forty, his life only got better. He often asked his grandmother to come live with him and his wife in one of the wealthiest counties in St. Louis, which she refused every time. This was her house and she wasn't leaving it was the typical response she gave her son. He explained how horrible her neighborhood had gotten. And it was going to continue to get worse was his story. She didn't care. She would tell him to keep providing a nurse to help her around the house, and she would be just fine. As more time passed, he really hated visiting the city. He hated seeing his people in the condition they were in; even worse, he hated the idea that they enjoyed wallowing in the muck. His visits became less and less frequent. Then the change of his life occurred, which initiated a chain of events that caused the entire black population to reinvent themselves.

On May 21, 2010, he visited his grandmother at her home. She was doing as fine as expected for an eighty-two-year-old woman. Trenton, his wife Christine, and their son Travis were all sitting at the kitchen table in Mother Branch's home, when Travis asked to go outside to play with some of the other kids. Trenton walked to the front door, peered out, and saw a group of kids approximately his son's age. He then told his son to have a ball but don't wander too far from the front of the house. Travis happily obliged. He ran out and quickly joined whatever game was being played by the band of kids. Trenton and his wife continued their conversation with Mother Branch, laughing every time she confessed to not understanding the young generation with their drugs, saggy britches, lack of respect, and laziness. She would then explain how in her time those kids and parents alike would starve or either be shunned because of their worthless activities. She continued by denigrating the girls, saying all they want to do is have babies by any man just for a welfare check. Then she would ask Trenton, "What's wrong with 'em, boy?"

His answer was always the same. With a chuckle, he would respond, "I don't know, Grandma."

Then she would finish as usual and tell him how proud she was of him and how glad she was that he didn't end up like old so-and-so (either one of his many good-for-nothing childhood friends). He would smile, give her all the credit, and continue laughing. He didn't visit as often as he should, but he always loved seeing his grandmother.

Everything transpired as usual when all of a sudden, they all heard a series of loud bangs. For about three seconds, there seemed to be a constant rally of gunfire. After the first sound, Trenton was on his feet running toward the front door. The gunshots didn't scare him much; neither did they frighten the grandmother. Growing up in the ghetto, one gets acclimated to the sound of firearms, but he had to be sure Travis was safe. After the gunshots, he then heard tires peal rubber on the asphalt and an engine roar as a vehicle plowed down the street. He ran to the front door, pushed it open, and leapt down the steps. He looked to his left then his right and calmed once he saw the little kids standing around. He slowed his pace and started walking toward the group to inquire about the gunshots. To his dismay, as he approached, he saw the kids all in a circle looking down. His heart began to bang louder than any gunshot in his ears as he approached and realized his son was not a part of that circle. When he closed in on the circle of little ones, he realized why Travis was not visible. His son lay in the middle of the group with all of the kids gawking at him, with gaping mouths and wide eyes. Trenton ran to the spot on the sidewalk and slowly shoved a couple of kids out of his way. That's when all logic left him, and emotion took control. What he saw resided in his head for the rest of his life. His first sight was of his son sprawled on the ground, with his head moving from side to side, coughing up blood. He screamed to the little kids, "BACK UP, BACK UP, GIVE HIM AIR!"

Trenton quickly lowered to his knees. By this time, Christine was looking out the door and ascertained the situation. She ran to his side, and Trenton yelled at her, "Go back to the house and call the ambulance." When he saw that she didn't or couldn't move, he yelled even louder "NOW!"

Trenton scanned his son's body, too terrified to touch him in fear of making a terrible situation a lot worse. There was so much blood covering the boy's shirt he didn't know where the entry point could be. Trenton slowly lifted his son's shirt and saw a massive hole squirting blood all over his hands. The red fluid diffused from the center of his son's sternum at an alarming rate. He had to keep face and be brave for his boy. He looked in his son's eyes, which were streaming with tears, and told him to be still. He then told his ten-year-old son that he had to press down on the wound. He timidly covered the wound with both hands, but the blood flow did not falter. There was so much life fluid spilling. His son muttered, "D-a-d-d-y," in a mixture of cough, cry, and belch.

Trenton told his son, "Don't speak, baby. Daddy's here. I got you, boy."

Trenton used all of his manly power to hold back the waterworks waiting in his tear ducts. He held the palm of his hand over the massive wound all the while watching the tears stream from his son's eyes and blood and spittle leaving his son's mouth. By this time, a larger crowd was appearing. Trenton didn't notice.

Then his son tried to speak once more, "Daaa, Daaa, Daaa . . .," the last unpronounced word coming in a gurgling rasp, announcing the departure of his son's soul. Trenton just sat in the same position, still trying to cover the wound. He saw what just happened but couldn't budge. He continued to stare into his son's eyes, which were absolutely lifeless now. He couldn't look away nor could he say or do anything. He was stuck, stunned, and bewildered. His wife's scream woke him up. Christine ran and dropped to her knees on the other side of their son and grabbed the lifeless body and brought it to her bosom. Blood was everywhere.

Moments later, sirens could be heard. The crowd that had assembled parted to allow room for the ambulance and police, which happened to both show up at the same time. The first responders immediately assessed the situation and ran for the boy. They tried to gently pry the lifeless kid away from his mother to no avail. Trenton finally grabbed some of his old logic and told his wife to give Travis to him. She slowly relinquished her grip, and Trenton passed his son to the paramedics. The guy and girl team laid the boy on the stretcher softly and, after checking for vitals, tried resuscitation. Trenton held his wife as she sobbed, screamed, and wailed in his chest. He watched the responders do their best to save his son, but he knew success was not an option. He watched his son's soul leave the shell that lay on that stretcher.

The police came and cleared the scene. They put the yellow tape all around the perimeter, and a couple of officers approached Trenton and Christine. Once they got close enough, Trenton could see that one of the officers was an old childhood friend.

"I am so sorry, Trenton," he said. "I know this is a horrible time, but I have to ask you some questions."

Trenton, now in a daze and really in a dream state, just nodded to his old friend.

The Hate

THE IDEA OF these creatures, supposed human beings so lost of heart, so void of conscience. These wretched souls that spit on the gifts that life has bestowed. I cannot share the same blood as them, God, please tell me I am more. I have learned to hate my own people . . . These ideas, along with others far worse, filled Trenton's mind as he peered down at his son in the casket. He held his wife tightly to his chest and tried his best to console an inconsolable woman. He shed not one tear during the funeral. All cried out.

They shut the casket one last time, and Trenton watched the caretakers lower his boy's coffin into a perfectly dug rectangle and could only think of the size. Why did they need such a big hole for such a small casket? He wiped that thought away from his mind then squeezed his wife. This was the worst time in his life. He logically assumed that his wife was in no better shape. She certainly seemed on the verge of dehydration from a constant stream of tears. She really hadn't stopped crying since the first day the murder occurred. The fact that the police never caught the culprit really didn't help. That lingering situation just made the entire ordeal more painful. The senselessness of it all.

Their only child wiped off the face of the planet. He finally shook his head and kindly tugged his wife while backing away from the scene. Trenton, so engrossed with his negative thoughts, was totally oblivious to how much time had passed. Trenton's best friend, Manno Gully, his freshman-year roommate at UMR, was one of the few people still at the burial. Manno walked up and put a hand on Trenton's shoulder then softly spoke.

"If you ever need anything . . . anything, Trent, just let me know." Manno's eyes were bloodshot, but the tears were gone.

"No doubt," came a programmed answer from Trenton. His mind was elsewhere. There was so much anger building. The sadness was gone and was replaced with rage. With that rage came hatred, and those emotions combined caused dark ideas to run through Trenton's mind – ideas and images that his polite mind conjured for the first time ever. Trenton was no saint, he certainly was no killer either, but his present ideas would have disputed that fact. What he wanted to do to every inner-city thug . . . no . . . to every inner-city dreg crossed the lines of sanity. He just wanted to hunt every one of them down then filet 'em . . . kill 'em. Really dark thoughts pervaded his psyche as he watched chunks of mud cover his son's casket.

"Why aren't you talking to me?" his wife asked. "It's been seven months, and you've said less than seven sentences to me. I am hurt too, but I am trying to move on. I need you, Trenton." Christine was crying, not sobbing, tears merely gleamed in her eyes, and a few trickled down her cheeks. "I need you to move with me."

Trenton stared at his wife, really eyeing her like she was a pest. He didn't intend to have that look, he just couldn't remove it. "I am here, Christine. You got me. What do you mean you need me?" he finished, giving the impression that she sounded insane.

She dropped her head and shook it from side to side, then she slowly raised her gaze to meet his, speaking, "Something's got you, but it certainly isn't me, Trent. First off, since when have you called me by my full name? You used to call me pet names or one of the cute forms of Christine. Now you're calling me Christine? And every time you say my name now, you sound like a stranger. You are not here . . . and I don't have you, Trent. But I want you, babe, yet I can't wait for you forever. You have to remember, you are not alone in this."

Trenton was not in the mood for her bitching at the moment. His mind was rationalizing one of the many philosophical reasons for righteous murder. That's all he could think of lately along with the ways how. Yet he went to work and maintained an extremely fake façade of contentment while there. His coworkers all knew what happened to his son, but no one would have believed such a horrid thing occurred by his corporate demeanor. He still behaved the same way he did prior to his one month of bereavement absence.

He couldn't hide his pain and anger at home though. Christine caught the brunt of it, expressed through extreme distance. He said nothing to her; barely acknowledged her when she said something to him. He hadn't touched her or shown any affection since the funeral. Anytime he did say something to her, it was short or argumentative. Though he knew the aforementioned to be true, he couldn't stop himself from responding harshly. "Are you serious? You are fussing at me about calling you, your name . . . I don't have time for this shit," he shot at her. His wife broke down with some serious crying and stormed off. He went to his computer room and read more stories from city papers. He truly didn't care anymore.

He incessantly thought of vengeance of the worst kind. He consumed himself with the news, local and national (what occurred overseas didn't concern him). He filled himself with news from differing black neighborhoods. He studied all American news, yet he focused on black newspaper articles primarily. He began analyzing every bit of text regarding black debauchery. After he found his trend, he began performing tons of research. All of the research dealt with the crime increase in black neighborhoods. He studied the crime rate, but he more so focused on the murders. He noticed that there were always so many murders in such a small area. He asked himself what was the cause.

Is poverty the reason the black population would turn toward murder? He threw that notion out of the window immediately. He researched numerous cities and districts. He delved deep into the different economies and found white cities down south living in equally poor (if not poorer) conditions. The one thing that the poor shared was their affinity for highly addictive and dangerous drugs. Trenton could understand the reason for high drug use in poorer areas. The answer being very simple: the folks wanted an escape from their seemingly worthless position. With the drugs and lack of funds to support those drug habits came more theft (even that was far more aggressive in poor black areas). Poverty also attributed to higher dropout rates, higher teen pregnancy rates, and a higher percentage of children being born to unwed parents. The poor shared a lot of negative trends whether they were black, white, red, or yellow, but the pervasive anomaly in the poor black neighborhoods was the exorbitant murder rate. This disrespect for life, this lack of understanding of an important fact: you can steal a person's belongings and you can always give it back, yet if you steal a man's life, it can never be returned.

Another theory Trenton concluded was the idea of a bad apple syndrome. Every citizen within these violent neighborhoods wasn't a criminal. In all actuality, most inner-city dwellers were law-abiding people and just wanted to live their lives. Yet most of these people would live in fear because of the few in the neighborhood who didn't share this civilized sentiment. A few of the fearful were kids too scared to take certain routes to school, people too terrified to leave their homes after a certain time, witnesses too intimidated to help authorities solve crimes, and much more. This fear and intimidation was all caused by a few punks roaming the "set". If someone could just clear the city of these purveyors of crime, then the resulting situation would have to be a peaceful neighborhood. That last thought made Trenton think of his favorite superhero, Batman. He loved the idea of Batman: a person void of alien abilities or mutant powers yet acquiring the responsibility of cleaning an entire city. Trenton laughed at the thought of himself prancing around in tights and a Halloween mask. Even with Batman, Gotham was still plagued with violence and criminal activity, so being a vigilante wouldn't complete the true task at hand. What was the task? He asked himself. His answer – to clean up the black neighborhoods. Yeah, that was the job before him.

"I am willing to take on that responsibility," he said to himself alone in his office. The question he then asked was how.

Trenton shut down his computer and rose from his chair. His eyes were heavy from lack of sleep, and staring at the computer screen didn't help. He said aloud, "I guess I have to become Batmanesk." He laughed while leaving his computer room. He walked to his bedroom and lay flat on his back in the bed. His wife was already snoring; obviously, she had taken her sleeping pill/pills. Trenton's head hit the pillow, his eyes shut, and he slept instantly.

He was dreaming, at least Trenton believed he was dreaming because he stood on his grandmother's rooftop watching his son Travis play with his peers. Trenton wore black tights with a black mask. He lifted his arms to see nylon wings attached, connecting to his waist. It was nighttime, and each streetlight was malfunctioning, causing spells of complete darkness. The only source of consistent illumination came from nearby homes and the full moon, yet the kids had no trouble playing tag. The children all ran aimlessly having fun, when all of a sudden, a dark figure appeared next to the group. Trenton knew this was all wrong, so he instantly leapt from the roof, unconcerned with the drop. As he slowly fell to the earth, the dark figure approached Travis and drew a large Desert Eagle from his trench coat. He stood point-blank range upon the small boy and lifted his gaze to meet Trenton's. Trenton continued to fall ever so slowly to the ground, wondering why he felt so featherlike.

He should have landed and had time to reach this dark stranger before it confronted his son. Trenton then realized he couldn't change destiny. There was no saving his son. So Trenton kept his eyes on the dark figure, which after closer inspection showed a face with empty eye orbitals – black holes where the eyes should have been. No eyes must've meant this guy had no soul. The dark figure kept an empty socket gaze on Trenton, almost as if he was toying with him. Then a flash of light streaked from the barrel followed by a crack of thunder that sounded all too distant and all too real. His son's chest and back exploded in a spray of blood, flesh, and bone. Trenton finally touched down. He ran to his son, only to see him take his last gurgling breath. Trenton turned left then right, looking for the murderer, not noticing that the kids were gone. He caught slight movement going around the corner of a nearby house. Trenton darted in that direction, moving like a superhero ought to with wings fluttering after each beat of his arms. He turned the corner and could see the guy about ten yards ahead of him. The guy wore black saggy pants and a long black T-shirt (which was weird because before the murder, he wore nothing but a long black trench coat). Trenton caught up with the guy in no time. He somersaulted, landing right in front of his prey. The dark figure drew his weapon, only to have Trenton knock it out of his hands with a reflexive swipe. Trenton then grabbed the murderer and threw him to the ground. He hopped on the stranger's chest and started punching the eyeless face ferociously. He jabbed furiously with both hands while keeping his weight on the culprit. Because the murderer's arms were pinned, he could do nothing but catch each blow squarely to the head. Blood sprayed in all directions. His son's murderer was soon obviously dead, but Trenton continued bashing and hammering away. He wouldn't stop until this guy's face was one with the concrete. This was the first time Trenton had dreamed about catching his son's killer, and he was going to take full advantage. Trenton smiled contently as his own face became covered in blood from the backsplash of his furious punches. The metallic taste of the red goo that landed on Trenton's lips only made him grin wider. He never imagined he would be so happy while committing such a horrible act. He then realized this act wasn't horrible at all, it was needed. He was ensuring that this soulless dark figure would never hurt another child again.

Trenton popped up. It was daylight, and he could feel the smile he still held on his face. His wife was gone. Maybe working, but it was Saturday. Maybe shopping, but that wasn't her typical routine. Maybe she was with another man, good for her. He was happy for the first time since his son's murder. He finally understood what must be done. He would save the black population in this country. He would take on that responsibility, and he had a plan. This city doesn't need a batman; it needs a thousand Batmen, maybe tens of thousands. As he contemplated that idea, he rose from his bed and walked to the bathroom for his daily routine. He would clean himself up and go right up a protocol. He knew what the city needed, and he was just the man to initiate it.

He heard Christine open the front door. She was finally home. She had been gone all day. She walked past his office and stepped in softly, trying not to disturb him. He turned and smiled at his wife for the first time in seven months. Her eyes widened at the amazing response he gave her. She apparently expected him to ignore her as usual or snap at her with vitriolic words. The smile actually startled her. He rose from his computer and walked to his wife. She was stunning. She was a petite yet vivacious black woman with a tight belly and caramel skin. She appeared as though she had been to the beauty shop all day. Her hair was shiny and hung just below her shoulders. Her toenails glistened, matching her fingers, and she smelled of honey. He hadn't seen his wife in months. He knew she was present, but he hadn't truly seen her. He had forgotten how much he appreciated his wife and remembered that he needed her more than anything else in this miserable world.

After slowly approaching Christine, Trenton hugged her, and at first she stood with her arms at her sides. She was too shocked to respond, but she acquiesced and slowly lifted her arms to his side. She hugged him back hard. He kissed her softly while looking into her eyes without a word. He then swept her up in his arms like a newlywed bride and carried her to the bedroom. No kid around, so no need to shut the bedroom door. He undressed his wife while caressing and rubbing every inch of her body, then removed his clothes and made passionate love to his better half.

After the love making session, Christine asked, "I am certainly not complaining, sweetheart, but what just happened?"

"I had an epiphany, babe, and with that came a glimmer of joy," he responded, "and with that joy came the knowledge of my horrid neglect for the one person that truly loves me. I hope and pray that you can forgive me, babe, because I have some plans I want to put into motion, and I will need you to back me. I will need you to be here for me because I have some long nights ahead."

"What are you planning, sweetie? I mean what has gotten you so upbeat all of a sudden?"

He replied, "Well, my love, I'm going to make sure that no other family will ever have to face the pain we faced, nor will any child experience a senseless death ever again."

"And how do you plan to do that?" she asked, sounding like a child.

"I tell you what, you don't worry about that. Just know that I have something in store for these murdering thugs, and life is going to change drastically for the black community," he finished.

After that night, Trenton and his wife were on far better terms, and she couldn't have been happier. He spoke to her and took her places like he used to, and life seemed like it was going back to some sign of normalcy. The only thing that left her feeling a little uncomfortable was the fact that he forbade her to search his computer. She didn't like that he kept secrets, but if that secret left him happy and soothed their relationship, then so be it.

The Organization

TRENTON PRINTED FLYERS. The pages were not elaborate, but they were meant to catch the eye. The title, written in large, bold lettering, simply stated, FATHERS THAT LOST A CHILD. The words where covered in a gunshot design he found online, so each word held bullet holes. Underneath the title, the message became more apparent. The flyer asked, "Did you have a child that was a victim of murder?" The rest of the flyer then explained that a support group was starting for fathers of kids that were killed by violence. It was very simple and direct.

Trenton woke early one Sunday and traveled from church to church within the inner city. While at the different churches, he asked the pastors if he could hang his flyers. After they saw the message, they all said yes. The first part of his plan was coming together.

The night of the event arrived. He rented out the veterans' hall and stocked it with finger food, soda, snacks, and water. The hall was very quaint, merely a very small square building with a few tables and a microphone inside of a podium that stood in front. Each table had its own set of treats so the visitors would not have to move. It was seven o'clock (starting time), and he was still alone. He checked a copy of the flyer to make sure that the place and time wasn't ambiguous. After rereading the flyer for the thousandth time, he felt a little let down. For some reason, Trenton expected a nice turnout . . . maybe he was wrong.

He should have known; most black men are too proud to join a support group. The black man's idea of receiving mental help is akin to showing weakness. If they only knew that this particular therapy group was destined to be so much more than just a bunch of guys talking and crying in a circle. Then something happened that lifted Trenton's spirit.

Someone walked through the door. He was a nerdy-looking fellow, short, bald, big belly, ebony skin, and glasses. He wore high-water pants and a checker-patterned shirt tucked inside the tight khakis. Trenton thought to himself, "I expected a much better turnout." Then a couple more black men walked in, followed by a few stragglers. Trenton stood at the podium and gave each stranger a hearty hello as they stepped in. He waited a few more minutes then decided to lock the doors twenty minutes after the starting time. He didn't want them to be disturbed once the operation began. He also wanted others to learn that his function will always start promptly and not on CP time. The tables didn't fill up, but he had at least fifteen brothers waiting on him. They all looked skeptical and not in the mood for whatever was about to occur. Most of the guys just appeared upset about being reminded of their dead children. Trenton didn't want to waste their time, so he commenced with their first session.

"Hello, gentlemen, I will get us started. First off, I know this isn't an easy subject, and I also know that we brothers aren't big on the mental help thing. You all know what I mean: sitting in circles, singing Kum-bay-ya, crying on each others' shoulders, letting out your feelings until we all have some type of breakthrough . . . Ain't that type of meeting.

"I put this little thing together to encourage brothers to not let go of the rage that comes with a murdered child. Actually bathe in it, let it build, then when you feel as though you are about to burst with raw, white hatred, that is exactly what you do."

The listeners within the hall looked amazed at Trenton's introduction; it wasn't what they expected at all. From that moment forward, he had their undivided attention, and he didn't waste time. He jumped right into the heart of the reasoning behind his meeting.

"This meeting is for fathers of young men or women that were murdered senselessly. I did not start this function to help you cope with your negative emotions. Instead, I am here to help you remember the anger and rage you once felt and help you focus those powerful emotions into a laser beam. Then use that laser-like focus for a common task. What task? You may ask yourselves. Well, we will get to that later. Let's get to know one another first. I plan on taking all of you on a journey of unbelievable proportions, but we first must get to know each other and learn to trust one another. First I say if none of you brothers are willing to take this journey, I think you should leave now." The men looked around the room, not one of them willing to leave with such a beginning.

Trenton didn't have any words planned or written. He was shooting from the cuff and was amazed as the right words seemed to fall from his mouth almost perfectly. He was actually impressed by the response all the men gave him. He could feel that they were already hanging on every word. He could see in the men's eyes that they were waiting to hear something different. He himself wanted to hear something different than the typical moral or religious platitudes, (e.g., everything happens for a reason, God has a master plan, your child is rejoicing in heaven safe and sound). All of that crap meant nothing to a man built on logic. He needed to hear that he wasn't alone, and something could be done; he needed to feel that justice is truly being lashed out against the criminals. Those ideas and feelings are what he wanted to give to these men, and it seemed as though they all were very receptive. He continued.

"Though this team of men we have here and this meeting will be totally different than all others, we will initiate this meeting in the typical fashion. Which means we will all introduce ourselves and give a brief description of their child's murder. I, of course, will begin."

"I am Dr. Trenton Branch. I am a PhD scientist. I work for a pharmaceutical company. I am married, with *no* children now. I live in the suburbs, but my grandmother lives in the heart of the ghetto. You brothers know Evans Street and Whittier Ave.? Well, that was my old stomping ground, and that is where my grandmother lives to this day. Anyway, to make a very long story short, while visiting my grandmother almost a year ago . . ." Trenton began to grind his teeth, and his eyes almost got watery. He continued after a few seconds, "My ten-year-old son was gunned down by some gangbanger. He was an innocent bystander that got caught during a drive-by. Wrong place at the wrong time is the cliché I have heard every cop use. They never found the killer. I can go on and on about the incident for the entire scene is etched into my psyche. Whenever I close my eyes, my mind replays the event over and over. But to go through the gory details serves no purpose. So that is my story. I long to hear you brothers tell your stories. I long to get to know you all. And most of all, I long to take you all on a journey of purpose . . .," he teased his audience. "Once again, I get ahead of myself. I keep throwing out hints of what's to come, but that is for a later date, when we all have proven that we can trust each other . . . not only with our lives, but also with our dark secrets. Anyway, let's continue; I pass the platform over to the gentleman right there," he finished.

Trenton pointed at a tall thin black guy with dark-rimmed glasses over dark eyes, matching his dark skin. He wore navy slacks, white shirt, a tie to blend the ensemble, and a pair of Stacy Adams. The clean-cut gentleman looked startled at the prompting but obliged without complaint. He started with a slight southern twang, "Hello, all, my name is Marcus Huggs. I am originally from Nashville, Tennessee, but I have been in St. Louis for the last twenty years of my life. I was married, recently divorced. Our marriage couldn't survive the . . ." Marcus looked away from everyone's eyes for a moment then continued, "Our marriage couldn't survive the death of my little girl. Being totally honest, since moving from Tennessee, I stayed out of St. Louis City. I had been around young angry brothers before, but the breed up here was just a li'l bit angrier than what I saw down south. Anyway, whenever I traveled through the city, it was for a purpose, hopefully a quick purpose. I ain't one to be around a bunch of silly niggas. Well, one day, I had an overwhelming taste for some soul food. Good Southern-style cooking is hard to find up here especially in the burbs. I don't think collard greens and pinto beans are high on Chad and Buffy's eating list." The men chuckled at Marcus's joke, and he continued, "So I decided to visit one of the soul food joints a brother from my gig told me about. He gave me the directions; he added that I should only go during the day. It was called Sarah Lou's." Marcus could hear the sounds of the men remembering the place well and the great food that place offered. After the murmuring ceased, Marcus continued, "This place was on the corner of Sarah and St. Louis Avenue. When I got there, I knew it was one of the hot parts of the hood. I could feel it. I hate being around a bunch of niggas . . . Anyway, I rode down there with my little girl; she was just eight years old. I parked my car and got out. She got out . . ." Marcus smiled, remembering his little girl. He could see that she was totally oblivious to the environment. She had been raised in Clayton, a very safe suburb, so she was unaware of the many crimes going on right in front of her eyes. Marcus could pick out every wrongdoing happening as they walked from the car to the restaurant: a lady hooking on the corner, a guy smoking crack between two houses, a drug deal going on a few yards away, a group of young punks blasting the music from their car loud enough to wake the dead, little kids roaming the area totally unattended, and refuse and trash all over. Oh well . . . he figured they would make their visit a very short one. Marcus removed the thoughts from his head then continued his story.

"I go into the place and give my order. The service was atrocious as usual; the lady spoke to me like it was a bother to actually take my order. Y'all know how that is. Anyway, we hear arguing, loudly from right outside the place. My girl jumps on a stool to look out the window to see what's happening . . ." He paused a little longer this time. After he composed himself, he continued, "Almost as soon as she jumps on the stool and puts her forehead to the window, gunshots ring out. Before I could make a move" – he cleared his throat of the lump that was forming – "my little frail girl is flying off the stool. She lands on her back, completely motionless. The left half of her face was gone. I could see brain. I could see into her nasal cavity. I could see bits of her skull."

Trenton first figured he should stop Marcus from going on with the gory details but remembered he wanted these guys to remember that pain. He wanted them to wallow in it, so it would be for the best to allow this man to continue conjuring up those horrid images.

Marcus was trailing off now. "They caught the guy. He had at least eight notches on his belt. And the only thing I could wonder was how in the hell is an animal like this not locked up behind bars or better yet just wiped off the face of the planet. Fucking rules and stupid fucking regulations, worthless fucking judicial system, worthless fucking penal system. Am I leaving anything out?"

Someone yelled out, "And worthless fucking niggas!"

That brought an unexpected smile to Marcus's face. He almost chuckled. "Hell yeah, how could I forget, and worthless fucking niggas. I could go on about how that whole ordeal ruined my marriage, my job, and my mind. But let's keep it brief."

"And let's keep it moving," Trenton jumped in. "Thank you, Marcus." He eyed another gentleman. "You, young man" – he pointed to the oldest-looking guy in the group – "tell us about your situation."

A light-skinned black man, short and stocky, stood at attention. His hair was mostly gray, but it was full. He stepped into an at ease stance, which made it obvious that this guy was a soldier. The retired marine gave his account. It was just as sad and horrible as the previous two. He was on leave, and a young thug attempted to jack his car while his kid was in the backseat. Before he could respond the thug opened fire. The first bullet only grazed the back of the driver's head, so he reflexively sped away. The car jacker continued firing leaving the car looking like swiss cheese. The marine lived, his boy died. The entire time he gave his account, he didn't break up at all – a true soldier. He did finish with something that Trenton enjoyed hearing, "While I was over abroad fighting foreigners for nothing, I should have been here fighting these scoundrels." His name was Deak Charleston.

The introductions and the depressing stories continued. Trenton was sure to take notes on each guy. He facilitated and kept the meeting proceeding smoothly. The stories began to coalesce into one big nightmare, and eventually, it sounded as though the guys were repeating the same thing over and over. Two and half hours later and no one was ready to leave. After the last guy finished his description, Trenton thanked everyone for coming and told them that there was a lot of work ahead. He closed the meeting, and they all left. The first night was a huge success in Trenton's eyes. These men all seemed intelligent and on the verge of insanity. Just the type of warriors he needed.

Trenton went home that night with a smile on his face. He felt crazy, being excited after hearing such tales of unnecessary violence. While in his car, he put in some Marvin Gaye, cranked the volume, and listened to "What's Going On." After a short drive, he pulled into his driveway and exited his car. His wife was opening the front door for him as he slammed his car door. He walked in, gave his wife a kiss, and told her that his plan was coming together. She wasn't sure what his plan was, but she really wasn't concerned. It was nice to see her husband with drive again as well as a bit of happiness.

Trenton and his wife had another pleasant night, and it seemed as though their marriage was no longer on rocky terms. He constantly explained to his wife about his prior bad mood and ensured her that it was long gone. They made love and slept throughout the night.

Trenton went to work the next day totally unfocused. He had other items that he felt took priority over his mandated experiments. He toyed in the lab briefly, but the bulk of his day was spent preparing for his next meeting. He would begin to lead these men toward his way of thinking, or he would weed out the guys who wouldn't agree. Regardless, he was going to build an army, and he needed extremely loyal soldiers for the task at hand.

Meeting Two
Meeting number two was at the same location. The original fifteen attendees were all waiting outside for Trenton this time, and they were all early. The men gave their greetings, and after he unlocked the door to the veterans' hall, they all entered. They had twenty minutes to spare and

Trenton was shocked at such an early arrival by each man. He was prepared to start early and delve right into his topic, but the door swung open and two more guys walked in. Because he removed all of his flyers the day after the first meeting, he wondered how the new participants learned of the meeting. He soon realized it was by word of mouth.

Tony Hall, one of the originals, a forty-year-old computer analyst, smiled as the two men entered the building. Tony motioned for the newcomers to join him at his table. Soon after, three more guys entered, then another three.

All together, Trenton counted another ten guys added on top of his original fifteen. He planned on getting on his soapbox and providing a small glimpse of his future goals for this group. But with the newcomers, he figured he would stick to the earlier format, allowing these men to tell their stories. Trenton noticed that talking about their children's death seemed to help connect the men on some level. They all carried themselves as strong black men, but it was apparent that they all needed to get this stuff off of their chest. The clock struck 7:08, and he locked the doors and started meeting number two.

"Gentlemen, I had planned on doing something a little different this meeting, but with the arrival of these new brothers, let's just replay last week. Are there any objections?"

No one said a word.

"All right, we will introduce ourselves. The original fifteen will follow my lead, but for the newcomers, please explain why you are here. My name is Trenton Branch, and I started this group. I had a son. He was ten when he was murdered by some gangbanger. I am making this very brief because we all spoke in depth about our children last week. This is how I want the rest of you guys to introduce yourselves. For the newcomers, I want you to talk as much as you like and explain the scenario as much as you deem necessary."

The original fifteen followed Trenton's lead by providing their names and then gave a sentence or two offering information on their lost children. Afterward, the newcomers opened up and expounded on gut-wrenching scenarios very much like what they all heard the week earlier. Again, all the stories began to mesh into one big nightmare. The brothers consoled one another and allowed each other to shed tears without fear of condemnation. The anger was apparent in these new guys as well as the original fifteen. It also seemed as though every tale of murder just enraged the whole lot of them. Trenton enjoyed this process. He wanted them all to be thoroughly immersed in their anger. With that anger, it was going to be a lot easier to convince them all to join him in his attempt to make this country a better place. Once again, the meeting lasted over two hours. After the final guy provided the group with his tale of a lost child, Trenton concluded the meeting.

Before dismissing everyone, Trenton said, "Guys, could you please keep this group to yourselves this time. I am not opposed to helping all that need it, but this group is going to be a lot more than just a sharing of lost children. We are also going to do some work. I have big plans for us and I have tons of information to provide, yet I will never have the time if the group keeps growing. I want the group to grow of course, but I first want to get some things started. All right all, have a safe night, and we will reconvene next week."

The men departed, and Trenton began to clean up. As he cleaned, the doors opened, and one of the gentlemen reentered. It was Mathew Korn. His story was one of the saddest. His little girl, thirteen at the time, was gang-raped by a bunch of young thugs then strangled to death. He was a cop, so the response was immediate. His fraternity of police canvassed the city streets till they found a suspect. After locating the seventeen-year-old suspect, he was interrogated (quite viciously). He gave up no one. The teenage boy took the blame for the entire ordeal, totally unafraid of spending the rest of his life behind bars. Mathew begged for the death penalty, but the system would not sentence a "minor" to death. It would sentence this "minor" to life behind bars, but not death. Mathew vowed to avenge his daughter one way or the other. With such a traumatic story, Trenton knew that Mathew was going to be a very important member of his team someday.

Mathew walked over while Trenton was wiping a table clean of debris. "You should have asked for help, brother. I guarantee we would have all stayed to help with the cleanup," Mathew said politely.

"Oh, no biggie, my friend," Trenton started. "After these meetings, I kind of enjoy the quiet time. It allows everything to sink in."

"I understand," Mathew responded. "Well, I don't want to hold you, Dr. Branch. I just wanted to say that I ain't been able to open up like that since . . . well, since ever. I don't know what you got going on here, but it seems like we all needed it. I hate being reminded of what happened to my daughter, but it is nice getting it off my chest, dude."

"I am glad, my friend. But this team just started, Mathew. We will be doing a lot more than just getting stuff off of our chests. We are going to take back our streets," Trenton said with absolute positivity.

"Is that what this group is about? Trying to take back our streets? How the hell do you plan on doing that? We been trying to do that for eons, we meaning the police," Mathew said, sounding genuinely curious.

"Well, you guys have rules. I plan on building something a little different, and I am going to need you. I need you all, but I am really going to need you, Mathew. Can I count on you, my friend?" Trenton asked while looking Mathew square in the eyes.

Mathew had only met this guy last week, yet for some reason, he couldn't deny him. He felt something coming from Trenton. Mathew couldn't discern whether the energy he felt was positive or negative, but he felt great power none the less. "Dr. Branch, you ask, and I will do whatever I can to help," Mathew replied.

Trenton nodded, "That's what I like to hear. Don't worry, brother. Our kids did not die in vain. If it took their deaths to force us men to act as we are supposed to then so be it. But things have to change, and the change starts with us, Brother Mathew."

Mathew liked this Trenton guy more and more. He helped Trenton with the final cleaning while making small talk. The men got to know each other a little more, and then they walked out to their cars together. They said their goodbyes, and both went home.

Trenton drove to his castle happy yet again. The meetings were going very well, and he couldn't have wished for a better group of men. Trenton arrived home and let himself in. His wife was walking down the steps in his blue polo oxford. The shirt was open, and she wore nothing but small panties underneath – a great end to a great day.

While walking to his wife's open arms, he thought about the best way to propose the colossal goal he had in store for his band of men. Trenton had already laid out the master plan in his head a long time ago – absolutely nothing on paper. No one would ever have proof of what was about to come.

Meeting Three

"How are you guys doing today?" Trenton greeted everyone. The group of twenty-five men were all accounted for and ready to roll promptly at seven o'clock. No one else entered or knocked after the starting time. Trenton heard a quick response of salutations from the gentlemen, and then he commenced.

There was a video curtain pulled down the wall behind Trenton. In front was a table holding a video prompter. Trenton had the specific cables running from the prompter to his laptop on the podium in front of him. He would persuade his audience to his way of thinking the best way he knew how – via a PowerPoint presentation. Trenton thought about just talking to the crew of men but remembered that pictures provoked more emotion as well as helped to convey one's ideas a little better. He turned on all of the gadgets; the computer screen glowed to life, and the projector showed what was on his laptop screen. He was ready to start with his presentation.

To the left and behind Trenton was a picture of a little handsome boy – thin but tall. The kid was in a baseball uniform posing for one of many photos that day. "This is my son," Trenton said without batting an eye. "He was gunned down by some unfound gangbanger. Do you see how I can tell you this without flinching? Because I no longer feel any sadness for the atrocity committed to my son. I feel nothing but anger. I want you gentlemen to join me in this shedding of the sadness. How many of you feel nothing but constant sadness right now raise your hands."

About five guys raised their hands.

"How many of you feel nothing?" Trenton asked the crowd.

About ten men raised their hands.

Finally Trenton asked, "How many of you are angry?"

Trenton counted seven.

"Well, the ones that are angry, I want you to hold onto that anger. You are going to need it for the goal at hand. Everyone else, I want you to get angry."

Trenton went on to explain his philosophy, "Sadness never accomplishes anything. It is an emotion we all feel, yet it is a worthless emotion, and apathy is its close cousin. Now . . . those are the two emotions to be expected after experiencing the death of a child, but they are by far the most useless emotions a man could experience. Sadness kept me in my underwear and in my house all day every day. I was disheveled and wreaked of week-old funk."

He continued explaining worthless emotions, "Apathy . . . I felt that too, gents. You begin to believe that an absence of all emotion is better than feeling the gut-wrenching sadness that has a hold of your soul. The problem with apathy is that some of us stay there for the rest of our lives. That is what makes apathy a horrible emotion. Once it is there, it can stay with you until death. It is hard to turn on emotions when they have been turned off for so long. The number one reason to remove apathy is that it is another useless emotion."

Trenton started connecting the dots, "Useless emotion . . . you are asking yourself what the hell am I talking about. What is a useless emotion as opposed to a useful one? OK, I will show and explain, gents."

"This is sadness," he tapped a key on the laptop and a white woman wrapped in covers on her bed popped on screen. A closer view of her face showed tears. "Look at her," Trenton started, "She's just lying there . . . no telling how long . . . doing nothing . . . just wasting her life away, crying." He tapped the button again. On screen came a transient lying on a park bench. "This is apathy," Trenton said, pointing at the bum. "This man has gotten to where he really doesn't care what happens to his life. He eats filth, and he craps in public." He pressed the button again. On screen showed a full view of a suicide note written by a man. "This guy is really sad. The note is poetic and literal at the same time. Who'd think that when a guy says he can't live without a woman, he really means it?" The next picture on screen was the writer of the suicide letter with his brains on the wall behind him, while he was slumped on a chair with half his face missing. "This is sadness. What a worthless emotion. Killing yourself is just weak. That is the ultimate failure. Unless you are dying slowly of cancer or something crazy, killing yourself because of one small moment in your life is asinine. Time goes on, but sadness will lead you to believe that time doesn't, that this is your only way out . . . worthless! I bet this chump could have found a better woman in a bar that same night. But will he ever find out?" Next picture . . . another bum. "This guy's wife divorced him and took the house. Instead of him moving on, he shut down and stopped caring about everything. Now he just exists on the street not caring whether he lives or dies . . . worthless!"

"Now don't get me wrong, we all feel both of these emotions at times. We are human, we are not automatons, but those emotions should reside in us for a very short period."

Trenton then switched gears, "I am not saying it's the best emotion, but if you got to feel any, let it be anger." Trenton could see some weird looks from the crowd. "I know," Trenton pacified, "anger is supposed to be a sin and can lead to some terrible consequences. Yet anger will get a person off of his or her butt. Anger causes action. There is no lying in bed when you are angry, you got too much energy you need to use. There is no killing yourself when you are angry. There are too many others needing to die. Anger leads to action." He hit the button. A band of men in white sheets and hoods marched down a dark southern road. "Now do these men look sad to you? Maybe they look depressed or apathetic," he paused for effect. "No . . . These men are angry, and they are focused. Now no one in this room likes what these men did with their anger, but we all know it got them out the damn bed." The next picture had the same sheeted and hooded individuals being chased in the opposite direction by a larger group of southern black men. "Now this is anger too. These black men were so enraged they joined and fought off the KKK in the middle of the fifties. That was unheard of. That was anger."

Next picture – a battered woman in her casket. "This woman just didn't care anymore. She was beaten so often that she went from sad to feeling nothing. Instead of anger or even fear, she stayed in this extremely abusive relationship until she was beaten to death." The next picture was split in half, one half being John Wayne Bobbitt, and the other, a penis pump. Before Trenton could say a word, the room roared with laughter. "I see you guys are getting my point," he said, laughing with the crowd. "Now this man's wife got very angry with him."

Next, Trenton showed more photos but without his commentary: there was a picture of Malcolm X marching with a bunch of men behind him. The next was another fifty-fifty split – the top picture was a depiction of the Boston tea party, while the bottom was the Boston massacre. Then came a picture of Moses slamming stone tablets to the ground with the background showing Jews worshipping a golden calf. The pictures kept coming till Trenton spoke again. "This is the last one," he stated then hit the proceed button. It was a painting of Noah's ark. "I don't know how many spiritual people we have here, but I am a believer. This is the ultimate reaction to anger – the destruction of all living things. I really want you all to take note here. God was doing what we will call cleaning house. I want you all to get use to that term because that is going to become our undercover mantra . . . cleaning house. But I digress. Bottom line, God destroyed the world not because he was sad or unhappy. He destroyed the world because he was angry. I say once more that anger moves one to serious action. So if you are feeling lost or sad, try to replace those worthless emotions with one of action. Fall into anger, my brethren."

The hall was completely silent as he concluded his presentation. Everyone present was beyond attentive. They had never heard such advice, and they hung on his every word. The men appeared to absorb Trenton's ideas without any disagreement or objections. Trenton knew that in order for his ultimate goals to reach fruition, he would need followers with no resignations. Not one man seemed to shy away from his teachings, allowing him to believe that they may follow him to his dark places.

"OK gents, unless there are any questions or comments, we can adjourn and reconvene next week," Trenton ended.

"Dr. Branch," one guy said, beginning a question. "That was real interesting, but what's the point? I love coming here to these . . . these . . . meetings, I guess, But I guess that is my question, where we going? You never said what we're here for." He continued, "Are we like a support group or like the 'Big Brothers,' a volunteering group, or a small church? Or are we just coming here to listen to you speak?" He quickly added, "Which I don't mind, 'cause you a bad cat on that mic. I can listen to you all day. I feel you big time; every word you say makes damn good sense to me, bruh. For real, man." He finished his accolades and asked, "So Dr. Branch, you just trying to bring some uplift to some broken brothas or what?"

The man with all the questions was Luke Chodi. He was a carpenter and had the physique of a laborer – broad shoulders, big arms, and a pot belly. He was tall, dark, and clean shaven.

"Well, first off, Luke, (Luke looked shocked hearing Dr. Branch address him by his name), you all are not *broken brothers*." Trenton continued, "You all are wonderful and strong brothers. We all have endured a serious crash course on pain in our lives; for no parent wants to bury his child. But I don't see one broken man in this room. If I did, I would remove him because the goal of this group is not fixing broken brothers. I brought you men here with me to make sure that no one else has to feel the pain of losing a child through senseless violence ever again in the black community."

"So that's what we doing, or that is our thing, we want to stop gang violence or stop the crime, something like that?" Luke asked again with a touch of condescension.

Trenton knew he had to tread carefully here because he couldn't lose Luke. He couldn't lose one man because that would encourage others to leave, and this plan of his would end before it started. So Trenton got on his soap box and spoke with the type of passion one only hears from supreme leaders, "Luke, my friend. I hear and understand your question, and I even hear the slight sarcasm in your tone. I am not offended because I understand what you are saying. This stop the violence, this war on drugs and war on gangs crap is a big joke. A lot of brothers and sisters have had negative incidents occur in their lives and tried to change the world with little to no effect. I have seen a number of societies and organizations burst open with grand ideas of affecting status quo, only to see those ideas and dreams squashed by status quo." Trenton looked down and took a deep breath then continued, "Well, that is because of the one major flaw each of these organizations possessed. They tried to tackle only one issue, maybe its drugs, maybe its gang violence, maybe its teen pregnancy, or even illiteracy in a country where information is a click away." Trenton paused again, slammed his fist on the podium in front of him, and started speaking strongly, "Well, that is not going to be us. We understand that all of those societal destroyers are all connected, and you cannot change one without changing the other."

Trenton continued speaking strongly, "We are at a time of decisions, my brothers. We are on a ledge, and I am ready to jump off into an open abyss. What I plan on creating is unheard of and has never been attempted. We twenty-six brothers will bring forth the renaissance that is sorely needed in the black American culture." Trenton was almost preaching now, "Like the Europeans during most of the past millennium dwelling in the dark ages, that is where we are now. It is time to wake our people up, and we twenty-six will bring the alarms my brothers. We will spark the black American renaissance." The men listened at the edge of their seats with faces all contorted in an expression of disbelief as Trenton continued, "I know that task sounds daunting. I know that the idea of affecting so many sounds crazy, but who would have thought that a thirty-six-year-old black man during the height of racial unrest could affect a world so? I'm talking about MLK here."

Trenton continued with the support, "Listen, guys . . . We are capable. I have the ideas. I have a massive group of real men using anger as a limitless source of power. If you all take me seriously and only if you all are willing to work your fingers to the bone will I be able to guarantee you success. We are going to do this. I just need to know if you guys are with me. Are you guys with me?" Trenton shouted the second time.

A resounding cacophony of "yes's," "I'm with you," "we got your back," and many other terms of agreement were yelled out along with claps, chants, and whistles. The hall only held twenty-six men, but from the outside, one would have thought a platoon of three hundred was in the small building. The men didn't know where this guy was going, but they wanted to be with him. Not one man in that hall could remember feeling so exhilarated. Every man wants to be a part of something monumental, but most never see the opportunity. The twenty-five men in that hall were on one accord, and all realized that Dr. Trenton Branch presented them with the chance to do something earth shattering, and for some reason, they believed him capable. The man exuded a can-do attitude matched by a powerful presence that none could deny. They wouldn't leave the group without at least knowing where he planned on taking them.

Luke, with his constant curiosity (Trenton thought he was going to have to start calling this guy Doubting Thomas), had one more question. "One final question, Dr. Branch, how do you plan on doing these things you talking about?"

"I have some serious plans as well as some serious planning to do, but I am not the only intelligent person here, so I also challenge you guys to think of ideas. Now that you know what this group is all about, think about what you would do if you could fix black America. Though every detail isn't prepared at the moment, Luke, I will tell you not to fret for there is a master plan," Trenton finished.

"Well, it don't matter to me, Dr. Branch. I'm in it for the long haul. Still really don't know what we doing, but if we can stop just one more kid from getting murdered, I'm in," Luke said with a wide grin.

Trenton spoke a little longer and allowed the guys to partake in manly discussions before saying, "Well, this was a damn good meeting, gents. Let's adjourn and reconvene next week. I will have more information to relay, so I hope you guys are retaining a little of this stuff," Trenton finished. "Have a great week, guys."

They all got up and left. Again, Mathew stayed behind to help clean and to converse with Trenton more.

"Dr. Branch, that was a very powerful presentation. I'm sure just like everybody else here, I don't know where you are going with all of this, but if you work as well as you speak, I think we might be in for a surprise," Mathew said. Mathew had a soothing demeanor about himself. He was tall and thin, though muscular if ever seen without his shirt. He was married with two boys at home. His middle kid, his daughter, had been murdered.

"I am very happy to hear that, Mathew. The goals I have planned for us will not be accomplished in a short time. So I need you guys to stay motivated and passionate, and if it takes some good words to move you, I will yell until my throat is bleeding, brother," Trenton joked.

"I hear you refer to your plans a lot. Are you going to let us in on any?" Mathew asked.

"Of course. This is as much your group as it is mine. I accept the role as the head and leader, but I am not king here. And I only take lead because someone has to. I also don't think anyone would ever try to implement the moves I have in store, Mathew," Trenton said.

"There we go again, that mystery. I hope you start filling us in soon," Mathew looked at Trenton seriously.

"Don't worry Mathew and enjoy the buildup while you can, because once the action starts, you won't have time to sleep, brother." Though Mathew chuckled at what seemed like a joke, Trenton said it without cracking a smile. Mathew stopped giggling after seeing Trenton's serious expression.

"Go home, Mathew. Enjoy your life because once the shit hits the fan, friend, your time will belong to this group. I expect much from all of you, but especially you," Trenton said with genuine care.

Mathew didn't leave; he continued helping Trenton with the final cleaning steps, and they walked out together. They said their farewells, and they both departed.

Meeting Four
"Good day, my fellow collaborators. Are we here to take on the world or what?" Trenton started this meeting with a little more gusto than the others. "OK, guys, I have some stats for you, followed by a couple of questions. I will talk of course, but the floor will be open for most of this meeting. Is that cool with you brothers?" Trenton asked. He got the answer he expected – no objections. "OK, let's get started."

Trenton used his laptop and projector for effect again as he spoke to the men. "Have you brothers seen the dark statistics on the black population? No pun intended. Well, they are atrocious, and what makes it worse is that they are not improving. Either the negative statistics are getting worse or just staying plain old bad. Are you all ready to hear these crazy stats?"

He started with the worst of all crimes, "First off, my ultimate hated crime, well I guess *our* ultimate hated crime . . . murder! Let's look at the places of the highest murder rates in this country." He pulled up a list of cities with the highest murder rates for the past ten years. The same cities were seen over and over. Sometimes, those popular cities ranked number one, sometimes, number ten. Regardless, the same cities stayed extremely dangerous. St. Louis was in the top five for the past ten years and won the gold twice.

Trenton explained the murder statistics further. "All of these murders were recorded in big/semi-big cities, but most of the action is generally focused in a small area, which makes the statistics a lot worse than what is actually documented."

Trenton then said, "I am quite sure that you guys know these cities, and I am also sure that you all know that the dangerous areas within these cities are predominantly black. That may not sound nice, but it is a fact. So I ask, really . . . what is causing this black-on-black killing at such an alarming rate?" (Someone raised a hand) "Oh don't answer yet. Let me finish this line of info, then we will have a discussion."

"Next up, teen pregnancy. Again, we take the gold there. Not saying other nationalities don't have their issues with pregnant teenage girls, but per capita, we win hands down. A lot of people never realize the serious trouble this causes. A child raising a child, how do any of you expect that to turn out?"

Trenton continued with his list of destructive statistics, "Robbery. Now this is touchy subject for me because we are labeled as the race that has the stickiest fingers. Though there is another race that wins in that area, thievery occurs so often in the black community that it isn't shunned. Robbing a man is even cool for some kids. And a lot of us have had a drug-addicted relative raised along side us in our homes; watching them steal whatever wasn't bolted to the floor. This also allowed thievery to become a societal norm within the black community. Well, it's not, and it should be condemned."

Trenton continued, "Incarceration . . ."

"Wait up, Dr. Branch," one of the guys in the crowd interrupted, "What race has the stickiest fingers? You can't just leave us hanging there."

Trenton answered the interrupter, "Well, let me answer your question with a question. What is worst, 1,000 kids of one race stealing 1,000 TV sets, or 1 man of another race stealing the pensions of 1,000 people? I guarantee you, the trifle crap that has been snatched by blacks isn't a drop in the bucket when compared to the real money white men have been stealing for centuries. Robbery is not an area we have conquered. The system may label us as a bunch of thieves, but that is absolute propaganda. The truth is, there is no better or greater thief than the white man. Eighty percent of America's wealth is in 1 percent of its citizen's pockets; go look at the recipients. Ha . . . if that isn't the result of some good ol' robbery, then I'm the fool."

The group all offered their agreement as he continued with his list, "Now where was I . . . oh yeah, incarceration . . . enough said." He glared at the men like that subject needed no clarification as he continued, "Next on the list of negative statistics . . . educational values. Absolutely poor. First off, America ranks seventeenth in science and twenty-fifth in math, and that is out of 34 countries. So America as a whole doesn't value a good education. America's disinterest in a good education compounded by the black youth's absolute spurning of intellect lowers the black school's statistics far worse."

Though the men hated to agree with Trenton, no one could disagree with the facts. He continued on to his next subject, "Next . . . unemployment; we wear the crown again. There is not one city in America where our employment rate exceeds our white brethren, which I think is attributed to the last negative statistic on my list . . . health. We tend to be more susceptible to strokes, cancer, and viral infections than the people living in third world countries."

Trenton put his hands on both sides of the podium and hung his head low. It appeared as though he had to hold himself steady by locking his arms in place. The information he just relayed weighed heavy on his soul, and the weight became quite palpable for a second. After that second, he looked up, eyes weary, with a distant look as though he had served time in some horrible war. And for the first time, the troops saw an exhausted leader. It was as though each one of the aforementioned calamities was a load on his shoulders, and speaking of them just added more weight. He gathered himself and began again.

"So," Trenton started, "why are we the worse in all categories? Especially the murdering, why are we taking the gold in most negative American societal stats?"

Trenton looked around at the attentive faces and provided their queue, "That is where you guys chime in."

Curtis Tarver raised his hand then stood. "I have an opinion," he started, "I believe it's all the music these kids are listening to now. I also think it's all of the TV too. All this music and TV is encouraging these kids to be what they are," The cable tech sat down with a look of satisfaction and pride, believing his answer was the correct one.

"OK, I will write that down," Trenton said while quickly scribbling a short version of what Curtis said on a broad pad standing on an easel. He wrote large enough so that all the men could see.

"I believe it's the system. I blame it on the system. The white man or the system, which is the same thing, be keeping us in chains. They charge us more for stuff we wanna buy, pay us less for any job we do. Demean most black men by putting some young white chump or blonde over us at work. They set up the hood so that the only thing these young cats out here think they can be is a ball player or a dope-dealing gangsta. It's the system, people," Ty Jackson, the physical therapist, concluded.

"Writing that down," Trenton quickly wrote under the first bullet, *the system.*

"Now we can stand here and squabble, my fellow gentlemen, but a wise man knows that history is the reason for all things," Malcolm Banks started, "The black American population lacks all essential cultural connections because of the slavery institution. We were stolen, put in bondage, robbed of culture, and mentally destroyed. This subsequent mass of the lost is what remains of what was once a noble tribe of people. You ask why are we the worst of the worst, Dr. Branch? I say the only undeniable, true and factual answer . . . slavery!" Malcolm Banks, a short, pudgy, dark-skinned guy balding with round-rimmed glasses was dressed in a buttoned oxford and khakis pulled just a tad too high. He was the perfect picture of what one thinks of when picturing a black nerd. He was an accountant and obviously a smart and poignant speaker.

Malcolm sat down to some hoots of agreements. No one stood nor said anything after him. After a few seconds of silence, someone yelled out, "Well, looks like we have ourselves a winner!" in a game show host's voice. The hall erupted in laughter.

"Very well said, Mr. Banks," Trenton said, "and I certainly wouldn't disagree with that," he stated while writing *slavery* on the list. "Well, I really can't disagree with any of your theories," Trenton continued. "The TV, the media are factors – serious factors when considering negative black behavior. The system, better yet, the white man's system has undoubtedly influenced the path of the black American culture." He paused while pointing at his pad then began again, "Then there is slavery. And whether slavery occurred 200 or 2,000 years ago, it is the worst institution a man can inflict on his brethren. There aren't many things out there more cruel than a slave master for he has deprived a man of his only true gift. The gift that all cognizant, sentient beings should possess . . .," he paused for effect, looked around the hall, and finished, "Freedom."

That was followed by a bunch of "yes, sirs" and other affirmations.

Trenton stayed on track, "The horrid treatment a slave receives leaves the victim physically broken and mentally destroyed – void of any real semblance of man." He shook his head while saying, "Slavery . . . uhn . . . uhn . . . uhn . . . now that is a good answer. With such a bad start, how can you expect a happy ending?"

Trenton then added his reason, "Why are we the worse in every category? If I could add one myself, I would like to add the crack epidemic. I am sure that if we all think back to black neighborhoods pre and post crack, we can see two totally different places. I am not saying the impoverished and poor black neighborhoods were pictures of a thriving mainstream America precrack, but I do know we weren't running around treating each other like animals. Yet one year after the introduction of that white chunk of evil, our neighborhoods turned to war zones. Everything changed: we began seeing our young boys easily pulled to the bosom of gang violence, we began to see groves of mothers and fathers falling prey to crack's relentless grasp, and that's when all of these negative statistics began to sky rocket. And those kids that were born of that crack era . . . we are dealing with them now."

Trenton prepared to take it home, making a connection to his original question, "I could go on forever about the detriment of the crack era, but I only wanted to add another to our list after slavery to show that there are numerous circumstances we could tally as answers to why we fail so."

While Trenton wrote crack on the easel, Ty Jackson chimed in, "You just brought up crack, and that just proves my point." Before Trenton could ask *what point,* Ty finished, "There's supposed to be some proof that the CIA shipped in over forty tons of cocaine to the inner cities of us black people. That proves that the system is the number one answer for our negative behavior, which proves my point," Ty sat back down, feeling superior.

Trenton smiled because Ty would help him make his point, "You could be right, Ty, maybe it is the system, but I ask one final question . . . so what?" Trenton said in a quizzical voice while shrugging his shoulders. He looked around the room at a lot of lost faces while waiting on a response. Then he repeated, "So what, Ty?"

Everyone slowly looked around at one another, hoping someone would have something to offer, when Anthum Williams, a martial arts instructor, said, "I don't think we all understand what you mean. What are you asking us?"

Trenton clarified, "OK, we just offered a lot of reasons why we believe our people are plighted . . . I ask, so what?"

Providing more clarity to his final question, Trenton went down the list again, "Number 1, most of our music is misogynistic and glorifies deplorable behavior. Why should that make us fall into traps? It's just music. Number 2, the system is trying to keep us down. So what? If it's obvious that the system is holding us down, when are we going to decide to live outside of the system? Number 3, slavery – that was over one hundred fifty years ago. How long are we going to use that as a crutch? Five hundred years from now, we could still throw slavery out there as a reason to be worthless. When will slavery be considered an excuse and no longer a reason for failure? I don't know if you guys know this but we are not the only people that experienced slavery. So I say . . . we were slaves once . . . So freaking what?"

Trenton continued on the same path, "When will these social woes no longer have an automatic connection to our pathological deviance? When will we stand up and say enough is enough?" By now, Trenton's voice was a tad louder, and with a bit of bass he called up from his diaphragm, he continued, "I ask you, Ty, so what if they ship in the drugs? Who said it's mandatory that we indulge? So what if they won't give us a job? We will make our own jobs. When we realize that we don't need the system, the system needs us." He calmed the level and tone of his voice to its typical speaking sound and finished, "So I ask again, so what? We need to start using these problems as stepping stones and not crutches, and that is what

I am here to encourage, my brothers. Please think about that. I no longer want you guys to ever accept anyone's reason why they are doing bad. If anyone offers you a sob story, tell them to convert it into a story of victory. Do you all catch my drift?" The men agreed yet again.

"All right, brothers, that's my time," Trenton said with sarcasm and a comic bow. After the applause ended, he asked, "Did anyone have anything they wanted to add?" After a couple of seconds of silence, Trenton then said, "No takers, OK, I will see you all next week, my friends. Keep it safe, keep it secret." Trenton smiled as everyone began to pile up at the door.

Another night ended well. He could see that the men were just as ready as he to make a difference. Affecting one's community is something simple. Anyone can do it. It just takes courage and typically involves greatly changing a conventional method. He and his compatriots were about to make some drastic changes to the community and make a big difference.

Black Boogiemen:

Approximately Ten Meetings After the First

THOUGH TRENTON WAS glad to see that all twenty-five men were on time, his grimace was solemn. There was a quiet ruckus of prattling, but once the clock struck seven, the room fell silent. Everyone expected Trenton to start on time as usual. He didn't. He merely sat in his chair in front of the hall with everyone staring at him. He posed motionless in his seat with his legs crossed and his hands folded atop his knees. His head was slightly angled downward as though he was praying, and his eyes held a vacant gaze. No one was willing to break his trance so five minutes went by with the hall in complete silence. They all just waited for Trenton to open the floor. Though no words were uttered, everyone could discern the difference in the atmosphere. There seemed to be a heavy weight inside the hall, and everyone felt it. Finally Trenton stood and approached the podium.

"OK, men, we have been meeting for a while. We have gotten to know one another quite well, and it is now time to truly come together as one. It is time to coalesce as a true faction, as a true unit. And the organization we start here will be bigger than anything any of you have ever seen."

Trenton continued to boast about what the future held, "What we start today will affect the country more than any election. The group that starts here will be more powerful than the police force, yet more covert than the CIA. This organization will free more blacks than the Emancipation Proclamation. We will not be known by name only, like the NAACP. We will not be known by reputation only like so many of our so-called black leaders. We will not attack the only injustices that provide media coverage; on the contrary, our work will support those the media ignores. We will be the purveyors of light while simultaneously extinguishing the dark that plagues our people. Men . . . what we are about to do here has only been seen in comic books. Years, scores, and decades after our task is complete, tales and legends about us and our amazing feats will be disseminated from generation to generation. We will leave more than a mark, gentlemen. We will make this country anew."

Trenton stopped to take a breath and observe the crowd's reaction. As usual, he had their attention with such an electric start.

He continued, "But with all things, there has to be a beginning. And like most beginnings, this will be our most challenging time. Like pushing a heavy load, the static friction is the most difficult force to overcome. Once that load is past that initial start, it becomes easier and easier to push. I liken our movement to that analogy. Getting started with so many opposing forces will seem daunting, even impossible at times. I am here to say that failure is not an option, neither is quitting; there will be no retreat, gentlemen. Once we began to move, the task will get easier, and the road will get smoother. I want you all to know and understand that we will succeed; we just have to persevere."

Trenton used his typical passionate voice without speaking loudly. Then he quieted a little and got extremely serious.

"I need to know that you all are with me 100 percent. Before I ask for your unfettered support, I must first inform and forewarn you all of what's to come."

He explained the rules, "First and foremost, anyone in here may ask all the questions he desires. Anyone in here may offer advice and even oppose some moves we will make. Just know and accept here and now that I am the head, and I make the final decisions. Anything with more than one head is a monster and doomed for failure. We will never have that issue here."

He explained more expectations if the men were to join his team, "I will be requiring a large load of your time, blood, minds . . . and also your money. Please be well aware that you are following me to a place of no return. What I may ask of you at times may seem like the most outlandish thing you have ever heard, but it will be for the greater good of our people."

He then told them, "I have come to know and love each and every one of you men. Moreover, I have come to trust you all with my life; I want you to do the same with me. Trust me. That is the only way we will succeed."

Trenton then reiterated, "As previously mentioned, you may see some of the moves we make as absolute craziness. Yet we all know that we are in dire times, and dire times cause for desperate measures."

After a ton of hinting and teasing, Trenton finally divulged the ultimate goal. "What you guys will officially agree to tonight is taking on the responsibility of changing the mind-set of the black American race. Not 10 percent, not 20 percent, but the entire culture – every black individual in the United States."

Finally someone chimed in with an obvious question, "Are you serious? You want us to change the mind-set of these niggas? All of 'em?" Ty Jackson asked as more of reflex than anything. He finished by saying, "I am so sorry for interrupting, but how do you plan on doing that?"

Trenton, not jostled by the interruption, responded, "Ty, my plans are foolproof, but before I divulge an iota, I need to be sure that you are onboard with everything."

Trenton explained why he waited so long to explain his goal. "What I will ask of you will not be any mere community service. There will be times I may ask you to do things that are against the law. Some things will be brutal, others will be unheard of. I will even require some of you to do things only seen during war times. And if that sounds scary, then my job is done. I want it to scare you. You all have to understand that we twenty-six men will start the new era of black America, and there will be a lot of eggs broken to make this omelet."

Trenton finally quieted. He looked into each one of the gentlemen's eyes. He saw bewilderment, wondering, and confusion. That was to be expected.

What Trenton didn't see was any trepidation in the men's eyes. To be sure, he said, "Now with all of that being said, is there anyone ready to leave now? Please don't be afraid. If you are not up to the task at hand, please leave, because once you are with us, there is no way to leave us."

Not one man stood, no one even looked apprehensive. He was fortunate to have a crew of real men with him. They all appeared ready to tackle any assignment he presented.

Trenton slightly smiled for the first time that night and explained what was coming next. "If all of you gentlemen agree to join this organization, I will need you to recite an oath and sign an X on the document in front of each of you."

The men having already noticed the manila envelopes in front of their chairs now understood what they were for.

"Look inside the large envelope and dump out the contents carefully," Trenton nicely ordered.

The men obliged. Each one opened the large brown envelope and pulled out a sheet of paper. The only other thing inside of the package was a new, unused scalpel still in its plastic wrapper. The sheet was an opulent piece of golden resume paper. There were two words calligraphically written over the top half of the page. The beautiful, large words simply stated *THE OATH.* At the bottom of the sheet of paper was a line with *signature* underneath it.

The men all glanced at each other with befuddled countenances. Then they began to softly murmur to one another, inquiring about the blade and how to sign the paper without a writing utensil.

Trenton interrupted the quiet rumbling and gave one example of his future outrageous supplications. "Gentlemen, before we go any further and before you agree to join this organization, I will let you know the first thing we are doing. It is one of the biggest requests I will ask of you."

The crew sat tentatively, awaiting this first request. Trenton continued, "As you all know, I want us to separate ourselves from the norm. The most important aspect of achieving this goal is to first free ourselves of this innate love of money. If you are born here in America, your first love affair is with money, whether you know it or not. This country loves to portray itself as a Judeo, Christian nation, but what we really worship is the almighty dollar."

He then distinguished their group from all others. "We, as the founders of this new organization, will reprogram our thinking and rid ourselves of this insane infatuation with money. No longer will we put money before our loved ones or even our neighbors. To initiate this change, we will have to again do something extremely drastic."

"This is what I propose," Trenton stated. "More so, this is my first request as the leader of this group. So before you sign your names to those oaths, this first request will help you understand the magnitude of my expectations."

Trenton got quiet for a couple of seconds, and as he made his request, he was sure to look each man directly in the eyes. "I ask that each of you give half of your salary to this organization."

For the first time since the group's inception, Trenton heard serious disapproval and sounds of dismay. He could hear a cacophony of statements like "Half our salary?" "Now you lost me," "Don't tell me that this was all about getting my money," and of course, "Aww, come on, man!"

Trenton could hear all of the men talking at once, but his efficient brain was able to separate and understand each statement. Though he knew that he was on the verge of losing a lot of his audience, he noticed six men that were quiet and awaiting the command to sign their names. He new these men would be his dark disciples.

"Men . . . men . . . please . . . let me continue . . . let me finish . . .," Trenton said, trying to regain some order. Once the crowd quieted, he continued, "In return for you relinquishing half of your salaries, all of your bills will be paid."

Again, the crowd erupted, even louder this time, almost repeating the same statements, "What," "How can you do that," "No way is that even possible," "I am so lost," and of course "Aww, come on, man!"

"OK," Trenton yelled over the commotion, "Now you can interrupt, and you all can ask your questions." After the offer, Malcolm Banks was the first to stand. So Trenton pointed his direction, giving him the floor.

Malcolm Banks took his hands out of his pockets and spoke plainly, "I have to admit, Dr. Branch, for the first time since this group's commencement you have completely lost me. How do you propose we provide you with half of our salary and expect that insufficient amount to take care of *all* of our bills? That's preposterous. Instantly, Dr. Branch, I see so many issues with this idea." Trenton listened and smiled, all the while enjoying Malcolm's poignant delivery. Malcolm continued, "Some of us make substantially more than others. Obviously we will give far more. Some of us are more frivolous or are more frugal than others, how will you account for those differences? I have at least fifty more questions, but I will let you answer those before I occupy all of your time," Malcolm finished and sat back down.

Trenton offered everyone a smile, hoping it would put them at ease. "I have to admit guys, I am glad for the questions, and I am glad for the concern and even a little dissension. For if you all followed blindly, I guess you all wouldn't be real men. So please don't apologize for having apprehension and a little distrust. Hopefully, what I say next can somewhat put most of you at ease, at least a little."

Trenton then said, "I know it is hard to imagine handing over half of your salary. I know it's even harder when you know that your earnings are far greater than the man sitting next to you. Your sacrifice will seem greater . . ."

Trenton stopped there, switched gears, and then explained his reasoning behind such a crazy request, "Listen, guys, I just don't want you to worry about day-to-day living. Because I am going to need most of your time and all of your attention, I don't want any of you to think twice about the necessities of life. Shelter, food, heat, electricity, even transportation – all of these things will be covered. Now that is the why; here is the how. I will perform the necessary calculations to see what we expect to bring in, and what we expect to pay out. If I find that there is a discrepancy and more needs to go out than what is coming in, I will begin to draw from *my* own savings to ensure the goal is met." Trenton didn't know it at the time but that last statement cemented the deal.

The fact that Trenton was willing to deplete his life savings for the cause was apparently what the naysayers needed to hear. If he was willing to sacrifice all, then they could certainly sacrifice half. Trenton explained more, "Let's think about this seriously, gents. For some of you, keeping half of your salary as discretionary funds will be a serious lifestyle improvement, for I know that some of you are barely making ends meet. Well now, those ends will be met without worry. For others, this will be an adjustment; your bills are already paid. You own your house, car, and boat. The money you bring in is all yours to do with what you please. You all will certainly feel as though you're getting the short end of the stick. And you know what . . . maybe you are. Oh well, you will have to change your way of thinking."

Trenton explained his viewpoint further, "We are no longer random black men meandering about. We are now brothers bonded in a common goal. We are family, and it is our job to ensure that everyone in this family is well taken care of. This sacrifice will be the start. Money or lack thereof will no longer be a burden nor will it be your sole reason for making the moves you make in this world. Money will soon become like a household chore; you know it exists, but it will only come to your mind when your wife nags about it." For the first time since the beginning of the meeting, the crowd laughed. The atmosphere lightened some.

Trenton started again, "Giving up our love, infatuation, and worship of money will be the first step of our evolution, gentlemen. No longer will money be the sole purpose for every single thing we do; from this moment forward, any and all things we do will be for the greater good of our race."

After that long speech, Trenton turned around, reached down, and grabbed a glass of water that sat behind his chair. He raised the glass to his lips and swallowed long and hard. His exhaustion was evident. Trenton continued slowly, "Now," he said sternly, "If you are with me, let's continue. But if any of this is beyond your comprehension . . . no worries . . . you can walk away now."

Trenton then quickly said, "I know how crazy all of this sounds. It sounded crazy to me while saying it. Yet I also know that this is the only way."

Terrance Phillips, a truck driver, interjected, speaking in a suspicious tone, "This sounds like communism to me, Dr. Branch."

"This certainly isn't communism, Terrance," Trenton quickly responded, "But it is akin to a form of socialism." He saw a few stressed looks after he used the word socialism, so he inquired, "And really, what is wrong with that?"

In an attempt to pull the men to his way of thinking, he expressed his viewpoint, "Capitalism vs. Socialism. Even if I didn't know the two concepts, knowing the root words, I would choose socialism any day. I hear capital, I think of money, I hear social, I think of people. Capitalism is about the individual, while socialism is about us all."

Trenton clarified his objective, "Let's not make sure that one person eats; let's make sure that we all eat. There is enough to go around. When resources truly become scarce, I guess then we can behave selfishly. We live in a country where everything is plentiful, so why should only the top 5 percent truly indulge in what life has to offer while the rest of us fight over the scraps from Longshank's table?" Trenton couldn't help but laugh at one of his favorite *Braveheart* quotes. He continued, "Capitalism is also about capitalizing. Let me capitalize on fear, on ignorance, on a person's drug addiction, on this person's hardships, even on people's basic needs. Capitalism breeds greed and that innate love affair with money. Capitalism is money over humanity." He could see the frowns leaving and understanding starting to show up on a lot of faces.

He continued, "While the rest of America can live by those ideas, we as the black race can no longer afford to place money over our brethren. We all are connected, your welfare does affect my well-being, and I will die trying to shove that message into our people's mind."

Staying on topic Trenton followed with, "So with all of that being said, the first thing we should do is consolidate our cash and ensure that each and every one of us is fed, sheltered, and clothed . . . with absolutely no help from the government. You all get that last part; we will not become dependent on handouts from the government. Getting handouts removes your drive to sustain your own living and makes you weak. Don't get me wrong, we will use what the government has to offer to help us in this endeavor, but no handouts."

Trenton continued, "So I say yes, this will be a form of socialism. Let's call it pseudo-socialism because we will ensure that we all are financially secure. If I eat, we all eat."

Trenton wanted to explain another idea, "Please don't get it twisted, excuse the slang . . . don't get it confused. I certainly don't believe every man should receive the same wages for different jobs as communism suggests. But I strongly believe that any honest job is honorable, and if a man works, he should be able to take care of his family without issue. Let me clarify; there are some jobs that are more demanding than others, and yes, that person should be better compensated for that job. For example, a doctor has to spend the bulk of his life in school, he has to work tirelessly to achieve his status, and if he is really good at his job, he can allow you to spend another ten to twenty years with your ailing grandmother. So yes, doctors are very special people and deserve accolades and a special salary."

The men seemed to agree with that sentiment and really began to pick up what Trenton put down. He continued, "So I am not trying to make us all equal; truthfully, we all are not equal, *but* we all are connected. And if this man beside me is comfortable, I don't have to worry about him trying to snatch the food from my plate."

Trenton went to drink another swallow of water; no one said a word while he drank. He smacked his lips, wiped his mouth with his hand, and began his closing argument, "I conclude by repeating my goal in this request again. I want to free you all of your ingrained love affair with money. We will change black America, but we first must change ourselves if we expect anyone to follow. We will not be like so many republicans, basically telling people to behave one way, while the leaders behave another. We will lead by example. We will change black America, but we must first change ourselves."

Trenton was finished. Now everyone could see why he needed that first five minutes for meditation. He had explained things in a way no one in the room had ever thought. He showed them things they'd never seen. One way or another, they all did have a secret love affair with money: whether they were unhappy because they just never seemed to have enough, unhappy because they had enough but still wanted more, or unhappy because they were really willing to do almost anything to get it. They all finally understood that it would be nice to free their minds of that burden. And if they could help the man next to them while undergoing rehab for their addiction to money, that's just a plus. Once again, Trenton opened their minds to ideas they never conceived, and maybe they could change the world. They would follow this man. They had tried everything else; it was time to try something new and crazy, and Trenton seemed to be that thing.

Trenton finally stated very candidly, "Sign if you are in, please leave if you are not."

The men all looked at one another, waiting to see if anyone would leave. Mathew stood up, stretched, and started walking toward the door, which obviously shocked everyone, especially Trenton, who could not hide the dismay in his face. When Mathew got to the door, he turned and smiled, said just kidding, and briskly walked back to his seat while asking, "How the hell do we sign the sheet? I didn't bring a pen. And what is that scalpel for?" as he reached his chair and held up the packaged blade.

Trenton smiled along with others who even laughed. Then he said, "First, you must say the oath for it is not written. Everyone stand and repeat after me with your fist against your heart. Listen, repeat, and understand the words you are reciting."

Trenton started the oath, "I, state your name," (repeated by all) "Solemnly swear to uplift the black American race. To shine light on the dark and devour the wicked. To stand with the righteous and destroy any wrong doing when and wherever I see. I will remove the shackles from my mind, freeing my thought process and allowing my third eye to see clearly. Finally I vow to be the best black man I can possibly be, taking on the responsibility of being an entire race's template and representative. I understand the magnitude of this endeavor and vow to work on these goals until my dying day. All of these things I vow to do here, now, and forever."

After everyone repeated the last part, Trenton then stated, "Now open your scalpels. Please prick yourself; the blades are all new and sterile. Now make your best efforts to write your initials on the dotted line . . . in blood of course." He watched as the men tried their best to follow his orders. He added one quick bit of advice, "I have already done this, so I know it isn't easy. Just try your best to make it as legible as possible."

Trenton could see a couple of guys finish and still holding the scalpels, so he gave further instructions, "If you look to your left or right, you will see a small biohazard receptacle on each table. Carefully dispose of your scalpel properly. Allow your signature to dry then put your oath back in its envelope and leave them on the table."

The men all complied, and then they all began to look around the room at one another. After a few seconds had passed, there was a wave of energy that traveled through the hall. Everyone felt it. No words could possibly describe the emotion they all were feeling at that moment. The best attempt would be to say they felt the ultimate connection – a oneness from many. Even the few gentlemen in the group that were fraternity members or part of the Masonic Order couldn't recall feeling so connected to a group of men. This was something special; it was as if they had been baptized, and all resurfaced anew, rekindling relationships with their long-lost brothers.

After all of the envelopes were closed and all the scalpels were properly disposed, Trenton left the podium up front, walked to each table, and picked up the oaths while tossing little plastic bags of sanitary medicated cotton balls to each man. The men, still standing, grabbed the packages and opened them. They all swabbed their little cuts and waited for Trenton to give further orders.

Trenton returned to the front and then inhaled a deep, meditative breath with his eyes closed. Afterward, he calmly asked, "Can you all feel that?" Before anyone answered, he then said, "Please sit, guys. We are ready for the next phase. Operation . . . What's up, my brother?" Trenton interrupted himself, "Billy . . . are you all right, my brother? I know the slight laceration probably hurt but not bad enough to cause tears, my man," Trenton said jokingly when he saw Billy trying to fight tears that were slowly streaming down his face.

Billy attempted to offer a smile to the joke but couldn't. Just like anyone who is trying to fight back a crying fit, once they are questioned about why they are crying, that is when the tidal wave begins. That is what happened. Billy really began to sob. He was not a crier, so witnessing his meltdown stunned everyone in the room. No one knew what was going on with their newfound brother. He finally gathered himself after ten seconds of hard sobbing, and then he stood.

He said with slob in his mouth while wiping tears from his eyes and snot from his nose, "Fellas, I am so sorry for this, but I just couldn't help it. I been goin' to church prayin' and prayin.'" He stopped for a brief second to fight another crying fit then continued, "Look, I ain't like a lot of you brothas. I didn't make a lot of the right choices in life. As a matter of fact, I made a lot of the wrong ones." He really started gathering himself, and the tears began to cease. He took a deep breath then continued, "I ended up in the joint for two years. Man . . . it's hard enough being a black man, but trying to get a job with a felo on your record? *Damn!* The crap I did, I did almost fifteen years ago. But I still got to work two temp jobs just to make a little change. Child support is hitting me up, and the system is threatening to send me back to the muthafuckin' joint. Me and my wife . . . we try bruh . . . we try so hard, but it is impossible to get out of this rut. I been talkin' to God like, 'Look, Lord, I am trying to be a good, God-fearing man,' but it ain't working. I just can't make it. Bottom line, I was on my last leg and about to do something real stupid . . . forreal."

He looked down, his face began to frown up, and tears began to well up in his eyes again. "But this plan you said would give me half of my checks back, and the bills will be paid too. That is so much more than I could have ever hoped for. Dr. Branch, I will consolidate, I will go to class, I will do whatever it is you need me to. Thank you, Dr. Branch, and thank you, brothas, forreal, thank you all. You all don't know what this means." Billy stopped and sat down.

"Well, the first thing you are going to do is quit one of those jobs, Billy," Trenton quickly stated.

Billy tried to add something, "But . . . but . . . I'm still gonna need . . ."

"What I am going to need is you, Billy," Trenton interrupted Billy's stammering, "And I can't have you if you are working two jobs. I have always said that no man should ever *have* to work two jobs to provide. If a man is working two jobs, it should only be because that is what he wants to do. Life is not about work and work alone. Everyone needs time for other curriculum. That is what makes well-rounded men and helps them build good families. A father should have time to see his kids on a regular basis and not just when they are sleeping in their beds before he crashes in his. If a man is working two jobs, he doesn't have the opportunity to spend time with, enjoy, or raise his children. He loses his connection with his wife, and they are sure to grow apart and realize they no longer know each other. No, I do not expect any of you to work two jobs; as a matter of fact, you *won't* be able to work two jobs."

Billy just sat in his seat, shaking his head from side to side with an amazed expression. Things couldn't get any better for him.

Trenton, feeling charged and proud of his group, then asked, "Do you all see that? You see what happens with just a touch of unity. We are just getting started yet have ensured that this brother and his family will be secure without him returning to a life of crime."

Trenton then focused on Billy and made a side note, "I know criminal activity isn't a first option, but it is an option, and that is something we want to take off the table for our brothers. Billy, don't feel bad about thinking of making your money through illegal means. Think about it . . . if you grow up in the inner-city, you will see more dope-dealing hustlers and thieves than actual honest workers. So we grow up thinking criminal activity is a job and no different than working at a corporation. Yet we know where all of those transgressors end up. But I digress."

Trenton then returned to the subject, "I just want everyone to see how happy we have made Billy. His wife will be happier, and so will his kids too. He will now have more time with them, and that is what is really important."

The men sat with their chests swelled with pride. To see their efforts instantly affecting lives gave substance to Trenton's ideas.

"All right, guys," Trenton returned to his topic, "The Restoration of black America has commenced. This production will be broken into groups; certain individuals will be responsible for each action item. I will provide you with my list of those items tonight but will go no further than that. It has been a long night, and I want you guys to go home and ruminate on everything that you agreed to tonight."

Trenton heard someone whisper very softly, "What does room-a-mate mean," he smiled while hearing the neighbor answer just as softly, "It's ru-mi-nate, and he means just think about it."

Trenton held up his index finger and stated, "Number 1: Cleaning house; Number 2: Educating our people; 3. Beautifying our neighborhoods; 4: Emotional reparation." He allowed a few seconds for those action items to sink in, then he continued, "Go home tonight, gents. Think about each one of those four areas of attack. Think about the one you may want to focus on. Think about ideas that can assist in accomplishing those goals. Think."

Luke interrupted, "Those all sound very generic like a bunch of clichés. I don't know what 'emotional reparation' is, but the others just sound really simple."

Trenton, undisturbed by "Doubting Thomas", responded coyly, "You know what, Luke, these goal topics do all sound like overused ideas." He stopped focusing on Luke and started addressing the entire group again, "Regardless, these are the areas of attack. I have ways of completing each goal, but I also want ideas and thoughts from you guys. Bring me all ideas, no matter how crazy you may think one is. The only ideas I don't want to hear are the old, overused ones. You know like boycotting, marching, letters to the government – the things that have been done over and over, typically with little reward. Also remember that this is about us fixing us, so no statements about what the government needs to do. Meeting adjourned, guys. Good night all."

The men stood and ambled out of the hall while talking to each other. They all shook Trenton's hand on the way out and offered their goodbyes. Though they all thought the same, only a few of the guys took the time to include compliments about the night's meeting. They were energized, and the charge emanated; a passerby saw the men leaving the hall and could feel the love from across the street.

Before Malcolm Banks could leave, Trenton grabbed his shoulder and asked, "Malcolm, can I keep you for a minute?"

Malcolm separated from the group of men leaving the hall (with a few of the men turning to watch him walk with their new leader) and followed Trenton to an empty table in the back corner.

Mathew stayed behind also. "I was gonna help you clean up as usual, Dr. Branch, but if this is a private discussion, I'll let you guys have the hall to yourselves," he stated.

Trenton knew that Mathew was going to be one of his dark disciples and didn't want to dissuade him in any way. So he stated, "Mathew, there will be very few discussions that are private within this organization. We will all be privy to what the others are doing. Very, very few secrets my brother. And this most certainly isn't a secret discussion. Please join us if you will, or begin picking up, do whatever you feel," Trenton expressed nicely.

Mathew walked over to the table and sat, "I'd rather be nosey and listen." The three men laughed at his brash honesty.

After the laugh, Malcolm just sat quietly, curious as to why he was needed. He, like the rest of the group, looked at Trenton as more than a mere leader. Actually, a few of the men were in awe of Trenton and saw him as a present day Martin Luther King. A few of the men could listen to him orate all day. Malcolm was one of those men and was quite nervous having to sit there and talk to Trenton one on one. He silently thanked God for Mathew's presence. Malcolm didn't know what Trenton wanted, but he already knew his answer would be yes.

"Malcolm?" Trenton started.

Malcolm lifted his head with his lips poked out and eyes wide. "Uhn-huhn" was the only thing that came out of this articulate man's mouth. He didn't know why, but Trenton made him feel like a teenager talking to an old pastor. He felt so little next to him. "Snap out of it," Malcolm told himself. "This guy is one year younger than you."

While Malcolm tried grounding his nervous energy, Trenton divulged his reason for holding him late. "Malcolm," Trenton said again, "I am going to need a whole lot of help from you. To get all of this started, money is at the root. I am no fool. I know the world we live in, and we are going nowhere if our money situation isn't strong. That is where you come in. I figure, you having been an accountant . . . for how long?"

"Uh . . . uh . . . twenty-one, no . . . twenty t-two years," Malcolm barely stated.

Trenton continued, "With you being an accountant for twenty-two years, you should be used to crunching numbers and handling loads of paperwork.

By now, it should be almost a part of your nature. Even if it isn't something you enjoy, you have to be a guru. It is not the prettiest aspect of this endeavor but by far the most important. Bottom line, Malcolm: I place our money situation on your shoulders, and I want you to spin gold from hay."

With both hands unseen under the table, Malcolm used his fore and middle finger from his right hand to check the pulse in the inside of his left wrist. His heart was beating fast, and he already felt the weight of the world on his shoulders. He knew he was going to fail the group. He was going to fail Trenton. His blood pressure felt like it had to be 200 over 200. "Calm down," he told himself while listening to Trenton speak. Why was Trenton relying on him? He had never been in charge of anything in his life. He continued to feel the quick throb of his pulse as he attentively listened to his leader.

Trenton, unaware of Malcolm's anxiety, continued with his script, "You will be head of all financial affairs. Whatever help you need, you let me know, and I will make sure you get it. I will share everything in the matters of money with you. Oh yeah, you are not just in charge of the money's coming in and the bills going out. There are other capital ventures I have in mind, and you will be my accountant for those as well. None of us will really worry about money, but you will, and for that I apologize. But know that some of us will surely deal with more horrid nightmares than keeping a money trail." Trenton turned toward Mathew and cut his eyes. Mathew felt a cold chill run down the base of his spine after hearing that statement and catching Trenton's quick glance.

Trenton continued with the forewarning, turning to face Malcolm again, "I am sorry for placing this burden on you, Malcolm, for this will be your cross to bear, the bane of your existence. It will be a heavy load, my friend. I want you to know that and understand that I know it too. As I previously stated, this is the most important aspect of our goal, and we all will be at your beck and call. So after that long-winded statement, are you OK with this request?" Trenton asked as though it wasn't mandatory.

Malcolm, completely caught off guard, was tongue tied at first. He didn't expect such a request, nor did he expect Trenton to be so different one on one. Malcolm believed that Trenton must have been a cool kid in school. He being a nerd throughout his academic years could see a cool kid from a mile away. Malcolm realized he was taking too long with a response. Scared that Trenton would take his silence as reluctance, he then blurted, "Yes, sir. Dr. Branch, I take you very seriously." Malcolm started to slow down so he could begin to make sense. "I think you really want to do the things you say.

I think you do want to make a profound change to black America, and for some insane reason, I believe that you can. And if handling the monetary affairs of this organization is the role I need to play, it actually pales in comparison to the role that you play. I will do my best, Dr. Branch."

"I expected nothing less from you, Malcolm," Trenton stated. "I don't want you thinking about anything other than money. I want you to focus on your upcoming task. Now go home and relax . . . and thanks again. Good night, Malcolm."

Malcolm comically jetted up from his chair right when he was told to go home. One would have thought that he was a marine. Malcolm then took hold of Trenton's extended hand and shook. "Good Night, Dr. Branch, and you too, Mathew," Malcolm said and cleared his throat. He turned and briskly marched out of the hall. He closed the door gingerly on his way out. When he stood outside getting his keys for his car, he felt silly being in such awe of that man. Yet the feeling never left, and he was relieved to be out of the presence of such power.

Inside the hall, Trenton slowly stood with a smile on his face and walked over to the front where he kept his waste bags. When Mathew rose to his feet, he reached for one of the biohazard containers holding the used scalpels. Trenton quickly reached out and told Mathew, "Wait up, brother. Let me take care of those. Not that I think anything is wrong with anyone, I am just a safety nut. I have gloves and a special way of disposing those containers. Here . . . take this bag and collect the papers and cups and stuff like that. I will get the biohazard waste." Trenton was walking to Mathew while holding a white Hefty trash bag in his right hand.

Mathew grabbed the trash bag and happily obliged without one question. Trenton walked back over to the front and grabbed the box that would house all of the small scalpel depositories. He set the box in the middle of the hall and began collecting the biohazard containers and setting them in the thick cardboard box. The box was brown with a big yellow and red biohazard marker on the front. He was going to make sure everything would be disposed of properly.

"Are you surprised, Dr. Branch?" a genuine question from Mathew directed at Trenton.

"Why do you ask that?" Trenton inquired, completely lost as to Mathew's subject matter.

"The response you are getting from the men, are you surprised by that?" Mathew succinctly explained.

"Am I surprised . . . ? That is a really good question. I have to say I am happy, I am proud, I am ready. But surprised, I never thought of that." Trenton stopped what he was doing and put his gloved hands on his hips. He looked down and made some thinking faces.

Then Trenton finally replied, "I guess I would have to say yes . . . and no. I am not surprised that there is a group of men out here ready to avenge their murdered children. But agreeing to the actuality of my plan, relinquishing half of their earnings, I am surprised that I didn't get much of a push back there." Trenton continued cleaning.

Mathew said while wiping a table with glass cleaner, "In case you didn't know, I'll let you know that these brothers are yours, and so am I, Dr. Branch."

Trenton made a peculiar face, nodded, and then said, "You know that you can call me Trenton, Mathew," Trenton told his friend.

"Nahh, I would rather call you by your earned title. I would even ask you not to encourage anyone to call you by your first name. Keep this powerful, leader persona you got going on, Dr. Branch." Mathew was on his last table. Packing the white bag with the last of the trash, he further clarified, "We all look at you as our leader. Your title is a piece of that."

Trenton made a curious face, rarely being able to hide his thought process, and said, "I don't want to seem all powerful and unapproachable. I will lose people."

"Well, if you seem like one of us, you will lose people. You have to understand, we follow you because you *are* powerful. You got something none of us got. Don't give it up or take it for granted, Dr. Branch. Keep that powerful thing about yourself going." Mathew was staring Trenton in the eyes by the end of his advice.

Trenton, once again showing his thoughts through facial expressions, nodded his head and simply stated, "Duly noted Mathew . . . Dr. Branch it is. Thank you for that bit of advice."

They were finished cleaning and were walking out with the waste containers. Dr. Branch carried the box to his trunk, and Mathew took the trash bag to the dumpster in the alley. On the way, more conversation commenced.

"Dr. Branch, I know where you are going, and I am with you," Mathew stated.

Dr. Branch, realizing that Mathew had a very cryptic way of speaking, again asked, "What do you mean?" It was like Mathew expected him to read minds.

"I know one of the major things you want to do, and I am on board," Mathew said again. After he saw Dr. Branch lift an eyebrow, he explained, "You've said it before, and now you say it again as one of our main objectives.

You use the term clean house. Cleaning house usually means getting rid of something. And if *it* is what I think it is, I am on board." Mathew didn't elaborate any further.

Dr. Branch and Mathew just kind of eyed one another with a telepathic-like connection. They both knew what the other was thinking. They left the subject alone. "Well, Mathew, I think it's time we call it a night," Dr. Branch stated.

They both said there farewells and hopped in each car and left the scene.

Next Meeting

"Let me have your ideas, gentlemen." Dr. Branch started the meeting without any small talk.

Ty Jackson started. He raised his hand and waited until Dr. Branch nodded in his direction. He then made his argument, "Well, I thought real hard, but I couldn't seem to get pass the basics. We need to keep fathers in the household or at least around. We need to have families raising their li'l ones. But that would be like controlling people, and we can't control people's behavior."

"You shouldn't offer a solution and shoot it down in the same breath, Ty," Dr. Branch admonished. Ty looked down and took his seat. Dr. Branch enlightened, "Changing behavior is our overall goal. We couldn't expect any of our plans to come to fruition without some serious behavioral changes."

More men offered suggestions but they lacked substance. And after Dr. Branch heard what he believed to be the last of the ideas, he closed the floor and began reciting his plan for changing black America.

"All right, gentlemen, here is what we are going to do. First off, we are attacking the education system. We will create what we will call the Inner-City Private School. We will build this school with funds we receive from pooling our money and government school aid. Public schools are always in debt, yet they never have anything to show for the money they receive. We will convince wealthy black brothers and sisters to contribute, and we will combine all of those funds with the funds we receive from the government.

"This school will be from the first through the twelfth grade. The curriculum will be a step above the best schools in the country, and the education style will be our own. We . . . I see your hand, Patrick, what's up?" Dr. Branch broke his stride.

Patrick, one of the older gentlemen, made a brief statement, "First to the twelfth, Dr. Branch, I don't know. Kids are cruel . . . putting twelfth graders with first graders . . . Well that could turn out downright bad." Patrick was retired. He was a short, stocky sixty-five-year-old man who looked twenty years younger than his age. His hair was cropped neat and matched the more salt than pepper appearance of his full beard. He wore overalls with cowboy boots, a cowboy hat, and a blue oxford, leaving the top button undone. He had the look of a laborer that worked all his life. Patrick continued with his point in the same broken cadence, rubbing his beard at each pause, "All kids are cruel . . . Black kids make it even worse . . . The gangs and what-not . . . The older ones could rub off bad on the li'l ones . . . With the droopy britches . . . You might want to keep some age groups away from others . . . That's all I'm saying, Dr. Branch," Patrick finished.

Dr. Branch offered his answer, "Thank you for that input, Patrick. Trust that I have thought about this process long and hard. Our children are our most important asset. We have to believe in them, trust them, and more than anything, teach them. I honestly believe if we teach our older ones right, they will be compelled to pass on those lessons to the younger ones. I again am not blind. I know kids will be kids, and I will let them be kids. I also know that older kids teach the younger ones how to be cool. And if getting straight A's, being articulate, and going to college is what the younger see the older ones doing. They will want to follow suit. Do you understand my point, Patrick?"

"I didn't think of it like that, Dr. Branch, I'm sorry for interrupting. Please keep going." Spoken like a real man.

"Please don't apologize, Patrick. Those were very good points you made. And to anyone else, if you have any questions, don't think twice about chiming in," Dr. Branch told the crowd. "Now let me continue . . . We will first start with our school, but the process will spread to others. Our disapproval of underachievement will infect every school nearby . . . We will make that happen one way or the other. That is how we will attack education."

Dr. Branch continued going down his areas of attack, "Next, we will beautify our communities. This again includes a lot more than just planting some flowers along the roadside. What this includes is fixing up homes, cleaning lots and removing loiterers. I know I say the latter like its simple. I know the complications that come along when people are involved. People will get on board or else."

"Next is emotional reparation. We are a broken people. There are no if's, and's, or but's about it. So many of us refuse to seek psychiatry or talk to someone because of the stigma attached to it, especially us black men. Yet when you think about it, if there is any group of people that need to unload, it's us. Who else has been so abandoned, beaten, who has felt uglier, or more worthless than us? Motherless, fatherless, no family, no history, feeling loss, depressed, alone – we need to repair our emotions; we need not feel what others choose we will feel. We will require most people to seek emotional help . . . or else."

"Finally, the subject I have been really hesitant to bring up for it is the darkest part of this crusade. Those who join this team will be doing a horrible thing, but by far the most necessary if we are to accomplish our final objective. We will call this Operation Cleaning House. If you are a drug addict, you will clean up or else. If you are a drug dealer or gang banger, you will change your ways or else. If you are committed to making your money through nefarious and illegal means, you will cease immediately or else. Bottom line, we will no longer allow these characters to exist in our story, either you will be a productive member of society . . . or else."

By this time, the entire crowd of men all had peculiar looks on their faces. One gentlemen chose to speak up, "What do you mean by *or else*."

Dr. Branch thought for a couple of seconds on how to approach this subject, he put both hands on the podium and began talking slow and deliberately, "Guys, this is where things get really difficult. What I divulge here is a wrong doing and I know this. The only reason I choose this dark path is because I see no alternative. This thing I speak of is truly on the cusp of insanity."

The men stared at their leader with curious eyes, and Dr. Branch attempted to clarify his meaning, "OK . . . during the creation of this new era, there is no such thing as some; it is an all or nothing deal. Either a person is on board, or there is no room for him. This new world will have rules, guidelines, and laws . . . either you are on board, or you are gone," Dr. Branch said the last part sharply.

"Sound like you talkin' 'bout killin' people, Dr. Branch," Luke said.

Dr. Branch replied candidly and somewhat coldly, "We have to know that everyone will not be on board with what we propose. For the opposition, there is only one way to deal with them. It is to remove them from the community . . . permanently. Let me reiterate, I am not talking about killing old ladies here. But I am talking about killing the destroyers of our people. I won't mix words; killing is a part of this objective. That is why we call it cleaning house." He repeated the word *kill* multiple times to ensure no one was confused about his intentions. Then he used a gentle metaphor to soften the term. "Think for a minute, gents. You cannot save a bunch of apples without casting out the bad one. You cannot save a human without excising the cancer. We cannot save black America without first removing the cancer that plagues our body." He hoped that would do, but he was sure there would be further issues. As always, Dr. Branch was prepared for said issues.

There were murmurs of opposition . . . Luke spoke up again, "I don't know if I can get down with this, Dr. Branch. You actually talkin' 'bout killing people. Sounds kind of crazy . . . What about the repercussions? What if we get caught? We all could end up in jail. What if we *kill* the wrong person? We could start a war with the wrong people." Luke finally had his chance to place true doubts in the crowds head.

"I am not asking any of you to murder. I just don't want to play games with anyone here. You all should know the overall goals of this group, including the dark ones. With that being said, if no one is willing to help, I will commit the acts of *cleaning house* myself. You all just need to know that it will be a part of what we do," Dr. Branch informed. That seemed to satisfy Luke for a minute, but another person spoke up.

One man stood, he shook his head from side to side slowly while speaking softly, "I don't know if I can be a part of group that murders, even if I ain't the one doing the killing."

Dr. Branch, knowing each of his participants by name and lost child, called Joe by his name, "I tell you what, Joe," he stated candidly. "Before you make your decision final, let me show you something. And after seeing this thing I want to show you, if you still want to disband from the group, you may. Though you have already given me a blood oath, I will not hold you to it. How does that sound?" Dr. Branch finished.

Joe just sat down without saying a word, very curious as to what Dr. Branch would present. Dr. Branch turned around and started retrieving his laptop out of its bag. He pulled out wires and began attaching wires to their designations until he had completed his task. His laptop was connected to the projector as it had been in the earlier meetings. Once all of the connections were complete, he used his mouse to open a file folder and pulled out a group of pictures. He put the first picture up. Joe instantly grew somber because the picture was of his kid, wearing his peewee league baseball uniform. The sweet picture melted many hearts. He was such a cute little boy. Dr. Branch looked directly at Joe's face while the picture was up. He saw the sadness and dismay in Joe's eyes. Dr. Branch didn't want somber, he wanted anger, so he clicked to the next picture. This picture was of the kid's crime scene. How Dr. Branch got the picture, Joe could only imagine. The picture showed a kid with one eye open and large holes in his shirt, and a blood pool under the sprawled body. The scene was horrific and caused a slight gasp from the crowd.

"That's not right, Dr. Branch," Joe said with an angry look.

Dr. Branch wanted more anger, even if it was pointed at him for now. Anger is the motivation Joe needed. Dr. Branch did not respond with words; he simply continued Joe's personal slide show, while eyeing him tenaciously. After a couple more shots of the crime scene, the next picture was of the murderer's mug shot. Though all black men have their differences, this guy resembled your default black criminal mug shot. He held a mean facial expression with scruffy, unkempt half-braided hair and a hairy face with a beard having small patches that resembled the mange. That's when Dr. Branch saw the facial expression he had been waiting for. He began clicking more images of the youth. There they all saw the teen holding two AK-47s (one in each hand) with smoke rising from a blunt that he held in his mouth. Next were pictures of the kid shooting one of the guns. They could only see the kid and the gun with a flash leaving the muzzle. The kid wearing the black youth soldierly uniform, long, dingy T-shirt with pants hanging to the ankles, was caught in midfire, his body weirdly angled because of the recoil. The target was unapparent, leaving lots of room for an imaginative father.

Where Dr. Branch tracked those pictures down from was of no concern to Joe. His focus was on the kid in the picture. Joe's face was hard and held the look of a hungry pit bull. Dr. Branch finally saw his opening. "This kid got ten years for killing a ten-year-old. Does that make any sense to you, Joe?" Dr. Branch asked coldly.

Dr. Branch spoke angrily then added, "This worthless piece of shit is kicking it behind bars. Two hots and cot, perhaps some jailhouse puntang, and all the drugs he wants for we all know that there are more drugs in the prison system than out on the streets. This is his punishment for gunning down a small . . . defenseless . . . unintimidating . . . well-raised . . . highly intelligent child." Each adjective was spoken separately for effect. Dr. Branch could see the tears of hate forming in the bottom of Joe's eyes. He concluded with passion, "Joe, I am talking about this." Joe dropped his head, and Dr. Branch yelled, "Look at him. He will be back on the streets around the time your son would have been graduating from college. He will be back to terrorize more young children in the near future." Dr. Branch said the last part as though it were a matter of fact.

Dr. Branch shut the projector down. He turned from Joe and spoke to all the men, "These kids nowadays have no respect. They know absolutely nothing of honor. We as black men can no longer allow this. We will gather each and every one of these lost souls, teach them, and show them the light. The ones who wish to continue in a destructive path will be removed. Again, plain and simple . . . removed"

Dr. Branch focused on Joe once more and asked a question, "Joe . . . what did you want to do as you looked at those photos of your child's murderer."

"I wanted to kill that muthafucka," Joe quickly responded in a monotone, soft voice.

"Come again, a little louder."

"I wanted to kill that muthafucka," Joe said more loudly.

"One more time, Joe. But only if it's the truth"

This time Joe yelled with control, "I wanted to kill that muthafucka!"

Dr. Branch quickly responded just as passionately, "And you are not alone." Dr. Branch continued far more calmly, "See, Joe, this is what I am talking about. You are not alone. I guarantee you if we played out that same scenario with any man in here, we would see the same show. Even the super saints would pray for vengeance."

Someone said "Amen," and a few of the men chuckled. Dr. Branch smiled and continued with his typical passionate yet analytical demeanor, "Every black American is sick of this shit. We all know what needs to be done, but no one would ever admit it. We need to start anew. Purge the old and start anew. While everyone complains about this or that, we all know the truth . . . nothing will ever change. In order for things to change, we have to be the ones who bring forth that change."

Dr. Branch continued, "Listen . . . we shall start judging our own. Our kids will no longer be meat for the table. Think about it. The entire judicial system exists because of our kids. Go to a court room. You see black kid after black kid marching in and out of those places. They are chained like slaves or wearing the orange jump suits signifying criminality. We all know that if it weren't for us, the penal system would be 90 percent smaller. We fill the prisons. Well not we . . . but our kids keep thousands if not millions employed within the system. That is why it is so hard to truly change the inner city. No one really wants anything to change, because if it did, a lot of people would be out of a job. But I digress."

Dr. Branch got back on track, "I can go on for hours upon hours on why we need to commit this horrid act. I also understand anyone's apprehension about this matter. Regardless, it is a part of our overall process. I will not force anyone to join in any of this, yet I don't want any secrets amongst us. You all will never hear of the gory details or witness anything abhorrent, but I do want you to be aware that it exists. I also want to be forthright from the very beginning. This is Operation Cleaning House and is about eliminating our cancer."

After much deliberation and discussion, Dr. Branch saw that it was time to conclude the meeting, "All right, my brethren, we will have to end this soon or we will be here all night talking about the same thing over and over. I just want to conclude with a couple of points." He held up his index finger while saying, "Number one, Malcolm is compiling all of our monetary data and will inform me of his final analysis. He will let me know what we all need to do to ensure that our pseudo-socialistic idea works." He then held his index and ring finger up in a peace sign saying, "Number two, I have another request to ask of you all." The hall got deathly quiet, and then Dr. Branch stated, "I am going to ask everyone in here to prepare to move." Again, Dr. Branch saw the disdain in faces and heard a few audible gasps.

"This is what I need," Dr. Branch started. "For those of us that live in the county, I will need you to move to the city. I am hoping we will all be able to move in the same neighborhood and begin our process there." Before he heard any dissension, he quickly added, "Before I hear any complaints, I want you all to think for a minute. Can you imagine a neighborhood in the city with twenty-six black men? I say again, black *men* . . . Not niggas, thugs, hustlers, pimps, or transients . . . but twenty-six black men with common goals and aspirations. That hasn't been seen since the fifties. We, working and living together, will help our impact greatly. It will also cut our cost because living in the city is a lot cheaper than living in the suburbs. Some places in the city the state will probably pay us to go and live." The last statement he said with a chuckle.

"Dr. Branch, you asking for a whole lot," someone from the audience said.

"I know, and this group started with me informing you guys that I was going to ask for some outlandish things," Dr. Branch returned. "I even stated that some of the things will be unimaginable. You all must realize how huge our goal is. No one can take it lightly. I certainly don't underestimate what is needed to accomplish this feat. I said it once, but I have no problem reiterating: to complete our mission, it will take tremendous sacrifice from each and every one of us." Dr. Branch spoke the next part softly but with an extremely serious edge, "This is not a cult nor is this some beginning of a new religion. We are a society, a society of black men that are literally going to change the world. You cannot expect to do that without doing something crazy," Dr. Branch said, throwing up a quote symbol with his fingers in the air.

"Listen, guys," Dr. Branch was wrapping up, "Reaching our main objective will only be accomplished through tackling smaller goals. Keeping all things in perspective, this is a smaller goal; moving to one community is just logical. It increases our chance of success in every aspect. And you all will be my neighbors. Now, is that really so bad?" Though Dr. Branch was being sarcastic, the question still caused some to sway.

"Where will we all live?" one of the men inquired.

"Now that is something I don't know as of yet," Dr. Branch answered. "I have to first find the most optimal spot to initiate this process. Anyway, I really need to get you all out of here . . . one final thing, though we will continue this weekly meeting, I will begin speaking one on one with you guys. Meeting adjourned, gentlemen," Dr. Branch said while eyeing his watch. He said damn under his breath, knowing his wife wasn't going to be happy with him getting home so late again

While the men were departing, Dr. Branch slapped one of the gentlemen on the back and yelled to everyone, "We *are* going to fix a broken people, my brethren. You will see. We really are." There were some cheers of agreement and fist pumping, and Dr. Branch stood smiling, while everyone left the building. Of course, Mathew stayed and helped with the clean up. They chatted and closed up as quickly as possible.

Dr. Branch drove home a little faster than usual. He arrived home and opened his front door to a clean, quiet house. Most of the lights were off, and the alarm was set. He typed in the necessary code to disarm the alarm and tiptoed upstairs after resetting it. He saw his wife with her back facing the door as he entered their room. He took off his clothes and slid in bed. She would be mad, but that was nothing he couldn't repair with a good breakfast in bed in the morrow.

Around nine o'clock Monday night, Dr. Branch was cradling a cold beer in one hand with the remote control in the other. He heard the door bell sound off with its cute birdlike ding-dong. He waited on Tom Brady to finish his third down play before rising off of his couch. After seeing Randy Moss catch a fifteen-yard pass from Brady, Dr. Branch finally stood. He cheered as he took one step away from the couch. By the time he took a second step, his wife was descending the stairs. He quickly flopped back on the couch.

After a few seconds, he heard his wife saying, "Sweetheart, here is Mr. Banks." Then she stepped aside to let Malcolm enter the TV room.

Malcolm, while entering the room, smiled and politely stated, "You have a very beautiful home, Mrs. Branch." He looked all the nerd in his high-water blue slacks and navy blue oxford. He even had two pens in the shirt pocket.

Christine smiled and turned to walk away. Before she was completely out of the room, she responded very condescendingly, "Yeah, it is a nice house . . . isn't it?"

Malcolm, a tad confused by her tone, thought he offended his leader's wife. Now somewhat shaken, Malcolm slowly walked toward Dr. Branch while extending his right hand. He held a black folder that was full of documents under his left arm. Dr. Branch yelled at the TV, and it startled Malcolm. He jumped from the unexpected excitement from Dr. Branch, and the folder slipped from under his arm. The folder fell with a thud, and the papers splashed in a circle around it. Malcolm quickly dropped to the floor to gather the papers. Of course with all of the bustling, Dr. Branch finally gave Malcolm some attention. Dr. Branch rose from his couch and approached the mess. Once Malcolm saw that Dr. Branch's focus was on him, he instantly started apologizing.

"Sorry . . . Dr. Branch, the files slipped. I got it . . . Please don't help. Sit back down and enjoy your game. I got it I just need to uhhh . . . I uhhh," Malcolm pushed out while gathering the papers.

Malcolm was stammering. He didn't understand why he was so intimidated by this man. He felt like a high school freshman hanging with the coolest senior in school. Dr. Branch just seemed to emanate power. Malcolm actually believed he felt light energy radiating from his leader. Even seeing Dr. Branch in his house clothes and slippers did nothing to mitigate this reverent feeling. Malcolm saw this man as honor and power incarnate.

"No need to apologize, my friend," Dr. Branch stated as he happily obliged Malcolm's request by returning to his butt groove on the couch. "Come on over here and have a seat, Mac. You don't mind me calling you Mac, do you?"

"Absolutely not, Dr. Branch," Malcolm stated while organizing the last of the documents and sliding them back in the folder. Malcolm got up off of the floor and sat on the adjacent love seat. Not being a huge football fan, he feigned interest not wanting to rush his leader. When the next commercial came on, Dr. Branch finally gave Malcolm his undivided attention.

"All right, Mac, what do you have for me?"

"Here you go, Dr. Branch," Malcolm stated while handing over the full folder.

Dr. Branch looked at the paperwork with disdain. Malcolm saw the look on Dr. Branch's face and a cold chill ran up his spine. He thought he was about to get reprimanded for something. In that instant, he thought of everything he could have done wrong with the paperwork and felt stupid. He started screaming to himself (in his head), "Stupid, stupid, stupid." Before he could continue denigrating himself, Dr. Branch turned from the papers and offered praise.

"This was a lot of work. Even more than I assumed it was going to be," Dr. Branch started. "You do know that when we all move, some of this info will change," Dr. Branch stated while looking at more documentation.

"Yes," Malcolm responded confidently, "I have taken that into consideration. I have the cost of everything now and the estimated difference once we all move to the city. Our cost will be cut dramatically once we all get settled in the inner city. Of course, living arrangements in the areas you want us to live will be far cheaper than most of our suburban dwellings," Malcolm informed, finally sounding like a confident man. He knew numbers, and when speaking on numbers, that is when he felt at peace. Numbers don't lie. Malcolm then added one final statement off subject, "By the way, sounds as though I offended your wife. I hope you both can forgive me. She sounded really unhappy with me."

Dr. Branch released a huge, robust laugh. Once he finished and wiped away the tears that were forming from such a hard chuckle, he placed Malcolm at ease. "Mac, it certainly isn't you that has my wife in such a foul mood. She is pissed because I've recently informed her that we were moving to the city really soon. You have to realize Mac that she put a lot of work into this house, and of course, she doesn't want to leave it to move into the city, especially where I will be placing us."

Dr. Branch then said, "I truly understand how she feels, but you and I know that this isn't about what we want. This thing we are doing is greater than any individual or their wants. This is even bigger than my marriage." Dr. Branch didn't hesitate when making that last statement. Back on subject, Dr. Branch then said, "OK, Mac, explain what I am looking at. Better yet, give a brief synopsis please."

Malcolm began to provide all of the pertinent information regarding everyone's salary and their cost of living. He tried not to focus on the minutia, but when he did, Dr. Branch would steer him toward the bigger picture. After a two-hour discussion with a few football interruptions, Malcolm transferred all of the important monetary matters to Dr. Branch. Before he finished, he left Dr. Branch with one concern.

"Dr. Branch, I just have one issue. There are some of us that will end up giving too much, while others will get too much . . . If you know what I mean."

Dr. Branch quickly retorted, "Let me stop you there, Mac . . . None of us will ever be able to give too much, but we can take too much. Please explain your issue." Dr. Branch began rubbing his chin, waiting on the response.

"Well, for instance, I'll start with Winston," Malcolm began. "Winston drives a Mercedes-Benz, car note . . . 850 dollars. Yet he only brings home a little more than twice that. He really doesn't need that vehicle, and little changes like that will aid our, um your cause."

Dr. Branch reflexively interjected, "You were right the first time. Our cause! Now continue."

Malcolm, pushed back by the strength of the interruption, slowly and softly began with the rest of what he was thinking, "Rod . . . Every penny he makes goes to bills, so if he wanted to feed himself and his boy, he would actually have to forgo a bill for that month. He is always behind. Phillip, he is taking care of three kids and a wife that works at white castles, living in North County, barely making ends meet. About three fourths of the group is living check to check, yet they continue to attempt living above their means."

Dr. Branch leaned back on the couch, took a look at the football highlights, and pondered for a quick second then said, "So is 90 percent of America." He continued, "That is very beneficial, and I want you to know that I truly count on you for opinions like the aforementioned, never hold back what you are thinking, Mac." After the uplift, Dr. Branch made a peculiar face then asked, "Is there some good news you can give me, my friend?"

Malcolm pushed his glasses back before they slid off of his face and offered Dr. Branch a very slight smile. The smile disappeared instantly, and he told Dr. Branch, "Though three fourths of the group is basically struggling to stay afloat, the combined estates of three in our group could sustain meager but comfortable living for the twenty-six men and our families." Malcolm sounded as shocked then as he did when he first found out.

Dr. Branch's eyes grew large. His brows raised, and his faced showed the conflict of being amazed and confused at the same time. "I have to ask, Mac, who?"

Malcolm, knowing the people and their info by heart, informed, "First, there is Fred Conch; he is retired from the military. He apparently made some smart investments as well as lived below his means. He has some property that brings in a nice amount of money. Then, there's Barry Youngblood. He's a salesman for a technical company that does very, very well. Last, there is Woody Daniels, the wealthiest amongst us." Malcolm cleared his throat before proceeding, "Well, Dr. Branch, Woody is a trash man, yet he has a substantial sum of money in the bank." Before Dr. Branch could ask, Malcolm was pulling a file out of the folder and passing it over.

Dr. Branch took the piece of paper and looked at it. He saw a number circled in red, and again, his eyes grew in surprise. He looked at Malcolm wondering was this the right number. Malcolm confirmed with a nod of the head.

"Well, that is wonderful. We have a little more than I was expecting."

"Then you and I are the next members living quite comfortably," Malcolm threw that last tidbit in to confirm his commitment to Dr. Branch's objective.

"Well, this is some good news," Dr. Branch began. "Moving to the city will save a substantial sum. And from what I hear, there are even some incentives encouraging folks to return to the city and fix it up. Make sure you look into those incentives and ensure we get every bit of monetary help we can, Mac."

"I certainly will, Dr. Branch," Malcolm responded.

"This is great work, Mac. You should be immensely proud of yourself. It's because of you we will achieve success, my friend," Dr. Branch poured.

"Thank you, sir," Malcolm quickly responded. He left the house swelled with pride after receiving such a compliment. He believed in Dr. Branch and would do far more than his share to see that man's plan come to a reality.

The Twenty-Six

THE TWENTY-SIX BEGAN to become really close. Though they still retained their old friends prior to joining the group, those relationships began to take second place to the newly attained friendships within the group. The Twenty-Six were linked tight, and certain members began to get really close to others and formed cliques. The men would be seen together at all types of venues: Little League games supporting a member's child, band recitals, or even for a few drinks at a sports bar. They started to take care of one another like brothers. Their united cause separated them from the world. They were truly becoming a family. Each began to share and hear very personal things about the other. Family members became well known, and the entire bunch became one connected community. Though cliques were forming, nothing excited the men more than their weekly meeting. No one could deny the power within the room when the Twenty-Six were together and on one accord. It was like being at an NFL football game surrounded by 70,000 people all cheering for the same play. The energy in the meeting hall was almost visible. And listening to what the men coined Dr. Branch's weekly sermons became the highlight of each week.

Correction . . . there **was** one thing that excited the men more than the weekly sermons. It was actually witnessing Dr. Branch's ideas becoming tangible.

Dr. Branch spoke to each member of the group separately about the necessary and immediate changes that needed to occur. After a lot of cajoling and some unintentional psychological mental manipulation, every man acquiesced to the immediate demands placed upon them at that time. Because every man obeyed without question (well without dissension), the plan began to take form. All of their funds where pooled (some of the men reallocating their funds without their spouses' knowledge). They all began to move into the same neighborhood. And teams within the Twenty-Six were forming for future missions.

Dr. Branch rejuvenated the men's passion on a weekly basis. He was sure to keep their minds off of remedial worries. *The little things* is what he called them (the day to day stresses that plague all hardworking men and the stuff that provides most black men with an unhealthy dose of hypertension). Week by week, the men received action and not just words. They also understood that each one had a role to play and neither wanted to let the group down. With Dr. Branch's ideas and their combined dedication, the smaller goals were getting accomplished. Though living arrangements where reduced for some, life did become a lot easier and noticeably different for most. In the beginning, the only major difficulty was reconnecting to the city lifestyle.

West Side St. Louis was the group's destination. Dr. Branch found a vacant school perfect for his educational plans and wanted to have the surrounding area prepared for the building's restoration and subsequent occupancy. Finding places to live around that school really wasn't difficult because group members and connecting families accepted less than accommodating domiciles. The area wasn't the safest, but that would soon change is what the men truly believed.

The one thing that ensured change within the mind-sets of the Twenty-Six was the weekly meeting. The weekly meetings would include lessons, behavioral and emotional. Men received lessons from other men but mostly from Dr. Branch. Dr. Branch would include lessons on priorities and what was really important. It took patience, and at times even tough love from Dr. Branch, but the men began to firmly grasp hold to his concepts. There were times when he needed to completely revamp a person's perception and way of thinking, but it was all for the greater good.

Some meetings would include Dr. Branch describing what needed to be changed. During one gathering, he mentioned the fact that some men would have to trade in their current vehicle for a less expensive one. Winston, feeling like he was certainly going to be on that list, jokingly replied "Anything but a Neon, Dr. Branch," the crowd roared with laughter. Though there was jest in that statement, Dr. Branch knew Winston wasn't joking. He saw this as an opportunity to touch and change Winston's way of thinking forever. So in a one-on-one meeting with Winston, Dr. Branch demanded that he trade in his Benz for a Neon (the color was Winston's choice). Winston adamantly protested, stating that he could not be seen in a toy car. Dr. Branch let him know that he was unconcerned with Winston's trivial, egotistical desires. Dr. Branch was determined to show Winston the things that were truly important, and the type of car you drive was nowhere on the list. Winston fought tooth and nail, and he and Dr. Branch ended their discussion with Winston strongly telling Dr. Branch that he would never trade in his car for a damn Neon. Dr. Branch merely nodded and left Winston's home.

The next meeting, Winston pulled up in his new all black Neon. Unhappy with his new car in the beginning weeks, he slowly fell in love with his little toy car. The neon used at least one fifth as much gas. He no longer received the looks and glares he once got from others while driving past in his Benz, but he no longer needed such attention from the outside world. Winston, like everyone else within the Twenty-Six, slowly began to see and accept Dr. Branch's teachings, and having a vehicle that turned heads was so unimportant to him now.

Dr. Branch was truly amazed at how well everyone got along. He coined that time frame the *connection phase:* a moment in the group when everlasting relationships were built. Everything was coming together, a tad too slowly for Dr. Branch, but coming together nonetheless.

Throughout the connection phase, teams where decided, and personnel was established. During one meeting, Dr. Branch circulated a sheet of paper with the team names and all members of the Twenty-Six wrote their names under the team they wanted to join. He also told the men to try and make teams of six. Regardless, he certainly wanted each man to join the team that he was most enthusiastic about. After everyone wrote their designations, the paper was passed back up front. Dr. Branch studied the resulting list and was surprised. Though he didn't expect to see any names under the *Cleaning House (CH)* objective, he saw six. They were his six dark disciples.

Dr. Branch turned his back to the audience and wrote on an erasable white board with a purple marker. When he was finished, he stood back so the team could see the resulting list. Everyone was surprised to see the CH team with a complete set of participants. Everyone who wasn't going to be a part of the team all looked at the soon to be members with questioning glares. All of the men on that list just shrugged their shoulders as if saying, "Well, somebody's got to do it." Even Joe was on the list. He first seemed to oppose the idea of cleaning house, but he was on board after much consideration.

Dr. Branch then said to everyone, "We will need a leader for each team. Though I am leading this entire operation, I will also lead the CH team. I'll lead because the nature of that work is going to be a heavy burden on someone's soul. It's just right that I hold the majority of that weight."

A few guys volunteered for the leadership positions. Luke Chodi, volunteered to lead the *Beautifying the Neighborhood* (BON) objective. Luke, a carpenter of twenty years, would surely know how to repair a damaged area. Deak Charleston, a Vietnam vet, chose to lead the *Emotional Reparation* (ER) objective. This pleased Dr. Branch because if anyone could understand a damaged mind, it would be someone who spent time in actual combat. The final objective of *Educating Our People* (EOP) was chosen by Shannon Progress, a man who taught at Harris Stowe, a junior college. Dr. Branch could not have chosen better leaders for each objective and was glad he didn't have to oppose any of the volunteers.

The men spoke a little longer about how they wanted to begin the true aspect of their endeavor: what they were going to tackle first, when these things would be done, and of course, how would these goals get accomplished. They were all impressed after listening to Dr. Branch for he had an answer for each question, and he already had specific ideas on accomplishing those goals.

Dr. Branch concluded the meeting by saying, "Once again, guys, great meeting. A lot was accomplished tonight. We have a few more ideas to discuss and some specifics we need to look at. Regardless, I see us really diving into this process within the next couple of weeks. So spend as much time with your family as you can because once we start, we are going full speed with no breaking. All righty, gents, have a good night."

The men rose from their seats, all glowing with ideas of what was to come. They began to march out of the hall, and Dr. Branch held one back for a personal discussion, something that was becoming a norm, for he always needed to speak to individuals.

"Woody, would you mind staying after for a little while? I have some extremely important matters to discuss with you," Dr. Branch asked.

Woody Daniels, looked at the men leaving the hall then back to Dr. Branch and replied, "Of course, Dr. Branch. Is there anything you need?"

"Let's grab a seat," Dr. Branch said and began walking to a table in the corner of the hall. Though most of the men had exited the door, Dr. Branch still felt like they would have more privacy in the back of the hall. Woody, a quiet trash collector and a tall, very thin man with mocha brown skin and a clean shaven face followed Dr. Branch to the back corner of the hall and had a seat. He still wore his work jumpsuit.

Dr. Branch started, "Well, you know we have pooled all of our money together. After much consideration, I am actually feeling sort of bad."

"Why?" Woody jumped in sounding genuinely concerned.

Dr. Branch smiled and finished, "Woody . . . being totally honest with you, if it wasn't for your considerable sum of money, none of this could have happened. Though I never thought I would say something like this, I think you are giving too much. Your funds are supporting us and will be the main source of capital for our beginning . . . "

"I will be frank, Woody. Everyone provided bank account information and job information. Though a few of us are doing quite well, our funds combined with everyone else's couldn't sustain my idea for this pseudo-socialistic system. But you, you have enough money to take care of all of us, at least for now. With that being said, I have a few questions."

Dr. Branch spoke quietly almost whispering, "First, Woody, are you OK with being the primary source of money for the things we want to do? I mean we will be buying a lot of equipment and a bunch of other items that we could have never thought about getting without your monetary input. We will spend your money, Woody. I would typically say our money, but that wouldn't be fair to you. I feel bad. But if you say it is OK, that will give me some solace. And if you say it's not OK, I would actually understand. The type of money you have provided is a huge sacrifice." Dr. Branch rubbed his eyes and said again, "A huge sacrifice. I just wanted to be sure you knew that."

"Dr. Branch, after losing my kid, money means absolutely nothing." Trying to hold back emotion, Woody continued, "I was really wondering what to do with the damn money. If I can help support you and our team with it, that's perfect."

Dr. Branch just smiled and shook his head in disbelief. Woody needed no lecture on how to fall out of love with money. Dr. Branch then asked, "OK, another question. Why are you working as a trash man, if you don't mind me asking, when you obviously never have to work another day in your life?"

Woody looked at Dr. Branch as though that was a stupid question then responded like Dr. Branch should know the answer, "Because every man should work. Well, any real man anyways." Dr. Branch smiled and shook his head in amazement again while Woody finished, "And I like what I do."

Dr. Branch loved this man. He really couldn't remember hearing Woody say much throughout the hall meetings, and now he understood why. Woody was a man of little words but apparently of much action. His answers were concise and superquick. Dr. Branch then asked, "I also see you have a lot of property. Do you think we could have access to a few of your buildings?"

"You don't have to ask, Dr. Branch, just tell me what you need," Woody stated.

"Awesome. I am astounded, Woody. I only have one final question for you, brother. How did you accumulate such wealth? Simply put, how did you get all of that money, my man?" Dr. Branch inquired, speaking softly, almost as though someone was eavesdropping.

"I got the money," Woody responded blankly, looking Dr. Branch directly in the eyes.

Dr. Branch quickly left that topic alone. "Well, all I can say is 'thank you'. I thank you, we thank you, and the world will thank you when we are finished. I don't want to hold you too long, my friend. I just had to let you know what was going on. I'm about to close up. Come on, let's get out of here."

They both stood and meandered to the door quietly. Woody said nothing during the entire walk until he got to his Ford flatbed truck. Then he said, "Dr. Branch, do we have a name? Our group, we should have a name. It's important for any group to have a name."

Woody was one of the quietest people in the Twenty-Six, now Dr. Branch understood why. He was a thinker.

Goals truly were getting accomplished. New living arrangements were found for the entire bunch, and their money was all pooled together. The men allowed Dr. Branch to lead, and they all basically followed orders as well as soldiers. The first phase was complete. They could begin with the second phase: beautifying the neighborhood.

Beautifying the neighborhood was going to be a two-part process. The two teams were going to have to work together. The aesthetics of the neighborhood could not be improved if young street punks loitered. It is not a pretty picture to see seven or eight kids with their pants hanging, all posted in front of a house. Even if the house is a mansion, the wrong people standing in front of that mansion can make it look like a brothel. So team CH and team BON began meeting together more often than once a week. They rarely used the hall for discussing any agenda items; the hall was primarily designated for Dr. Branch's weekly sermons. They met at their new domiciles in the city to discuss business matters.

Dr. Branch would have leadership meetings with his three compatriots, Luke, Shannon and Deak. They would usually meet at his beaten down house. They discussed the paths each would take and the how's. And that information would get disseminated to the other members in their respective teams.

Dr. Branch also met with his six CH team members almost daily. One Thursday, the small group arrived at his house. Anthum Williams was the first to show up. Anthum was a spectacle; he was six foot six and two hundred sixty pounds of pure plutonium alloy. He was dark as night and held a facial expression of hate constantly. What made things worse was that he was a karate instructor and had trained uninterrupted for the last twenty years. He pulled up, parked about 20 feet from Dr. Branch's house and exited his car. He took a look around the neighborhood. He twitched his eyes at the hoodlums a little way down the street and walked toward his leader's home. He consumed his surroundings. While walking up the concrete steps to the concrete porch that night, he could have told Dr. Branch how many cars were on the street, the number of people out, and a lot of other information his eyes caught. Directly after rapping on the door, he turned back toward the streets to take it all in: the dilapidated shape of the homes, the many vacant houses, the numerous lots filled with trash and broken glass (no telling what else). He heard footsteps approaching and turned so Dr. Branch could see his face through the peephole. The old-fashioned wooden door opened after numerous locking mechanisms were heard. There, Dr. Branch stood in all his glory. This man was going to rid the world of this trash, this filth, and Anthum looked forward to bathing in the blood of these honorless creatures.

Dr. Branch stepped out and shook Anthum's hand. They stayed on the porch after greeting each other and watched as the other members all pulled up almost concurrently. This was going to be a good meeting. They had a lot to discuss, and each had already sworn not to leave until plans were finalized.

The men all shook hands and said their hello's. Dr. Branch, no longer having an array of rooms, asked the men to meet in the kitchen. Though the house needed some work (a lot of work), it was spotless. They all gathered in the small kitchen, sat around a table that was three-fourths the size of the small room, and started their discussion.

"So how do we go about cleaning the filth from our streets?" Anthum started, skipping the small talk.

"Yeah, I was wondering the same thing. I mean are we just gonna do drive-by's and stuff like that?" That question came from Larry Evans, a manager at Krispy Kreme's, and a man who goes nowhere without his seventeen-shot Glock, loaded with black talon bullets. He was a second amendment fanatic, especially after the death of his daughter.

After a slight chuckle, Dr. Branch answered, "Absolutely not. We are not a gang. We will not act like one. This is the one major covert aspect of our endeavor. Nothing will be done in the open. We will be as infamous as the CIA; all things will be done behind closed doors. We will have information before we act – nothing spontaneous and nothing that can be traced back to us."

Dr. Branch continued, "You guys know Mathew here is a cop. So, he is privy to a lot of information that we will need to know about the lives we plan to change. We have property out in the boonies, which is getting renovated for our plans as we speak." Dr. Branch rubbed the tiredness from his eyes and continued, "This is how we will do things. First, we will distinguish the murderers from everyone else. The murderers will be removed all at once. Then we will get the thugs and drug addicts and lock them up while purifying them through pain."

"You mean sit people in a room and haze 'em like some frat boys?" queried Joe.

"Honestly, that is the best picture I can provide," Dr. Branch explained. "Trust me, the hazing will be more like torture, and this isn't a movie." The coldness in Dr. Branch's voice made his point stick. He continued, "Afterward, we will give them their freedom under one condition. They join us. If not, they join the dirt." The men had never heard Dr. Branch sound so cold.

"What makes you think this will work, Dr. Branch?" Larry inquired.

"I'm glad you asked, Larry. Let me tell you guys a quick story. I think it will be quite entertaining." Dr. Branch told the story of the first experiment he performed right before he left his suburban home.

Subject Numero Uno

WHILE DRIVING TO work one morning, Dr. Branch noticed a young black boy. Because there were few black families in his neighborhood, Dr. Branch recognized all of the other kids. He would have especially remembered this kid, because he stood out. Unlike the other few young black boys in his township, this one looked like an inner-city youth. Dr. Branch estimated the kid's age at about fifteen or sixteen. He wore jeans sagging bellow his gluteus minimus with a colorful Ralph Lauren polo shirt. The outfit was very clean, including the spotless shoes. The ensemble would have been really nice if the pants were worn at the waist and the shirt wasn't three times too large. Though the style of dress caught Dr. Branch's eye, it wasn't the clothes that held his attention. It was the fact that the kid eyed Dr. Branch as though they were old rivals.

As Dr. Branch drove down the wealthy suburban street, the kid stared at Dr. Branch eye to eye until they were out of each others view. The entire scenario pissed Dr. Branch off to high heaven. Here he is about to sacrifice all to save the inner-city youths, and this one obviously wants to carry that ghetto attitude within him when there wasn't a need.

Dr. Branch didn't approve of the behavior or the attitude of today's inner-city youth, but he understood it. He grew up with it himself. When navigating through the treacherous waters of the ghetto, one had to look and act like everyone else. To be different was to stand out, and standing out in the ghetto usually meant trouble. But this kid was nowhere near the city and light years away from any ghetto. He was actually in one of the wealthiest regions in all of the St. Louis metropolitan area. So why this kid wanted to look and behave like something he didn't have to baffled Dr. Branch. Maybe this was a one-time thing. Maybe the kid was visiting a friend that lived in this area. Dr. Branch figured he would pass by this street at the exact same time the next morning to get an answer to the questions ringing in his head.

The kid was a resident, and Dr. Branch did see him again, this time with his book bag. The kid gave Dr. Branch the same response. As Dr. Branch slowly scooted pass the kid, the kid looked up, made direct eye contact, and glared at Dr. Branch as though they were at the OK Corral. Dr. Branch became infuriated. This kid represented everything he hated about his people.

That is when a light bulb went off, and Dr. Branch realized this kid would be his first project. Every morning thereafter, he was sure to drive pass the kid on his way to work. Dr. Branch left his house earlier each day to learn the kid's route, until he finally caught the kid exiting a particular house. It was a big beautiful house; apparently, his parents were well off. Why the kid wanted to portray that thug mentality confused Dr. Branch.

After a lot of planning and preparation, Dr. Branch finally set his operation in motion. His heart pumped twice as fast as normal when entering his car on that morning. He circled the area a few times, ensuring that there was no police presence, and he found a part of the kid's route that was the most secluded. Dr. Branch sat in his parked car, waiting on the kid, and then he began to get extremely nervous . . . cold feet. What was he doing? If anything went wrong, he could end up in a ton of trouble. No matter, this was not the time to lose heart. Dr. Branch knew that if he could not go through with this, he might as well abort the whole ordeal. Cancelling was not an option. It was time to see it through. Dr. Branch felt in his bones that if he could convert this kid, he could save every black soul that needed it.

That morning, he was sure to approach the kid from the back. He drove very slowly in his black and silver Grande Marque, which didn't make a sound as it crept along the black pavement. Dr. Branch focused on the kid's back as the kid walked down the sidewalk like he owned the street. The kid's boxers were visible from a distance. Showing Dr. Branch his underwear was like waving a red flag in front of a bull. If Dr. Branch had any trepidations, seeing the kid's saggy britches removed them. Dr. Branch allowed the car to roll right behind the kid, while he switched gears. He put the car in neutral and popped the trunk. He hopped out in one swift motion.

The kid heard the car door open and finally turned toward the sound. He was amazed to see an empty car rolling beside him. He attempted to examine his immediate surroundings but experienced a quick jolt of pain and everything went black.

Dr. Branch moved like a ninja. He ran behind his car and tapped the kid's back (near the kidney) with his taser. The kid instantly jumped with a quick grunt and fell limp. Dr. Branch caught the kid in midfall. He opened the trunk fully and hoisted the kid in, being sure not to be too gentle. He then shut the trunk while scanning the crime scene. Excellent, Dr. Branch thought; no one saw a thing. The kid's snatching took less than seven seconds. Dr. Branch dove back into his driver's seat and made his way home. He pulled into his garage, got out, and popped the trunk. The kid, appearing really small and frail while unconscious, laid in the trunk sprawled like a rag doll. Dr. Branch hefted his victim over his shoulders, the whole time thinking that he was about to have some serious fun – an experiment on a human subject.

Dr. Branch knew his logic was quite flawed. Using the results of this one experiment to hold true for all further test samples was illogical. Numerous experiments would have to be performed before experimental results could become expected results. Dr. Branch didn't care about his flawed thinking. If he could change this one kid, he could change the world. He already had a plan in mind. Fear. Throughout history, fear has been a common tool used when wanting to affect the masses. Dr. Branch would use fear, here, now . . . and always.

Dr. Branch walked down the steps to his basement with the kid still on his shoulders. The kid was slowly regaining his consciousness. Dr. Branch could feel the kid shaking his head, obviously trying to gather his wits. Dr. Branch carried the load to his basement and slammed the boy hard onto a wooden chair. The kid expelled an audible grunt. The kid's eyes were glossy but fully open, and he instinctively resisted as Dr. Branch tied his wrists to the arms of the chair with blue nylon string. The kid was still too groggy to even fight his ankles being laced to the front legs of the chair with the same material.

The kid shook his head one more time and finally seemed to gain full coherency. He looked around the small, enclosed basement room, trying to figure out what was going on. His head angled downward, allowing him to see his legs tied to the chair. He saw his wrist and began tugging while attempting to kick his legs. When the realization hit that he was someone's prisoner, he began to scream frantically.

"Help! Help!" the kid shouted.

Being unable to turn completely around and get a full view of the basement, allowed Dr. Branch to remain invisible from the kid's eyes. The only thing the kid saw in the room was a television about six feet in front of him. It sat on a stand with a DVD player on top. The kid struggled more violently this time and screamed more loudly. He continued wailing, and Dr. Branch had to struggle to hold in a laugh once the kid's pitch hit soprano.

They were in a small back room deep in Dr. Branch's basement, so he just listened to the kid scream himself silly, knowing nothing could be heard outside of that compartment. Then he finally let the kid know that there were at least two people in the room.

"A big tough guy like you isn't scared, are you?" Sarcasm poured out of Dr. Branch.

"Wha . . . wha . . . wha," the kid stammered.

Dr. Branch stepped from behind the kid and stood to his left. The kid jumped when first seeing Dr. Branch in his periphery. The kid turned to face Dr. Branch, and his eyes widened enough to look cartoon like.

"Have you ever heard that saying, 'Be careful who you fuck with'?" Dr. Branch inquired in a slow, deep, and menacing tone.

The kid, still tongue tied, just eyed Dr. Branch in utter amazement. Again, the kid tried to expel some words, but he had lost all communicative abilities. The kid pushed again, "Wher . . . who . . . wha . . .," then he began breathing too rapidly.

"Take a deep breath, boy!" Dr. Branch demanded. The kid obliged. He took a few breaths. After the kid gained some type of composure, Dr. Branch then repeated, "Have you ever heard the saying, 'Be careful who you fuck with'?" this time without the menacing tone.

The kid, still incapable of connecting his brain to his tongue, just shook his head from left to right. Dr. Branch stepped behind the kid and left the basement door. He quickly returned with a small three-legged seat. It was a short stool with wheels. Dr. Branch sat on the cushioned seat after shutting the door and rolled the stool directly in front of the kid.

"Let me enlighten you, little brother," Dr. Branch said with his face nearly touching the kid's. "Well, they always say, 'Be careful who you fuck with, because one day you are going to run into the wrong person.' Young brother, you have officially run into the wrong one."

"What did I do?" the kid blurted, finally able to find his tongue.

Dr. Branch quickly thumped the kid's bottom lip. The thump was violent enough to cause a slight abrasion. With the punishment came a lesson.

"Don't ever interrupt me again. You speak when spoken to," Dr. Branch snapped.

The pain caused the kid's eyes to well up and encouraged his lip to quiver, yet no sound escaped his mouth.

"Good, I see you have some control," Dr. Branch said with contempt. "As I was saying . . . that wrong one is me. I know you remember this face." He tilted his head slightly, waiting on a response. The kid just looked at him. "You can speak."

"Yeah, I remember you. You're the old dude that be staring at me every morning," the kid said.

"Me . . . Staring at you . . . I am sure it was the other way around," Dr. Branch informed. "I saw you, and you looked at me as though I harmed you in another life. In my day, we called it mean mugging, maybe even mad-dogging. We did it a lot, but we never did it to an older person. We had respect. And we certainly wouldn't have done it while living out here. Why are you behaving like that out here?"

Dr. Branch continued, not allowing time for an answer, "Out here people are not concerned with how *hard* you are. To them, you look like a fool, and you are perpetuating every negative stereotype we carry." Dr. Branch started getting intense, "So once again, I ask, and if the answer is not your truth, punishment commences, maybe even death. Why . . . did . . . you . . . mug . . . me?" Dr. Branch said, poking the kid's forehead with each word.

"I don't know," the kid said while starting to cry.

"Did you think I was in some opposing gang?" Dr. Branch yelled and poked.

"No." (sobbing)

"Was I homing in on your territory?"

"Noooooo." (More sobbing.)

"What was it? Why where you mugging me?" Dr. Branch screamed, voice sounding loud and deep.

The kid, never having been chastised by a man, had never felt the bass of a man's voice move through his chest. He felt such a thing then. Sheer terror took over, and he spoke the first words he could articulate. "I thought I was supposed to," was the truth that left the boy's mouth.

Silence.

Dr. Branch's excited demeanor instantly turned tamed and stoic, and then he said, "Now that is all I was looking for, just a truthful answer from you."

Dr. Branch switching subjects instantly said, "Now I need you to do something. I need you to scoot yourself back." The kid looked confused as Dr. Branch gave further details, "I need you to scoot back far enough until your butt is hanging out the back of the chair."

The kid faced Dr. Branch with wide eyes that were welling again. The kid softly pleaded, "Please, mister, don't rape me."

A robust laugh shot out of Dr. Branch, and he responded, "Kid, you don't have to worry about that at all. If you die today, it will be unspoiled, young brother."

"Die today? Why, mister?" the kid whined. "Why I gotta die, why you gonna kill me. Just for looking at you. That's crazy, mister. Please. I will never stare at anyone else. I swear. I don't wanna die, pleeeaaaasseee." The last plead lasting for three seconds.

"Kid, I am not killing you because we made eye contact," Dr. Branch actually spoke gently to the kid, like a father. He continued, "I will let you in on a little secret. Some big changes are about to happen within St. Louis. There is a group of men that thinks exactly like me, watching you kids, and we will no longer allow you to behave like a tribe of lost souls. I can tell you more, but that sums it up." The kid looked a tad baffled, so Dr. Branch added more, "We are going to make things simple for all of you; either you change your ways, or we will kill you."

"What?"

"No more questions. Poke your ass out the back of that chair," Dr. Branch demanded.

"What for?"

"Do it now, boy, or this day ends quicker than I planned!" Dr. Branch yelled.

The kid, seeing no alternative, complied slowly. He scooted back, allowing his backside to protrude from the opening between the back and the seat of the chair. Dr. Branch exited the little room. With the door being behind the kid, Dr. Branch could remain out of the kid's sight. The kid just sat there whimpering, waiting on Dr. Branch to return. Outside of his sniffles and sobs, there was absolute silence, and then, *wapp*! The kid screamed, more from fright than anything else at first. Once the pain set in, that is when the kid got an idea of what occurred. Before he could think any further, *wapp*! The kid screamed again, closely followed by a brief coughing fit. The kid was getting spanked by something . . . and that something was damn hard. The kid hadn't received a whipping in ten years. In turn, those two smacks on the backside caused the worse pain he could remember receiving in his life.

Dr. Branch, being a member of a fraternity, saved a few mementos from his college days. One item being an oak paddle, with an etching of three Greek letters, he used when hazing his pledges during his heyday. Dr. Branch learned very early that nothing trains a person, young or old, faster or better than the fear of brutal punishment. Though Dr. Branch knew that type of thinking could be considered abhorrent, he also knew when the end justified the means.

So Dr. Branch swung his paddle at the kid's posterior with fervor. He swung again, connecting solidly each time. He took another swipe at the kid's butt, but the kid scooted up no longer giving easy access to his wounded pride. The paddle hit the wooden frame of the chair with a loud thud, which displeased Dr. Branch. He took a step forward and stood directly in front of the kid. He then tapped the kid on the head reminding him what would happen if he used the peace of wood on the kid's head instead of his bottom.

"Either I can crack your skull and bury you in my backyard, or you and accept your punishment," Dr. Branch informed candidly.

The kid, outright blubbering like a toddler who's lost his candy, slowly slid his backside out the back of the chair. As soon as it was accessible, *pow*! Another solid connection from a wicked swing. The pain caused a little bit of brown stuff to leave the kid's anus. He inadvertently slid forward.

"Uhn-uh," Dr. Branch admonished.

The kid quickly caught himself and poked his butt back out. *Wapp*! One more powerful crack to the hindparts. The kid's sphincter lost all strength for a second, and more feces exited the boy's butt. He knew it, and Dr. Branch realized it after a few more seconds.

"Please, mister, I can't take no more," the kid begged, "Whatever you want me to do, I will do. Please stop. Pleeaasssssssseee," finishing with uncontrollable sobbing.

Dr. Branch meandered to the stool and perched. He set the paddle across his lap, and a bead of sweat trickled down the right side of his face. Because the stool was so low, he sat even with the kid. He attempted to look the kid in the eye but couldn't. The kid, too intimidated to return Dr. Branch's gaze, just cried and hung his head very low. Dr. Branch reached out with the paddle and touched the wooden object to the bottom of the kid's chin. He then lifted, raising the boy's head level with his own.

"What is your name, boy?"

"Donald . . . Donald Turner," the kid responded.

"Donald, a strong name. Well Donald, what is your story?" Dr. Branch inquired.

The kid just looked confused. He wouldn't dare ask a stupid question nor give a wrong answer. So he just waited for clarity from Dr. Branch.

Dr. Branch clarified, "Tell me who you are, tell me about you, where you come from, and what you are doing now."

The kid, wincing from some leftover pain, began to speak through his tears, "I'm from the north side. My momma always went out, so I spent most of my time with my friends that lived next door. My friends moved when I turned twelve, and that's when my momma gave me to my grandma and granddad."

"How old are you, boy?" another question from Dr. Branch.

"I'm fifteen, I'll be sixteen next year," Donald answered.

"Oh, so you think you will be seeing next year, how presumptuous," Dr. Branch toyed with Donald. The kid just looked Dr. Branch in the eyes with utter despair. He was defeated. Dr. Branch told the kid, "Finish your story."

Donald began again, with little to no tears this time, "My grandma and granddad been taking care of me ever since . . . That's it," he finished timidly.

"How are you doing in school?"

"Well, I'm doing OK I guess. But I might be getting kicked out," he said truthfully, not wanting to hold anything back from this man.

With no change in emotional tone, Dr. Branch inquired, "What reason would your school have for kicking you out?"

"Fighting," Donald said.

"Fighting or bullying," Dr. Branch tried to pry deeper.

"Both, I guess," the chastised boy responded.

Dr. Branch stood from the stool and said, "Bullying huh, let me show you how it feels to be bullied." He left the little room.

Donald could only hear his captor leave. He waited, terrified, wondering what else was about to happen. He began thinking about his grandparents and dwelled on the idea that he may never see them again. He thought about his few friends and wished he could play basketball with them one more time. Because it was well pass lunchtime, he thought about his granddad's fried pork chops with mashed potatoes, gravy, and garlic cheese bread, his favorite. Thinking that he would never get to enjoy those things again caused him to break into another crying fit. He yanked at his binds one more time, nothing gave. He only felt more pain. He never heard Dr. Branch reenter the room. He didn't know Dr. Branch saw his futile attempts of escape.

When Dr. Branch was bored of watching his helpless victim, he cleared his throat. The kid straightened. Dr. Branch didn't say a word. He just stood behind the kid, breathing dramatically loud. All of a sudden he grabbed Donald's head and snapped it back as far as it would go, exposing Donald's smooth, brown neck. The teenager's Adam's apple was just beginning to poke out. With his left hand, Dr. Branch slowly brought into view a large butcher's knife. The kid caught a glimpse of the knife and shuddered. Donald began to struggle, causing Dr. Branch to tighten his clawlike grip on his head.

"Stop moving, idiot," Dr. Branch demanded through tight lips. Dr. Branch continued talking using his best impression of a lunatic, "This knife is really sharp. I might unintentionally cut the wrong vessel." Dr. Branch then slowly lowered the blade to the kid's neck and rested it against his throat. Donald, too terrified to swallow, allowed his mouth to fill with saliva.

"Now this is some serious bullying here," boasted Dr. Branch. He continued passionately, "Does this feel good to you, getting bullied like this?"

"No, sir," Donald cried. By this time, sweat rolled down Donald's entire face. His eyes burned from a mixture of tears and perspiration, and his nose leaked snot like a broken faucet. The discomfort he felt from his eyes was greatly overpowered by the emotional turmoil he was experiencing. Donald felt a level of fear he didn't know existed. His overwhelming emotions mixed with a dire situation caused the teen to revert to a small child. With absolutely no base in his voice and sounding like a prepubescent, he begged more.

"Please, mister, please let me go. I won't tell nobody. I swear."

Dr. Branch, finally seeing some true openness in the kid, removed the knife from Donald's throat. He released Donald's head with a shove. Then Dr. Branch said, "I tell you what, little Donald. I am going to play a program on that TV there." Dr. Branch pointed at the television set in front of the boy. He continued, "Afterward, I will ask you a bunch of questions. If you are able to answer them all correctly, I will let you go." Dr. Branch stood there, picking his teeth with the knife. The image could have been in insanity's hall of fame.

Donald, believing his prayers being answered, merely nodded frantically. "Yes, sir," was the only thing he pushed out. His tears slowed to a stop, leaving him with a severe case of sniffles.

Dr. Branch walked to the TV set and turned it on. He pressed the play button on the DVD, and the blue screen jumped to life. Just when Donald thought he would be free of Dr. Branch, that is when the person that presented himself on screen was none other than the one and only Dr. Branch. As the TV set Dr. Branch began his narration, the live Dr. Branch exited the small room.

The program Donald viewed was a two-hour educational peace on black American history. It started with a brief introduction given by Dr. Branch. He provided a brief synopsis of what was to come. The gist of the intro informed the viewer that they were going to learn about the true history of the black American people.

Once the intro finished, the on-screen Dr. Branch dove into a history lesson. Starting with Kemet, ancient Egypt, and ancient Ethiopia, Dr.

Branch provided facts on the origins of black people. Mixed with pictures, maps, and excerpts from other programs, the lessons provided were deeply informative while also being extremely enthralling. After the ancient African history lesson, the program described Africa's progression. Then the topic jumped to the colonization of Africa by Europe and the subsequent slavery holocaust. Next was a deeper focus on the slave trade and the start of America. The lesson progressed to the black American emancipation and the many hardships thereafter. After a deep lesson in segregation and the civil rights battle, the DVD concluded with the many accomplishments of blacks throughout history while primarily focusing on the black American contributions to the world. The conclusion continued with the great sacrifices of prior generations but finished with the horrid state of black America presently. The end showed how the present-day black American people have shamed their near and distant ancestors.

Exactly three seconds after the show ended, the live Dr. Branch entered the room. As he turned off the television, he inquired, "So what did you think of the piece?"

Donald answered honestly, "It was good."

Dr. Branch smiled at the compliment and stated, "We have a deal boy; you answer my series of questions, and I will let you live. You will be free. If you fail, you are mine forever." Dr. Branch couldn't end that statement without a maniacal laugh.

Donald shuddered and nodded his head. Initially, Dr. Branch began with a few very easy questions that Donald answered correctly. Dr. Branch progressively asked more difficult questions until he chose one that would surely stump the boy. Donald fumbled searching for an answer, the correct answer, but could not remember the specifics Dr. Branch required. Once Donald realized he'd lost his last opportunity of escape, he merely hung his head and asked for a second chance.

"Ask me something else. Please, I'll get the next one," he spoke without tears and with a somber sense of acceptance.

"We had a deal, boy!" Dr. Branch shot back at the kid. He continued, "In the last two minutes of your life, you will stand true to your word. You will die with some honor. Don't beg, your life is mine. You didn't understand nor appreciate what you had, so it all shall be taken away, young Donald."

Dr. Branch then brandished that same giant butcher's knife. He flashed it so quickly it seemed to have appeared out of thin air. While standing in front of the kid, Dr. Branch performed some strong practice strikes off to the right side of the chair. The fervor he put into each practice thrust gave

Dr. Branch a gladiator's appearance, preparing for battle. Donald surmised that if Dr. Branch struck him with one of those knife jabs, the blade would pass through his chest easily and would probably go through the back of the chair as well. Dr. Branch then jumped directly in front of Donald.

"Well, you have shown yourself unworthy of walking on this Earth," Dr. Branch stated robotlike. He continued, sounding blank and detached, "I will find another kid that's actually willing and ready to grow. May God have mercy on your soul."

"Please, mister," yelled Donald. He saw the instant change in Dr. Branch's demeanor. Dr. Branch was crazy, but there was always some emotion. This was the first time this crazy man appeared disconnected. Donald knew this was it. He saw Dr. Branch cock his knife wielding arm back to a prone position, full of potential energy. Donald screamed his last words, "I will do better, I promise. Please." With his left hand on Donald's shoulder, Dr. Branch took on a fierce striking pose and held a facial expression to match his stature. Donald saw the knife hand leave its static position and head toward his sternum with blinding speed. Though he could only catch a glimpse of the knife, that microsecond lasted another lifetime to him. In that flash, his eye caught low-level light reflecting off of the blades jagged edge. He could make out letters carved into the blade. His eye even caught the color and wood grain pattern of the handle. He saw all these things while simultaneously thinking about his life. He focused on nothing but regrets. If he could've, he would've done so many things differently. Fucking with this crazy old man would've been at the top of the list.

Donald felt a hard, solid blow to the center of his chest and instantly felt warm liquid flowing and filling his seat. The only bright side was that the pain wasn't what he had expected. Nevertheless, tunnel vision ensued, and little Donald whispered a prayer under his breath. He didn't fight as the darkness consumed him. His last vision was of Dr. Branch's blank scowl looking down upon him as he passed.

slap!

Donald began to stir. His eyes slowly opened. He looked around the room not understanding anything. He was lost as to how he was still alive. He peered down at his chest and saw no blood, yet his bottom half was soaking wet. That is when a realization hit him. He wasn't stabbed by Dr. Branch, but the climatic scene caused him to release all of the contents he held within his bladder. Here he sat still alive, in piss and shit, but still alive. At the last second, Dr. Branch reversed the knife's direction and hit the boy's chest with the handle and not the blade.

"You passed out on me, boy," Dr. Branch told the obvious, he then spoke compassionately, "Listen, I think you want to do better, not only here but in life. Am I right, young Donald?"

"Yes, sir, gimme another try, sir, please I will answer everything right, I promise," Donald explained while waking from the darkness.

"I will do you one better," Dr. Branch said. Dr. Branch walked to the TV set and hit play again while saying, "I want this stuff to stick, learn it for your life depends on it. Not just here but always and forever young brother. No more practice tries." All of the sting was out of Dr. Branch's voice. He spoke calmly, "Listen to me, Donald, this lesson is telling you where we come from. Don't watch this like you are getting answers for me. Listen as though you are finding out all of the answers to your own questions, and you will be capable of answering mine. Do you understand?"

"Yes, sir," Donald's only response as the program started. Donald watched the same program, reinforcing the information he had just learned. He also caught a lot of facts he missed on his first viewing. The show was better the second time. By the end, he was quite confident he could answer any question Dr. Branch presented.

The program ended, and again, Dr. Branch walked in within three seconds. Dr. Branch walked past the kid and turned the television off without words. He turned toward Donald and smiled. He studied the kid as Donald sat in his own piss and shit. The sweat and snot that weren't washed away by tears sat dried to his face, slowly flaking. The smell coming from the kid filled the room; Dr. Branch thought he could actually taste the odor. The kid looked horrible, yet he sat with his head up prepared to show Dr. Branch that he had learned something. Dr. Branch attacked . . . with a question. He started with something he knew Donald could not answer. Instantly deflated, Donald did not attempt to guess. He merely looked Dr. Branch in the eye and said he didn't know, but he added a quick tidbit, signifying he knew something about the subject. Dr. Branch merely widened his smile and brought out his knife slowly, without the dramatics. He walked to Donald and dropped to one knee. With no attempt to scare or trick the boy, Dr. Branch simply took the knife to the binds and sawed until the boy's hand was free. He went to the other side and did the same. Donald, stunned beyond all comprehension, made no sudden moves. He was too tired and weak to do anything stupid. He slowly brought his hands around and rubbed on his soar wrists. Dr. Branch removed the binds from the kid's legs also.

"Now don't do anything stupid, boy,"

"What are you about to do now, mister?" Donald inquired, stretching his limbs.

"I'm about to take you home."

Donald's eyes widened like two eggs. He stood up, hoping this was no final bit of punishment. To dash his dreams now would send him over the edge.

"Sit back down; I don't like you standing over me," Dr. Branch demanded. Donald dropped to the seat with a splash of leaky contents. He saw that some of his juices reached his captor. He rolled his eyes at himself and pushed out a humble apology. Dr. Branch just shook his head and informed the kid, "I'm going to get you some clothes, and you will take a shower and put them on. Afterward, we are going to my car, and I'm driving you home." Donald nodded. "Please don't try anything. We're done, you have proven yourself worthy of life. Don't do anything stupid. I don't want to have to hurt you for real. Stay here, seated. Don't move."

Donald nodded, and Dr. Branch left the room. In that instant instinct took over, and Donald almost jumped out the seat to escape. After reconsidering, he changed his mind. His captor wasn't dumb, and why take a chance? For some reason, he believed what the man was telling him, and he knew he would be free in a matter of minutes. So he sat patiently, awaiting the next command.

Dr. Branch walked in and threw some clothes at the kid, which slipped through Donald's fingers and fell to the floor. Donald picked the clothes off of the floor and was instructed to follow Dr. Branch out of the room and down the hall. To the right was a half bathroom with a small shower. Dr. Branch pointed, and Donald obliged. He walked in the bathroom and shut the door. After his shower, he felt new, free, and certainly different. He looked at himself in the mirror and saw a changed individual. He would get so see his family and his friends again. While thinking those happy thoughts, he put on the clothes Dr. Branch provided, and somehow, they were very close to his size. The clothes weren't name brand, but they would do. He was just happy to be clean and alive. He opened the door to Dr. Branch, standing like a parole officer. Dr. Branch told the kid to follow him out of the basement to the first floor. From there, they both entered the garage. They slid into Dr. Branch's Grande Marque with no words between them. When Dr. Branch opened the garage door and the kid saw the world that he thought he'd never see again, his heart jumped to his throat, and he had to hold back tears. That's when Dr. Branch and Donald had their final conversation.

"You understand what happened here today, Donald?" Dr. Branch genuinely asked.

"A whole lot happened, sir," Donald answered, hoping not to say the wrong thing when so close to freedom.

"You tell me in your own words, young man. Sum this all up."

"You wanted me to respect you and other adults. You wanted me to understand what I got, and I do. You said you wanted me to prove that I'm worthy to be living here." Donald had a lot more he wanted to say, but he was a tad too young and inarticulate to formulate the words. He just stopped there, and it sounded as though he had more to express, but he cut himself off.

Regardless, Dr. Branch was quite satisfied with the answer, but he wanted to make sure the kidnapping was nothing that could come back to haunt him. He also wanted to ensure that Donald understood everything, so he told Donald the absolute truth, with some embellishments of course. "I agree with everything you said. I do want you to respect your elders, especially your grandparents. I certainly want you to understand and appreciate all the things you are blessed with. And you have proven yourself worthy of life," Dr. Branch said, echoing the boy's sentiments. He continued with more, "Donald I also want to let you know that by enduring the process and choosing life over death, you have joined me and my group. So you are one of us now. Us being a group of black men going around making great changes to our people. You have pledged your life to this cause whether you knew it or not, and a whole lot is expected from you, young brother. You are no longer allowed to backslide into your old ways for you have seen the light, and you are only allowed to see the light once. You are no longer Donald Turner, young, motherless, fatherless black teen from the inner city of St. Louis. You are now Donald Turner, member of an elite task force charged with the overwhelming duty of curing your deceased people. This idea may be a little over your head, but I'm sure you understand the fact that now great things are expected of you, Donald. I will not sit by and watch you squander your greatness. None of us will. We will be watching you even when you don't know. We may be under your bed or in your closet," Dr. Branch jested.

"Like the boogie man," Donald threw in.

Dr. Branch slightly chuckled at the statement, "Just like the boogie man," Dr. Branch echoed. "You will be watched, as I am watched," he added, letting Donald know that no one was above judgment, including Dr. Branch.

Donald could not help but to interrupt again, "You had to go through what you just did to me?"

Dr. Branch offered a genuine smile though his eyes showed intense sadness, and he responded, "Donald, in order for me to see the light, I had to experience something far more painful than what you have just endured." Getting back on subject, Dr. Branch kept on, "As I was saying. Just as you are being watched, so am I. We have black men that are a part of this change everywhere." (A huge exaggeration) "If I don't behave as I should, I will be removed, and so will you if you don't do what you're supposed to." Donald looked nervous, so Dr. Branch put his soul at ease, "No worries, little Donald, for I see the change in your eyes. You have transcended, young brother. And just like our brothers are out here to ensure we don't fall, they are also here to help hold us up. All the help you need will be a phone call away. Anything you need, well anything of importance, just contact us. Don't call for the new Jordans."

Dr. Branch, wanting to lighten the mood, offered the joke, and the kid responded with a smirk. It was amazing seeing the bond between the two after such a horrible scene a mere twenty minutes ago. Any notions Donald had of giving this man to the authorities departed after understanding the meaning behind his capture. Donald especially liked the notion of being part of a secret group. He still wanted some specifics on what he should do. He didn't know whether he was supposed to kidnap people in the same way, whether he should run around trying to stop crime, or spy on folks. He hoped Dr. Branch would volunteer the information for he didn't want to ask too many questions. Dr. Branch said nothing more at that time. He cranked the car and backed out of his driveway. The drive was short for they were in the same township. As they pulled close to Donald's house, Donald had to know, so he asked.

"Sir, what do I do now? How do I help?"

Dr. Branch put the car in park in front of the kid's huge, beautiful home and grabbed his wallet. He reached in his wallet, pulled out a card, gave it to the kid, and said, "If you need me, call. Everything is fine, your grandparents don't know a thing, and your school has reasoning for your absence." Donald took the card, not expecting much more of an answer, when Dr. Branch finished, "Right now, Donald, we just want you to do the best you can in school. No more bullying, try your best not to fight. We're not expecting you to sit and get pummeled. Protect yourself but start using your brain, young man. Donald, just be you, but be a better you. You know right from wrong, do what's right. It's that simple. When we need you, we will call." Dr. Branch stated and reached his hand out for a shake. The kid, no longer scared of Dr. Branch but still somewhat intimidated, slowly reached his hand out, and the two black males shook hands while looking eye to eye. No more words were said. Dr. Branch unlocked the doors mechanically from his driver's side panel, and the kid opened his. He hopped out, shut the door, and Dr. Branch instantly popped on some classical music to soothe his nerves. The perfect piece was reaching a climax, Carmina Burana done by Carl Orff. He listened to his music and watched as Donald slowly walked up his walkway. The kid started with a slow waddle but sped up the closer he got to the door, until he was at a full sprint. The scene went perfect with the singing of the sopranos, the brass instruments, and the drums, all joining together musically, symbolizing a great ending to a great story. He watched the boy enter the house and slowly drove away.

The Work

Dr. Branch finished his story regarding his meeting with Donald. Throughout the entire tale, the men sat like they did in the hall, quiet and attentive. They all sat around the table, wordless for about thirty seconds, passing glances to one another, thinking of what to say next. Anthum Williams was the first to speak.

"Dr. Branch, that was raw. What an idea! So this is a scared straight tactic that you want to take global huh?" Anthum said.

"Not global, just nationwide, Anthum," Dr. Branch responded, "Of course, we have to start in our immediate vicinity first."

"We could certainly start with that crowd you got on your corner, Dr. Branch, if you like."

Dr. Branch enjoyed seeing Anthum's enthusiasm, "We certainly can."

Fred Conch, being an ex-military man, brought up a good point, "Have you looked into the logistics, Dr. Branch. If we performed in a likewise regiment, meaning one kid scared straight per day, that is only a little over three hundred kids a year. I thought we were looking for a much greater impact." Fred was a older man, but like most military men his physical features said otherwise.

"I am not talking about getting one kid a day. I am not talking about keeping them for one day only. I am not talking about kids only," Dr. Branch informed. He continued, "Fred, this is going to be all-encompassing. The scared straight tactic, as Anthum so poignantly coined it, is going to be used for the people that are on the cusp. They aren't really bad. They just have no discipline. We will give them a heavy dose of discipline; whether they are locked up for a day or more will depend on their rate of change. Trust me, the teens will be easy."

Joe chimed in, "So if they don't convert, we will just kill them?" He asked that question sounding like a shy boy. Joe was a dark skinned man with full lips and a cleanly shaven head. He was 5'11" and of average build.

"I am more than positive that any kid we want to scare straight will change his ways. We will either turn the heat up or hold him until he sees the light," Dr. Branch answered. "The problems come when we will deal with men. Men aren't easily scared nor do they change their ways without sooner or later reverting back to their old ways. Honestly, we won't know what to expect until we start, gentlemen."

The men continued their conversation in Dr. Branch's small kitchen into the middle of the night. Not concerned with work, they all stayed until they were on the same page. Ideas had been discussed, and Dr. Branch told them within two weeks that the work being done at one of their new properties would be finished. It was built specifically for team Cleaning House and for what they had in store. When their session ended, the men all departed together. They stepped out of the house one after the other, peering down the street. It was a little past midnight, yet the corner was full of hoodlums.

Anthum was pissed. He hated the fact that his leader had to deal with this. He felt that Dr. Branch had enough on his plate and shouldn't have to witness street punks loitering all night. He couldn't hold his tongue. As the men were entering their cars, Anthum said to the men as well as to Dr. Branch who stood on his porch, "Won't you be glad when all these li'l niggas are gone." He purposely said it loud enough for the youngsters to hear if they were listening.

They were listening. Two of the hoodlums turned toward the loud voice and slowly began to walk in Anthum's direction. Anthum's heart jumped for joy. They could start the cleaning tonight.

"What's up, cuzz," the one on the right said. The one on the left began to reach behind his back as he kept pace with his counterpart. The hood on the right was a tall thin boy wearing sagging jeans and a long T-shirt, and his shoes were some tattered tennis with no laces. He looked like a shiesty individual. His partner in crime was a short, stocky dark-skinned kid, wearing close to the same attire, the only difference being a baseball cap atop his head turned to the right. The gaggle of friends stayed on the corner laughing while watching the scene play out. They were all ready to jump in when the time came.

Anthum shut his car door, and the men that were already sitting in their cars began to open their doors and got out. Mathew did not have to exit his car for he stayed behind with Dr. Branch. They stood together on the porch, shoulder to shoulder. He looked at Dr. Branch and could see the anger building in his eyes.

Mathew was right about the anger but wrong about the direction in which it was pointed. Mathew believed Dr. Branch was angry with the hoodlums, but that wasn't the case. Mathew was about to attempt to quell the situation using his police tactics, when Dr. Branch took charge as he always did.

Dr. Branch, living in the neighborhood for over a year, had learned most of the faces well (he actually learned a lot more than faces). The kids sort of recognized him, so when Dr. Branch spoke, they somewhat listened.

He spoke directly to Anthum, "Anthum, why are you messing with them dudes? Let them be." Dr. Branch purposely attacked Anthum. He knew the kids would be far more responsive if they didn't have to submit first. Then he said to the two young hoods, "Be cool, young brothers. My friend is a little intoxicated."

The hoods, already in the mood for chaos, couldn't let it go. The tall one spoke again, "I heard him say sumtin 'bout *when we gone*." The tall boy spoke sarcastically and with authority as he continued, "What that mean, 'when we gone,' where we going, cuzz? You gone take us out, cuzz? You snitchin' or sumtin, cuzz? Whut's up, cuzz?"

Anthum, fuming by now, was ready to charge headfirst into the young punks. He knew he could get to the stocky one before he pulled his heat. Anthum also knew that if no one had a gun, he could break the neck of each of them loitering chumps, even if they tried to take him on at once. In the few seconds it took the tall boy to finish his verbal challenge, Anthum had run the complete scene through his mind: he would attack with blinding speed, ensuring that each blow would be deadly. He would take out the stocky kid, then the lanky one. Afterward, he would run to the party corner and Bruce Lee the whole lot of them. No mercy for these dishonorable vagabonds. Anthum moved his foot behind him to make the bums believe he was retreating. He also did it for leverage and a speedy attack. The moment of truth approached, the boys were five cars away.

Dr. Branch, watching the entire scene play out, was truly baffled as to what to do to stop it. Not knowing what to do was abnormal for Dr. Branch, and he realized he needed to think fast. He saw Anthum getting his body prepared for an attack, he caught his other friends turning off cars that were previously ready to go minutes earlier. He even caught his second amendment fanatic, Larry, reaching for his concealed weapon. That is when Dr. Branch reacted with split-second decision making. He yelled at Anthum.

"Anthum, get in your car now and go home," he demanded.

Anthum, not wanting to take his eyes off of the two dangers walking his way, quickly shot Dr. Branch a snide look. But after seeing the utter anger in his leader's eyes, he turned quickly, opened his car door, and hopped inside. He started the car and rolled off. He did it all in one smooth motion. With Anthum leaving, the other members of team CH returned to their prior places, and all started leaving as well. Mathew still stood on the porch, waiting on an order from Dr. Branch. The two hoodlums merely threw up their hands in victory and yelled some crude words to the leaving vehicles. After the vehicles were out of sight, they turned their attention to Dr. Branch. The same talker offered some interesting advice.

"You need to let them old dudes know who set this is old man," the tall one said. Not hearing a response from Dr. Branch, he added some authority, "You feel me, cuzz."

"I got you, young brother. It won't happen again. As I said, my partner was quite inebriated," Dr. Branch humbly responded, giving all the power to the two hoods. They were satisfied and started walking back to their crowd. Dr. Branch finally heard the shorter guy say a few unkind words.

"Damn, cuzz, you scared that old dude so bad, he started soundin' like a white man." Both of the boys started laughing emphatically.

Mathew stared at Dr. Branch, amazed by his humility when dealing with the two perpetrators. He waited for Dr. Branch's next move, saw it, and followed his leader back into the house. While they were walking into the house, Dr. Branch told Mathew to dial up Anthum on the phone. They saw Christine coming down the steps to the front door as they entered. She inquired about the commotion, and Dr. Branch put her mind at ease by minimizing the occurrence. She said he needed to come to bed, and he told her he would be up soon as he sent Mathew home within the next five minutes. She yawned, grabbed the banister, and stumbled back up the steps to their bedroom. Mathew waited until he heard her shut the door and hit the dial button on his phone. Once he heard it ring, he handed it to Dr. Branch. Anthum answered on the second ring.

"Hey, Matty, I should've broken some bones huh," Anthum said, sounding too excited about the whole ordeal.

"Do you understand discretion, Anthum?" Dr. Branch said, surprising his overly anxious friend.

"Oh, Dr. Branch, yes, I do. I mean I was trippin', Dr. Branch."

"Listen, no one can know a thing, Anthum," Dr. Branch admonished. "Usually, people say you can't show your hand, meaning your cards. Well Anthum, with what we are doing you can't even show *one* card. Do you get me?"

"I understand, see Dr. Branch I was just . . ."

"You have over what, twenty years of martial arts training," Dr. Branch interrupted, "If there is anyone I expect to see with discipline, it's you." Dr. Branch completed his point, "You have shown an extreme lack of discipline, Anthum, and I don't expect to see it happen again. Do you understand?"

Getting hit where it hurts, Anthum could only provide one response, "It will never happen again, Dr. Branch."

"I know my brother, just please use your head before choosing to use your body from here on out, all right Anthum. Have a good night." Dr. Branch never changed the tone of his voice.

"Good night, Dr. Branch," Anthum returned. He loved Dr. Branch even more now. This was a man truly worthy of following. He was a natural leader. Very few men would reprimand Anthum, yet Dr. Branch did it smoothly and honestly. Anthum couldn't get upset, especially after Dr. Branch pointed out the discipline aspect of Anthum's training. He was right. Anthum should have shown more discipline. Anthum made a promise to himself that it would never happen again.

Dr. Branch handed the phone back to Mathew, and they began to have a brief conversation in the hall.

"Dr. Branch, are we going to add more people?" Mathew asked.

"Of course. We will not be able to change everything with just us. It's a big city," Dr. Branch chuckled.

Mathew then told Dr. Branch about his fellow police partner, "Well, I am sure my partner will want to join. He's been working in the city for ten years, and he's tired of the B.S. He told me he felt like he was wasting his time. Nothing ever gets better. I agree with him. I wanted to tell him about us, but I know I can't. I also know that I if I did, he would be on board 100 percent. What do you think?"

With most of the preliminary work being completed, Dr. Branch knew it was time to build the body. He certainly would need more men, and another police officer would be an excellent addition. He responded, "Mathew, don't be blunt, kind of hint about our group and our goals. Then see if he would be on board. Afterward, I will talk to him personally if he wants to join us."

The men shook hands, and Dr. Branch escorted his friend out of the front door. He watched him to his car, knowing it was unnecessary. He walked upstairs to his quaint bedroom and lay with his wife. She turned to face him, and they kissed. She was unhappy about the living arrangements but rarely showed it. She made due with the little house. The spouses wrapped their arms around one another and stayed in that position until Dr. Branch dozed. She let him go and tucked him in. She noticed that he hadn't been getting much sleep because he worked from the moment his feet hit the ground until the late hours of the night. So when he slept, she didn't disturb him. She turned on her stomach and fell back to sleep herself.

The next morning, Dr. Branch was with the complete Twenty-Six at Phillip's new house in the city making some extreme repairs. The men were led by Luke. Luke surveyed the property weeks ago and had determined what needed to be fixed. Then he spoke with Phillip and his wife about their aesthetic aspirations. After combining the two, Luke drew up some crude schematics and was out directing the Twenty-Six's movements. He spread the men throughout the house, working on the places needing actual repairs first. The men worked hard, while Luke and another two worked on the roof. The men all worked diligently, and all were surprised by their efforts. They hadn't realized the type of work that could be accomplished by twenty-six men all working together at once. Everyone worked, no one stood idle. When one completed a job, he moved to wherever he saw help was needed. Tasks were being completed quickly. A few people passing the team would stop and watch the men as they worked. Some of the junkies watched, hoping for an opportunity to snake a tool or two.

Within six hours, the porch had been completely rebuilt, tuck pointing had been finished, pipes had been replaced, outside painting was done, and the new roof shingles were almost set. A kid that sat on his porch across the street from the work watched and was amazed at how quickly the house changed before his eyes. He walked across the street and caught one of the Twenty-Six's attention. It happened to be Dr. Branch.

"That look nice, cuzz," the youngster said.

Dr. Branch thought to himself, "Is 'cuzz' the only word these kids know?" He responded, "Thank you very much, young brother."

"I guess that dude rich, paying all y'all to fix his house like that?" The kid stated and questioned at the same time.

"Naw, not at all. The supplies cost money, but the work is free," Dr. Branch responded.

The twenty-something kid squinted his eyes with confusion, one would have believed that the kid never heard of the word *free*.

"Free! Y'all doing that for free. Why?" The boy was genuinely lost.

Dr. Branch explained to him and a few other people walking up, "That man right there is my brother. He needed my help so I am helping him. It's that simple."

"So y'all just his friends and y'all rebuilding his whole damn house," the boy stated, still incapable of understanding what was going on. "Why y'all doing that? It looked fine to me."

"Young brother, this house looked bad," Dr. Branch corrected. "How does your house look to you?" Dr. Branch inquired, trying to get a bearing on the kid's perspective.

"It look fine to me," he said without thinking.

"But your porch is missing two steps, and your door is three different colors," Dr. Branch said without sounding condescending. Though Dr. Branch was not trying to snap on the kid, the people listening began to crack up with loud laughter. So he quickly added, "I'm not trying to be mean to you, young man, so don't take it personally. Please, look up and down the street. Most of the houses need some serious rejuvenation. The houses are nice, old buildings. They just need some love, and that's what we wanted to give our brother's house," Dr. Branch said. He finished by introducing himself to the people standing around.

The boy quickly responded, "You a doctor! You must live out in the county somewhere in a big ass house, hunh."

"Well, first off, I'm not a medical doctor if that's what you're thinking," Dr. Branch continued, "And no, I actually live right around the corner, a few blocks from here."

"What, we ain't never had no kind of doctors around here. How long you been living here, cuzz?" The boy sounded excited, almost as though Dr. Branch was some celebrity.

"It'll be a little bit over a year since my brothers and I all moved here," Dr. Branch answered. He also said, "We are all moving back to the city."

"What? Rich people moving back to the city?" he asked.

Dr. Branch chuckled then said, "Naw, young brother. I mean 'we' as in black men. There aren't enough of us in the city. You need to see a PhD, a brain surgeon, a carpenter, and a plumber living next door to you. You need to see men built of hard work, and men built of stature outside of your house. When you look out of your window, you shouldn't just see junkies and thugs, young brother." Dr. Branch noticed he was beginning to preach, and even though the crowd got a little larger, he made his conclusion, "It should be black men like each one of us outside your door. And we are here to see that idea become a reality, young brother."

Dr. Branch always noticed how enthralled the rest of the Twenty-Six would be when he spoke during his sermons, but he thought it was because they all shared a horrible common bond. For the first time, Dr. Branch realized that his speaking must be a little more captivating than he previously assumed. He watched as the kid, along with the small crowd, just stood there flabbergasted after his last word. Finally the kid said something.

"That's cool, man," exclaimed the kid. "Y'all be careful though 'cause it's crazy around here." The boy looked around his immediate area and peered into the small crowd, ensuring that the wrong ears weren't present, then he said, "Cause it's some crazy niggas around here, cuzz. They'll shoot you for no reason. Then y'all gonna be moving back out to the county." The kid then turned to look at his house and wondered if he could make some repairs. He inquired, "How much would y'all charge me to help me fix my grandma's steps?"

Hearing the operative word, help, Dr. Branch responded kindly, "Young brother, we will do it for free. We will even use the left oversupplies that we have sitting around here." The boy smiled in amazement, while Dr. Branch gave him instructions, "Go back and put on some work clothes. By the time you are ready, we will be over there."

The young man walked back to his house and went inside. Dr. Branch, staying true to his word, sent Andre and Peter to the boy's home. As the men walked to the boy's steps, he exited the three-toned door wearing old blue jeans and a long sleeve T-shirt and old boots. The pants drooped low of course.

The men introduced themselves, with the boy responding as politely as he knew how. Peter told the young man that it would be a lot safer if his pants were worn correctly, and without argument, the boy quickly pulled his pants up and buckled his belt tighter. The two men began the work, showing their apprentice how to perform simple repairs. Soon they allowed the younger the opportunity to saw, hammer, and paint. They coached while he yanked and pulled the old wooden planks from his faulty steps. They let him measure and saw new boards for the replacements. The young man slid the replacement boards in place and drove the nails in through the porch. They all painted the old and new steps, along with the three-toned door a cream brown. Even with teaching the kid the ropes, the entire fixing process only lasted a little more than an hour. With the work completed, Andre and Peter grabbed their tools and began walking back across the street. The young man, Jeoffrey, yelled out to them.

"Thanks, cuzz," Jeoffrey said, peering back and forth from the men to his home.

Before the two men completed their journey to Phillip's porch, Peter turned and said, "You are welcome and please stop calling us cuzz. We are men. We are not your young pals. You should speak to us as men."

Truly not knowing what to call those old dudes, he walked close to the men to stop yelling and asked, "What do I call you, cuzz . . . I mean, what do I call y'all?"

Andre finally responded. He was probably the quietest of the Twenty-Six but always had some insight to bestow when speaking, "You can call us, sir. We introduced ourselves, so Mr. So-and-So would have been acceptable. The point being, you talk to men differently than you would your young friends. Did you know that?"

"Well, cuzz . . . I mean, Mr . . . ."

"Reid," Andre reminded.

"Mr. Reid, it ain't no men like y'all around here," Jeoffrey shot back. "The men around here is mostly crack heads or gone off that water. The only other dudes that look a little bit like y'all just stay in their house. And when they come out and see me and my boys, they just look at us like they hate us, like we stole something from 'em. I mean somebody probably did steal something from em, but it wasn't me."

"Where is your father, Jeoffrey?" Andre inquired, jumping subjects.

Jeoffrey laughed at the question as though he heard a punch line from Richard Pryor. After the quick chuckle he responded, "Man . . . Mr. Reid, we in the hood. You know ain't none of us got no dads. Some of us ain't even got no mommas. I got my grandma, that's all. Fuck my dad," Jeoffrey said, showing a glimpse of his hate.

Andre, wanting to put the kid's soul at ease, especially after seeing the anguish of missing parents, told the boy, "Jeoffrey, you now have real men among you. We will not shun you. We will teach you. You all are about to start seeing some different things around here. I got to go, Jeoffrey, but if you want to learn about being a man, come here Thursday." He handed the young man a small slip of paper with the veteran's hall address on it. It also had the time the meetings started.

Andre finished his goodbyes with Jeoffrey, turned, and joined the men within Phillip's property standing around the house. The work was finished. With twenty-six men working for twelve hours straight, only stopping to eat, all of the plans that were on Luke's paper were completed. Dr. Branch called for a quick meeting within the house for it was getting dark outside. The men went inside, and Dr. Branch instantly congratulated them all on the work. He especially noted the fact that they affected a watcher. He reminded them of what could be accomplished when they worked together and without shame. They peered around the house seeing the absolute difference they made and swelled with pride. Finally they were touching the community. The operation was starting. The next day was Sunday; he told them to rest up for Monday as more work would ensue.

On Monday, Dr. Branch met with Shannon Progress and the rest of team Educating Our People (EOP) in Dr. Branch's kitchen and was informed about their progress. On the educational front, their goal was to get the money and later the resources to start a school in the old, abandoned school building within their neighborhood. Dr. Branch's plan was to have the immediate area clear, clean, and super safe by the time everything would be finalized. Their tactic for getting the school started was unheard of. They wrote to every wealthy black person they could think of multiple times explaining their goals for a new educational system within the black neighborhood. Each letter was personalized for the recipient. Dr. Branch spent a lot of time researching and contacting the black multimillionaires, and the one black billionaire. He informed them of his intentions within the letter and also included diagrams with charts explaining what the money would be used for. The message was articulate and elaborate and left no questions for the reader. When concluding, he reminded the reader that they would receive all of the accolades for the school's many successes. He also mentioned that no government funds would be accepted, so that no politician could ever boast that they were the reason for the changes. The government wasn't needed for this endeavor and wouldn't receive credit for its positive results. The letter ended, providing all of Malcolm Bank's contact information. They were sent more than once, ensuring that the package would eventually reach its destination.

"So team EOP, what do you have for me," Dr. Branch inquired.

The team, all looking to Shannon, just listened as he and Dr. Branch conferred. Shannon responded, "We have enough money to get things started, Dr. Branch. We cannot expect to have the work completed by the beginning of this upcoming school year but maybe the next." Shannon was a native from New Orleans and maintained his creole look. He was part black and part french leaving him with really light features and a head full of curly, jet black hair.

Dr. Branch was elated about the money but disappointed about them not being able reach his deadline. He chose to speak on the good news first, "We have the money to get started, seriously? That is wonderful. Damn good news. So our rich brothers and sisters are contributing?"

"Some are giving quite handsomely. It appears the people that received your letters began communicating, and after they concluded that this was no scam or farce, we received five pretty big checks. One being from the rapper, Melly. He gave in rare fashion. Apparently, he is really behind educating our kids." Shannon informed. Though they only recognized old school rap artist they new Melly because he was a St. Louis native.

"Are you kidding me? Melly gave how much?" Dr. Branch said, still surprised.

"He gave . . .," Shannon wrote on a sheet of paper.

"Hot damn!" Dr. Branch exclaimed, "I knew I loved that young brother for a reason. That is extremely generous. I didn't know he had money like that to give." Dr. Branch was excited from seeing constant success and couldn't contain his jubilee. Then he thought about the bad news. His demeanor changed and his smile turned straight. He said, "Now why aren't we going to be able to open by this year?"

"Well, Dr. Branch," Shannon responded, showing no sign of intimidation, "You are asking for too much to achieve by the desired dead line. Listen please, when speaking about getting a school started, getting the basic essentials takes time. Adding the special items you want slows the process even more."

"What do you need, Shannon?" Dr. Branch inquired.

Shannon responded, "These are just a few of the items we have to procure prior to having an active school. We need to get the repairs and remodeling done. That will take a lot more than the Twenty-Six working day and night. We need a staff. We need students. We haven't started the interviewing process for any as of yet."

Slightly switching subjects, Shannon reminded his leader, "The money has just started coming in, Dr. Branch. We could start nothing without the funds. Now we can at least begin the work. I would like to open the school this year, but the time between now and then is too short. It can't be done." Shannon said candidly and continued, "With that being said, if you allow us the remainder of this year and some of next to complete all of these goals, the school will be more than ready the next school year." Shannon finished. He and the rest of the team looked at Dr. Branch awaiting some form of anger.

Instead, he spoke with understanding and compassion, "If you say so, Shannon. He looked at the rest of the team. If you guys don't believe it is doable, I accept that conclusion." Dr. Branch spoke more, looking at the bright side, "Hey, it will give me more quality time with the wife."

One of the men jokingly apologized, and the table laughed together.

"All right, then tell me what to expect when the school does open," Dr. Branch told Shannon.

Shannon brought out the schematics of the school and began pointing in differing areas while explaining what would go where. He let Dr. Branch know that the school would house the ninth through twelfth grade, but each level could only have a certain number of students. He pointed out the cafeteria, gymnasium, lab areas, and other main facilities.

After the virtual tour, he then explained the school's expected amenities. Shannon told Dr. Branch that the school would house the finest and fastest computers available at the time. The school would also contain the best scientific equipment that's priced right, and that the biology lab would stock one cadaver a semester. Learning two languages (other than English) will be mandatory, and the curriculum will rival any other school in the nation. The history taught at the school will be totally revamped and formulated for the young black mind. Shannon continued explaining until he could think of no more. That is when one of the other men, added a few items Shannon forgot. After he finished his points and the men felt Dr. Branch knew everything they knew, the meeting concluded. They all said there goodbyes and departed.

Dr. Branch loved the progress and saw that in their own way, each team had commenced with each plan. Five houses were completely remodeled, the school had already been excavated, other men began to attend the weekly sermons (some even helping with tasks), and the CH headquarters was receiving its final necessary touches. Goals were truly getting accomplished. Dr. Branch was ecstatic as he sat having dinner with his wife. He apologized to Christine often because he believed her upset due to his new job monopolizing all of his time. To make a preemptive strike, Dr. Branch told his wife he would be sure to have at least three uninterrupted dinners a week with her. Christine raised the stakes and added a guaranteed kiss before and after he entered the house. He happily obliged his wife's request and wished he could do more. He would do more, but he couldn't at that moment.

Christine could see the guilt all over her husband's face. She wished she could take it away, but she knew she couldn't. No matter how many times she told him that she understood why he spent so much time away, he would still feel guilty. She also knew that he couldn't stand himself for putting anything before his wife. She consoled him the best she could.

Christine enjoyed her dinners with her husband, because as of lately, those were the only times she got to stare into his eyes. They used to be so bright. Now his eyes looked too weary. She couldn't see him lasting much longer at the pace he was currently moving.

Christine also had mixed emotions she couldn't show her husband. She longed to have her husband as she did in the past, yet she understood the circumstances. She also admired the task he had taken on and the way the men respected her husband. Actually, seeing the way her husband lead was astounding. She had never known her husband to have such authority and knowhow. It was kind of amusing to her; every man she now saw looked unto her husband with reverence and called him by his professional name. She merely saw this *Dr. Branch* as her sweets, or honey, or sweetheart, or plain old Trent, her nerdy scientist, devoted husband, and loving father. She understood the role she should play, and she played it well. She rarely nagged about the lack of time and supported all of the moves he made.

Witnessing his ideas come to fruition dazzled her. She still couldn't believe what her husband had completed in such a short time, and she could do nothing but admire the man sitting across the table.

"So how are things with the 'Twenty-Six'?" Christine asked then added, "You know you guys really need to find a better name."

"We are doing very well, my Christine," Dr. Branch responded. "Let's not trifle over the affairs that keep me away from my wife. Better yet, lets focus on the celestial grace God has blessed me with by sending me his most beautiful and prized angel." Dr. Branch smiled while flattering his wife.

"Oh how poetic, but you know I'm not one of the members of your group, moved by flowery words dripped over charismatic rhythm," she said tartly.

"Oh yes you are, actually, you are quite easier to move with flattery, gorgeous," he said.

"Well, you are right about that. When you know me, you know me. Now tell me more about my eyes." Christine began to flutter her eyes as they both laughed at her easy acquiescence.

"How is everything going for you, babe?" he genuinely inquired.

"Things are going fine. My boss will never understand why we moved from the suburbs to this part of the city," she said.

"How does he know that?" Dr. Branch asked.

"Dear, when we were first leaving our old house, you didn't give me much to go on. So I did a bunch of complaining to who would listen. My boss and I have a talking relationship, so I bitched to him. I hated it when we first moved here. I complained constantly. Everybody in my department probable knows where we live," she finished.

Dr. Branch merely shook his head from side to side. He wasn't upset in the slightest. He understood her issue. He didn't explain much as he initiated the Twenty-Six nor as their endeavors first began. He learned from that mistake and kept her somewhat informed on the team and their works (leaving out team CH). After hearing about a few of their goals and later seeing a few of their completed accomplishments, Christine instantly showed a joint passion for her husband's commitments.

Again, Christine missed the hell out of her husband, but if he were to change the world as he was professing, who was she to stand in the way of something like that? She wouldn't dare impede a process of such magnitude; instead, she would support it and help wherever she could.

She started adding her help by meeting with the wives and girlfriends of the other team members and encouraging the other partners to support their respective spouses in this major transition. She threw card games, sandwich parties, and even sex parties to keep the women entertained when they missed their counterparts.

"The women really miss their men, Trent," Christine said after taking a sip of her wine.

"I am sure they do babe, as do you." Trent responded, "Can they see what we have done so far?"

"They can see, but what they see is small," Christine explained, "They can see a few remodeled houses, but if it wasn't their house remodeled, its not major news. They are not at our house where they can see the constant meetings and hyper activity. Nor do they attend your Hall meetings, so they don't see how your numbers increase weekly."

"They aren't happy about the bills being paid?" Dr. Branch inquired, sounding a little pushed back by the direction of conversation.

"Of course they are, but you miss another point there," she explained further, "You are talking about women who were use to living check to check. They fretted over bills and money issues regularly. Now without those things to worry about, their minds are searching for other things to keep their thoughts occupied. And you know a woman's brain, time to think and nothing to think about is a bad combination. We need to worry about something, or we will cause something to worry about."

Dr. Branch, completely lost, just nodded as though he understood his wife's explanation. Dr. Branch, being a natural scientist, didn't relate to a lot of natural human emotions. When adding women's emotions into the mix, his mind would spin from utter befuddlement. He remembered arguing with his wife in their beginning years, and it baffled him as to how this intelligent woman could sound so ignorant. After he aged and gained some wisdom, he understood that emotion had a lot to do with a woman's logic. Being a hardened man with a third world upbringing, and receiving little to no help caused a serious lack of emotions. This compounded by a genetic predisposition to follow logic before all else culminated to an emotionally challenged man, and he could not wrap his mind around his wife's essential point. He believed that women would complain even if all of their demands were met.

"Is there anything I or we can do to help?" he asked seriously.

"No worries, babe, its just conversation. They will all be fine," she said, "Just start remodeling those houses a little faster. Some women are getting jealous. And now that we are on that subject, why is our house not done, and why weren't we first, anyways, Sweets? I mean, you are leading this thing, right?"

Dr. Branch simply responded, "Babe, just because I am leading this, I don't want to get the big head. I don't want people to start carrying me on their shoulders and blowing a bunch of smoke up my skirt." Dr. Branch departed some leadership lessons to his wife, and she listened, "Babe, the second I begin to request and receive constant preferential treatment, that is when one of my men will betray me. They have to always offer, and I have to refuse most of the time. That is the only way I will continue to get the support from the men, and more importantly, their loyalty and love."

Christine looked down at her drink, swirled the glass, and emptied the last of the wine. She finally realized why these men followed her husband so. This was a really smart man. His brain and the wine began to turn her on. She reached for his hand and took it into hers. She dipped his finger into his glass of wine, and brought it to her mouth. She sensually sucked the red liquid from Dr. Branch's finger and watched his face instantly blush. The waiter was coming with more wine and their entrée. She could save the rest for later.

Her husband blessed the food after the waiter left their presence, and they ate. They conversed a little more after dining but soon left. The moment they entered the house, they ripped each others clothes off and made love like their younger years. That hour he was suppose to give his wife turned into a complete night. He cut the volume on his phone. He laid with his wife the entire night with no interruptions. She purposely fell asleep with her head on his chest so that Dr. Branch couldn't leave if he wanted. He wasn't going anywhere. He rubbed her hair while thinking about the many things he needed to do the next day and slowly drifted into a dark slumber.

Dr. Branch and the other six members of team CH all met at his house, which was scheduled for its remodeling the upcoming weekend. They all wore business attire. Dr. Branch, in his shirt and tie ensemble, greeted the men once they all were seated in his kitchen.

"Hello, gentlemen, welcome to my humble abode," he started. "You guys know what today is right?" He asked not trying to sound patronizing.

Joe responded, "We are getting a lay of the land."

"We are going to our headquarters," Fred Conch said, "We are going to see what the headquarters look like and how it's going to be used."

"Exactly, gentlemen, the plan today is for you to see where all, and I mean all, of our negative activity will take place." Dr. Branch brought his gaze to Anthum when reiterating, "Absolutely nothing we do will take place away from our headquarters. Do you get me?" More of a demand than a question, and the men all nodded with some verbal form of agreement. Dr. Branch continued, "We will all ride in Mathew's Navigator. It can hold us seven, and he is less likely to get hassled by his fraternal order?"

The men grabbed their suit jackets, waited for Dr. Branch to say his goodbyes to his wife, and then they followed him out of the door. The men exiting Dr. Branch's house in church attire caused a few stares from the neighbors. A few of the same punks were on the corner, peering in Anthum's direction. Anthum gave a quick look in the punks' vicinity, but he didn't stare. Anthum didn't want to disrespect Dr. Branch by disobeying his previous orders. Dr. Branch noticed Anthum's calmer demeanor and patted him on the shoulder with vigorous approval. They all hopped in Mathew's giant SUV, with Dr. Branch riding shotgun. The truck pulled off slowly, and the men were on their way to a place that would change their lives forever.

Dr. Branch navigated as Mathew drove completely through St. Louis County via highway 70. After exiting the highway, they hopped on a two-lane road that was small enough to be a one-way street. While the drive took place, the men spoke seriously about their plans for this horrid operation. Then Joe asked a question.

"How far is it Dr. Branch?" Joe inquired.

"Just a little bit further," Dr. Branch said.

Dr. Branch pointed his index finger to the right, giving Mathew some new directions. They were well outside of the St. Louis area and on an outer road that was a mixture of dirt and gravel. The road went up a small hill, and the moment the hill was peeked, a building popped into view. Dr. Branch told Mathew to go to that building. Mathew made a right turn onto another dirt road that led the team to the bland structure. The dirt road slowly morphed into smooth pavement, which was for parking. The rectangular building sat within a giant C-shaped parking lot, allowing ample parking for a nice-sized work force. Mathew rode around slowly until he caught sight of the building's main entrance and pulled the truck up to the curb. The building was a flat, rectangular one-story box, with the entrance and back having the short sides. There were windows all around the building, but they were darkly tinted, and no one could see in. Mathew shut the engine down and unlocked all of the doors. The men exited the vehicle and stood erect while stretching away the long drive.

"You guys go on in. I need to smoke," Phillip, a handsome man of caramel complexion, said while removing a Newport cigarette from the pack. He lit the cigarette and took a powerful drag while taking in the secluded, wooded surroundings.

The rest of the men watched as Dr. Branch retrieved a set of keys from his pocket and inserted one into one of the large double entrance doors. The men heard the sound of a locking mechanism giving way to the key's turn and the final click signifying the door was then unlocked. He opened the large thick glass door, and they all entered. Outside, Phillip was still enjoying his menthol flavored nicotine. Once inside, each man exhibited some outward symbol of the surprise they all felt. None expected a building near the size they were seeing, nor did any of the men expect to see an actual completed inside with such a newly refurbished look. Upon entering the double doors, the men were encased in glass. To the left and to the right were sheets of glass leaving a hallway leading straight to the back of the building. Directly straight ahead, at the end of the hall, was a door leading to what appeared to be a janitor's closet. Each encased side had two separate doors for two different entry/exit options.

Dr. Branch, being the tour guide, went through the first door to the left, giving access to the entire left side of the building. This side appeared to be a technician's wet dream. It held small cubicle areas and small offices but lots of open space for robotics and computer equipment. The men heard a sound and swung their heads in its direction. It was Phillip entering that same door. Phillip attempted to enter quietly but bumped into a large piece of machinery, causing the metal monstrosity to drag along the floor, the sound similar to the screech of a tropical toucan hitting a high note. Phillip merely shrugged his shoulders, and the men laughed, their voices echoing throughout the vacant facility. Phillip finally joined the group of men and asked a question no one had asked yet.

"What's all of this, Dr. Branch?" Phillip inquired. He said what all of the men were thinking. "I thought this place was gonna possibly get bloody, but it seems like a real office building."

"This is a real office building, Phillip," Dr. Branch responded. He continued, "Don't you guys think we need some type of cover for the actions that will take place here? Please think about it: seven black men riding out to a giant vacant building every now and again, out here in the boonies. It may seem a little suspicious, wouldn't you think? But if the facility is being used regularly . . . if it were a place of business, our coming and goings would seem natural."

"So business will really go on here?" Phillip asked. "What type of business, and what is all of this stuff?"

Dr. Branch figured this was as good of time as any to enlighten his partners. From that moment on, he added words to his tour. Dr. Branch walked up to a robotic arm, rubbed his fingers across the smooth metal, and began talking.

"Even before initiating the Twenty-Six, I had an idea of an invention running wild in my head for a while, but I never had the guts to bring it to light. Once we started meeting, and my confidence reached an all time high, I figured I would try to make that idea a reality. So I drew up some crude sketches, and I met with an engineering friend who used my sketch along with my words to complete a finished three-dimensional model on his computer. The device was completed and is in the process of getting patented. I was approached by some giant industries wanting to buy the device. They all offered some good, really good money. I respectfully declined their futile attempts on purchasing my idea. Their efforts showed me that the device could possibly be bigger than I even thought." Dr. Branch was walking while he spoke, allowing the men ample time to see the entire left side.

The men were exiting the left side and entering the right side when Fred Conch, finally spoke up, "So what is this device, and what is its purpose?" He inquired, sounding like a soldier. Fred said little but listened and watched everything.

Dr. Branch described the device and its purpose, and the men stood there shocked.

"I can't believe nobody thought of that yet," Phillip continued, "Damn, Dr. Branch, you are going to be rich."

"We are going to be rich, Phillip," Dr. Branch corrected, then continued, "We are all in this together." Dr. Branch walked to a copier and hit some buttons for no particular reason. He then began explaining the two sides of the building to his team, "So the left side will house the engineers, and they will construct the devices. The other side will be where all of the business is done: the finances, the filing, the archives, and all of the other paperwork that's necessary to run a corporation."

The men then walked through the right side, which was completely different than its opposite side. The right side was full of cubicles, offices, fax machines, copiers, and other necessities for a functioning office. It was a pen pusher's heaven. Dr. Branch pointed to the large glass separating where they stood from the hall way. He was directing their attention to the other side.

"If you guys will notice," Dr. Branch started, "I wanted glass separations so the engineers could have a clear view of their counterparts and vice versa. I believe this will encourage more team unity. It's pretty amazing, but as you all can see, the facility is almost complete. I have hired my good friend to be CEO of the group with me being the owner. He told me that he already has 75 percent of the working crew right now. He's already hired engineers, a lawyer, an administrative assistant, line workers, and a janitor. He said he needed to find a good salesman and other essential components to get the business going. I told him I am looking to get the place going within the next two weeks, but he is apparently having a hard time selling the money arrangement."

"What do you mean?" Joe inquired.

"In order to work here, the employee has to agree to our pseudo-socialistic ways." Dr. Branch answered, "There are a lot of people who quickly agree and sign on to the idea, especially in this economy, but there are also people thinking that we are trying to rob them, when in fact, we are attempting to free them. Oh well." Dr. Branch returned to his previous subject, "There is still much needed to get this place up and running, but it will be finished in two weeks even if I have to do the work myself."

The men all stared at Dr. Branch, and then they looked at one another. They returned their gaze to their leader. All amazed at what Dr. Branch was telling them. Then Phillip spoke.

"Are you fucking kidding me, Dr. Branch?" Phillip said, sounding outdone. He continued, "You been leading the Twenty-Six with everything we been doing, and you done got a robotics business started too. You also got enough money to get that school started next year. Holy shit," was the only way Phillip could conclude.

"Do we need to get you some blue and red tights and paint an S on your chest, Dr. Branch? Jeesh, man," Anthum said with some sarcasm.

With a jestful tone yet a very serious undertone, Joe then inquired, "Dr. Branch, when do you sleep?"

The men all looked at Dr. Branch, waiting for a response. Dr. Branch merely smiled and shook his head. That is when the men truly took a closer look at their leader's face. They saw a weariness that only a man twice his age should have. The bags under Dr. Branch's eyes were more apparent, and far more gray could be seen in the man's hair. Dr. Branch finally spoke up.

"I get enough sleep, Joe," Dr. Branch started. "I just want to make sure I do my part, gentlemen. And sacrificing a little sleep here and there is small potatoes. I can't dare ask you guys to commit if I'm unwilling to do the same."

After hearing of their leaders constant sacrificing and seeing the physical results of the apparent stress, the men's adoration and love for Dr. Branch increased even more. Wanting to get back on track, Fred spoke up.

"Returning to the matter at hand, Dr. Branch, please explain how we will share these facilities with civilians, sir, especially considering the nature of our operation." Fred spoke concisely, with no humor in his voice, strictly business.

"Good question," Dr. Branch said, smiling. He continued, "Well, Sergeant Conch, the tour isn't over." He brought his attention to the rest of the group when saying, "Let's get out of here. This way, gentlemen."

Dr. Branch walked to the door within the huge glass window separating them from the hall and pushed. The door opened, and the men entered the quiet hallway. He then led his crew to the end of the corridor, right to the door marked janitor.

"Why do we need to see the mop closet?" asked Joe.

No response. Dr. Branch just reached for the knob and slowly turned. He pulled on the door, and it opened ever so slowly. The men actually began to get excited, believing the door would open to some secret room, but they were all let down when the door opened to an actual janitor's closet. The small room was dimly lit by one light bulb crudely hanging from the ceiling by an electrical connection. This room by far was the most unattractive place in the building. Even the bathrooms looked new in comparison to this janitor's closet. The gray paint and the dim lighting could cause any sane man to fall under a state of instant depression. There was a large sink to the right, and on the left was a small shelf holding unopened cleaning supplies. Straight ahead was a gray wall.

"This is where we will do our deed, fellas," Dr. Branch said, holding his hand toward the small closet.

The men all looked baffled. The room could barely fit two men, three if they weren't planning on any movement. How could they deal with serious perpetrators in a space made for wringing out mops? Anthum spoke up this time.

"Dr. Branch, how do you expect to handle business in there?" Anthum said, pointing at the closet. "I can barely fit in there by myself."

Dr. Branch pulled a small black object from his pocket; it resembled a keyless entry device typically seen on a key ring. He then smashed a button on the small device, and the gray wall in front of them slid to the left slowly. On the initial movement of the wall, Joe and Larry Evans jumped because of the sound. Fred and Anthum stood still as statues, not easily jarred by abrupt sounds. Behind the wall was a large metallic door with a keypad right where the doorknob should have been. The men looked at Dr. Branch and laughed at his snide smile.

"Pretty cool, isn't it? I am having one of these made for each of you," Dr. Branch said, referring to the small remote.

He walked to the key pad and pressed a six-button combination. A little red light switched to green, and a great hiss came from behind the door. The sound was quite similar to an airtight seal being broken. Dr. Branch pushed on the door, and it gave way quite easily. The smooth movement of the door shocked the men, for they all could see that it was metal and quite thick. Behind the door was a small floor, then steps leading downward. The space was cramped, and that area could've caused a claustrophobic person to have an anxiety attack. The walls were close, and it was very dim, though there was light coming from the bottom of the stairs. The suspense was killing the men. Dr. Branch purposely took his time walking to the steps then down them, knowing the men were overly excited. The men all followed one behind the other without words. They walked down the long staircase where it quickly became far more illuminated. They all gathered at the bottom of the staircase and took in their surroundings.

The basement was very similar to the floor above it. The staircase ended with a white wall six feet away from the last step. Heading in the opposite direction of the staircase was an unfinished pathway of dirt that was the exact length of the first level's corridor. This lower-level corridor headed straight back to a giant metallic door. On either side of the corridor stood more metallic doors, though a lot smaller than the one at the end of the walkway. The doors that lined the walls were similar to the refrigerator doors of old – huge, rectangular, silver objects with a long lever toward the middle. The doors also had a small circle cut around eye level for peeking purposes. Larry Evans, who had so far been extremely quiet, was the first to meander over to one of the large doors. He grabbed the lever and pulled. Again, the sound of an airtight seal decompressed as it swung open.

"Be careful, Larry," Dr. Branch advised. "If the door closes, you will be trapped. It only opens from this side."

Larry, still not saying a word, just nodded in understanding. He opened the door wide and peered inside. The other men were just as curious and left Dr. Branch to stand behind Larry. What they saw was quite unimpressive. The room contained one uncomfortable looking metallic chair somehow anchored to the dirt floor. The walls separating each identical cell seemed thick and layered with stuff one sees in an insane asylum. The back of each cell was a dirt wall. The floors and the periphery of the basement weren't covered at all. No work had been done to either. It gave the basement an ancient dungeon vibe. The men separated, each looking in cell after cell, until they all made it to the far end of the path and waited for Dr. Branch to open the big door. Dr. Branch came and opened that door without needing to unlock anything. He did need to pull a huge lever, and the door opened like a safe. Again, the sound of decompression.

"Why are all of these rooms airtight, Dr. Branch?" Anthum inquired.

"This is really the only true airtight room down here, and it is for cleaning house," Dr. Branch answered emotionlessly as he stepped aside to let the men enter.

The room just resembled a much larger version of the other cells. Except this room had more chairs stuck to the dirt floor, and they were all facing the front. Joe thought it looked like a classroom after a nuclear holocaust had occurred, and it gave him the creeps.

Anthum thought he noticed Joe shudder yet paid it no attention as he asked another question, "Why are fire sprinklers only in this room, Dr. Branch?" Anthum continued, showing his attention to detail, "I didn't see any others throughout any of the other cells."

"This is the only room that will need them," was Dr. Branch's only answer.

The men walked in the eerie room and slowly ambled about obligatorily, then they all piled out anxious to leave the death room. After they exited, Dr. Branch spoke.

"Well, guys, this is where we will be doing our deed," Dr. Branch spoke matter-of-factly, "The cells are where we will keep our victims. They will sit in those chairs until they have seen the light. They will eat, shit and piss while in those chairs."

Dr. Branch spoke a little longer about how the facility would be used and the necessary moves everyman had to make, and he greatly harped on discretion. He then told the men to get ready for their next meeting because that is when they would know who their first victims will be. The men all left the basement. They all watched as the janitor's wall returned to its proper place, showing no sign of falsehood. They walked through the upper level hallway, still impressed by the look of it all. Phillip smoked a cigarette before they all got in the truck, and Mathew drove everyone back to Dr. Branch's house. They said there goodbyes from there and set the date and time for their next meeting.

For the next meeting, team CH showed up to Dr. Branch's new-looking, refurbished home. The house was of its own class and now stood way out from every other house on the street. The necessary tuck pointing, new windows and doors, and the new roof instantly gave the house stunning curb appeal. With the landscaping complete, it was amazing to see what one could do with a little elbow grease and a lot of determination.

This was to be the last meeting before actual action ensued. The men met that night to receive Dr. Branch's detailed plans. The men all entered the house looking at their recent handy work. Impressed, they walked to their meeting place, the kitchen. Though the room now resembled something from a magazine, it was still small. They sat at the kitchen table, which was littered with folders and papers.

"What's all of this?" Anthum asked.

"This is all of the information on the boys we are grabbing during our first trip out," Dr. Branch answered.

"Why? I thought we were just grabbing random thugs and . . .," Anthum started.

"No," Dr. Branch interrupted. "Everything we are doing is calculated. Every kid or adult we grab will be known to us . . . What if we grab the wrong kid merely because he looks thuggish?" Dr. Branch asked and then continued, "That would not be fair. Absolutely nothing about this is random, you guys. We will know our murderers, we will know our gang members, and we will know our drug dealers. Oh yeah, and our drug users. They are going to have it the worst . . . probably"

"There are a lot of people here, Dr. Branch," Fred spoke, poking through the files.

"These are opposing gangs in our neighborhood," Dr. Branch said, giving the history lesson he received from Mathew and his partner days ago, "These boys have been warring in this area over these same streets for decades now. Their size grew as well as their violence. Their colors have evolved, changed, and even disappeared, but the quest for money and respect has remained. A lot of the boys outside on my corner are in one of the factions. We take care of these kids, and we will greatly affect this neighborhood immediately."

Dr. Branch turned toward Mathew, patted him on the back and said, "Men, we really have to thank this man right here. He has done true detective work in acquiring files on each one of these hoodlums."

Mathew quickly diverted the accolades away from himself saying, "My partner used his resources to get a lot of this info, guys. I can't wait until we let him join."

"We will thank him in due time. But you are here now, so we thank you now, Mathew," Dr. Branch said, continuing to pour on the praises. Then Dr. Branch picked up a folder from the table. The folder contained more than one file. He grabbed a file at random and threw it down face up while speaking of his soon to be victims. "Every one of these kids has done some serious criminal activity, but there are those who have lived by the sword. They will be separated from the others and thrown upon that same sword."

"This is a lot of people, Dr. Branch," Joe reiterated, pointing to the many files on the table, "Won't people notice this?"

"I suspect people in the neighborhood will," Dr. Branch answered, "but I don't think that they are going to mind these guys being absent from their corners. Regardless, I plan on returning a lot of these boys before anyone notices that they are missing anyway."

"Returning 'em?" Anthum said, sounding shocked.

"Anthum, this is not a killing spree," Dr. Branch admonished, realizing Anthum may be a little overzealous, "This is about changing our people, not wiping them off the face of the planet. Do you get me, Anthum?" Dr. Branch reached to his right and put his hand on Anthum's shoulder, saying, "I say this to everyone here, but especially to you, Anthum. What we are about to do is horrendous. Don't be overly excited about killing. I am quite sure

Sergeant Conch will agree, we are about to sacrifice far more than money and time, gentlemen. Our souls may be at stake." The men's faces grew grim at that last statement, and Dr. Branch continued, "Please understand this is not about avenging our little ones. It's about leaving them a legacy. And though God will see the horrid atrocities we commit, hopefully he will soon see the glorious results and find forgiveness for even the likes of us, gentlemen." Dr. Branch ended that portion sounding like a priest.

The men studied the photographs and the files as they discussed each kid. They determined the best routes and hangouts the boys ventured. They went over each intricate detail of Dr. Branch's plan ad nauseam, and then again. When each man felt they were up to complete speed, the meeting ended. The men said their salutations and departed.

Anthum gave the boys on the corner a quick look, nothing more as he stepped into his car. Their time was coming, and Anthum almost salivated at the thought. The next time team CH met, it would be during their first escapade. Anthum shot off in his car with his music blasting, too excited for words.

Dr. Branch met with Malcolm Banks at his apartment. Malcolm moved into a place down the street from his leader. Malcolm lived in a top-level apartment within a four-family flat. He was unconcerned with the remodeling and told the team to fix his place last. With Malcolm living so close, they saw each other daily, and Malcolm's impression of his leader couldn't have been more inflated. The feats the man performed were legendary, and Malcolm couldn't believe the wealth Dr. Branch had accumulated in such a short time. He was able to get money from rap artists like Melly, huge grants from extremely wealthy stars like Opal Winifrey and William Bosbie, donations from wealthy athletes like Wizard-Johnson and Cloudwalker-Jackson. He even received funds from black CEOs and other black-owned businesses, all contributing to his model of the new inner city. Again, whenever Dr. Branch felt he wouldn't get the funds from a particular person, he would remind the solicited that absolutely no government funds were being accepted in this endeavor, and therefore only they would receive credit for the changes that would ensue.

Somehow, anyone Dr. Branch spoke to couldn't say no to the man. Though the philanthropist knew that their money was used strictly for education and renewing the neighborhood, they had no idea that the money was supporting Dr. Branch's socialistic principles. He kept that information to himself.

Malcolm also watched Dr. Branch weave a tapestry of black networking that improved black-owned businesses substantially. He learned of all the black-owned businesses within the city, especially within the immediate vicinity, and spoke to each owner personally. He, along with multiple members of the Twenty-Six, would have a powwow with owners of these businesses, and the message would be the same. They make sure that they buy their products from black producers, and he would make sure that everyone would shop with them. He negotiated and encouraged but never forced. The only time Dr. Branch seemed somewhat forceful was when he dealt with the neighborhood supermarket owner. He and all of team Twenty-Six, minus Mathew (for obvious reasons), strolled into Pop's Sursave and demanded to speak to the owner. Dr. Branch, knowing that the supermarket's owner would be there, demanded his presence. Finally the owner showed, and Dr. Branch told him to look at the condition of his market. It was unacceptable: lights flickering, cracks in the floor, a giant dead cockroach in the center of one of the aisles, and the meat was one day too old to sell. He told the owner this place should entice the taste buds, not nauseate. Even worse was that this was the only market available in the vicinity. Dr. Branch told his men to wait outside while he and the owner had a talk in the office. Within the office, Dr. Branch told the black owner that if he would begin to fix up the place, Dr. Branch would help. He also told him that if he started getting his meat and farm supplies from black farmers and began using black-owned trucking companies, Dr. Branch would ensure that everyone in the neighborhood would buy the groceries from his market. The man's eyes twisted in suspicion.

Dr. Branch left the man with this quote, "If you buy black, so will we."

Slowly but surely, everything Dr. Branch said was coming to pass. It was amazing for Malcolm to see these things first hand. How his leader affected everyone he spoke to and how he instilled belief in anybody. He deserved nothing but adoration.

Today, they were going over the giant account. Malcolm had separated the accounts into numerous different categories. This way, he could keep tabs of the many bills being paid off as well as the funds they received from donation and the interest accrued from those moneys. He also had to remember to prepare for the funds received from future profits from the business. That was another thing to go crazy about. This man also invented a widget that everyone wants or will eventually want. His leader was a genius pure and simple. Some men are special, but there are some things that are special that happen to be men. Dr. Branch was something special that happened to be a man.

Malcolm quit thinking about the majesty of Dr. Branch and focused on the meeting's subject. Dr. Branch wanted to see how things were looking, and Malcolm provided a brief synopsis of their money situation. With other people incorporated under their monetary system, everything was still holding quite well. Malcolm informed his leader that with the excess money from the huge donations, the living arrangements of every working soul underneath his socialistic umbrella was at peace. The cost of living in that area wasn't expensive at all. Because the homes were not humungous mansions, the heating and cooling costs were cheaper as well. When inquired about his living arrangements, Malcolm humbly thanked Dr. Branch for his concern but always let Dr. Branch know that he was quite comfortable.

He reminded Dr. Branch of future meetings with a few other philanthropists that actually sought them out.

"Debra White somehow learned of our academic plans, and she wants to meet you, Dr. Branch," Malcolm informed his leader.

"How did she find out about our school?" Dr. Branch inquired.

"I'm not sure, sir. I received a letter with an invitation to Martha's Vineyard with hopes to build a better school for the poor kids in the inner city," Malcolm explained.

"That is amazing," Dr. Branch said, honestly baffled at his fortune. "Typically, a man has to beg for funds. Now people are seeking us out to give. I have to know why. Get in contact with her people and set up a meeting please, Malcolm."

"Absolutely," Malcolm agreed.

"I need to get prepared for tonight's lecture, Malcolm. Is there anything else of great importance? If not, I just need a couple of hours of sleep before the meeting."

Malcolm pulled out an electronic notebook and pressed a few buttons. He looked up and said, "Nothing that cannot wait until tomorrow."

They said their farewells. Dr. Branch walked out of Malcolm's home and spoke to the other tenants that happened to be standing outside, a mother with her two young kids. The mother returned the gesture and forced her children to do the same. Dr. Branch made his way home and walked straight to his bed. He took his shoes off and sat with his back against the headboard. His eyelids slowly drooped until his wife made her way into the room. He perked up, intent on sacrificing his two hours of sleep for his wife. She simply sat down, put his feet in her lap, and began to rub them. He was snoring within five minutes. She covered him with a blanket and shut the door as she left.

That same night, Malcolm pulled up to the hall and could not find a place to park. The weekly sermons had been getting more visitors weekly, but there had never been so many cars outside. Malcolm walked to the door, and the youngest member of the Twenty-Six stood there. Leroy was the man's name, and though the youngest of the bunch, he wasn't a young man.

"How's it going, Leroy?" Malcolm greeted his team member.

"What's up, Mac?" Leroy responded happily. Leroy was lighting up a cigarette as he gave Malcolm directions. "Bossman want us to stand in the back."

"What do you mean?" Malcolm inquired.

"Come on, Mac, don't you see all these cars?" Leroy said as he blew out smoke. He continued talking, "Bossman is getting big. Look inside there. It ain't nowhere to sit. So he don't want us taking up all the seats. He want the Twenty-Six to stand in the back, let the visitors get front row. It's all good. They need to get enlightened. Yeah, that's the word, enlightened." Leroy repeated himself as though he wanted to show Malcolm that he learned a new word.

"All right, well, thanks for the information, Leroy. I'll see you in there." Malcolm shook Leroy's hand and walked in.

The place was beyond full, and Malcolm believed that they far exceeded the maximum capacity load about fifteen people ago. He saw his team along the back wall except for Anthum and Mathew. They were up front. As of late, whenever either wasn't working their worldly jobs, they both stuck to Dr. Branch like glue. Anthum and Mathew both felt the need to protect Dr. Branch, and they slowly began to become bodyguards. They were always sure to be an arm's length away from their leader.

Malcolm waved to the two centurions and Dr. Branch as he walked to the back wall. Dr. Branch smiled and waved back to Malcolm, Mathew waved also, and Anthum merely nodded his head in acknowledgment. Malcolm greeted his fellow team members as he walked to the back wall of the hall, and they all responded in kind. He squeezed between Larry Evans and Shannon Progress. The hall was loud with many different conversations, and Malcolm needed to talk directly into Shannon's ear to be heard.

"This is a lot more people than the last two weeks. Are we expecting this growth to continue?" Malcolm said.

Shannon bent his back a little, being taller than Malcolm, and responded in his ear, "This is what occurred, Mac. A few of the Twenty-Six invited a couple of people from the neighborhood to one of the weekly sermons. After they heard Dr. Branch's word, they invited others, who invited others, and so on and so fourth until we now have this huge crowd we see here tonight."

Shannon, being an analytical person, added a little more for Malcolm to ponder, "Mac, you know Dr. Branch is a prolific speaker. I still haven't met one person who doesn't love to hear that man talk. One of the younger attendees actually said this and I quote, 'I would listen to that man talk about what he had for breakfast." Both men laughed as Shannon continued, "Seems like our leader is getting well known." Shannon shrugged his shoulders as he looked up front and rhetorically asked, "Well, Mac, you didn't think we could keep a man like that contained to just us, did you?"

Malcolm smiled then turned away, wishing that they could've kept Dr. Branch as theirs and theirs alone. He found himself being a tad jealous, especially knowing that his leader would have to spread out his attention further as more people joined. He knew that Dr. Branch needed the city's support, which would necessitate his networking and seeing more people. He also knew that team Twenty-Six was just the beginning, and eventually, they would grow. Malcolm understood these eventualities . . . yet understanding didn't mean he had to like them. Malcolm just hoped his time with his leader would never get short changed. He then saw Dr. Branch walk to the podium, and he quit dwelling on himself as he tuned in to the speaker.

Dr. Branch stepped up to the podium, prepared to give his speech. Anthum and Mathew stayed seated behind him listening to his words while waiting on any wrong doings. Dr. Branch began his speech slowly and softly. He started with a recent incident.

"Hello, all, I see we have an amazing crowd tonight. Are you all ready to change black America, everyone?" The crowd excitedly responded in the affirmative. Dr. Branch continued, "Well, for all of you newcomers, let me forewarn you, this is not a church sermon. I am not here to get you to commit your soul to Jesus, though I think that's a good idea. I am not here to tell you to give your life over to Allah, as my Muslim brothers would encourage. Neither am I here to bash white America. No, these meetings are about us, black America, and what needs to be done to finally see some serious improvements. And I think we can agree religion has been pushed forever yet has done nothing but put money in the leaders pockets." Again the crowd erupted.

Dr. Branch left his intro and jumped to something else, "Let me tell you what my wife and I did recently. Remember this because it is the basis for tonight's sermon. My wife and I ate dinner a few weeks ago at a really fine restaurant. The place was five-stars nice, yet it was in Chesterfield. You all know where that is, well those of you without warrants." The crowd laughed. He continued, "It's out there a little bit past Ladue, the place where if you are a black man, you are guaranteed to get pulled over and harassed. You guys do know that we are one thousand times more likely to get pulled over than our white brethren while driving out there. That is not an exaggeration. We are literally one thousand times more likely to get pulled over out in Ladue or other surrounding counties than a white man." After repeating his point, he then said, "Obviously, they don't want us out there. And you know what? That is OK, because if they don't want us out there, we shouldn't want to go out there. But the problem usually is that we *need* to go out there."

Dr. Branch looked out at the crowd then said, "Why is it if we want anything nice, if we want to go somewhere nice, or want to see nice things, we have to go to where white people are? Aren't you guys sick of that?" Though rhetorical, some audience still answered. He continued.

Sounding as though he switched topics, he then said, "You guys know that my thinking is quite different than Martin Luther King Jr. He wanted to unite us, us being blacks and whites. But I say if white people don't want us around them, then we shouldn't strive for that unity. See, MLK was a modern-day Moses, and I won't dare say one bad thing about such a great man. But I will say he had one thing wrong. He set a precedent that caused us to go in one direction when we should have been going in another."

After making that statement, the hall was quiet as a cemetery at midnight. The audience all wondered where Dr. Branch was going with an MLK disagreement. He noticed the silence yet continued with his point, "MLK boycotted the busses and wanted blacks to have the right to sit where they chose on white-owned busses. Eventually, the system caved because we were the main patrons of the bus company. After winning that battle, from then on, we fought hard to get included into white society." Dr. Branch looked back and forth, watching the crowd, then made his point, "Imagine if instead of boycotting the bus company, he with some other black folks somehow started their own bussing company. The money that they gave to the white people, who hated our existence, could have been going into some black family's pocket." The men were shocked at their agreement. "Imagine that," Dr. Branch kept going, "I mean really imagine that, gentlemen. If from that moment forward, we chose to fight not for the right to join their society, but for peace in ours. What if because of their decisions then in the1960s, we here now in 2012 didn't need white people for anything?" Eyes widened, and heads shook back and forth with the thought. "I know it's hard to picture but please try to wrap your minds around us actually having control of our own lives," Dr. Branch said with a little sarcasm. He continued, "Wouldn't it be amazing if all of that money we give to rich white people that own everything was actually coming back to us?" A lot of the men appeared dumbfounded by the idea, too many years under a system.

It hurt Dr. Branch to see his brothers in such disbelief, yet there were others with understanding in their eyes. Encouraged, Dr. Branch continued, "Really guys, what if we didn't need the government nor white America for anything other than protecting our borders? And please guys, know that I don't want you to focus on the idea of us being separatist. That is not my goal at all. I want you all to focus on the idea of true independence. We depend on white America or the government for everything. And they give us just enough to keep us begging for more. We need them for jobs (good or bad), we need them for food, water, electricity, and I'm about to bring it home . . ." Dr. Branch said the next part slowly, reminding the crowd of his initial story, "Even if I just want to go to a good freaking steakhouse, then I need them too." The crowd roared with agreement and amazement.

Dr. Branch banged on the podium while saying the next part, "Well, I'm sick and tired of being sick and tired. Are you all sick and tired too?" The crowd roared with most of the men rising to their feet. The Twenty-Six hadn't heard any of tonight's lecture, so they listened with the same elation as the newcomers. The hall roared with at least one hundred black men applauding and chanting. The energy was wonderful.

Dr. Branch had the answers. "Brothers, it is time for action. All the talking is over. There are simple activities you all can to do to help with the revolution. Actually, I am begging you guys to follow me and my efforts." The men were shocked that such a powerful man would beg them for anything as Dr. Branch continued, "Number one, quit traveling way out in the county to buy your clothes. There are five black-owned clothing stores in North St. Louis. From here on out, only buy your clothes from these five places. Number two, Pop's Sursave is upgrading everything. Please buy all of your groceries from there."

"But his stuff be old, and the Schnuck's is just cleaner," someone yelled.

Another man in the audience yelled out, "And those clothing stores you talking 'bout be just as expensive as the mall's, bruh."

Dr. Branch, always quick on his feet, quickly responded, "Well, Pop's has been upgraded and is continually getting building improvements. He is also getting fresh products from a network of black farmers now." Dr. Branch wasn't finished. "The clothing stores I'm referring to are lowering their prices as well as selling clothes from actual tailors that live here in St. Louis City."

That quieted the questioners and stunned the crowd. Dr. Branch had instantly shown that not only did he have effective words, but he had the motivation and know-how to put plans together. It also showed that he had already been active in the community. He had the crowd locked.

Dr. Branch then pointed to the back wall and said, "Look at my fraternity of men back there. We have already started what everyone thought was impossible. The Twenty-Six will change everything, men."

Dr. Branch spoke a lot more that night and then closed by saying, "All right, everyone, that's the end of tonight's sermon. I need to speak with the Twenty-Six." He purposely excluded everyone, knowing it would cause a lot of them to yearn to join even more. Nothing drives a person crazier than being excluded from a cool group. He continued, "I want you guys to implement the ideas I have shared tonight. I will reiterate: keep our money right here with us, so go shop at Pop's Sursave and buy your clothes from these neighborhood black-owned shops. Help them grow because they will help us grow," he finished, "Also, clean your surrounding area. Don't wait till trash is piled up to the curb before picking up. Go and ensure that your area is clean enough to eat off of. As you all can tell, the Twenty-Six has already started beautifying our neighborhood, but we cannot do it alone. We need your help."

He then said, "By doing those two things, you all will help us greatly. You guys have a safe trip home, and we will meet again next week. Invite whomever you want, just remember that we are still a men crowd only. We will soon get the women involved, but we as men still have a lot of work to do on ourselves before we could ever advise women on their actions." The crowd hated to agree, but truth reigned supreme in the hall, and they all nodded to his point. "Have a good one, gentlemen. Young men are most certainly welcome too."

The huge crowd rose with one man yelling up front to Dr. Branch, "Hey, brother."

"That's Dr. Branch," Anthum said coldly.

The speaker, a middle-age black man in jeans and a jacket his height at about five foot seven, looked up at the six foot six Anthum and quickly complied to Anthum's demand.

"Um . . . Dr. Branch," the man said.

"You had my attention when you called me brother, go on then," Dr. Branch replied.

"Can we join the Twenty-Six?"

Someone in the crowd jokingly said, "If that happened, they would have to change to the Twenty-Seven."

Even Dr. Branch laughed before saying, "Of course you can join but make sure you know what you are joining before you make a request. This is a blood in/blood out fraternity. Once you are in, great things are expected of you. You are looking at men who live on at least four hours of sleep a night because of all the work we do daily. And if you don't hold up your part, you will be removed." That statement made the men truly yearn for the opportunity to join.

Not only were the Twenty-Six an exclusive group, but their gangster mentality just fortified the men's hunger to join. Getting removed just sounded gangster, and though the Twenty-Six would never claim themselves to be a mafia, black men love the idea of anything slightly resembling a mafia setting. They were hooked.

"Just come to the next meeting, and I will begin the arrangements to have you guys start your process," Dr. Branch said.

"You mean we got to go through a process like a Freemason or something?" that same jacketed man asked.

"You have to earn the right to say that you are a member of the Twenty-Six. We have been working long and hard, and no one is just going to run up and take credit for our work. You have to earn our trust because once you are in, you are a brother for life. And we will expect you to behave as a brother would. Do you all get me?"

"I understand that, bruh." He looked at Anthum's cold gaze and corrected himself, "Uh . . . I mean . . . Dr. Branch."

Dr. Branch closed, "Good night, men. Please be safe." To his team members, he said, "Twenty-Six, I need you guys to stay a little longer. We have some critical business to discuss."

The men slowly departed the hall, everyone too excited to leave quietly. The newcomers were astounded and thanked their friends for the invitation. The last man finally closed the door as he left the hall, and Leroy locked up behind him. After Dr. Branch was sure that all the cars had driven from the parking lot and street, he started.

"OK guys," Dr. Branch spoke just above a whisper, "I just wanted to let you all know that our first bit of cleaning house is about to commence, and we will need all of your help."

Shannon Progress quickly chimed in, speaking somewhat loudly, "Though we all knew that your team would have to eventually do this one day, you told us we would never have to get our hands dirty."

"First off, Shannon, when discussing this, please keep your voice down," Dr. Branch advised. He continued, "I am not asking any of you to get your hands dirty. What team CH is about to do takes a lot of preparation and a lot of effort. Though none of you are needed on the field, you are sorely needed in a different capacity. Just listen and let me tell you how all of this is going to go. I have a list of the first kidnapping subjects, but I need more information before I pull the trigger, no pun intended. I also need certain supplies and a ton of work done prior to the due date to ensure this goes off without a hitch. You all get me."

"We get you, Dr. Branch. Just tell us what you need," Woody Daniels said. He looked at team CH and said, "You guys got the hard job, so we will certainly do what we can do to help."

Dr. Branch thanked him, and the men talked into the middle of the night about operational planning. Dr. Branch truly embraced this time with his team for he knew the next time they all were together, he and the rest of his sub-team would be murderers. A morbid thought, but he couldn't shake it.

Boogie Night

THE SANDWICH HUT is a restaurant whose look fits its name. It was a small structure with enough room to house cooking necessities, a cash register, and a small area to order and wait. Of course, the register and waiting area were separated by bulletproof plexiglass. This was Darryl Brown's favorite eatery. He spent much of his blood money buying burgers from this place. He especially loved their wings. Darryl was an interesting character. Killing was no problem for him; as a matter of fact, it was how he got paid. Jacking fools for their shit was Darryl's motto. He was the type of person that could perform armed robbery, brutally murder every witness with no remorse, and then go eat a burger and fries with blood still on his hands.

That particular day while exiting the Sandwich Hut, he walked out to a cop ambush. Two uniformed cops had their guns drawn and told him not to move. He would have gone out firing, but his gun was in his car. Damn the luck. One of the cops ran up smacked the bag out of Darryl's hands and cuffed his wrists behind his back. Darryl didn't think about it, but there weren't any flashing lights nor did he see a police car. He was shoved over to a Dodge Intrepid but still was unalarmed. When Darryl realized that the cops didn't read him his rights, he was actually happy believing it would be his reason for a mistrial. The two cops hopped in the front seat and pulled off. Darryl looked out the window, wondering where the two cops were taking him, and then he felt a sharp sting around his knee. When he looked down, he could see that the passenger cop was removing a needle from his leg. Before he could complain, everything went black.

Nathan Norfolk. Nasty Nate is what his friends called him. Nasty Nate is what everybody else called him as well but for different reasons. Nasty Nate was an actual pimp. It's hard to imagine that actual pimping still exists, but that is one game that hasn't changed at all. Nasty Nate learned his pimping game from the old school, which meant a lot of punishment to his whores, as well as lots of drugs to keep them hooked. Even worse, he had killed and dumped more Jane Doe's than he would ever admit. It was well known that he raped women and young girls on a regular basis. His whores gossiped that raping a woman was the only way Nasty Nate could get his rocks off. If you asked him, he would probably agree. He didn't know why he loved to hate women so much. He just did.

This night, it was dark, and Nasty Nate was leaving one of his many living quarters. He spotted a young scantily clad girl standing across the road. He called out at her, and she smiled wide enough to be seen in the dark. He thought to himself she was going to be easy, she already dressed like a hooker. As he walked toward her, she started walking into a nearby alley. The closer he got, the more he could smell her perfume and see her youth. He pegged her at fifteen. Perfect. He licked his chops as he followed her into the dark alley. Without knowing her intentions, Nate already unzipped his pants and was fondling himself. He would have her regardless of how she felt about his plans. She walked close to a dumpster, and he walked over to her.

"Pull your pants down, daddy," the little girl said.

She sounded so young, and she already knew the whore's lingo. Nate was ecstatic. This fresh meat must've belonged to someone else is what he was thinking as he dropped his britches. He said, "Bitch, this gonna be the ride of yo life. Turn that pretty ass 'round cause I'm about to . . ." *Thud.*

Nate was cracked over the head with a night stick by a giant in all black. He was slung over the giant's shoulder and wisped away as though weighing less than ten pounds. Before the masked giant left the scene, he winked at his little cousin, letting her know that her efforts were appreciated.

Richard Drake was a strong name given to a weak person. Unable to think or talk his way out of any situation, Richie Rich would always rely on his three eighty to do the talking. Richie Rich, at the age of twenty, already had over twelve undisputed notches on his belt. Because no one would

my stun gun. I figured this way, no paperwork." A slight and rare smile lined Mathew's face.

Leroy just leaned against his car, unconcerned with the broken glass under his tail, and said as though in a daze, "I see now. I see why Dr. Branch wanna just take these dudes out instead of helping 'em." Leroy followed Mathew as he joined his partner, and Leroy watched as they tossed Richie Rich into the back of their police cruiser, saying, "Man, y'all should have seen the look in his eyes. It was like he was a possessed man. What y'all gonna do now, Matty?" Leroy asked, always changing someone's name.

"Mathew looked around and watched as people started gathering around the scene. Staying composed, he said, "Well, Leroy, we are going to take him to the station and lock him up." His corporate tone, plus the way he looked directly in his eyes, let Leroy know he was BSing.

"OK, well, am I free to go?" Leroy asked as sirens could be heard coming their way.

"Actually, that would be best," Mathew told his teammate. "Take your car quickly and get out of here."

Leroy briskly obliged, hopping into his car and driving away. He was turning down the opposite street as more police showed up. The band of cops got a quick explanation from Mathew and his partner as they lied about some car that just got away. The other officers quickly took pursuit, in search of a ghost. Not one cop noticed the guy lying in the backseat of Mathew's cruiser. No matter, Richie Rich would be gone in less than five minutes anyway.

There were a few other single-person kidnappings like the aforementioned, but the larger mass of participants they received came from the bulk captures. Team CH's first bulk capture came from attacking the gang that always resided on Dr. Branch's corner. Team CH would rid his corner of those hoodlums first. Afterward, they would attempt to capture their rivaling gang, which rallied a few blocks east.

As usual, Dr. Branch's corner was littered with the typical crew along with some other vagrants. They were having a blast that night. They all drank, smoked, and played craps . . . loudly. Every few minutes, a zombie-looking drug addict would timidly approach the gang and speak a few soft words. After one of the thugs would peer up and down the street (looking for any sign of the authorities), he would nod his head toward one of his friends and give him a quick hand gesture. That friend would then walk to the alley behind them and approach a dumpster. In a small crevice near that dumpster was a stash spot. It held crack, heroine, prescription pills, and horrible weed. The hand signal the boy received from the initial guy let him know what to grab and how much. After getting the drugs, that person would walk back into the crowd and slowly walk over to the addict for a solid handshake. That dap is where the exchange of merchandise and money would take place. The addict would then scamper away, elated that he had received his *precious* for the time being. That scenario replayed itself all day everyday, and the night was way worse.

The crew on that corner even learned and adapted over time. While crack was a top seller, they were sure to have an ample supply. But as of late, most people wanted heroine, and this crew was never the type to disappoint. They had the best heroine in the city. They also showed their impudence to the authorities, often by getting arrested only to return a day or two later to that same corner. If that thug didn't show up, a look alike would just take his place. The cops ceased policing that intersection, and after the futility truly set in, police even stopped responding to 911 calls involving that corner and that crew altogether. With no police presence, the crew became even more disrespectfully loud and unabashedly overt in their illegal activities. This night, the crew seemed to be in rare form, and a passerby would have thought a midnight block party was going on.

Dr. Branch and his entire sub-team sat some ways down the street in a giant brown old van. They all went over their plans as they watched the hoodlum festivities. The team wore SWAT gear acquired from good money and even better connections. Mathew was the only one that had a badge that he would display at the right time, which they hoped would be good enough to fool the boys. They knew they would have to be quick, because they were sure that a couple of the boys on the corner would draw their weapons.

The plan: Dr. Branch and Mathew would drive the van up while the other men would slowly creep up to hiding spots blocking any escape routes. After the men were all set up, the time to execute presented itself, and the men leaped to action.

The van darted from its parked position and swooped up as Mathew flashed his badge. He and Dr. Branch appeared as mercenaries with their faces covered and submachine guns held in military form as they exited the vehicle. The fake SWAT team screamed the typical drills, "Don't move, get down, freeze," and a few other specials. A few of the street punks noticed the gear and badge and figured they would die if they ran, so they stood still and dropped to the ground. Others followed their first instinct and darted. One kid tried to run westward until Fred popped out from behind a car and fired a round into the air as he approached from his hiding spot. That kid stopped in his tracks and walked back to the group. Larry approached with his submachine gun pointed at the crowd from a totally different angle, discouraging other would-be runners. Phillip ran up like a crazy man chasing another escaper back into the bunch, with his gun pointed at the kid's back while screaming obscenities. Phillip did his running and screaming while a cigarette hung from his lips. It was a wonder his face mask didn't catch fire.

Another kid ran into the ally and got some distance between him and the cop scene, so he thought himself safe. He continued running while looking back to see if he was followed and as soon as he turned forward he was smashed by the butt of one of those automatic weapons. The force he received from Anthum's strike combined with his forward running momentum sent the boy's head backward, with his feet continuing to go forward. Blood squirted from the boy's mouth as the plastic and metal gun crashed into his jaw. He hit the ground with a thud, and a tooth was coughed out of his mouth. Anthum simply grabbed the boy by his shirt and dragged the assailant back to the group.

As Anthum joined the rest of the group with his prisoner in hand, Dr. Branch only shook his head at his friend's over exuberant tactics. The other hoodlums were all getting their hands cuffed behind their backs. Not one person escaped. The tactics that team CH used gave the impression that it was far more of the fake SWAT than there really were. It was Dr. Branch's tactic, and surprisingly, it worked. The hoods all thought this was a typical drug bust, so no one really resisted. Expecting to be back out on the streets, they all complied after the attempted escapers were rounded up. Especially after they all looked up at a giant Anthum walking back carrying one of their friends like he was a rag doll. Blood leaked from the kid's mouth, and a broken tooth was stuck to the kid's collar by his own serum and saliva. No one attempted to cuff that one kid. Knowing that Anthum busted the boy up, team CH believed the lad would be out for a long time (they really hoped that the kid wasn't dead). They all walked the kids to the back of the van, slowly pushing each inside. There were no seats, so the thugs all sat Indian style or just with their knees bent and their butts on the hard metal. Ten guys in all, so it was somewhat cramped. Of course, they all voiced their issues.

"What y'all doin'? You know we gone be back tomorrow don't y'all. I 'ont even see why y'all wastin' y'all time." The bulk of the talking came from the same mouthy guy that had that spat with Anthum a long time ago. He must've been the leader or a leader of some type because the others simply echoed his sentiments or followed his same line of banter. "Look here, pigs, y'all let us go, and I got a thousand dollars y'all can split. I know it's more than y'all make in a month. I make that in a hour." The crew all laughed.

Dr. Branch merely listened to the insults while driving and looking forward. Everything worked out great, and he and his team were relieved. So many things could have gone wrong. If seen impersonating an officer of the law, they all could do serious time. Mathew, who sat in the passenger's seat, would even be in more trouble for aiding the impersonators. Those worries left as the two drove to their next destination.

"Y'all awfully quiet, officers. Don't y'all wanna talk about how y'all wastin' everybody's time?" The talker again attempted to use some psychology. Starting to get a tad more rambunctious, the talker then yelled, "Y'all ain't gonna take off y'all masks? You better not show me yo face or you know you as good as dead." That threat did get a response, and both men looked at the talker, then each other, but still no words were passed between the two. Finally seeing a response from the supposed cops caused the thug to continue with his negative banter until the van pulled into a vacant lot. Both CH team members quickly exited the van, and the young guys attempted to get to their knees to see what was going on. After a few seconds, the passenger front door was opened, and a small round canister was thrown into the back of the van. Instantly the thing exploded, and gas erupted from the small grenade-like object. The gang all tried to get to the front, climbing on one another with their shoulders and knees, attempting to get some fresh air. They yelled and screamed until the only thing they could do was cough. After each one inhaled enough of the gas, the coughs turned into silence. Gas expelled from every small opening of the van and blew in the direction of the wind. From the outside, it appeared as though smoky souls were all leaving the old van at once. Dr. Branch knew that wasn't true . . . yet. Those boys were merely sleeping, and this was another job well done. It was now time to get the opposing gang.

The next group of guys that would soon be under attack resided on a basketball court. This was a hangout as well as another serious dope spot. Dope spots in the ghetto were like McDonalds. You could find one everywhere. Clearing this scene would greatly change the immediate area and therefore cause another massive improvement to the neighborhood. There was a need for more planning because the basketball court was open and ill-placed for a sneak attack. Police were more likely to show up there as well, unlike the last place team CH attacked. Special tactics were needed for this endeavor, and more members were going to be a necessity.

Again, Leroy volunteered even after his last episode. He was told how smoothly the last gang raid went and expected to be part of the same type of adventure. He was going to be a driver. Because this group of thugs had to be nabbed quickly, many cars and drivers were needed for a quick grab and go. Each member of team CH would have his own car and driver. The driver was a volunteer from another sub-team. Dr. Branch gave tons of appreciation to his volunteers for they did not choose to be a part of the dark side of this operation yet stepped in when times called. To make certain he didn't have a similar episode like what Leroy experienced, he ensured that all members of this operation were armed. Not only were the CH team members carrying automatic submachine guns, but the drivers were carrying pistols as well. The plan was to park in the street on three sides of the basket ball court (the fourth side being too far away), and then attack when the time was right. The men waited for their queue from Dr. Branch, which they received via a walkie-talkie.

Time to get started the walkie-talkie said, and the six cars pulled up in varying spots. Two parked along the curb on one side of the street, while the other four cars parked similarly on the other two sides of the street. They felt they covered most of the possible exits. They looked at the basketball court and saw a few young girls being harassed by a group of guys. These guys totaling eight looked exactly the same as the last group of thugs they picked up. All unkempt, pants sagging down to the ground, most of them had dreds, and none of them looked like they gave a damn about themselves nor anyone else. Not one of the boys looked like someone any responsible parent would be proud to call their own. The gang would smack the girls on the booty, flash a wad of cash, or just call the girls out of their names. Demeaning women was a must if you were a thug, and this crew took serious pleasure in it. The girls were no better, for they appeared to be gluttons for the punishment. The girls, not having much respect for themselves, simply saw the cash the boys often showed, and allowed the gang to treat them like waste.

Dr. Branch and the others were dressed in their SWAT uniforms, and all waited for the action to begin. Dr. Branch saw that the street was clear except for the group of kids within the basketball court. He gave the order on the walkie-talkie, and all of the men hopped out the car they were in. They all approached the court with guns drawn. Dr. Branch and Mathew, being the first to get to the gate's entrance, announced their presence.

"Nobody move, get on the ground, everyone!" Mathew yelled in his typical cop fashion. "This is SWAT!"

A few of the guys instantly complied and hit the ground as soon as they heard the commotion, others waited until they actually saw the uniforms and the badge Mathew showed. Never being part of any type of ambush, the girls dropped to the ground, crying and fearing for their lives. Everything seemed to be running like the last bulk kidnapping, when all of a sudden a bald-headed young kid removed a nine millimeter from his waste in a flash and opened fire. He was only a few feet away from the fake SWAT and was able to release two rounds that both struck Mathew. One bullet hit him in the right pectoralis, and the second shot hit him directly in the center of his chest. Mathew flew back from the powerful force of each bullet and landed hard on the concrete. The kid saw his damage and then pointed at Dr. Branch. Dr. Branch didn't waste any time. He squeezed the trigger and seven rounds left the small machine gun quicker than he had expected. Four of the shots landed home, riddling the boy's right side. The boy's contorted body then dropped to the ground. Dr. Branch looked down to see Mathew with his eyes closed and fingers still gripping his gun. He turned to yell at his driver, which was Tony Huggs,

"Come out, grab Mathew and put him in the car now!" Dr. Branch frantically screamed to Tony.

Seeing the commotion as an opportunity, two more of the young men stood from their lying position and drew their weapons. Dr. Branch hit the ground when the two boys fired their guns. One had a Glock, and the other had a 50-caliber Desert Eagle. The Desert Eagle sounded like a cannon, and Dr. Branch actually heard the bullets whizzing past his face as well as bullets ricocheting off of the concrete around him. The firing started before Tony could drag Mathew into the waiting car, so he just hopped over him to shield him from further damage. By this time, the other CH team members were running up from their positions. The two shooters continued firing in Dr. Branch's direction while trying to flee in the other.

One thug ran to the right and the other to the left. The one boy that ran to the right looked forward and saw Phillip in his SWAT uniform. The boy, feeling as though there was no alternative, fired his Desert Eagle at Phillip. He only got off one shot, because Phillip squeezed his trigger and let bullets fly. That kid caught more than fifteen bullets in his midsection and danced before he hit the ground. Phillip ran up to the bloody mess and kicked the fifty caliber pistol away from reaching distance.

Leroy sat in the driver seat of his car watching the entire scenario play out and focused on the two boys shooting at Dr. Branch. He saw the one turn and get destroyed by Phillip. Then he saw something he believed should have been on someone's movie screen. The other kid stopped shooting at Dr. Branch and ran in Leroy's direction. Anthum had just left the car, so he was between the car and the kid with the gun. Leroy sat stunned as the kid unleashed what bullets remained in his magazine in Anthum's direction all the while Anthum continued running full speed directly at the shooting youth. Anthum not only ran at the kid, but he threw his gun to the ground as Leroy watched the kid continuously letting round after round go. Everything moved in slow motion, and Leroy couldn't believe that Anthum hadn't been hit yet. Anthum took a few more large strides, closing the distance between him and the kid, and lunged forward. He hit the ground, performing a complete roll, looking quite small being tucked like a ball. He then sprung up to full height, grabbing the gun with his left hand and the kid's throat with his right. He twisted the kid's shooting arm until something snapped and the gun fell. He lifted the boy in the air by his small neck and whispered into the kid's ear.

"I wanted you to live, so we could kill you later, you little fucking piece of shit," Anthum said as he held the boy a foot off of the ground by his windpipe.

The kid gasped for air as his neck felt crushed between Anthum's massive fingers. Anthum's strength seemed unreal to the boy, and he didn't know whether to cry for breath or cry out in pain because of his broken arm. Anthum continued holding the boy while taking inventory.

The rest of the crew was present and accounted for. Mathew was finally inside one of the cars. There were two dead bodies on the ground with six others alive but not moving and two whimpering girls. Anthum's main concern was Dr. Branch. He could see that Dr. Branch was all right and helping Mathew. No one seemed to know what to do, so Anthum took control.

"Cuff 'em and let's load 'em up quick." He shouted at the other members. They quickly did their jobs cuffing and running the guys to their respective vehicles. Again, Anthum needed no cuffs for the guy he held, and before he turned to take his prisoner away, he spoke harshly to the girls that remained on the ground, "Get up and get the hell out of here. If I hear about any of this, I'm coming back for you. If I ever see you hanging around thugs like this again, I'm coming back for you." Anthum turned and drug his prisoner away.

The girls stood and saw the carnage around them. They were tempted to scream but saw Anthum's giant back as he jogged away and thought otherwise. They both just ran away from the scene as quickly as they could. Trying to wipe away the memories the same way they constantly wiped away the tears that streamed down their faces. Neither girl ever told a soul that they were at that crime scene, and neither was ever seen with a thug within that neighborhood again.

Two blocks away was a police car. Two white officers sat in a parking lot eating burgers and fries as the gunshots began. Officer McCullin, a buff, six-foot, blonde-haired rookie heard the gunshots and threw his food out of the window.

"Let's go, Rogers!" the rookie eagerly told his old and learned partner.

"Do you hear that, McCullin?" Officer Rogers, old, short, and pudgy retorted. He continued, "Those are Uzis, and that other thing sounds like a freakin' cannon."

"Come on, Rogers, it's our job to serve and protect," Officer McCullin said, hoping to stir his older partner just a little. He finished, "So let's serve and protect."

"Listen here, rookie," Officer Rogers said, preparing to tell his partner some words to live by, "I don't know about what you and your next partner will do, but while you are with me, you will not run into an obvious volatile situation. I mean, come on, let the niggers kill who or what they're going to kill, and we just go in and clean up afterward . . . you get me?"

Officer Rogers looked sympathetic as though he truly cared about this rookie cop. "It may sound harsh, but I've lived fourteen years in these St. Louis streets, and nothing has ever changed, rookie. And if you want to last as long as I have, you never run into a volatile scene in progress. It never lasts long . . . See, sounds like the shooting has stopped," Officer Rogers said as he stuck his ear out of the window, attempting to hear more shots.

"OK, let's go now," the rookie said sounding impatient.

"Did you call it in . . . call it in, rookie . . . you know protocol," Officer Rogers said to his partner as he continued eating his burger and fries. "You shouldn't have thrown your food away, rookie. This burger is awesome."

Officer Rogers chowed down on his food and sipped his soda through a straw as his young partner yelled into his CB. Officer Rogers seemed as though he didn't have a care in the world while his partner screamed out codes and street names. After calling for backup, Officer McCullin frantically changed sitting positions as though he was unable to get comfortable in his passenger's seat. Officer Rogers finally finished his food, licked the last of the salt and ketchup off of his fingers, and tossed the bag in the backseat.

"I hate littering . . . hint . . . hint . . .," Officer Rogers told his young partner. "Next time throw your crap in a trashcan, rookie."

"Sorry Rogers, I just got excited. Can we please go now?" Officer McCullin pleaded.

His partner responded by turning the key to get the engine roaring. Officer Rogers then turned on his siren and shot toward the noise. Being his district, he knew it was the basketball court that housed the action. A shooting happened there at least once every week. Even if no one was shot, there was at least someone shot at. It was home to one of the most notorious gangs in St. Louis, "so what did you expect", Officer Rogers always said.

As he and Officer McCullin were pulling up to the shooting scene, off in the distance, they could hear numerous vehicles driving hard, tires screeching loudly.

"I just saw a car shoot down Page Ave. Rogers, let's go chase 'em," the rookie offered.

"Naw, they will kill themselves or somebody else in the very near future, and we will just get them then. I am quite sure they left some evidence on the crime scene. Either way, it's no big deal," he said as he parked next to the basketball court. They got out, and Officer Rogers said, "See, rookie, it's just two more dead niggers. You will see this often in this district, so be prepared. God-damn, look at this one," Officer Rogers said as he caught a glimpse at Phillip's work. Officer Rogers added more, "These guys must've really pissed someone off."

Reiterating his point, Officer Rogers then said, "Listen to me, rookie, these niggers will kill one another until there isn't a one left. Don't you dare run into a hostile environment or second guess yourself while you are working in these streets. Do you get me, rookie?"

"Why do you have to use that word?" Officer McCullin inquired blandly.

"What . . . rookie?" Officer Rogers asked, his attempt at a joke.

"No, the N word, you dolt," the young officer shot back. He continued, "I thought you liked Briggens, Johnson, and Bradford," Officer McCullin called out some of the black cops he and his partner knew and respected.

"Yeah, I love those guys. But I don't compare them to these dirt bags. Those are hard working men." Officer Rogers nudged one of the dead boys with his boot and said, "This right here is a worthless nigger. And I don't think anyone will cry over his death." Officer Rogers was quite wrong. Though most of the people that attended the kid's funeral would've said they expected him to end up in a casket at a young age, they all still cried hard at the loss of another black kid to the cold cruel streets.

Dr. Branch sat in the backseat with Mathew as they sped away from the scene. He was so appreciative that Anthum picked up where he dropped the ball. Dr. Branch didn't foresee any of the stuff that just happened. He smacked himself on his head a few times yelling out "stupid, stupid, stupid," as his driver peeled rubber to their emergency destination. Dr. Branch had established safe houses if the situation necessitated a quick getaway. He looked at Mathew, whose eyes where yet closed, and saw the holes in his outer jacket. Forgetting that they all wore bulletproof vests, Dr. Branch forgot to check for entry and exit wounds. He assumed the worst. The driver said nothing as Dr. Branch ridiculed himself and the operation. Though he didn't take full credit for the successful operation earlier, he took full blame for this failure here. He heard a sound and glanced downward. Mathew was opening his eyes and saying something softly to Dr. Branch.

"Don't worry," Mathew whispered.

"I'm not worried," Dr. Branch said, trying to be strong for his friend, though he was very worried.

"Did everyone get away?" Mathew asked.

"Just got confirmation over our com links." Dr. Branch held up his walkie-talkie and then continued talking, "You got shot, and there are two boys dead out there, and little girls saw what happened. We barely got away."

Mathew was glad no one else was around to see their leader so shaken. He himself had never seen Dr. Branch so psychologically frail. After Mathew gained more focus, he sat up straight and removed his flat jacket. Underneath was his kevlar vest, which held two slugs. The fifty caliber slug had penetrated the vest and touched Mathew's skin.

"Those are gonna leave a serious mark," he said to himself and Dr. Branch.

"Oh my god," Dr. Branch said, sounding dramatically relieved. "I would not have known what to do if you were killed, Mathew."

"You would keep this party moving, Dr. Branch," Mathew informed his leader. He was surprised that his leader needed to hear this yet said the words anyway, "One monkey don't stop the show, Dr. Branch. We all know what we have signed up for, and if something happened to any one of us, you keep this train moving. You get me?" Mathew said, giving orders to his leader.

Dr. Branch really needed those words and was quite receptive. He seemed to calm a little and responded, "I get you, brother Mathew."

"I am fine, and the dead gangbangers on the ground were going to meet their maker soon anyway," Mathew continued uplifting his leader. "So there is no need to fret, everything is still on schedule. We have all of the bastards we set out to get, and we are done for the time being. And trust me, my friends on the police force won't know a thing. So let's get all of these punks to the spot and go from there, Dr. Branch." Mathew merely advised Dr. Branch to continue with the plans he had already drilled into each of his men's ears.

Though Dr. Branch was a great leader and appeared to all as never having a weak moment, he was yet human and needed uplift and confirmation as every man does. After Mathew's speech, Dr. Branch regained a lot of composure, especially after seeing Mathew alive and well. Mathew's words went a long way and were greatly appreciated. The men had worked very hard that day and succeeded in their endeavors. They had all of their victims; it was then time to transport them all to the headquarters.

Junior, real name Joey Jacobs Jr., wasn't a really bad boy. He hung around his hood friends and participated in a few of their illegal activities, but it was more so for acceptance than anything else. He wore the street colors so he was definitely affiliated, but there were no records of him in the police files nor did researching the neighborhood provide any negative notes on the kid. Him waking up in the CH headquarters was purely the result of being at the wrong place at the wrong time.

He was one of the kids at the basketball court. All he could remember was a crazy shootout between the cops and his boys while he lay on the ground. He was snatched away to a black magnum, and then everything went dark.

Junior slowly gained his faculties, and a picture began to come to view. Things were blurry from drugs still leaving his system, so the objects he saw had a wavy motion to them, and he thought he was going to puke. His mind cleared more, and things began to make sense. He was in a small room, like a jail cell, but the walls were padded. He saw a huge metal door directly in front of him, and that's when things got scary.

He attempted to rub his head to help it clear, yet his arms felt tethered. They were both tied together behind his back, and his ankles were chained to the front legs of the chair. A quick tug let Junior know that he was going nowhere. The metal chair he sat in actually was constructed upon legs that were drilled many feet deep under the ground, so the single chair was not budging. Of course, Junior didn't know that and tried using all of his strength to kick or break his way out of his binds to no avail. He was at a loss as he sat and pondered what kind of police station he sat in. He had never seen anything like it. There weren't any cameras nor was there that two-way mirror he'd always seen in movies. Just him – tied to a damn metal chair.

He heard a noise: it sounded like there was someone at the door. There was a metallic clang signifying the pull of a lever, and the door opened. There stood a giant in a black, SWAT suit wearing the matching black mask. Junior couldn't see the behemoth's face. His testicles retreated into what felt like his stomach, and he swallowed audibly hard. A deep voice rang out.

"Do you want to live, boy?" was the only question from the tall giant.

"I . . . I . . . where am I?" Junior asked.

"Well, Junior," the giant, showing his knowledge, asked again, "I am never going to repeat myself again. The question is simply . . . do . . . you . . . want to live . . ., boy?"

"How do you know who I am? And the police ain't suppose to tie people up," Junior said, knowing his rights.

Junior barely saw the giant move from the doorway. He just caught a blur then felt a ground shaking crack against the side of his face. He felt like he had been hit by a Mike Tyson punch, but it was only an open hand slap. The smack rocked Junior, and his lights went out for a couple of seconds. He felt a trickle of blood leave the corner of his mouth, and from that moment on, he was terrified.

A room over Jesse Botwin, a twenty-five-year-old do-nothing, sat in the same situation. But instead of seeing a giant at his doorway, he saw a medium-sized man in all black with a mask and a hole in the mask. The hole was at the mouth, and in his mouth was a cigarette. Jesse thought the guy looked funny and laughed. The masked smoker first, tilted his head like a confused dog, and then he blew smoke out of his mouth. Most of the thick smoke stayed in the mask and exited from the top. He appeared as a man with his head on fire. He then walked up to Jesse and dropped to his right knee. The smoker lifted Jesse's left pant leg, quickly snatched the cigarette from the hole in the mask, and shoved the burning cherry into Jesse's shin. The noxious smell of burning flesh mixed with tobacco smoke was nauseating, and things became a lot less funny to Jesse. All Jesse could do was scream out in pain, and he did so loudly. The masked smoker then bounced up like a jack in a box and looked at Jesse. Once again he tilted his head like a confused dog. The masked figure emanated darkness and insanity. Jesse was terrified.

Hershel Macky, another boy who wasn't extremely bad, found himself in the same crazy situation. At his door was a short, stocky person in all black and wearing what looked like a ski mask over his face.

"What the fuck is going on?" Hershel spat at the short person.

The masked person didn't respond. He simply walked from the doorway and dropped down to Hershel's feet. Hershel could feel the person doing something with his sneakers, so he attempted to make it difficult. He tried kicking, but because his legs were chained, there wasn't much room to move. He wondered what was going on until he could see that his right shoelace had been removed. Then he saw the masked person get behind him and drop the shoestring around his neck like a gold chain. The masked person tugged on the string tightly, and then tighter and tighter. Hershel felt pain, and his air supply cut short. He tried to struggle, but the crazy positioning left him at the behest of the masked man. As things began to get dark, the strangler let the string go, and air rushed into Hershel's lungs. The air rushing through his bruised windpipe hurt like hell. He didn't know what was going on. The only thing that Hershel knew was that at that moment, he was the most terrified he had ever been in his life.

There were guys like Junior, Jesse, and Hershel waking up the same way. The total number of guys captured was twenty eight. Fourteen of the detainees each woke in a separate room. Some woke to a ski-masked sadist, instantly torturing the victim, while others woke to absolute silence, wondering what was going on. Of course their wait didn't last long.

Team CH spread the love and would leave one room in order to visit another, providing their style of torture to the new victim. Every member of team CH was present and accounted for, and they all took the task quite seriously. They all kept in constant contact and ensured perfect coordination throughout the process. What was the overall goal? To scare these people straight. Hopefully a lot sooner than later.

Within the confines of their area were thirty rooms. Fifteen identical rooms being directly across from each other. And then there was the larger room at the end of the hallway in the making of a classroom. Within the classroom, there were fourteen chairs total. In front of those chairs was a small table with one chair behind it, appearing as the teacher's desk. Behind the "student" chairs were two large silver panels with one large metal handle on each. They resembled giant laundry shoots. The wall and the ground inside of the mock class room was dirt. The ceiling housed no light fixture, only fire protecting sprinklers that poked out looking like little metallic pods. The dark-colored ceiling along with the dirt walls gave the room a dismal look, and the dank was something a man could taste. It seemed like a dungeon of old, one that could be seen in ancient times. The only light source came from a small, cheap-looking lamp that sat atop the front desk. The light bulb emitted a soft twenty-watt power output and merely illuminated the room enough to add to the depressed feel.

The classroom is where the other fourteen kidnapped victims found themselves. One by one the likes of Darryl Brown, Nasty Nate, and Richie Rich opened their weary eyes and awoke to a groggy scene. The age of the people in that room ranged from seventeen to twenty-eight, yet they all pretty much reacted the same upon seeing their situation. They all first opened eyes and then tried to bring their hands to their face only to realize that not only were their hands bound, but also their ankles were on lock down too. That's when the yelling commenced. The victims that were still unconscious were waking to the yells of a few that were already aware of their disposition. They soon joined in with the hollering. After a good hour of different people begging to know what was going on and yelling to get out of there, one of the captured announced his presence.

"Shut the fuck up," Nasty Nate demanded. "Y'all crying like a bunch of my ho's."

"Fuck you!" one of the murderous members of the bunch said.

"Listen, you dumb fuck," Nate told the tween. "You been screamin' for like three fucking hours," Nate said smoothly, sounding like a pimp. "Ain't nobody coming 'til they come, dumb ass. You think they don't know we down here? You got my muthafuckin' head hurtin'."

"Where the fuck we at?" Darryl inquired when he regained consciousness.

"It looks like the cops got us you young chumps," Nate said, taking on the mantle as leader. He crudely informed, "Just chill out and don't do no damn snitching, and we will be out in a few hours or days." Nate thought and added, "It don't matter me none, I ain't gotta be out on the streets to make my money."

"Man, this don't look like no damn police station," Richie Rich said, adding his two cents. "I been to a lot of police stations, and I ain't never seen nothing like this."

"Bullshit," Nate spat back, "Young chump, this is a police station. They just poor," Nate said, making poor sound like po'.

"Well, why they got us chained up down here?" a different juvenile inquired.

"Listen here, young chump," Nasty Nate demanded then continued, "They just trying to scare us. Getting us in here all talking and shit. Next thing you know, they got cases on all us." Nate sounded as though he had the game figured out, "Now just sit back, relax, and enjoy the show." He offered the last bit with a little too much confidence. That confidence bled into the rest of the murderous crew, and they all calmed slightly.

"Damn, I'm starving," one of the heavier set lads admitted.

"You would be, you fat fuck," Nate spewed. He kept on antagonizing the chunky murderer, "Chew on your bottom lip. It look like a fat hot dog, you fat stankin' fuck you," Nate finished, being his typical crude self.

Except for the chunky fellow, the rest of the room busted out in laughter, which caused them to calm even more.

The friends within the room began exchanging words. There were four guys from Dr. Branch's corner, and there were three from the opposing gang from the basketball court. After getting bored, they all began talking, first to one another then at each other.

"A cuzz," the light-skinned leader from Dr. Branch's corner said, talking to one of his partners, "Where's the shit?" he asked, referring to their stash of drugs and money.

That kid looked around at his crew and back to the leader, answering, "I don't know. Scotty was the last one with it, and he ain't in here."

The light-skinned leader, Zero, looked around the room for the fiftieth time and compared the number of his gang members captured versus the number present within that gloomy room.

"That's crazy. Why ain't we all in here then?" Zero thought out loud.

That question sparked a conversation between the leader and the few members he had present with him. They held their discussion quietly, trying to keep secret what they could. While they conferred, the three members of the opposing gang conversed as well.

"Hey, Lando, did you see how they sprayed up Mike and KK?" a sleepy-eyed, dark-skinned kid said, talking to his compatriot.

"Yeah, that shit was crazy," Lando responded. "Did you see Chin?" he asked then said, "You went out like a soldier, Chin." That compliment was pointed at the kid with the broken wrist.

Chin winced in pain as he tried to put a smile on his face. His hand, wrist, and forearm were swollen badly, and the pain the skinny boy endured was obvious to the crew. Trying to restrain his anguish, he shot back, "Yeah, but that big muthafucka broke my arm. And he head butted me with that big ass head of his. So my fuckin' arm killin' me, and my head hurt like hell, blood."

After hearing about his rival's pain, the light-skinned leader from Dr. Branch's corner stopped his conversation with his crew and then threw a major insult in Chin's direction.

"Yo head hurtin' cause you a bitch ass nigga," he spurted.

"Nigga please, that big muthafucka broke my arm, and they ain't took me to no hospital or nothing." Chin tried to plead, not wanting to look soft, forgetting that pleading would make him look soft.

"That big muthafucka broke my arm," the light skinned leader said in a high-pitched feminine tone, mocking his rival. His crew all started laughing, even Nasty Nate added a loud unique laugh to the mix.

"Fuck you, faggot ass nigga," Chin shot back.

"Nigga, you the fag, crying like a li'l baby over there," Zero retorted.

"Nigga, that's why we taking all yo fiends, all yo money, and we blew that nigga Corey's brains all over his mama's door," Chin said, purposely hitting below the belt.

Corey, being one of the Zero's best friends, was murdered two months ago. Chin's comment enraged Zero and they started slinging obscenities at each other.

"Nigga, fuck you," this time one of the other boys from Dr. Branch's corner spoke up. "That's why I still got T-bones's blood all over my shoes."

Both gangs let their hate fly. The dimly lit room was filled with the blue banter of the opposing gangs, and it reached a crescendo when the boys attempted to spit on each other. That is when they all heard clanging on the other side of the large metal door. They quieted, and after a few more loud mechanical noises, the door slowly opened. They all sat motionless wondering who or what was about to enter. That is when Dr. Branch, still wearing his SWAT suit without the ski mask, walked in.

Dr. Branch slowly strolled into the room with his laptop tucked under his arm. He didn't even look at his audience; he merely made his way to his chair and pulled it out. He then placed his laptop on the table and sat down. The chained boy's all glared at their captor, waiting on some words. No one wanted to break the silence until Nasty Nate spoke up.

"Hey, man, you ain't allowed to detain us like this." Nate spoke with a little knowledge of the law, "We at least get our one phone call."

Dr. Branch said nothing in response. He acted as though no one had said a word. Dr. Branch simply opened his laptop and started typing.

"Hey, I know you," Zero said, "You that dude from my hood. You been a cop all this time?" he asked.

Dr. Branch continued ignoring his prisoners. He continued with his preparations until everything was in complete order, then he looked up from his laptop menacingly. He still didn't say a word; he merely eyeballed each vagabond one at a time, holding their gaze for almost fifteen seconds each.

Chin, sitting in absolute pain, said something timidly, "Y'all caint just break my arm and not take me to no hospital. Look at it, it look like it got a gallon of juice in it, man."

"Yeah, cuzz, y'all can't do stuff like that, that shit ain't right," Darryl said, taking up for his new friend and purposely heckling what he believed to be a cop.

Unable to stay quiet after Darryl's statement, Dr. Branch finally said some things of his own. "Darryl Brown," Dr. Branch spoke in his deepest tone, "Do you really think you have the right to tell anyone what's right? To you Chin, real name Charley Jackson, I will admit my team member was probably a little too aggressive in his efforts to capture you. But you were shooting at him, so what do you expect?" Dr. Branch said, showing absolutely no compassion.

"So you gonna let us know where we at," Nate spoke with no fear. "What po' dunk police station we in?"

"Ahh, Nasty Nate, or should I call you by your name given at birth, Nathan Norfolk," Dr. Branch lavished. "You are one of my top prizes."

"What the fuck are you talking about, and how the fuck do you know who we are?" Nate responded, using his colorful language.

"Nathan, Nathan, Nathan," Dr. Branch said, as though Nathan should be ashamed of asking such questions. He continued, "Nathan, I know all about your pimping. More importantly, I know about other things." Switching subjects, Dr. Branch said quickly, "I have something to show you guys."

Dr. Branch, always reverting to his PowerPoint slide, connected his laptop to a projector and showed the slides on the wall behind him. He then stood so the picture show could be seen clearly by his captive audience. Dr. Branch pressed a button, and the screen popped to life. After another button pressing, a picture came into view. The first picture was of a murder scene. The picture was of a young man, with his eyes and mouth frozen open in fright and pain. The body was sprawled in a gutter. No one saw the irony. The shirt the corpse wore was some indiscernible color that had been washed a different shade by pints of blood. The bullet holes were not apparent because the vast quantity of blood was the eye-catching part of the picture, and it covered everything.

The next picture was the same crime scene with a wider view showing a peace of the street the gutter belonged to. It was Dr. Branch's neighborhood. That is when the most amazing thing happened. One of the hoods bragged about the murder.

"Aww, I thought I recognized that nigga," Chin said, happy he could throw more stones at his rivals. "That's li'l Trey," Chin reminded his enemies.

Of course, Zero and his followers had already recognized their dead homie on the wall but kept quiet. Chin's outburst just caused them to release the fire they were holding within their chest.

"What you got to say about my nigga?" Zero inquired with lips curled back in a snarl.

"Nothing but he dead," Lando said, and he and his crew laughed.

"Nigga fuck you, cuzz," Zero said while yanking on his chains, wishing he could get one hand on his rivals. Not caring anymore about snitching, Zero told it all.

"That nigga right there know what happened to my man up there," he said, nodding his head in Lando's direction.

"Aww, so you snitching now," Lando said to Zero and continued, "Well, fuck it, yeah I iced that nigga."

Dr. Branch chimed in after the confession, "So you proudly admit to murdering this person on this screen? Interesting." Dr. Branch merely shrugged his shoulders and pressed the button to call up the next picture. The next picture, very similar to the first in its gory disposition, contained a boy and a girl. They both lay side by side with their shoulders touching in a pool of blood, and one could not tell where the boy's blood began nor where the girl's ended. It was summertime, and they wore little clothing. The bullet holes were quite visible and riddled throughout their bodies. The way the two laid in the grass gave an image of a macabre wedding photo. The scene was gory and would cause any man to cringe – anyone but the people in that room. Zero raised his head and poked out his chest in pride while taking credit for the murders.

"That's me, cuz," Zero said proudly. He laughed and continued boasting, "I mercked that nigga, Ced, and the bitch he was with." The pride and the hate in his eyes shined bright.

Before more could be said about that picture, Dr. Branch continued on. The next photo was of an old corpse, contorted and folded within a cabinet. Everyone, knowing that story, slowly turned their attention to Darryl Brown. Darryl Brown just smiled his evil grin. Because the other thugs were claiming their horrors, Darryl figured he'd take credit for his as well. Not that he could deny it, considering everyone in the room had already given a strong hint that it was him.

"That nigga shorted me some funds and tried to hide out," Darryl explained as though the dead kid deserved his horrendous fate. "I had to do what I had to do or other muthafuckas was gonna think I was soft."

Dr. Branch finally chimed in again, "That is a perfect reason for murder, young Darryl Brown. You did what you had to do, young brother."

Though Dr. Branch sounded genuine, Darryl felt sarcasm hiding deep within the statement.

"Let's continue," Dr. Branch said, sounding like a teacher.

He pressed the button, and another horrible picture popped up. This one of a young girl, and she wasn't lying in a bloodbath. She actually rested in a field and was recently freed from a sixty-gallon, black trash bag. The sad girl had dark rings around her neck, signifying strangulation, and her face was battered and bruised. Her left eye was swollen, and both her lips were split. More pictures showed the sixteen-year-old girl's body, which was tattered. The body held numerous teeth imprints around the shoulder and neck area from deep punctured bite wounds. The body showed multiple gash marks received from beatings with a belt buckle, and it held a litany of perfect circular marks from cigarette burns. The frail girl was obviously tortured brutally before the murderer finally allowed her peace.

That was the first picture that incited a bit of emotion from the audience, and no one took credit nor bragged about being the attacker. Everyone, knowing Nate was a pimp because of all of his earlier bragging, turned toward his seat slowly – some with disbelieving eyes.

"Damn, cuzz, is that you?"

Zero asked Nate.

Nasty Nate merely gave the questioner an angry look and responded, "What the fuck did I tell y'all earlier. This muthafucka just want our confessions." He spoke loudly and with a lot of fervor. With spit flying from his wide mouth he screamed, "I ain't saying I did shit, if you gonna arrest me, then arrest me. Until I see my lawyer, I ain't saying shit."

"My young brother Nathan," Dr. Branch continued, speaking with a soft, sympathetic voice as though he truly understood and cared, "We have all the proof we need that this is your doing. But you have one thing mistaken, Nathan. I am no cop, and you are not under arrest. You are under detainment."

"What?" Nate said. "You ain't no cop? Well what the fuck are you doing then? Let me up out of this muthafucka," Nate said while pulling on his binds.

"In due time, Nathan, I will set you free," Dr. Branch admitted. And though he sounded sincere, Nathan sensed a dark undertone in that statement. Dr. Branch continued, "Guys, I am a scientist, and I am researching murderers. I know everything that you all have done. I just wanted to see the reaction you all would provide when confronted with the results of your vicious attacks."

"Aww, so you ain't no cop, this is like we on candy camera, and you wanna see how we react to seeing those pictures," Lando clarified in layman's terms for himself and anyone else that may have been a little lost.

"I think you mean *candid* camera, and yes I guess something like that," Dr. Branch said.

"And you gonna let us out after you done with yo experiment, cuzz?" Zero asked.

"When this is all done, I will most certainly set you all free, my young murderous friends," Dr. Branch said, and though most of the captured sighed in relief and some even cheered, Darryl and Nate, being the darkest of the bunch, could sense the dark intent in Dr. Branch's statement. Needless to say, they did not cheer, and they both began to feel really uneasy.

"Let's see more," Dr. Branch said as he caused a new set of pictures to show on screen. This was very similar to the first, another young black male lying in a puddle of sticky red liquid with his skin tone just a little lighter from having lost his life fluid. This time, another kid took credit. He didn't brag, but there was no remorse in his tone at all. He even laughed at the way the victim danced as he was catching the bullets.

On the outside, Dr. Branch was as smooth as a cucumber; on the inside, his heart was going to explode from the red hot anger welling in his soul. Listening to these animals confirmed Dr. Branch's belief that it was too late for these blood-lusting beasts. These people were lost, and there was no saving them. He continued showing crazy crime scene after crime scene. Until something different occurred.

Dr. Branch brought up another photograph of a dead kid, yet no one took credit for this one. Dr. Branch made eye contact with the young person that caused the death.

"What's the matter, William, you are not proud of this one?" Dr. Branch asked, sounding confused.

William was another who couldn't figure if Dr. Branch was being serious or sarcastic. It didn't matter because he couldn't hide his emotions. William kept his eyes on the ground, and then all at once, his body began to shake as though he was having a seizure. Dr. Branch didn't budge, He merely continued watching the kid, trying to determine what was going on. Then William released a god-awful bellow that caught everyone off guard, causing the guys closest to him to jump. When William finally lifted his head, his eyes were full of water, and his entire face was wet and shiny. William could barely get words out because he sobbed so badly. He more than sobbed, he wailed like a banshee. Within in a few seconds, he was attacked by the wolves.

"Hey fag, shut the fuck up," Chin said.

"Yeah, you see anybody else in here crying like a li'l bitch?" Zero added, finally agreeing with Chin about something. "What the hell you crying for?" He asked the question Dr. Branch was wondering.

The sobbing William could barely contain himself, and Dr. Branch noticed that whenever he tried to talk, he would look at the picture and breakdown again. So Dr. Branch pulled up a blue screen, hoping this would help William explain his issue.

"I didn't mean to do it," was the first thing he squeezed out, "He killed my brother, and I was pissed. My brother was into all of that gang shit, but I wasn't, not until he got killed. I confronted my brother's killer. That dude that was up on the screen 'cause I knew he did it. We got to arguing, and he told me that he killed my brother and he would kill me too if I didn't get out of his face. Next thing I know, he is lying on the ground, and I am running with a pistol in my hand. I am sooo sorry, I wish I could take it back. I hate myself, I caint sleep, I caint eat. I caint stop thinking about it. I begged for forgiveness, but I don't think God will forgive this. So I just gave up and started hanging with Lando and 'em. Drinking and smoking helps me not remember, but that picture up there is the same picture I see in my head if I ain't drunk or high." Tears flowed the entire time William spoke.

"So you mean to tell me you are not proud of what you did?" Dr. Branch asked, sounding disappointed.

William spoke genuinely, "There ain't one day I don't wish I could go back and change what I did. I will never do nothing like that again, I caint do nothing like that again." He broke into another sobbing fit.

Dr. Branch moved from in front of the room and made his way toward William. He got close and said, "You don't belong. You are not worthy to be in here with true killers." Dr. Branch said the last as though he was proud of the murderers in that room. "Let's get your soft ass out of here," Dr. Branch finished, giving the impression that William's removal was some type of punishment. To worsen the matter, in a flash, a taser appeared in Dr. Branch's left hand. Before William could plead, Dr. Branch was already touching him with the hot end. William gave a quick yelp, a quick jump, and then he slumped over in his chair unconscious.

While Dr. Branch slowly made his way back to the front of the classlike room, he was whispering something softly into a small handheld device. Before a minute had passed, they all heard the clanging of a giant lever being pulled and then the sound of air pressure being released. The door opened, and two guys wearing the same gear as Dr. Branch quickly strode in, one with a key, and the other with a giant blade. With timed precision, one unlocked the chains on Williams legs while the other cut the material that kept his hands bound. Once William was freed, they hefted him up and carried him out, shutting the big metal door behind them. The process took less than forty-five seconds.

No one said a word throughout the whole ordeal, they all merely watched in awe wondering what the hell was going on. Eventually, someone spoke up.

"What the fuck was that about?" Nasty Nate asked.

"Oh, he didn't belong in here with you guys, that's all," Dr. Branch answered.

"What do you mean?" Zero asked.

"There are killers, and then there are killers," Dr. Branch explained. "He may have murdered someone, but he is not a killer. Not like you all in here."

"So y'all gonna set him free early cause he failed the experiment?" Nasty Nate asked, trying to get an understanding.

"No, he didn't fail the experiment, Nathan." Dr. Branch answered his tone never changing.

"So what y'all gonna do with him?" This time, Darryl had the question.

"Let's not worry about William, gentlemen. Let's finish our course." Dr. Branch said.

No one dared to debate with Dr. Branch, especially after seeing his quick dispatch of William, so they went right back to the gruesome pictures. They viewed crime scene after crime scene, and the chained people continued divulging a lot more about themselves than they thought. No one else appeared apologetic about their dirty deeds. They all talked about each crime scene as though they were discussing movie plots. No one seemed turned off by the gruesome pictures, and even worse, some seemed to get giddy when seeing the results of their murderous activities.

Toward the end, Dr. Branch's head swam in a sea of amazement. How people could become so desensitized to murder baffled him. He knew that what he was doing was also akin to murder. As an honest man he couldn't lie to himself. But he truly believed that his purpose was of noble intent, which separated him from the people sitting across the table.

After the last photo was shown, Dr. Branch slowly proceeded to shut down his computer. He looked to the crowd and spoke.

"We are done here," he said.

"Good, cause I been holding a piss for a hour," Nasty Nate said.

"Yeah, me too," Darryl said, adding, "Are we getting out now?"

"William may yet have the opportunity to get out, but why would I allow the likes of you all back out into my neighborhood?" Dr. Branch said.

"Hold up, what the fuck you talking about?" Nate yelled, "You said you was gonna let us out."

"Correction, Nathan," Dr. Branch said. Still speaking calmly, he replied, "I said I would set you all free. There is a big difference."

"What the fuck is this, what's going on here?" Chin inquired frantically.

"Calm down, guys. It's time for me to be completely honest with you all," Dr. Branch said. He leaned his buttocks on the table and explained exactly what was going on. "Young men, things are changing in the inner city. The neighborhood is sick and tired of dealing with all of the social woes that coincide with living in neighborhoods like ours. They are sick of the constant fear, they are sick of the crime, they are sick of the trash, and they are especially sick of you all. Black men of St. Louis have united, and basically, we have taken on the charge of cleaning up the city, literally. That not only means transferring trash from the streets to waste containers, it also means clearing the streets of the likes of you. We want our neighbors to feel free enough to walk around at midnight, unconcerned with getting jacked and murdered. We want our kids able to walk to school without seeing a litany of criminal activities before they are even halfway to the building. We want our children to look out their doors and see doctors and businessmen, not gangbanging drug dealers or shady pimps. We want our city back from you all, and I aim to get it."

Dr. Branch was interrupted by Nasty Nate, "So this was all bullshit. You *are* just taking us to jail." Feeling like a genius he then said to everyone else, "I told y'all he was gonna do this. He just needed y'all confessions now he gonna lock all y'all up. But I ain't confessed to shit, so you can let me out," Nate said with conviction.

"You still don't get it, do you, Nathan?" Dr. Branch said more as a statement than question. He continued, "We are not the police, young killers." He then balled his fingers into a tight fist while saying, "We are retribution. We are anger. We are wrath. We are the saviors of black America. And we have concluded that the only way we can clean black America is by eradicating our neighborhoods of guys like you," Dr. Branch finished.

"What . . . eradicating," Lando repeated, and trying to get some comprehension, he then asked, "Don't that mean kill?"

"I like to use the euphemism *getting set free*," Dr. Branch informed, "But kill is the most accurate verb to use," he finished, always speaking in the same blank and emotionless tone.

"What the fuck is you saying, cuzz?" Zero asked plainly.

"I thought I spoke as simple as possible." Dr. Branch stated. He reiterated with the most basic language he could provide, "Please listen and understand. You all are bad. We don't want you around anymore, and we don't want to fight you. So we are just going to kill you all. I don't think I can simplify my point any further," Dr. Branch told the murderous bunch.

"Come on, man, you got to be bullshitting, blood," Chin yelled.

Actually Chin was not the only person yelling, the room was filled with loud talking. Everyone spoke at the same time, wanting some more reasoning, and Dr. Branch just waited until there was some semblance of order. After one person took control and spoke alone, Dr. Branch finally listened and responded.

"Shut the fuck up," Nate screamed to the room, and then he spoke directly to Dr. Branch, "You don't have to do this." Nate actually sounded soft and afraid. "I want to live, bruh. If you want a confession, then yes, I killed those girls and even more than you probably know about." Nate offered, hoping his honesty would get him off of the hook, then he repented, "And I am sorry for what I did, just like William. You let him out, you gotta let me out too. That's just fair." Nate stated thinking he could use his typical silver tongue to help his situation.

"Nathan, you are not sorry for anything," Dr. Branch sharing the truth, "Please don't lie."

"Please let me out of here," Nate begged almost in tears.

That's when the others began to beg as well. Every last one of those hard core gangsters turned to babies with the knowledge of their eventual demise. A few even began to cry after truly realizing the reality of it all.

"This is something I have always found amazing," Dr. Branch said coming from left field. "It amazes me how a person that has killed multiple people cry when they are about to undergo the same torment. Where is that brutal person that walked around taking lives? Did you yield when people begged you for their lives? No . . . Well, I believe you all should receive the same justice you dished out. You guys have all lived by the sword, so there should be no shock that you will die by one." Dr. Branch felt that they deserved to know everything.

There was more pleading, and finally Dr. Branch raised his hand, quieting everyone in the classroom. He spoke softly, "Guys, I am sorry, but you all have been convicted and sentenced. Death is your penalty for forsaking your people. You all have sold harmful substances to your people, removing mothers and fathers from their children. You have robbed and stolen with gun in hand, intimidating our people and leaving them too scared to leave their homes. Yet these are not the crimes that have made the decision final. What has made the decision final is the worst of all crimes. You all have taken a life, you have spilled blood. Not only affecting your victim but everything they were connected to. Make your peace, gentlemen, for there is no escape." Dr. Branch shook his head with absolute shame and said, "Murder is the most abhorrent act man can do to his brethren." Dr. Branch concluded and grabbed his laptop. He said nothing else; he merely walked to the giant door pulling it open.

That is when the yelling started again, but Nate's voice resounded above all others.

"That's bullshit. What the fuck do you call what you about to do to us? You about to murder all of us," Nate screamed with tons of foam forming on the corners of his mouth, making him look like a mad dog.

Dr. Branch stood at the doorway with the giant metallic beast open. He pressed a small button on a remote in his pocket, and the sprinkler system kicked on. Thick clear liquid began to rain down over the loud people in the room as well as all over the floor. At first, everyone thought it was water, but the drops felt a lot denser than water. Then the smell wafted to their nose. No one could pin point the substance, but it contained a strong chemical odor. Not one thug in the room would know that the compound leaking on their heads and bodies was liquid napalm.

The screams got louder and louder. All of the urine and feces that were being held at the brink splashed from their respective orifices. Mouths were agape with the sounds of pain, anguish, and fearful anticipation. The toxic liquid splashed in eyes, got into mouths, and covered skin. The slightly corrosive material gave the skin a cool feeling first, then there was a mild burning sensation. The cacophony of voices in utter torment caused great sadness in Dr. Branch, and for a second, he reconsidered. Just as quickly, he maintained his resolve and finally responded to Nate's final words.

"This is not murder, this is disinfection," Dr. Branch said that last bit and slowly walked out, reaching his hand into his pocket. He shut the door behind him, but right before the door shut completely, he tossed a lit match into the room. The match landed right on a puddle of the volatile liquid, and the door shut with an air tight seal just as the room ignited.

If Darryl's skin wasn't melting and sloshing from his muscles, if the moisture in his eyes weren't boiling and about to cause his eyeballs to explode from their sockets, and only if the unbelievable pain from this fiery demise didn't exist, he would have said that the initial ignition was the most beautiful wonder he had ever seen. The flame opened and surrounded everyone like a bright omnipresent blob. Then the blob turned into a fiery blanket that covered everything in that room. Though the room was airtight, the dying soul's bellows could be heard throughout the bottom layer of the building. Dr. Branch didn't look back.

The members of team CH that were in cells with victims, stepped out of each room to look at Dr. Branch as he stumbled through the walkway. No one said anything as they heard the screams of the damned, nor did Dr. Branch look at any of his teammates as he passed them. He walked to the staircase and slightly swayed, feeling light headed as he reached the first step. Anthum ran to his side to steady him, and Dr. Branch snatched his arm from Anthum's grip and staggered up the long flight upstairs. He exited the secret compartment and drunkenly meandered to the front of the building, leaning on the giant glass wall the whole way.

He opened the front door, and God smiled on him. There was a thunderstorm underway with an extreme downpour; just what he needed. He walked out with his hands held out beside him as though on a crucifix, and his head bent backward with his eyes to the sky that sparkled with lighting and boomed with thunder. He allowed the cool flood of rain to bounce off of his face as he just stood silent. Then he dropped to his knees and screamed as no man has screamed before. All of his teammates had followed him upstairs without his knowledge. They watched as he exited, and they all heard his exasperated outcry. They all looked at each other and then to their leader. They whispered a few comments, and then they decided to let their leader have his much-needed alone time. They left Dr. Branch outside and went back to their reconstructing duties.

The Business

WHILE MAKING HIS way to Ankeny, Iowa, Manno Gully rested his head on the cushion of the plane's seat. He sat in business class wearing a fresh Kenneth Cole suit and sipping on a glass of vodka and cranberry juice. He relaxed and allowed his mind to drift. He laughed at himself falling victim to his best friend's uncanny ability to get anything he wanted. Trenton would never admit it, but throughout college, whenever he had a craving, it was sated. Manno remembered watching numerous times as his friend finagled classmates out of their completed homework problems (so that Trenton could copy), convinced a girl to give up her precious pearl, or even coerced professors to change *C's* to *A's*.

Trenton's tongue was gold, and now here was Manno, a victim of the same old Jedi mind trick. He was a man that left his comfortable living arrangements in Atlanta, Georgia to become CEO of his friend's new company in St. Louis. With the hefty startup money supplied by the owner, Manno was able to hire his staff without any major issues. More workers would soon be a necessity, but he could get the ball rolling with the few people he had. Manno thought that the widget Trenton invented was ingenious and couldn't believe he was the first to put that idea into manifestation. Manno travelled to and fro advertising the device, and the item was actually selling itself. Within the first month of operation, profits were rolling in. The business' only issue was servicing such a quick demand. They had to grow, and they had to grow fast. He could no longer keep track of finances and business affairs, so he would have to find a CFO. He also needed many more line workers to build the product. His engineers could build the special order widgets, but most businesses wanted to equip their desk workers with the standard device. He knew an assembly line with a standardized system would be needed.

Though Manno had two things working against him, he still found willing applicants for his high-profile positions. Number one hardship for Manno: Trenton demanded that all personnel had to be willing to live in the city. Number two hardship: Trenton demanded all personnel must submit to the new pseudo-socialistic system. These principles were easy for the lower-level employees to accept, but for the higher level employees, it wasn't so simple. Most blue collar employees already lived in the city, but most white collar employees lived in the suburbs, so they always felt as though they committed the far greater sacrifice. And the higher-level employees saw their monetary sacrifice outweighing their subordinates. Even with such great deterrences, Manno had little problem finding people to fill those all important roles.

Manno was amazed to see people so willing to accept such an idea. He himself thought it was outlandish to commit to this socialistic philosophy. But his friend expressed a dire need for his presence and his business acumen. And in order to take on the mantle of CEO, even he had to put his money into the community pool run by Malcolm Banks. This didn't please Manno at all. He was a businessman living quite comfortably in Atlanta. He was single, childless, and wealthy. Those qualities alone made him a superstar in the A.T.L.

With a man to woman ratio beyond skewed, he held a stable of dime pieces that would have made Wilt Chamberlain beg for a second youth. His life was awesome, and he loved his job. Making money was the American way, and if a person was incapable of handling their affairs, why should Manno assist them? He didn't like the idea at all, but he loved the idea of running a company. Being CEO of a company superseded his dislike of the socialistic principles, so he committed half his salary to the cause. Manno Gully surmised that in the present economic situation, most people would agree to be a socialist too for a paying job.

Though Manno was accustomed to seeing Dr. Branch's powers of persuasion, it still amazed him when witnessing it up close and personal. They were able to snatch some of the most high-ranking business men in Wall Street to join their small business. Mitchell Whenthorpe, one of the most successful black businessmen in America, was one of their first aggressive recruits. Manno informed Trenton of Mitchell's business prowess and explained that with him the business was a guaranteed success. Trenton believed his friend and told Manno to go get him. After many attempts, Manno had no success acquiring Mitchell's participation. Mitchell did not want to give up his current position to join a startup company, nor did he want to relinquish his funds to their socialistic efforts. Manno even remembered Mitchell using the word communism. And Mitchell finished by saying that if they thought he would give up his million-dollar home to come live in the treacherous city of St. Louis, they could keep dreaming.

After Manno informed Trenton of Mitchell's staunch stance, Trenton instantly brought a plane ticket to New York for the both of them the next day. Trenton caught Mitchell at his home.

Mitchell started by saying they were wasting their time. Manno merely looked in Dr. Branch's direction, and his friend commenced to use that magical mind manipulation he so wielded until Mitchell could see no alternative. Trenton somehow gave the impression that Mitchell could save all of black America or either condemn it with his one decision. The man had no choice but to say yes with such a heavy burden placed upon his shoulders. Manno, amazed, pictured Trenton saying, "You will work for us," and then Mitchell responding in a zombie's voice, "I will work for you." He laughed to himself. He never knew his friend dreamed so big or that he had such courage and heart to attack anything ahead of him. Manno had a newfound respect and admiration for his friend.

The business opened and was named Satelite Sciences. The first days were the roughest, yet the most exciting. With the business just getting started, the engineers and the line workers had most of the early work, while most others twirled their thumbs. But as days passed and accounts began to come in, along with questions and more business, they all became more busy. Manno rarely spent his time at the facility because he was always on the go, grabbing new business. But when he made it back to the facility, he was always stunned when first entering their unflattering building in the middle of nowhere.

The building was no different than any other corporate or manufacturing business in America. It contained a variety of cars in the parking lot, a couple of delivery trucks in the back, a manicured landscape, and a giant sign atop the front with their name and logo. The logo was a space satellite with little lines coming to the antennae.

There was one huge difference and that is what continued to blow Manno's mind every time he walked into the building. It was all black. From the housekeeping staff up to the CEO, the complete body of Satelite Sciences was all black. It baffled Manno that something like this existed. He had read about and been to numerous black-owned businesses; most being restaurants and hair salons. He appreciated those small businesses and hoped for their success, but something like this he had never heard of. This was the first black-owned engineering and manufacturing firm in the country. There was a staff of forty, and they would have to double that number in order to meet their exorbitant demands.

Manno was proud as he entered the building, wearing his tailored made suits, looking debonair as Billy D. He would look from side to side enjoying Trenton's glass wall idea. Because of the see-through walls, Manno could see all or most of his employees as he walked to his desk, which was on the business side. He loved seeing all the black faces, yet didn't know what to expect in an all-black corporate environment. After a few days with his workforce, he soon saw that there was very little difference from any other corporate environment. Mostly everyone was content, yet a job will always have its complainers. Conversely, the super fans will also exist. Even though groups formed almost instantly, the entire staff seemed to get along well enough. And it was interesting seeing everyone's wardrobe. Though there was no dress code, the difference in the daily attires were obvious and again representative of typical corporate America. Most on the business side wore some type of khaki or slacks for pants and either a golf or oxford shirt with a nice shoe. Most of the engineers wore jeans with some type of pullover shirt. His handpicked administrators were two of the sexiest young black girls in St. Louis, and they dressed in a way to accentuate their feminine appeal. To Manno, everything seemed to move quite typical to any other business facility in the country.

Because he rarely frequented the building, whenever he entered, everyone appeared to be on their best behavior, but within his leadership meetings details of typical issues would be divulged. His management explained the fact that on a basic level, everyone held each of their team members in high regard. The fact that everyone was willing to contribute to a big pot to ensure that they all lived comfortably connected them on a level that none had ever felt before. Yet with that deep love within them, human emotion is always present, and feelings are always hurt. His management told him about a verbal brawl that got hairline close to breaking into a physical altercation. Manno couldn't help but laugh, then he asked what happened. His prejudice instantly put the line workers or janitorial staff in his mind first. He assumed the less educated would be the ones subject to fall into physicality. He was surprised and laughed when his management said it was actually the engineers. When Manno asked what sparked such a heated confrontation, one of his silliest leaders explained that one engineer said that Princess Leia from *Star Wars* was prettier than Deanna Troi from *Star Trek: The Next Generation* and all hell broke loose. He finished by calling the combatants, damned nerds. And the few men within the leaders' meeting broke into hysterical laughter.

On the plane, Manno sipped his vodka and almost spat it out thinking about that situation. He set his glass down and considered his luck, and how it felt to work at an all black establishment with other black intellectuals. He laid his head back figuring his salesmen should be doing all of this damn flying. Manno dozed as he awaited his next meeting with his friend, the owner of Satelite Sciences. He needed to inform Trenton of the business' extreme growth, and the extreme wealth that would follow.

Meanwhile, back at CH headquarters

D R. BRANCH FELT baptized and washed clean. He felt like a new man, now it was time to reenter the building. He was still on his knees in the midst of a thunderstorm, soaked to all hell. His arms were wrapped around his stomach as he knelt, curled up in a ball. He straightened, took four deep breaths, and rose to his feet. He then walked back into the building with a face of stone. He made his way to the lower level and entered the first room available from the bottom step.

The youngster in that room was Jason. He had already experienced torment from all of the other men and jumped when the door hissed open. He saw Dr. Branch and cringed in his chair looking like a timid cub. He began to shake. He didn't say a word. Apparently, already well trained. Dr. Branch had planned on releasing a rush of emotional energy on the helpless victim, but after seeing the bruises and blood, he chose to cap his energy and refrain from torturing the kid. Dr. Branch also realized that if he heard the shrieks of the boys that just fried, so did these guys. They all would have to be scared out of their wits after hearing people dying in extreme pain.

"Why are you here?" Dr. Branch inquired blankly.

The boy was shocked that he could see this person's face. He began to cry, believing that a facial appearance was the signal for death. Though horrified of Dr. Branch, he didn't beg for his life. He simply answered the question.

"I am here because I've been destroying my neighborhood and my people," the boy said through a quivering voice.

Dr. Branch, stunned, said nothing. He merely looked upon the boy, amazed at the quick training his team performed. If any of the other boys could answer a question before begging for their lives, then his crew was doing a better job than he hoped.

What Dr. Branch didn't know was that his crew *was* doing a fabulous job, maybe a little too fabulous. Their cruel tortuous tactics had many of their victims screaming in pain. Many times, the torturers going further than Dr. Branch would have encouraged. Nevertheless, the job was getting accomplished, and there were always civilian casualties in any war, and this was officially a war. Dr. Branch finally spoke again.

"What choose you this day?" Dr. Branch asked dryly.

"I choose life," the kid answered between sobs.

"Do you understand what responsibilities come with life?" Dr. Branch inquired.

"I'm willing to learn."

"Willing to learn . . .," Dr. Branch said, leaving room for Jason to complete his sentence.

"I'm willing to learn, sir."

"How old are you, Jason?" Dr. Branch asked, already knowing the answer.

"Nineteen, sir," Jason answered, his tears leaving.

"What are you doing for yourself?" Dr. Branch asked.

"Uh . . . Really just surviving, sir" Jason answered.

"I imagine you live with your folks, huh?"

"Yes, sir."

"Well, I hope you told them you loved them because you may never see them again," Dr. Branch told the boy.

Dr. Branch left the boy sobbing in that room and gave short visits to the remaining thirteen terrified young men. They were in pretty much the same emotional state. Half of the lot had one of his team members in the room administering their own special brand of punishment. While the other hapless souls sat in their locked cells waiting on their next visitor. Dr. Branch gave each kid the fear of God by showing his face to them all and then reminded them that they would never leave that place.

Each kid had already urinated on himself, with some even sitting in their own solid waste. Yet they all were taught to only speak when spoken to and not beg for their lives. After much training, they all complied. Dr. Branch took pride in his team's quick work. These boys all seemed ready for the final step in their transformation.

Dr. Branch called each one of his masked avengers for a quick briefing away from the kids. They met in the hall and discussed how to finalize the process and send the boys out with a bang. They told Dr. Branch that every kid acquiesced to his team's demands, not a one showing any sign of rebellion. They all simply wanted to get home at any cost. Mathew told Dr. Branch that their prisoners now had a true appreciation of life and would do anything to sustain that life. Dr. Branch heard their consensus and then told them of the final plans.

After listening to Dr. Branch's grand finale, the men all looked at one another in disbelief, thinking that final bit of punishment may be just a little too much. Even Anthum was stunned by Dr. Branch's demented thinking. Yet with all of their concerns no one dissented in the slightest, and they prepared for the final move.

Fred and Mathew took defensive positions out in the hall with their guns at the ready. Everyone else went into each room and unchained the boys. Each kid was told to stand right outside of his door and not to make any sudden moves, or they would be shot instantly. After being chained for so long, each boy merely stood straight and stretched his hands to the sky. They all walked to the doorway and took one step forward. They stood at their doorway awaiting their next order.

Dr. Branch absorbed his surroundings, everything appearing ethereal. After hearing the screams of his first kill, he'd been in a dream state, and the picture before him intensified that feeling. Seeing these so-called rough and tough kids now looking like a band of refugees after a long trudge through hostile territory, left him in a daze. They all smelled to be damned and held facial expressions of utter defeat. Not one attempted to flee. They all merely swayed while standing in place. Lack of food and sleep made them even more docile. They came out to the hallway, some holding their hands in front of their eyes because it was considerably brighter in the hall than their drab cells. Dr. Branch waited until he saw each lad out in the walkway and thought to himself that the scene mimicked the penal system. Guards standing at the ready and prisoners standing with their heads held low. Dr. Branch remembered seeing this scene in *Shawshank Redemption*. Once everyone was in place, the hall was eerily quiet. That is when Dr. Branch spoke.

"I believe you all have a very good understanding of your situation, but I will briefly explain everything with clarity one final time," Dr. Branch began. He continued talking forcefully to each down trotted kid, "We as black men have done you all a terrible disservice, my young brothers. We haven't done our jobs in raising you right. We have allowed you all to run wild as a pack of wolves. No training, left to the vices of a country that loves to devour you as a shark devours all in its path. Well, no longer, my young brothers. Every black man is uniting under one banner, and it is taking our streets back. With that being said, we know that cleaning our streets will take your cooperation, but we are not asking for it. We are demanding it. Now this is where we get to my point, boys. Simply put, either you are with us or against us. Either you will cooperate, or we will remove you from the face of this planet. There is no in between. Do you get me?"

"We get you, sir!" exclaimed one of the stinky prisoners.

"This is not the army, dumb ass," Anthum snapped at the kid, "If you scream in my ear again, I'm going to break your fucking neck," he finished. And even without seeing his face, the kid could tell that Anthum's lips were curled into a snarl.

"A simple and quiet 'yes, sir' will suffice, Antoine," Dr. Branch informed the intimidated kid. Getting back to the point, Dr. Branch asked the final question, "Do you guys want to live as a member of one of us, or do you want the alternative?"

They all voted for option A, though one kid had just a little bit more to say than the rest. His name was Alex, and he just couldn't bite his tongue any longer.

"I will join 'cause I wanna go home," Alex said, he kept talking, "But I know what this is. Its like MTV's scared straight, mixed with a rough boot camp. And I ain't gonna lie, I'm scared . . . but I know y'all ain't killing nobody."

After hearing such insolence Anthum made his way toward the kid. Alex tucked his head between his shoulders, terrified of the masked giant stomping in his direction. Before Anthum could make a move, Dr. Branch gave a cough and a shake of his head, signaling Anthum to belay his physical response to Alex's spoken statement.

"I must admit, young Alex; typically speaking out of turn like that would cause you to get some type of punishment," Dr. Branch spoke coldly. "Because your point was extremely valid, and because it actually took bravery to speak what was on your heart, I will let it slide. Honestly, young man, I am quite glad that you said that. Maybe others have assumed that this is some type of reality TV show and that there truly is no ultimate punishment. That is of no concern, for you all will see in due time that there is a place of no return when we are involved (Dr. Branch pointed at his compatriots while finishing that last statement). You break the rules, you die. And that is not a joke, young Alex." Dr. Branch said, focusing on the tall and skinny, curly haired tween.

"This is it," Dr. Branch said with finality. He continued, "You all will be put into a classroom. You all will be shown a documentary. Questions will be asked regarding the documentary. If you answer one question wrong, you will be killed. If you get them all right, you will be allowed to return home. No games, no confusion."

The boys all looked baffled – some starting to believe Alex's suggestion, for this did seem like a game. Who would kill somebody for not remembering something on a TV show? The whole thing sounded preposterous. Regardless, they all agreed to the terms and awaited their next orders.

"Look down the walkway," Dr. Branch demanded (they did), "You all see that giant door there." He continued as they answered, "Beyond those doors is a classroom for learning. Get in there and grab a seat." Dr. Branch stopped the kids as they attempted to obey and said more, "Hold up. It's not that simple, people. Your seats are dirty. You will have to clean them. There are large trash compactors in the back. Go open them by pulling really hard. The metal shoot will open providing access to the trash compactor. So before you all sit down to watch the documentary, make sure that your seats are clean. Do you get me?"

"Yes, sir," they all said, not too loudly.

No one knew what they would see when they opened those doors, and the members of team CH watched their leader in disbelief. What Dr. Branch was asking these kids to do was on the cusp of lunacy. Dr. Branch didn't think so. These kids needed to know the only conclusion when choosing the wrong path. The young recruits all lined up and walked to the giant metallic door. They didn't know whether to open the door or wait for instructions, so they just stood. Dr. Branch then spoke again.

"Pull the lever and go on in."

The kid in front pulled on the lever and pushed the door forward. There was that hissing from the seal breakage, and all at once, an acrid odor passed by everyone. The people closest to the door, including members of team CH retched and gagged from the strong smell. It smelled as if someone soaked human hair and skin in alcohol and motor oil and then barbequed that hairy, fleshy mix for hours. Dr. Branch thought the fans would take care of that, but it was quite obvious that they didn't. Well this was the first time the killing room was used, and it was apparent more work was needed. Dr. Branch covered his nose as he shoved the back kid into the kid in front of him. That caused a domino effect until the momentum flowed to the first kid.

"Get in there and do as told . . . or deal with option B," Dr. Branch demanded sternly.

The kid in front pulled his nasty shirt to his nose and entered the room slowly. What he saw made his heart freeze, and he stood motionless for what seemed like hours. It was only seconds because more kids entered and began pushing him in order to make more room for the others. What they all saw left them still as statues. They didn't know what to do.

They saw a room with a metallic table by the door, and the same type of metal chairs facing the front. The only light came from the open door, which added to the dismal look of the room. The table and chairs weren't special at all; it's what was in those chairs that stopped the heart from pumping. They housed contorted bodies all burned beyond recognition. Charred would be an accurate description. Each blackened face elicited an expression of utter agony, anguish, and incomprehensible pain. The boys glared at the dead bodies occupying each seat resembling three dimensional shadows. The smell was horrendous, but the visual was unbearable.

With no time to spare, Anthum entered the room just as amazed by the carnage. Yet he took no time to lament. He simply kicked Alex in the ass and said, "Get to work li'l fucker." Alex, not expecting Anthum's blow, flew headfirst into one of the seats. Alex's shoulder hit the head of one the dead bodies. The cooked neck muscles of the dead body must have been turned to brittle and weakened for his head flew off from the force. Alex screamed, which scared everybody, but no one else uttered a sound.

"Still believe this is just a game, Alex?" Dr. Branch inquired cynically.

"No, sir," was Alex's response as he picked up the charred head and took it to the giant trash compactors.

Alex slowly walked to the silver compactor handle and pulled. Another freaked out prisoner pulled on the neighboring trash compactor, and they both opened with a loud squeal. The two boys couldn't resist their curiosity and took a quick peak down. The heat emanating from the opened shoots almost singed their eyebrows. They both jumped back from the venting heat. The two trash compactors were simply laundry shoots that ended in a fiery furnace, and it was the boy's job to discard these dead remains into this final lavalike resting place. The idea was unreal, and the boys all stood in place, too scared to do anything.

"Get to work or end up like them," Dr. Branch yelled.

The boys jumped from the loud sound of Dr. Branch's voice and started getting busy instantly. They pulled up the bodies from the metallic chairs, with some of the body parts sticking to their seats. The boys were smart and worked together, two or three working on one body at a time. After numerous limbs were torn from intact bodies, the kids soon learned that the best way to transport the dead was to grab them by the shoulders and thighs. They carried them to the furnaces and dropped them in one by one. After the first four or five removals, desensitization set in, and the kids began transporting the bodies like men moving furniture. After the last corpse slid down the metal slide to a fiery inferno, they all sat down and awaited their next assignment with a catlike awareness. Alex no longer assumed that death wasn't an option. No one believed that. This situation proved to the youth that their captors truly were mad, and killing was certainly a part of their agenda.

Once things were prepared, Dr. Branch said, "You know what's up. Here is the documentary. Focus and learn. Questions are to follow."

Dr. Branch set up his laptop with the built in projector on the fireproof metallic table, and the wall flashed to life in front of the kids. The documentary came on, and team CH walked out of the room. The boy's watched the same program that *Subject Numero Uno* watched. Because the guy on screen was the same as their real life tormentor, it was first difficult for the kids to focus. After a few minutes, they were able to bypass that issue and absorb the lesson on screen. They watched in utter amazement and actually enjoyed the black educational program. For the two hours the program played, they forgot about the conditions they'd endured, they forgot about the torture, and they even forgot about sitting in seats that were just occupied by burnt corpses. The documentary ended, and upon completion, Dr. Branch and his crew entered the room. The kids sat quiet and motionless, awaiting their questions. Dr. Branch didn't disappoint, he went right to asking questions, the first being quite easy. They got them right. The questions got progressively hard, until he asked one kid a question that none of them could answer.

"Sorry, boy, you have failed, and instead of killing you, I think we are just going to get rid of you all," Dr. Branch said coldly.

The room broke into cries and pleads of a second chance. Some guys even threw the person under the bus for not knowing the answer. Some of the kids stood and took one step forward. That was when Mathew held his submachine gun at the ready; they all froze and sat back down.

"OK . . . OK . . ." Dr. Branch acting like he was changing his mind said, "I will give you all one more chance, but this is it. Do you get me?"

"Yes, sir."

"You all better pay close, well, closer attention. This stuff isn't for me, I know who I am. It's for you. Remember that." Dr. Branch left them.

Again, the documentary started and ended, and the staff reentered. Dr. Branch proceeded to ask the room questions. He started easy and got harder. They did quite well and even worked together by answering questions posed to their neighbors. Dr. Branch saw this and was satisfied. They were ready to go.

"You all are done. I am going to give you one last tidbit," he said this, and team CH left him alone in the room with the boys. Dr. Branch continued, "You all will be allowed to return home, but know that you all are free with duties. Instead of death, you have chosen its better counterpart. But with life comes responsibilities. Things will now be expected of you. Number one, you will start behaving as men or young men. No longer will you sell drugs to your brethren, no longer will you steal from your brethren. You will work for your bread as is meant for man. You will show your guardian respect. You will strive for an education. And when called upon, you will work for us. If these things aren't done, you will see us again. And if you see us again, that is bad news for there are no second chances. Remember, all . . . we are everywhere, and we are always watching. With that being said, know that we are also here to help. I congratulate you, boys." With that, Dr. Branch concluded.

He pulled the giant door open and left the room. The boys stayed seated, not knowing what to do. No one really believed they were about to see freedom, so no one showed any positive emotions. The door opened, and two canisters rolled in. More smoke bombs. After an initial spark of light and a small boom, smoke poured from both containers. Before the boys could run to the door, they were collapsing to the ground from their chairs in a deep sleep. The smoke cleared, and the boys were sprawled over the floor or slumped in their chairs. The giant door opened, and team CH entered. One by one, they carried each kid outside to a vehicle. Throughout the night, team CH delivered their first converts back to their respective houses. They dropped them off on the steps pouring alcohol all over their clothes, giving them each the look of a bum. The boys were delivered back to their homes safe and sound, still unconscious.

Alex heard the sound of birds chirping and dogs barking. Though his eyelids were closed things still seemed really bright. As he slowly opened his eyes, the brightness of direct sunlight penetrated the slit between his lids and lit up his world. He shut his eyes from the blinding light and turned his head only to try and open his eyes again. He did, slowly. As they opened, he absorbed his scene only to realize that he was at home, on the front porch. The birds were chirping, and the dogs were talking to one another. The morning dew rested on each blade of grass, and a fine layer of midst covered the vehicles on the street. Alex caught all of this and a lot more.

His eyes took in every detail, and his ears received every sound like giant antennae. Alex breathed in deeply as he raised himself from the ground. He was sore, groggy, and covered in his own filth. It also smelled like someone showered him in vodka. He slid to the front door and gave it a rap. The picture was unreal – the prodigal son returning home only after wallowing in shit. His mother answered the door and grabbed her mouth.

The mother thought something really bad had happened to her son. She had called the police to see if he was in jail. When there was no record of her son in prison, she just assumed the worst. So to see her son before her eyes left her beyond speechless. He looked like he had gone through war, but he was home, and that was all she was concerned with. He stank . . . really bad, but she hugged him anyway. Then she heard something amazing.

"I'm sorry, Mom. I will try and do better. Really." That was all it took to break her into tears. They stood in the door hugging, while the sun slowly rose and shone on them both.

Not every story was as heart warming, but every boy was happy to be home. They all had a newfound appreciation of life and a respect for life that none knew existed before then.

Dr. Branch saw the results of his first true Cleaning House event and was happy. Though the future held limitless possibilities, some being very bad, Dr. Branch was unconcerned. He merely dwelled on his team's first success. After much consideration, he told his team that they could quit their jobs and focus on doing work for team Twenty-Six full time. From that moment on, cleaning house headquarters was a revolving door of kidnap victims: most converted. Sadly, a few were killed.

Changes

It was a beautiful spring morning, and Dr. Branch was awakened by his wife.

"Sweetheart," Christine rubbed his head softly, saying, "You know I really hate to wake you when you are sleep. But you got a call, and it sounds pretty important." She finished and handed him the cordless phone.

"Thanks, sweetheart," he told her and brought the phone up to his ear.

"Hello," Dr. Branch started.

"Hello . . . Dr. Branch," the voice was young. Dr. Branch had no idea who it was.

"Dr. Branch, this is Donald Turner," the voice said. He continued, "I just wanted to let you know that I graduate next month, and I wanted to know if you could come to my graduation?" he asked.

"Of course I can," Dr. Branch happily replied, and then he gave instructions. "Here take down my address, Donald, and send me an invitation with all of the pertinent information. Can you do that for me?" Dr. Branched asked nicely.

"Sure, Dr. Branch," the boy said. "This might sound weird, but I am really happy you did what you did."

"No need to say anymore," Dr. Branch interrupted, not wanting the boy to divulge much over the phone.

The boy got the point, so he changed the subject. He asked, "How are the Black Boogie Men doing?"

Dr. Branched laughed as he got out of the bed and walked to the bathroom with the phone in his hand. Then he answered, "They are doing quite well, young Donald." He started urinating, still holding the phone and with that name ringing in his head . . . Black Boogie Men.

"Well, thanks again, Dr. Branch. My grades are better than they ever been, and my grandparents are so happy and proud of me," the boy said with jubilee.

"You will never know how much that means to me – to hear you say those words," Dr. Branch informed the graduating teen. He finished, "Well, I will be there, and I am honored that you asked. I got to get out of here, young brother. I will talk to you soon, OK?"

"OK. Bye bye, Dr. Branch," Donald said, sounding like a teenage boy. He hung up the phone, and Dr. Branch did the same.

While in the bathroom, Dr. Branch cleaned himself. Afterward, he threw on his clothes. Though team Twenty-Six was more active than ever, Dr. Branch was able to get more rest. He'd done what all great leaders do and bestowed leadership roles for each intermediary endeavor. It took him much practice, but he eventually learned to just trust the people he placed in power and not attempt to do it all himself. "Share the load," they all advised. He finally complied and soon saw the benefits.

Though he had less on his plate, there was still much for him to do. This day was no different – once it got rolling, it wouldn't end until it was time for him to get to bed. He had files of his next kidnap victims he needed to vet. He was obligated to meet with his leaders today. He had a chore for his new recruits. He also needed to cook breakfast for his wife this morning. Though the smell of pancakes told him he was too late for that one.

After getting dressed, he went downstairs and had a pancake breakfast with his wife. After they ate he tried to wash dishes but she wouldn't have it. They talked while she washed the few dirty items in the sink, and he informed her of his latest activities. As of late, he kept her abreast of all of team Twenty-Six's progress, well almost all. She was unaware of the darker side of their activities. She complimented him on their apparent success.

"I must admit, babe, I can actually see a difference in the immediate neighborhood." Christine said while putting the clean, dry dishes away. She continued, "People are working on their homes, and it looks really clean out there. And our corner has been empty and quiet . . . Thank you, Jesus," she said.

"Can you really notice, or are you just saying that to make me feel good?" Dr. Branch inquired, sounding far more human when with his wife.

"No, really dear . . . you can tell a big difference." She returned and kept talking, "I wish I would have taken some before and after pictures. It has only taken a little over a year, and houses are remodeled, streets are clean, and now our corners are empty. I don't know what you did, but people can't help but to notice that, hun," she ended.

"Babe, you have officially started my morning off right. Come here and give me some sugar, and I ain't talking about pure cane," he said as he grabbed his wife's waist and drew her near.

He and his wife kissed and hugged. Then they stayed intertwined, touching foreheads, and slightly swaying to music that wasn't there. After a few minutes, they broke their embrace, and he was off to start his day.

Dr. Branch had been so busy running the show, that he stopped noticing the slight changes occurring within his immediate area. He promised himself he would take inventory this morning and the whole day while taking care of business. He walked outside and sucked in a deep breath of fresh air. He stood on his porch and looked around. His house was no longer the only remodeled house, and the street was immaculate. He couldn't believe how clean his street was. Things were beautifying in his small neighborhood. More than that, somehow the neighbors knew he was responsible. So as soon as he exited his home, all outside neighbors waved in his direction or yelled out some type of greeting. He was shocked to see so many neighbors out manicuring lawns and painting porches, or others performing some small household chores. His street was beginning to look like a community. Without the immediate threat of corner hoods, people felt more comfortable leaving their homes. Old faces started poking themselves out of doors, and after seeing the change in the neighborhood, those people joined in the restoration process. Making things more aesthetically pleasing was infectious, and it was a bug that had bitten mostly everyone within his area.

He walked to Malcolm's apartment down the street. On the way, he caught other issues needing attention. There were still too many vacant houses and empty lots he saw throughout his walk. Also, young boys walked around showing their entire ass – he didn't want to see that anymore. He would think of a plan to cure the sagging syndrome these young boys exhibited. After a short walk and a lot of thinking, he was outside of Malcolm's apartment. The few people on the porch and the steps instantly made room by giving Dr. Branch a wide path to Malcolm's door. They all spoke, with one of the ladies telling her little girls to say hello. The place had been fixed up by team Twenty-Six, and the difference was profound.

Dr. Branch's wife was right. He and his team had made significant progress, yet he was too busy to notice the vast improvements. He even stopped praising his troops. He would have to go back to giving them the credit they deserved. His wife always kept him on his toes. Where would he be without her? He needed to give her the credit she deserved as well.

He knocked on the door, and Malcolm answered in a heartbeat. Malcolm greeted Dr. Branch with a hello while bowing his head slightly. Dr. Branch stuck his hand out, which Malcolm instantly grabbed. The two men shook hands, and Dr. Branch stepped inside instantly dropping his jaw. The apartment was amazing; Dr. Branch was almost jealous. He had forgotten how much he loved those old German style houses. He really liked the high ceilings and large rooms and how the length of the apartment was always twice as long as a person would expect. He wished he could explain to everyone that with something as simple as new floors, paint, and a few other small items, one could completely revamp their entire domicile. Dr. Branch strolled in, with Malcolm following. They made their way to Malcolm's sitting room making pleasantries. His sitting room was the epitome of basic. He had two same-sized sofas facing one and the other with one end closer than the other, giving the couches the look of a V. There was a small table in between them both. At the opening of the V was his fireplace. There was one green vase that sat on top of the fireplace's mantle, and there were no pictures on the wall. Yet Dr. Branch really liked the basic look. Everything was so symmetrical, it all made Dr. Branch feel at home.

"This is really nice; did I help when you guys did this place?" Dr. Branch inquired.

"No. You were in New York taking care of business," Malcolm responded.

"Oh, no wonder I am so astounded," Dr. Branch said. Then he made his way to one of the sofas, took a seat, and said, "So what do you know good, Malcolm, my brother?"

Malcolm didn't know if that was his queue to dive into the books or if that question was rhetorical. Being his typical self, he dove into the books. He hadn't sat down yet, so he walked over to his fireplace and removed the vase that sat atop the mantle. Unnoticeable to the naked eye was a loose brick in the wall behind the vase. Malcolm shook the loose brick until it wiggled out of its spot and then Malcolm stuck his fingers in the empty hole. He brought out a small, shiny and rectangular little object that fit in the palm of his hand. He then walked over to the opposing sofa and sat across from Dr. Branch. He removed the top from the small object, and it turned out to be a flash drive, which he stuck into his laptop.

"Things have truly changed, Dr. Branch," Malcolm started, "The list of people we now have that's a part of our system has grown substantially, and with most everyone living well below their means, our savings have skyrocketed. Once the profits from the company begin to show, things will really blow your mind." Malcolm then added, "I hope that is something good." He smiled.

"That is wonderful news, Malcolm," Dr. Branch said. "Is there anything I need to be aware of? Anything coming down the line I need to be prepared for?" Dr. Branch asked, then reminded, "Honestly, I have been so focused on my sub-team's project that I haven't followed everything else like I should."

"That's very understandable, Dr. Branch." Malcolm told him, "I know what you guys are doing, and I can only imagine the focus it takes. I certainly couldn't imagine the emotional turmoil it would cause or that it should cause. The only comfort that I can offer is to tell you to look outside, especially at night. Our corners are finally quiet, Dr. Branch. And the only gunshots I now hear are in the distance."

Dr. Branch, not wanting to stay on that subject, switched it quick. "So everyone that is a part of our little socialism project is being taken care of?"

"Yes, indeed. If I have their information, their bills are being paid, and their money is being directly deposited into our master account," Malcolm informed. "And with the donations for the school from the extreme wealthy, we could potentially start our own bank."

"Are you serious, Malcolm?" Dr. Branch asked.

"I am very serious. I have been doing some involved research, and if we cross a monetary threshold, it would actually be smarter to have our own bank than trusting our money with the crooks on Wall Street." Malcolm advised.

"Now that is enticing, Malcolm," Dr. Branch said, and then he praised his friend, "You never cease to amaze me with your constant efforts, Malcolm."

"Dr. Branch," Malcolm started, "I joined the Twenty-Six because I wanted to make a difference. Honestly, I wasn't expecting anything this grand, and when things started rolling, I expected them to flutter to a slow halt. But I see if everyone continues to contribute, there is no limit to what we can accomplish. I digress. My point, Dr. Branch, is that you never cease to amaze me. What I have accomplished, what we have accomplished is all because of your vision and your leadership. So whatever I can do to keep this ball rolling, I will."

Dr. Branch almost felt a lump in his throat. He didn't know why. He had received flattery from a lot of people, but for some reason, he was struck by the unreal dedication his team had given him. They were absolutely devoted to the cause and handled business even in his absence. Malcolm's apartment was a living proof of that. He swallowed that lump and said, "Malcolm, thank you, this is really starting off as a wonderful day. Thanks for the info. I will be heading to see Mathew now. Have a good one, my friend."

"You have a good evening yourself, sir," Malcolm said, and Dr. Branch walked out of the front door, this time to an empty porch. While he walked down the outside steps, Malcolm reminded him of a monetary meeting, "Don't forget you have to meet with Lance Briggins next week. He won't give us any money until he meets the head of the school."

"Shannon Progress will be the head of the school."

"Dr. Branch, if you want the money, you know that you are the one that needs to see Mr. Briggins," Malcolm responded.

Dr. Branch stopped at the bottom of the steps and said, "I am getting really tired of talking to all of these rich black people." They both laughed as Dr. Branch began to walk away. Malcolm turned and went back inside. Three doors down, one of the ladies living in the four-family flat poked her head out to ensure Malcolm had shut his door, then she spoke.

"Excuse me, sir," the forty-something-year-old woman said. She was completely dressed, with her hair styled beautifully, and her face all made up. Her tight jeans accentuated her healthy figure, and her shirt was open enough to show just the right amount of cleavage to be sexy, not trashy. She walked out to the porch with her index finger out, insinuating her need for just one minute of his time. "Uh . . . Dr. Branch, right?" The woman asked, making sure she got the name right.

"Yes, ma'am," he returned, looking somewhat confused.

"Uh . . . your friends told us we wasn't supposed to thank you," she said, "But it wouldn't be right."

Dr. Branch, still baffled, scrunched his face and asked, "Why do I deserve a thank you, ma'am?"

"Oh . . . well, when your friends was here fixing up his place," she pointed at Malcolm's door and continued, "They fixed everybody's place. Mine too. All I had to do was work with them while they worked inside my house. I thanked them all, but they said you did all of this. Everything. Like how our street is so clean, and how everybody's house look better. They said you did all of this. They said you the reason all this stuff is going on. So I just wanted to say thank you . . . Uhh . . . Wait here." The woman hurried and lightly jogged back into her apartment.

Dr. Branch, still stunned by the unexpected appreciation for something he wasn't a part of, just waited at the bottom of the steps. She soon came back out in less than a minute with a pie pan.

"I make a hell of a pecan pie; it's my family's special recipe," she said as she stepped down the steps carrying the pie in one hand, ever so carefully in her high heels.

Dr. Branch extended his hand to take the pie, and then he stuck his other arm out to help her safely descend the rest of the steps. She played the damsel role quite well.

"Oh thank you." She smiled with a full set of gorgeous white teeth. "By the way, my name is Patricia." She held her hand out.

Dr. Branch took her soft hand into his and shook it, smelling her sweet perfume. His wife was sexy and slender, this woman was sexy and thick. Ample bosom, wide hips, and the type of badunk they refer to in rap songs. Stevie Wonder could see that this lady was doing some serious flirting.

"Let me know how the pie tastes," she said, "If you like it, I will make you some more. Or just let me know if you want something else. Baking is my specialty," Patricia said the last sentence with a slight seductive tone.

Dr. Branch, not wanting to lead the woman on nor put himself in a compromising position, quickly told her, "I'm sure my wife and I will love it. But I will let you know how much we enjoyed it next time I see you, Ms. Patricia."

She smiled back, undeterred by the wife statement, and they parted ways with a kind goodbye.

Dr. Branch got home with the pie and informed his wife that it was from a female neighbor. Even without the details of the flirting, Christine tossed the pie right in the trashcan.

"She wants to fuck you," Christine said with her hands on her hips, swaying her head as only a woman of color can.

"Whoa . . . Chrissy, where did that come from?" Dr. Branch said with a smile on his face.

"This shit isn't funny; I will break that bitch's neck," Christine yelled.

His wife never cursed unless she was seriously upset, but he could do nothing but laugh when hearing it. He chuckled slightly while grabbing her in his arms and said, "Babe, come on, no one wants these old bones, and even if they did, I only have eyes for you," he sang the last part.

She kept her arms folded, not hugging him back but not spurning his affection, and said, "That's right. You better."

She finally smiled at his advances then responded by grabbing his buttocks and pulling his midsection close.

"This is all mine, Dr. Branch," she said his professional name mockingly.

Getting aroused, he responded by kissing his wife harshly, and they made some spontaneous love down in the front room.

Mathew was scheduled to show up to Dr. Branches house at 3:00 p.m., and he showed up at three on the dot. As of late, Dr. Branch dealt with Mathew and Anthum more than he did Malcolm. Malcolm appeared to be in control of all the monetary affairs, and Dr. Branch trusted him completely. Dr. Branch merely visited the places Malcolm advised and spoke to the rich people Malcolm solicited. With those small efforts the money poured in, and Malcolm organized and controlled the money's subsequent destinations. Malcolm showed a propensity for money handling that was unparalleled, which allowed Dr. Branch to focus on his main objective.

Because Mathew was still on duty, he stepped into Dr. Branch's house wearing his cop uniform. He and Dr. Branch greeted one another at the door and walked toward the kitchen. Christine was leaving the kitchen, so she spoke to Mathew while sneaking a quick kiss from her husband. Mathew greeted Christine with a show worthy of a first lady causing her to blush, then he and Dr. Branch sat down at the round table.

"What's going on, Dr. Branch?" Mathew started.

"I think I should ask you that question," Dr. Branch returned.

"We stay busy at HQ, if that is what you're asking," Mathew said.

"We can get to that later, Mathew." Dr. Branch said, "I have another subject matter to discuss, my friend." Dr. Branch listened for a second to ensure that his wife was not in voice range then continued, "Right now, I am far more curious about what's going on at your department. Are you guys looking for missing people?"

Mathew actually laughed while talking, "Dr. Branch, are you kidding me? I am sorry, I guess I have background information that you don't. Let me explain."

Mathew started, "First off, we always get calls regarding missing young black men or boys. Whether it be a mother or a baby's mama, some woman is always calling looking for her son or baby's daddy. So yes, we are getting a few more calls than usual, but the detectives are showing their typical level of concern . . . not much. Especially after the detectives see that the young black boys got a record. They really don't take the calls seriously. They can be pretty detached."

Dr. Branch said, "So we are off the hook regarding our dealings with the authorities?"

"Dr. Branch, I have been a policeman for seven years, and in that short time, I realized something. I realized that they . . . we . . . the police force . . . really don't care about cleaning up the streets. These young boys killing one another is sad and horrible, but you wouldn't believe how many times

I done walked into the most crude statements while at a crime scene. I seen crime scenes up close and personal. They are horrible, Dr. Branch. Anyway, one time I walk to this crazy scene, and the shirts are there cracking jokes about the bullet holes in a young kid's back. The kid looked like someone emptied three clips into him. The damn detectives sat there and made all kind of crude jokes about the dead boy. They said he look like Chester Cheetah and started calling him cheesy." Mathew elaborated more, "There was also a time when I visited another crime scene where the boy's head was opened from an exit wound, and one of the detectives said that the brains made him hungry for noodles. They don't take these little dudes seriously. To answer your question, I think we could keep up what we are doing forever, and they wouldn't give a care," Mathew finished.

"So you don't think throughout this entire process we will have any complications coming from your boys, Mathew?" Dr. Branch asked.

"Trust me, we ain't trippin' off the missing riffraff. In all actuality, Dr. Branch, it's job security for them," Mathew stated with pure surety.

"That is very good to know, my friend. We don't have to worry about the police," Dr. Branch was saying when Mathew interrupted.

"I wouldn't say that, Dr. Branch." Mathew corrected him.

"What do you mean? You said that they aren't concerned with the disappearances?" Dr. Branch reminded Mathew.

"They ain't concerned with the disappearances, but your name has been mentioned more than once around the station," Mathew informed.

"My name? Why?"

"It seems like they don't care about kids killing kids in our neighborhood, but once people start cleaning it up, that's when they need to investigate. Please know that every cop on this beat has noticed the serious change in our immediate area. When they started asking around, your name apparently came up. So they are a little worried about you cleaning up the neighborhood," Mathew concluded.

"Are you kidding me?" Dr. Branch asked rhetorically. It was hard for his brain to wrap around such an illogical train of thought. The pathology of the black community was obviously system deep.

"I come to believe it's the change," Mathew started. "Anytime anything changes, it's bad news, Dr. Branch." Mathew explained his point of view, "Whether something changes from bad to good or good to bad, it's the change that makes people pay more attention to something. Do you feel me?" Mathew asked when he finished.

"Actually, I understand quite clearly," Dr. Branch stated. "It's just hard for me to believe, Mathew." He said, "So please explain more."

"They know that you are the main reason for the neighborhood looking the way it does now," Mathew said, "They want to know where the money coming from for this and what you are doing to get the people to help. That is when I chimed in and told them that you started a small group that volunteered their time and money to help clean the neighborhood. I hope I didn't overstep my bound."

"No, you did perfect, if they are wondering about me, it's best that you announce your connection with me up front," Dr. Branch told Mathew, "And its even better that the connection is through charitable means."

"Yeah, it was actually a good thing, because a few of the other brothers on the force want to meet you and maybe dedicate some of their time to the rebuilding process," Mathew finished with a smile.

"Are you serious? You turned a suspicious situation into one of recruitment? That is a good job, Mathew," Dr. Branch praised his teammate.

"I told the ones that were interested to come to this week's sermon and hear your words, and hopefully, they could meet you afterward," Mathew said.

"That will work. I actually have a wonderful sermon prepared for this week." Dr. Branch quickly said. Then returning to the subject he spoke more, "So all of this is so interesting. They aren't concerned with the darker side of our objective, but they are troubled by the lighter side . . . mind boggling." Dr. Branch then switched gears, "So anything new at HQ?"

"Nothing out of the ordinary. Anthum is putting the fear of God into each of these little punks."

"Have any of our converts contacted the police about their entrapment?" Dr. Branch asked. That was another of his many worries.

"Not one," Mathew said, "I have been keeping up with most of them, in one form or another. Every last one is trying to get back in school. The others are getting GEDs or trying to get a higher form of education. They feel like they belong to something important now – something bigger than them. Some of them said that they feel like they got purpose now."

"Good," Dr. Branch said, "Make sure they are always helping with the cleanup and remodeling of homes. Give them the pride of beautifying their own neighborhood while keeping their hands and minds busy as well. Any complications?" he asked.

"Not really. We haven't performed any execut . . ."

Not wanting Mathew to say the word, Dr. Branch waved him off.

"Like I said," Mathew reiterated, preparing to change his verbiage, "We haven't gone that route yet. We been saving those for you."

Dr. Branch frowned after that statement, and then he said, "OK, I don't like how that sounds, but I understand."

"Don't take that the wrong way. It's not that we need you to do the deed," Mathew said, "We just want you to agree that the few we have saved for you are beyond change. If my hands are commanded to do the deed, I sleep well at night, but if I make the decision, and it's the wrong one, I may never sleep again." Mathew said.

"What if I make the wrong decision?" Dr. Branch inquired.

"You don't make wrong decisions, I ain't seen one yet," Mathew said honestly and without a bit of sarcasm.

That statement startled Dr. Branch. That statement opened his eyes to something he hadn't seen throughout their entire rise as a team. His team truly saw him as more than man. They saw him as infallible, and that was actually disconcerting for Dr. Branch because he didn't know how to remedy their paradox view of him without destroying the cause. This power they had bestowed unto him is what kept them all motivated. To explain that he was no different from the rest of them could send a shock wave through the entire lot, destructive enough to crumble their core. This epiphany would have to be discussed with his wife, for she was the only person alive that would allow him to remove his leader's jacket.

Seeing if he could persuade Mathew otherwise, Dr. Branch smiled while saying, "No one is always right, Mathew; we all make wrong decisions."

Mathew, not relinquishing his stance, quickly bit back, "Not you. Listen, I am not the one to believe in bullshit, Dr. Branch, nor would I keep following you if you weren't special. But you are." Mathew got closer. "Don't you remember me messing with you in the very beginning? I told you that you were something special then, nothing has changed. I saw it then, and I see it now, Dr. Branch; your spirit is made with something different. I don't know what, but every man who meets you will follow you to hell and back, and that special spirit is why." Mathew sat back straight in his chair.

Dr. Branch, remembering Mathew's accompaniment when leaving the hall on those first starry nights, merely nodded his head in agreement. He then saw that his efforts to lower his status would be futile, but he had a very important point to make because of it.

"Mathew, have you ever thought about what would happen to the cause if something ever happened to me?" Dr. Branch inquired gingerly.

"Of course, and I think we would fall to shit," he responded honestly.

Hating to hear that, Dr. Branch said, "No, please don't believe that."

"It doesn't matter, Dr. Branch, it's my job and Anthum's, to make sure nothing happens to you," Mathew said.

"But you two aren't with me all the time, nor can you protect me from death," Dr. Branch started, "You as a cop should definitely know that. And if something happened to me, I would hate to think that our efforts would be in vain." Dr. Branch looked Mathew in the eye with his lips curled and his finger poking the table and said, "If I die, and this safe haven we have built crumbles, I will rise from my grave with this special spirit and haunt you until your dying day," Dr. Branch admonished. Dr. Branch, believing his scorn would register some understanding in Mathew, only caused Dr. Branch to see the absolute loyalty of this man.

"Dr. Branch, if anything ever happened to you, I would go out in a blaze of glory avenging you," Mathew said without thinking twice.

Dr. Branch then understood Mathew's make up. He was a loyal follower . . . not a leader. And that was just fine. There are far more followers than leaders and no need to force the job to one who didn't want it. But one thing was clear, and that was that Dr. Branch would need a successor. It would be a travesty to lose everything they have built because one man was removed. Yet too many times that idea has proven quite true; remove the head, and the body dies. There was a way to prepare for even that eventuality. Always have another head in the making.

Dr. Branch laughed at Mathew, and getting ready to end their meeting said, "Hopefully it never comes to that, my friend." Getting serious, he then said, "OK, I will come by HQ tonight to visit and confirm the damned. It's also nice to know that my name is in more mouths than I thought. Is there anything else, my friend?"

"Uhh . . . nothing I can think of."

"Good . . . you can go and get back to your fake job," Dr. Branch said with a smirk.

The two men rose from the table and proceeded through the small hallway. Before they made it out of the door, Dr. Branch made a request.

"Could you send me eight boys from our first conversion, Mathew?" Dr. Branch asked.

"Sure, what time you want them here?" he said, without needing to know the cause.

"Around seven would be nice."

"They will be here at seven on the dot, Dr. Branch. Have a good one . . . See you tonight," Mathew said as he stepped out of the door.

"Be safe, my friend." Dr. Branch closed the door.

"Babe!" Dr. Branch yelled upstairs as he started walking up.

"What are you yelling for, Stinky," his wife said, coming out of the bedroom. "It's not like this house is gargantuan." She walked back into the bedroom.

He walked up the steps and joined her in the bedroom. For a while now, she was the only one he could be himself around, and that meant a lot. Showing no weaknesses constantly and always thinking extensively about every word leaving his mouth could get extremely tiring. It was nice to unwind and say the first crazy words that entered his brain as well as express some deeper concerns he couldn't share with anyone else.

His wife watched her husband grow and played her role well. Whenever in public, she would treat her husband as royalty, giving him the appearance of constant control. Yet when alone, she would allow her husband to unwind and at times be the manic person he was. She understood and indulged in his utter need for her, yet didn't use her power as a bargaining chip. They worked together quite well. She was his yen, and he was her yang.

"I think that the men believe that I am something more than just a man, babe," Dr. Branch confessed.

"What? You just now figuring that out, sweety?" she said coyly.

"What do you mean?" He asked.

"Babe, you have got to be kidding me. You have never seen the pure reverence these guys show you? When they are around, I think I am with the president." She continued explaining things he hadn't thought about. "You say something to grown men, and it is done without question. These grown men, some even way older than you, hang onto your every word and look at you like you give off some type of glow. Some of the men even look scared when they are around you. And now it has started affecting the damn neighborhood. You didn't notice all of those people waving at us when we went to the market the other day? They were looking at you like you are some type of celebrity."

Dr. Branch truly hadn't thought that deeply about any of what his wife saw. He led this endeavor so he expected his men to be compliant. He also felt that in any true neighborhood, people were supposed to speak to one another. He didn't notice his neighbors showing him any special attention, but maybe they were. Dr. Branch knew that he was a leader, but he didn't see himself as special, nor did he want to start thinking that way.

"I don't want to be that special, babe. How do I stay humble?" he inquired genuinely.

"I don't know, sweetheart. I've been wondering how you still show such humility though everyone worships the ground you walk on," she said.

"Stop exaggerating, silly," Dr. Branch told her.

"No really. How do you stay grounded when everyone is lifting you to the clouds, babe? That is a good question," she said, and then she answered, "By always remembering that there is something far greater and more powerful than you are, sweety."

He reached over and grabbed a handful of her crotch tightly and said, "What . . . this right here?"

She jumped by the unexpected, strong touch. She then smiled and pulled him close and said, "You better believe it. Oh my . . . forgive me, Jesus. You got me talking bad Trent. Stop that." She smacked him lightly on the face. Then kissed him were she had just smacked him then said, "No, silly, you know who is greater than all. Our father, the one who has blessed you with this apparent gift to woo all in your path, including your lucky wife." They embraced and made sweet love.

The seed was planted in Dr. Branch, and a constant reminder of who and what Dr. Branch worked for would keep him deeply rooted and hopefully control his ego. After the obvious visuals from his wife, he finally saw the true power he wielded. Dr. Branch knew that power was a serious corruptor, so he had two goals for himself. He would have to constantly work on keeping his ego intact and find a successor as soon as possible.

Saggy Britches

The sweet loving left Dr. Branch in a comatose-style sleep, and he was again awakened by his wife.

Rubbing his head as she always did, "Sweety . . . Sweety . . . You have company," she told him.

"What . . . who is it babe?" Dr. Branch yawned.

"I don't know, it's a room full of young men," she said.

He sat up, always more tired than he recognized, stretched more, and said to himself, "These old bones just ain't what they use to be."

Dr. Branch went to the bathroom, urinated, and cleaned himself up. By the time he walked down the steps, he looked like his typical clean-cut self. He turned the corner of the steps and entered his front room where the young men sat.

They were all dressed nicely. Some in jeans worn around the waist and shirts tucked in. Others in slacks and oxfords, one kid even wore a complete suit. The funny thing was that usually when a kid overdressed, he would get ridiculed, but this time, the others looked at him then themselves felt worried that they were underdressed. Things were changing, so was the mind-set of the youth.

"How are you young men doing today?" Dr. Branch asked.

"Just fine, sir," they all said.

Making small talk as well as being genuinely interested, Dr. Branch inquired, "So briefly tell me what each of you have been doing these last couple of months."

One at a time, they each spoke.

"Well, I been going to GED classes, and my GED test is in two months, and I want to go to junior college after that," one said.

"I'm back in Sumner (high school). I had dropped out, but I'm back in," another said.

"I just been helping my sick grandma around the house and working with Mr. Luke Chodi whenever he need me," another said.

That's when they all added "Oh yeah we all been working with Mr. Chodi."

Dr. Branch spoke to the kid who was only helping his grandma, "Why aren't you advancing your education like everyone else, Trey?"

The kid being honest said, "I just don't like school." He got nervous, but he admitted, "I can't do it." He quickly added, "But I ain't doing nothing bad. I ain't robbing, or stealing, or selling drugs."

"Well, what do you like doing, Trey?" Dr. Branch asked, not mad at Trey's honesty.

"I like working with Mr. Chodi," Trey said with assurance. He continued, "He is real smart, and I like working on houses. When you done working on a house, you can see your work, like yeah look at what I did."

Though his explanation wasn't easy to follow, Dr. Branch understood what he was saying. "OK, I understand. I tell you what, Trey. I am going to make you an apprentice of Luke's, OK? That way you will learn carpentry, and one day you can build a house from ground up. How would you like that?"

"That would be cool!" Trey said with enthusiasm.

"The rest of you, continue going forward with your education. There is nothing more important. If you all need any help with anything, and I mean anything, come see me," Dr. Branch said, then getting to his point, he said, "OK, now the reason I called all of you out here. You all have been drafted for a secret mission."

The boy's eyes widened, and they waited like little kids for information regarding this secret mission. Dr. Branch bent down and signaled them closer. They all leaned in, and Dr. Branch started whispering. First he asked, "Are any of you good shots?" They all looked confused, and he clarified, "With a gun, are any of you good shots at long range?" No one said a thing; they all sort of shook their heads. Dr. Branch continued, "Well, that is first, I will need you all to practice day and night and become class A marksmen."

"I thought you wanted us all to get away from that kind of stuff . . . uhh . . ., Dr. Branch," William said.

"You all are on the side of good now, young William," Dr. Branch said.

He walked out of the front room and told them to follow. They quickly obeyed, and he led them to his downstairs closet. He opened the door and reached in. They stood stiff as boards, not knowing what to expect.

He came out with three tall boxes, handing each to one of the boys. On the outside of the box was a picture of a rifle, a pellet gun. He also brought out more guns, enough for all eight young men, along with eight discs. He passed along the guns and discs to every young man in the room.

"All right, this is your goal," Dr. Branch informed. I want you to study these discs and learn everything there is know about becoming a sniper.

The boys all looked surprised in their own way.

"Uhh . . . Dr. Branch, are you for real?" Alex inquired.

"Dr. Branch, I don't think I can shoot anybody ever again," William said, looking at his boxed rifle.

Dr. Branch walked over to William and put his hand on his shoulder. In a reassuring way, he said to William as well as the rest, "Listen, young men. Do not forget you all have made an oath. Great things are expected of you, and I will not request of you anything that you cannot bear. Killing anyone is not in your near future, so don't trouble yourselves with the thoughts. Take these discs; watch them over and over for they are actual advanced military techniques for training triple A snipers."

They all stood surrounding Dr. Branch – mouths agape, not knowing where any of this was going.

"Don't worry about the 'why', lads," Dr. Branch soothed. "This is a lesson in learning how to trust your elders. Just do what's told, and all will come to light very soon. I give you all two weeks of constant training. The first week you will do nothing but practice what is on those discs, OK? So that means right after school, get right to shooting practice. Got me?"

"Yes, sir," they said. "What about meeting with our mentors and helping with the home repairs?" someone said.

"No worries, all have been contacted. Your focus is on what I have requested." Dr. Branch looked at the two that were still in high school and said, "Your teachers have been contacted as well, and if your homework slacks because of your dedication to this new task, there will be no reprimands." In closing, Dr. Branch said, "So I want you all to work together and practice when alone. Become one with your weapon, and when I see you all again, I want you to be able to shoot a lady bug off of my nose."

They all laughed and so did Dr. Branch. Not wanting the boys to be seen leaving his house with brand new pellet guns, Dr. Branch handed out large bags, telling each boy to conceal his box within them. Afterward, he opened his door. But before the boys left, he left them with one final word.

"Listen, young men," Dr. Branch said, preparing to bestow a nugget of knowledge, "if there is one thing I want you all to know, it's that you have the power. Do you understand what I am saying?" He poked one in the chest with his index finger, repeating his statement, "You have the power. You have the power to be something great, but you also have the power to be something pathetic. You have the power to own the car dealership, or you have the power to be the one washing the cars. You have the power to fill the jail cells, and you have the power to shut those same jail cells down. Do you understand . . . you have the power to do anything and don't ever let anyone tell you that you are powerless. I see great potential and power in each of you. I truly do . . . and if you boys follow me, I guarantee that you will accomplish feats so great your eyes will be incapable of registering them. Now get out there and come back here in two weeks with the type of skills the CIA would beg for." They left his house feeling that power.

Dr. Branch gained even more respect with the neighbors on the block that night. After they all saw gang members from opposing factions leaving his house talking and laughing together, they began to think this man was a godsend. The neighbors all peered in disbelief as boys that intimidated them in the past walked in a bunch, emanating a vibe of positivity. One of the ex-thugs even saw some trash on the ground and picked it up. Old Lady Jensen saw that and almost had a heart attack right there.

Dr. Branch didn't close his door immediately, in turn he heard something that troubled him. The boys were beyond motivated as they left Dr. Branch's house, and they joked about their new leader in what they thought was a quiet tone. Dr. Branch could hear them though.

"Man . . . who *is* that dude?" one said.

"Yeah, how did he clear shit with my teachers already?" another said.

"It's like he know everything," someone else said.

"Yeah, like he Yoda or something," one said, and they all laughed.

Dr. Branch heard that and smiled himself, but the next statement caused him to step back.

Another kid said, "Or like the emperor." Then he hummed the dark side music. "Bum . . . bum . . . bum . . . bum . . . bumbum . . . bum . . . bumbum . . ." The boys laughed even harder.

Though he knew boys would be boys and crude jokes was a part of their make up, that one went to Dr. Branch's core. It was just a joke . . . right?

Two weeks passed, and each kid showed up to Dr. Branch's door with their new, air pressured best friend. They all practiced shooting until their fingertips burned with blisters. Not one slacked, not one wanted to show up to Dr. Branch doors knowing he didn't give his all to this cause. Typically, neighbors would have been concerned with those same kids showing up in their neighborhood with big black bags but not any longer.

Dr. Branch got them all in and sat them down. Once everyone was there, he asked a question.

"You guys ready to show me what you all learned?" Dr. Branch asked.

"Yes, sir," they said.

"Well, let's go."

Dr. Branch got them all up, and they left out his front door carrying their rifles in the bags. Mathew was waiting outside, so was Anthum in a separate truck.

"Let's rock. Some of you get in that truck, the rest ride with Anthum and me," Dr. Branch said.

The boys that rode with Dr. Branch instantly recognized Anthum. Though he was masked throughout the entire time of their conversion, his stature and cold demeanor was unmistakable. Needless to say, the ride up was really quiet. Anthum led, and Mathew followed with his crew of boys as they went to the outskirts near CH HQ. They pulled up to a distant wooded area open enough for shooting.

The trucks pulled up, and everyone exited. They all looked like a band of rebels in the midst of a secret, wooded hideout. Dr. Branch then told the boys, "OK, let's see what you got."

The boys pulled out there guns, loaded them with pellets, and took a firing position. Dr. Branch liked what he saw. Each young man learned well from the lessons on the disc. The disc taught that every position wasn't right for every person, so individuals needed to master the position that worked for them. It was pleasing to see each member of his sniper crew choosing something different. Watching them all at their ready position was like watching life-sized green army men set up by some toddler. A few of the young men laid on their stomachs, while others stood straight up. A couple of young men even used the kneeling position with their elbow resting on their knee. There were eight life-sized paper targets and eight shooters. They all waited on his go ahead.

"Fire!" Dr. Branch announced.

The shooting began. The pellet guns were top of the line and only needed the first round pumped. Afterward, the guns discharged round after round without any more work. They were also the quietest guns money could buy, and the sound of the pellets hitting trees and whizzing around made more noise than the actual shooting action.

"Stop," Dr. Branch commanded after twenty seconds of constant shooting.

The young men stopped and relaxed from their sniping positions. Anthum and Mathew went to retrieve the targets while setting up new ones. They walked right passed the shooters and handed the paper bodies to Dr. Branch. Dr. Branch then stretched each holey poster on one of the trucks, studying the skill of each shooter. The young men each wanted to see their poster but waited in the back until called on. No one spoke out of turn. They all felt disappointment when they saw Dr. Branch whisper something to the other older guys while shaking his head from side to side. Dr. Branch then called the young men up.

"Come here, guys," Dr. Branch said sadly.

They all walked up slowly, prepared for his lecture of disappointment, but they were surprised by his statement.

"Look at this here, lads," Dr. Branch pointed at the targets while saying, "This is damn good." The targets all had a cluster of holes in the heart area, with some in the head. All of the young men showed remarkable marksmanship skill, the top being Derek Browning. His clusters were so tight, one would have thought he shot once with a really big bullet.

"OK, I think we found our leader," Dr. Branch said, "Derek, get up here. How did you learn to shoot like that?" He asked.

"I just followed the lessons. Breathing is the most important part, that's what the disc said," Derek said shyly.

"Good job, but there is one thing wrong," Dr. Branch informed his crew of snipers, "I want you all to aim just a little lower."

As Dr. Branch and his body guards dropped off the crew of snipers, he provided explicit instructions for them to follow. He spoke into a phone that was on speaker ensuring that his mercenaries in the other car received instructions. The vehicles drove past key landmarks and vacant homes that Dr. Branch pointed at while explaining the plan. The boy's smiled in amazement at the plan and its subsequent goal if things went as hoped.

"OK, first, I want you guys to use the quiet tactics of a sniper to hang a few signs. Then I want you all to get into your secret locations and help clean up our city. You got me?" Dr. Branch said, and all the boys were all returned to their homes.

Derek Browning, leading his band of young snipers, first waited until two o'clock in the morning before beginning their first operation. They used the walkie-talkies provided by Dr. Branch to communicate. They moved in teams of two, and they were all dressed in army's black camouflage. Derek and his band of snipers behaved as though they were Special Forces on a secret mission, and they all later admitted to having the most fun they ever had.

They moved from car to car, house to house, and tree to tree, making sure not be seen by anyone. Like covert operatives, they moved to strategic places, hanging up an identical small sign throughout their immediate neighborhood. They each made sure that no witnesses saw anything to give the idea that the signs just appeared on their own. The band of newly formed snipers completed the first task of sign hanging, and then they made their way to their secret locations. That is when the teams of two had to split up in order to cover more ground.

Derek's secret location was at the intersection of a heavily travelled corner. There was a large vacant house on that corner with a view from the top window that covered a large portion of the immediate area in both directions. Making his way to that top room in the middle of the night was one of the scariest things he'd ever done, but he sucked up his fears remembering his time in CH HQ. Nothing was too scary after that life-changing event. He watched intently as he went from house to house in the shadows, making his way to the vacant house. Though it was around four in the morning, and all should have been quiet, Derek heard the voices of the night dwellers: the zombies and addicts, never sleeping, always looking for their next fix. Not wanting to be seen by the walking dead, he slid his way into the house by way of an unboarded window and dropped into the first floor living room. He stood up and saw that it was darker and spookier than any Stephen King late-night scary movie. He pulled out a very small flash light and actuated the tiny instrument. It popped on, providing the sight of pealed plaster, insane structural damage, and scurrying pests. He crept slowly to the center of the big creepy house, flashing the light on movement in all directions. He saw a grandfather clock on the ground with a giant crack where the gears should have been. As soon as his light hit the clock dead on, the light reflected from a pair of eyes, and a black cat shot out. He jumped back with a quick yelp and tripped over trash, falling to his butt. Derek then pulled his pellet gun out and aimed it in all directions. Even though the gun wasn't a deadly weapon, it still made him feel safe. Derek stood back up, shaking off the goose bumps, and slowly walked up the steps. He passed the second floor, looking in all directions, then made his way to the top floor. Up there was only space for two bedrooms – one in the front and one in the back. He could use them both. Once he canvassed the attic and tore down most of the cob webs, he felt more comfortable. He sat in a corner right by the window, and he let his childhood fears of the dark fade as he focused on the quiet picture outside. He glanced at the street lamps giving off their ominous glow, he then observed the clean streets that were filthy just months ago. He peered from house to house, appreciating the remodeling jobs. He then set his gun up. He looked through the sight and figured he better take a practice shot. He pointed his pellet rifle at a street sign and let a round loose quietly. The pellet left his gun quietly, but it hit the street sign with a loud pang. The intense quiet amplified the sound, and he sat back, laughing quietly to himself.

That's when his communicator buzzed to life, almost shutting Derek's heart off.

"Was that you?" William said. He was positioned in a vacant house cattycornered to Derek and apparently close enough to hear the noise.

"Yeah, my bad I was practicing Billy," Derek said. "Stay in your spot, be quiet, and wait for tomorrow to put in our work."

"Yeah right, nigga, you just popped some rounds off and gone tell me to be quiet til tomorrow. Fuck that," William responded.

"If y'all fuck this up and we gotta answer to Dr. Branch, I will shoot you stupid muthafuckas with a fucking Russian Dragunov SVD from the fucking Arch," the new voice was Alex, he finished, "Now shut the fuck up and get ready for tomorrow."

"Exactly," Derek, attempting to regain control, stated, "Everybody calm down and let's do this shit. Remember, after each round, get down. Never shoot more than once. Only use these things for emergencies (he was referring to his walkie-talkie). Two fingers, niggas," he closed.

Grimey was his nickname, but his real name was Jacob Grimes. He wanted to be a gangster so bad, but with a good mother, it was hard. Yet he attempted to exude the gangster persona while on the streets, and dressing like one was essential. Jacob's jeans were well below his waist, and his complete pair of sky blue boxers was easily visible. While walking to the corner store with his boy Rocky, they both caught a glimpse of a piece of paper floating from a stop sign. The two boys walked closer, and after further inspection, they could read what was on the back of the stop sign. The paper had been torn, but it was still legible.

NO SAGGING WITHIN THIS AREA

The boys were outraged; Jacob ripped the rest of the paper down and threw the trash to the ground.

"No saggin'," Jacob mocked, his young sixteen-year-old voice sounding like Eazy-E. "I wear my cloths how I fuckin' want to," Jacob said to Rocky but loud enough to be heard by people some distance away. With that statement, he pulled his pants even lower and flipped the bird to no one in particular but also everyone in the world. Jacob felt so cool. At that time, some of the teenage girls from down the block were traveling in his direction. They were watching his tirade, pointing and smiling at him. His chest swelled with pride, believing the little girls would think he was so hardcore with this blatant act of rebellion. Jacob stood there, pants damn near hanging on his shoes and middle fingers to the air, when something stung his right butt cheek.

If the comical self butt slap didn't make you laugh and the high-pitched yelp didn't make you laugh, then the jump from the second sting on the opposite buttock would have killed you. Jacob, already squeezing his right buttocks, felt the same pain in the left and involuntarily leaped sky high into the air with a hand full of his own ass. He landed, bent over to pull his pants up, and attempted to run home in one uncoordinated move. His backside hurt more than he could share, and his penguin-style walk left him humiliated. The last thing he saw as he waddled home was the same group of girls pointing and laughing at him but not in a good way. He was beyond embarrassed. Even his boy Rocky joined the little girls, and he could hear them all laughing as he made his way home.

Jacob Grimes got home, and his mother was on the phone yelling. He limped in the house and fell face first on the couch.

"Mom," he yelled. "Mom," he yelled again.

"Yeah girl . . .," Jacob's mother said, talking to her girlfriend until she saw her son's condition, then she switched gears, though still talking to the girlfriend, "Girl, it look like they done got my boy too. Oh well, let's see if this start making these li'l niggas wear they damn pants right. Ha . . . All right, girl, let me tend to this fool. Talk to you later. Yeah I know." She got off of the phone and approached her boy. "What's wrong wit'chu, boy, why you acting like you done broke a leg or something?"

"Mama, something stung me in my butt, both sides. Mama, it hurts," Jacob spat out, gasping for air and being overly dramatic.

It took all of her love to keep from laughing at her son. He sounded like a wounded animal, and as far as she was concerned, he looked like one too. She had been trying to get her son to stop sagging since he started at puberty. If this is what it took, so be it. Hopefully, he learned.

"Jake, stop acting silly. What's wrong with you, boy?" she yelled as she slapped him on his butt.

Jacob howled like a wolf after his mother's butt slap, and she broke into hysteria. She laughed and laughed. As soon as she thought she was finished laughing, she laughed some more. Jacob, hearing all of this, just wailed, whined, and screamed the entire time.

"Mama, why you laughing at me?" Jacob snapped. "I'm hurtin'."

"Boy, ain't nothing wrong with you," she said back at him. She finally let him in on her little secret. "Jacob," she said as she pulled his underwear down. He didn't protest. After she saw the small, circular bruises on both of his buttocks, she released his drawers and finished her sentence, "You ain't seen those signs around the neighborhood. They say you caint sag no more. And if you do, somebody shootin' you in yo ass. And it look like somebody done gone and shot you in yo ass, baby." She fell out laughing again. Jacob could do nothing to heal his wounded bum, yet his pride hurt far worse.

"See, now if I go around shooting people in they butt, I would be in jail," Jacob said, trying to rationalize his anger. "But they shoot me in my butt, and you in here laughing."

"You sho right," was his mother's answer. She tossed him a bottle of aspirin and told him, "Take three of those, you will be all right, boy. How about you don't go walking around wit yo booty hangin' out no more? Maybe this won't happen again."

Jacob took the aspirin. He also tested the waters once more. He received one more shot in his right buttock for his bravery or stupidity. After that second incident, Jacob decided he would only sag in the confines of his house.

Occurrences like Jacobs became typical, and young men and boys all around Dr. Branch's immediate area were severely penalized for wearing their pants below the waist. Those pellet wounds angered the youth, but with whispers of something called "Black Boogie Men" creeping into St. Louis slang, no retaliatory actions were performed. Parents and guardians, actually happy seeing their kids with the pants worn correctly, never reported the incidents. Especially after realizing it wasn't a personal attack on their son or family, the parent would typically encourage their child to just pull their pants up. After too many booty wounds, their sons would soon learn and comply.

The small band of snipers performed their service with joy and pride. New territories were claimed daily by the Twenty-Six which meant that work was always abundant for the little band of brothers. New territories meant a larger area to cover; a larger area to cover meant more members would be needed. The small sniper group stayed relatively small, but more young brothers were drafted to the ranks. The snipers quietly became infamous in the inner cities of St. Louis, and their signs slowly began to get results without physical harm. When they saw their successful efforts supporting the change that Dr. Branch always spoke of, and they saw that his crazy idea actually caused their peers to pull their pants up, the band of snipers vowed to follow Dr. Branch until their dying day.

Man Lessons

Dr. Branch sat in the pastor's office of one of the largest churches in north city St. Louis. The office was elaborately decorated and could have belonged to some type of CEO. Mathew and Anthum sat in the office with him; they all were waiting on the clock to strike seven. That is when his sermon would start. They could no longer house the sermons in the old hall. They could no longer use the first church they began renting on Tuesday nights because it was now too small. So they moved to San Francisco Temple. It was a church of old history but in a newly remodeled building, ornately designed with garish tapestries and laced with gold throughout the ceiling. Dr. Branch didn't like using such a ostentatious venue, but it was the only place large enough to satisfy the large crowds he now pulled weekly. Also, after a few of his sermons, the pastor was so enthused he told Dr. Branch he could get the church every Tuesday night for free. The pastor told him that Dr. Branch may not be calling souls to Jesus, but at least he was encouraging those souls to do what was right. And in times like these, beggars couldn't be too choosy. The clock struck seven, and Mathew and Anthum looked in Dr. Branch's direction.

"You ready, Dr. Branch?" Anthum asked.

"As I'll ever be, my friend," Dr. Branch answered, he then asked, "Has anyone gone out? How many are out there tonight? I wonder, are there more than last week?"

"I took a peak a few minutes ago when I went to the bathroom," Mathew said, "Nice bathrooms by the way. Anyway, there isn't even any sitting room out there. You know if we charged, we would be rich, Dr. Branch," Mathew joked.

"You know what, let's do that – five thousand dollars a head. My words are worth it, right?" Dr. Branch laughed at himself as he stood. "Let's get out of here, my friends."

Dr. Branch walked out of the pastor's office and took the back way to the pulpit, with his bodyguards following close behind. He opened the door and stepped on stage to a chorus of magnanimous cheers. Mathew and Anthum snuck out behind their leader and made their way to two empty seats behind the podium. The cheers and applause continued, and Dr. Branch waved to each of the men that were in the audience as he slowly crept to the podium. After a few more seconds of applause, he waved his hands directing everyone to have a seat.

"Sit down everyone . . . sit down . . . sit down," Dr. Branch instructed.

The roar of the crowd slowly weaned as the men took their seats. There wasn't an empty spot on the pews, and some guys were even sitting on steps. The crowd was full of black men ready to hang onto every word spoken from their newfound leader. The black faces all held some type of anticipation written on their brow, some ready to cheer even before hearing a single word. Dr. Branch didn't make them wait long.

He started. "Gentlemen . . . gentlemen . . . I say, because we are all gentlemen in here. Honorable and noble creatures understanding our worth. Gentlemen, I say unto you, I have a question . . . My question is . . . Can you see it?" Dr. Branch yelled his question. "Can you see the change sweeping across our neighborhoods? Can you feel the change spreading from one street to the next, spreading from one home to the next, spreading from one man to the next? I am not talking about a change that we have to look for, or a change we can believe in. No, I am talking about a change that is real and quite visible outside on our streets right now as we speak. I am asking, do you see the change happening right in front of you?" The crowd roared with the affirmative. "Have you ever seen your neighborhoods so clean? Have you ever seen your neighborhoods so aesthetically pleasing? Have you ever seen your neighbors so happy? Me neither."

Dr. Branch asked, "And who did this?" (We did, was the response), "Did the government do this," (No), "Did religion do this?" (No) "Who did this?" (We did)

"I think somebody in here understands what I am saying." Being on the pulpit made Dr. Branch feel a little preachy, "We did this. Every able-bodied black man in this room decided he was done talking about what needed to be and started acting. As they say; don't talk about it, be about it. And with a combined effort from all of you men, our kids no longer have to look dope dealers in the face on their way to school. Because of you men, our parents are no longer too terrified to sit on their porches. Because of you men, our young boys now see true, manly role models outside their doors. Because of you men, our young boys are no longer just meat for America's table. It's because of you men we see a bright and shining future for all of black America." Dr. Branch yelled, "We do control our own fate, and we have taken our collective hand and said either we are going to live together and thrive, or we are going to die trying. Regardless . . . we will be together." The crowd roared in agreement.

"Do you all remember the Million Man March? OK, for the few of you that attended, you remember, but the rest of you, let me explain the feeling. Being at the Million Man March was like being around a million of your blood brothers. The feeling was unreal. There wasn't an ounce of animosity, there wasn't a dab of anger, nor was there an iota of hatred. Love and atonement showered each and every black male in attendance. If you weren't there, you have never felt such a connection in your life. Until Now!" The crowd erupted. "Instead of having a Million Man March, how about we have ourselves a Million Man Stand. Instead of a day of atonement and unity, we have a millennia of atonement and unity. Instead of a day of loving ourselves and one another, we keep that love going year after year. It's OK to love your brother. Every other race loves their brother, why can't we do the same? Look to your left and right. Those are your brothers. Whether they are Christian or Muslim, whether they are college graduates or high school dropouts, whether they are lazy or ambitious, whether they understand or not, they are your brothers. They are you. We are one. And together we can turn St. Louis City into the most prosperous and safest place in all of the country." Even though the crowd cheered, Dr. Branch still said, "Don't look at me like that." As though the crowd disagreed, "It's possible. Come to my neighborhood. I bet you can walk your dog at two in the morning. Now I wouldn't wonder too far outside of our little safe haven because you and your little dog might get jacked." The crowd laughed. "Yet if you guys can see how street by street the city is changing for the better, and if we continue down the path we are on, we will see something no one believes is possible – black people running their own shit," he said as he stepped back from the podium. With that, the crowd roared and clapped loud enough to be heard throughout the neighborhood. They chanted his name and applauded.

"OK . . . OK . . . Let's calm down before they come in here and take us all to jail. You know a bunch of black men in one venue might incite hostile government involvement. They'll come in here and melt us all." The crowd laughed.

After more energetic speaking, Dr. Branch added more information, "I just wanted to put peace in everyone's heart along with some reality before I let you go. Gentlemen, I want you all to understand my message that we are all connected. We are all brothers. Whether you like it or not, it is true. It's our job to protect and help one another. If we do that, we as a community will be successful. Now, with that being said, I don't want people to think violence won't happen." Some people in the audience pointed at suspected culprits when Dr. Branch said that, he continued, "Listen we are all men in here. We have emotions and attitudes. We have pride and honor. We have egos, and we have testosterone by the bucket loads. And honestly, we can be just downright stupid; I am talking about men here." The crowd laughed again, "Because of those things, tempers will flare . . . crude words will be slung . . . and at times, punches will be exchanged. But with this love of self and love of your brethren, no longer is running to your car for the deadliest of all weapons your first option. Nor is it your second, as a matter of fact, taking your brother's life is not an option any longer." Dr. Branch had been speaking softly to make his point more effective, he continued in the same soft tone, "So I have heard of a few conflicts and even a few brawls. Though I first say try your best to keep them to a minimal, I also say that they will happen. But as long as you know that we all are working together to form a more improved union within our neighborhood, we will be just fine. Hell, sometimes we all need a good butt kicking." The crowd laughed more.

He said, "Look to your neighbor." The men obliged, "Tell that man next to you that you love him. Give him a hug." The men obliged, "Hey, you all hugged just a little bit too hard," Dr. Branch said pointing to a random set of two which caused more laughter. "You know I'm just messing with you. You all can sit back down." They did, and he continued, "I asked you to do that to understand that there is nothing wrong with loving your brother. It doesn't make you gay to love a man as you would love your father, your uncle, or your brother. It's OK to cry on your brother's shoulder. That doesn't make you less of a man. I say that because there seems to be a lot of confusion about what makes a man, a man. Well the lessons have always been around, and if you haven't seen them, just keep coming here, and I will teach you. Continue working with the men you see lining the walls, the Twenty-Six," he said while pointing at his compatriots, "And you will learn a couple of simple rules about being a man. You will learn that being a man is not about how many women you have made scream, it is not about how many bastard children you have seeded, it certainly isn't about how many jail houses you've visited, it isn't about how much money you have made, nor is it about how many men you've killed. Being a man is about three simple things. It's about respect, responsibility, and sacrifice." He counted on his fingers as he said them,

He clarified, "That's it guys. What do we all want as men? That's right respect. You give it, you get it. It's that simple. That's paramount for any man. If a man loses his self-respect, he is akin to a child, spineless and easily led in any direction."

"Then there are the two characteristics that epitomize a true man. Responsibility… Be responsible for your actions. You made eight babies, you take care of those eight babies. You committed a crime, stand up and be responsible for the crime you committed. You are a regular everyday Joe with the wife, kids, and a job. Be responsible for your family. You take care of yours. You never shy away from the consequences of your actions. That's being responsible."

"Then there is sacrifice. Every great man has sacrificed something, and the greatest men have sacrificed the one thing that they could never recapture . . . their lives. Well there was one man that got his life back, but that's a different story . . . where was I, oh yeah sacrifice. To sacrifice is to give up or surrender for the sake of something else. You all hear that, to surrender for the sake of something other than yourself. That is what men have been doing for years. Working a dead-end job or two, working sixteen-hour days, sacrificing sleep, sacrificing what he wants for the sake of the family, even at times sacrificing happiness to ensure the happiness of others. Some men have even sacrificed their lives for a righteous cause. I won't start naming names, but we all know a martyr or two."

He continued with the man lesson, "I am telling you all, if you work on those three things, you will see a change. Respecting one another will only ensure less violence, and if you guys add responsibility and sacrifice to your repertoire, you will take one step closer to being honorable men. That honor will spread, and eventually, honor instead of riches will be held among the highest achievement in the black community." The room erupted one last time, everyone believing every word leaving that man's lips.

Dr. Branch said a few more words then closed, "OK, guys. We are closing out. You all be safe. And for the fifty of you that are ready for your final trials, stay here with us."

The men slowly herded themselves out into the parking lot and eventually made their way home after talking to one another about what they had just heard.

Dr. Branch waited until the fifty chosen men were left in the hall, alone with the rest of the Twenty-Six. Dr. Branch spoke to the huddled recruits, "Well, from what I have seen, you guys have done everything required of you. You have spent six months performing backbreaking labor and never requested one dime. You all are now ready. Please understand that much is expected of you, and you will be privy to things no one else will ever know. If ever there is a hint of treason . . . well, just know that there is only one way in and one way out. You all also now have a bond with the best set of brothers you will ever meet. None of you nor your families will ever have a need, but again I say remember that this is a blood in, blood-out group. Speaking of blood in . . ." Members of the Twenty-Six began to pass around packages.

"A lot is now expected of every black man in our community, but the fate of the black community now rests on your shoulders specifically," Dr. Branch said. He recited the oath, forced the new soldiers to sign their names in blood, and a celebration ensued. Their family was three times as grand now. It was more of a necessity. Because their neighborhood conversion was spreading, more men were sorely needed, which wasn't an issue for there were ample men working to join the Twenty-Six.

Clean Bodies

Within six months of team CH's initiation of their operation, the final piece of the puzzle was complete – that final piece being the absence of hoodlums. Inside of a fourteen-mile radius, there was an inner-city black safe haven established in one of the most unsafe districts in all of St. Louis. The change was astounding. The change in people's attitudes was even more astounding. Within the confines of that district, businesses began to thrive, and the new aesthetics gave the neighbors a new perspective on life. The people within team Twenty-Six's district began taking serious pride in themselves and their surroundings. Change had happened, and it was time to spread to neighboring districts in the same fashion. But before they could do that, Dr. Branch saw the need for a final task within his area.

"Dr. Branch, these are the last two chumps in our hood that wanted to be gangsters," Anthum told his leader on a late Tuesday night.

They were at CH HQ, all of the cells were empty but two. All of the ruffians within their district had been converted or freed. So their list of kidnap victims substantially dwindled. That's why they were down to their last two neighborhood thugs. The two men were chained in separate cells, and they were at the end of their process. They smelled of that typical mixture of piss, shit, and unwashed body odor. Those two victims were both in their thirties but not yet men. It was always harder converting older guys than younger. Older minds weren't as malleable, and at times, unable to relinquish their old ways, but most anyone will submit if the alternative is death.

Dr. Branch wasn't concerned with the two converts; he met with his team to discuss a separate matter. This matter involved the one aspect he had taken too lightly. It was the drug addicts. Dr. Branch felt that if the drugs weren't available, then the drug addicts would leave the neighborhood, but they didn't. They were truly like roaches – everywhere and always in abundance at night. Dr. Branch was disgusted and felt it was time to discuss the matter with his team. Cleaning house was their department, and the junkies were now pest, infesting a very clean house.

"I have a plan to take care of the junkies," Dr. Branch said.

"That's a tough call, Dr. Branch," Mathew said, "Typically, I say once a crack head, always a crack head. If crack exists, they will find it."

Dr. Branch had a very quick flash back to his mother, "I know," he said, "That is why it's time to kidnap them."

"Really," Anthum said. "If you think these niggas stink after days of being here, just imagine how those damn crack heads gone smell."

"First off, guys," Dr. Branch said to everyone in attendance. "A drug addict's process will be totally different than the gangsters. We are not trying to take the hard out of these people. We just want to get them off of the drugs. So once they are here, just lock them in a cell and leave them. Feed them if they will eat and empty their waste bucket if they use it. Otherwise, leave them alone while they detox. Being alone during a horrendous detox will be punishment far more horrible than we could ever inflict."

"How long do we hold them?" Anthum asked

"A week of cleansing will remove the physical dependence of most drugs," Dr. Branch said, "The battle then becomes keeping their minds off of the substance. The body is free, but the mind remembers what it was like to be high, so it wants to go back. If put into a different environment, then the addict can get through those mental cravings as well. They will have to stay busy, stay occupied, which will be easy for our converts because we got more than enough work for them to do."

Dr. Branch reminded the men of their true job, "Remember, guys, none of you can imagine the shock to the system these people will endure. There will be nothing we can do for them, so please do not add to their torment by being dicks. Always remember that these are our brothers and sisters, and our overall goal is to help our people the best way we know how."

That raised a question from Phillip who puffed on a cigarette. "Sisters . . . we getting women too?" he asked.

"Yes, we are getting women this time too," Dr. Branch responded.

"That should be interesting," Anthum said.

"Very," Dr. Branch added. "Anyway, we will attempt to gather our neighborhood addicts in one night. Get them all here together, suffering side by side. Once they are coherent enough to understand what is required of them, we will explain what happened."

Dr. Branch reminded the men of the apparent hardship, "You all have to know that getting off of these drugs will bring some of our prisoners close to death. So keep an eye out and just try to make sure none of them dies. At the end of their process, they will also need to see the history lesson." Dr. Branch closed, "Are we clear?"

"Crystal," Phillip said with smoke leaving his mouth.

Dr. Branch didn't like being around Phillip's smoke, but Phillip spent more time in the bottom of CH HQ than anyone. So Dr. Branch didn't nag about the bad habit.

"I have plans in motion now. You guys be ready on Thursday night to abduct these poor souls," Dr. Branch said.

Dr. Branch actually had a little more pity on the drug addicts because he would see his mother's face whenever thinking about them. He looked down and thought about one of the last times he saw his mother. He was thirteen and was on his way to his junior high graduation. He hadn't seen his mother in weeks. Yet on this night, while dressed in a cheap suit bought with his grandmother's medication money, he finally saw his crack-addicted mother. That wasn't the last time he had seen her, but it was the last time he allowed her actions to hurt his heart.

Dr. Branch and his grandmother were getting into a cab when he heard his mother's voice from down the street. She was talking to some young man from the neighborhood, and her words came in a blur. While fast talking with the guy, she walked just as quickly as her mouth moved, keeping pace with the much taller man. Once Dr. Branch saw that it was his mother, he quickly yelled out to her. He yelled that he and his grandmother were going to his graduation and that he wanted her to come so bad. She responded very dispassionately that she would be there in time to see him cross the stage. Then she asked what school was it; she didn't even know what school her son went to. His grandmother merely tugged on his shirt, telling him to come on and get in the cab. He did, and tears flowed from his young eyes on a supposed joyous occasion. That was one of those eye-opening moments for Dr. Branch. He knew his mother was lost to him, and he would hate her for the rest of his life for choosing drugs over her son.

Dr. Branch had been staring down for fifteen seconds, not saying a word, when Mathew placed a hand on his shoulder.

"Dr. Branch, you still with us?" Mathew asked.

Dr. Branch snapped out of his sad memories and focused on the matter at hand, "Sorry about that, guys, I was elsewhere. Anyway, that is the plan. Any questions?"

Thursday night, Dr. Branch placed a couple of his young converts on the block dressed like their old selves and appearing as drug dealers. Dr. Branch felt it was going to be an easy operation. Dragging lightweight drug addicts away shouldn't cause too much commotion. He was right.

Anthony Barnes, one of the young men Dr. Branch recruited to be a fake drug dealer, stood on Dr. Branch's now empty corner and posed as a youthful gangbanger. He talked to his friend Barry, nicknamed Biggums, while they portrayed themselves as young dope dealers. Out of sight was a large van with Anthum in the driver's seat. Joe was parked nearby as well. Mathew was on cop duty that night, so he wasn't available. Dr. Branch and the rest of the crew were in attendance and all close by. Then an old addict approached the drug dealing duo and started talking to the young men as though he were waiting for them for eons.

"Holy shit, where y'all been all my life?" said the heroin addict. He was skinny, his hair was nappy, and he smelled as though a bacterial colony was undergoing evolution under his arms. He continued talking, "Man, I heard some nigga named Branch done scared y'all away. It's nice to see some real niggas stuck around here." He laughed in that dry, hacky smokers cough and then mimicked a rap song while dancing a jig, "I ain't never scared, I ain't never scared." He laughed some more and attempted to flatter the two, "That's y'all two young killers right there, y'all ain't never scared. Ha." He finally broached the subject, "What y'all got for me?"

"Calm down, old man. We got you covered," Biggums told the old addict.

Anthony had already waved his hands in Anthum's direction. That was the signal, so while Anthony mocked the movements of a drug dealer, Anthum was making his way to where they stood. Anthony walked back into the alley, behaving as though he was retrieving his stash. He came back and held his hand out for a drug dap.

The heroin addict slid a twenty into his hand during the handshake and looked at Anthony in the eye after realizing there was no merchandise being exchanged. Before the heroine addict could snatch his hand back and gripe about the lack of barter, Anthum was already standing behind him. Anthony held the addict's hand, while Anthum hit the back of his neck with a karate chop that would have broken cinder blocks. Needless to say, the bony addict dropped like a sack of potatoes. Anthony saw Anthum, and a quick chill ran down his spine . . . memories. Anthony was just happy that he was on the same side as that big black beast this time.

Anthony watched as Anthum hefted the bony drug addict over his shoulder and carried him back to the van.

That same scenario played itself out over and over until mostly all known neighborhood addicts were getting driven back to CH HQ. Once Anthony and Biggums's job was done, Dr. Branch showed up.

"You guys did great tonight." Dr. Branch told his fake drug dealers. He continued with the accolades, "Your neighborhood loves you for it, and you both will never comprehend the immense help you have provided your people. Keep this between us, and I will be calling you both later for some assistance in the near future."

"Yes, sir," they both said.

"Now get back home to your families, and if asked, just tell them you have been working hard cleaning up your neighborhood," Dr. Branch advised.

"Yes, sir."

The young men pulled their pants up and made their way to their respective homes. Dr. Branch then got on the road and followed his team to the headquarters.

Once at the HQ the team unloaded all of its unconscious kidnap victims from the cars, dragged them through the facility, and tossed them into individual cells. They nabbed eighteen men and seven women.

Dr. Branch helped with the transporting of the addicted prisoners and was astounded by the odor most of them already emitted. When they were done dropping the poor people in their cells, Dr. Branch held his hands to his nose and sniffed. He almost gagged at the smell stuck to his fingers. He was stunned by how easily the horrendous fragrance resided in his clothes and skin. He was even more amazed to see that some of the women smelled worse than the men. Dr. Branch honestly didn't know women could smell that bad. They smelled as though they wore old rotten fish for underwear. He couldn't believe people could allow themselves to fall to such a pitiful state. His mother never smelled like that, or did she and he never noticed?

When the cells were all locked and Dr. Branch and his team gathered in the walkway. Dr. Branch spoke softly.

"Damn, they stink," Dr. Branch said with a lot less articulation that usual.

"I told ya," Anthum bragged.

"Well, at least it caint get no worse," Phillip said.

"I hope not. How can a person allow themselves to get so bad off? I mean, damn," Dr. Branch said sniffing himself more. "Now I smell like a shit mix."

The men fell out laughing, not used to Dr. Branch speaking so crudely.

"I haven't asked, but how are all of you doing?" Dr. Branch inquired, changing the subject for a quick second.

"I'm cool," Anthum said,

"Fine," Joe said.

"All right," Fred said.

"Ditto," the rest said.

"Is anyone having a hard time dealing with what we are doing?" Dr. Branch asked. "Any sleepless nights, any horrible nightmares?"

"Actually, we've talked about that often, and surprisingly, none of us are having any issues," Fred said. "For me, this is nothing compared to life in the bush with the Vietcong. But for the others, they all take comfort in the reasoning."

"Explain further Fred, please," Dr. Branch asked.

"Well, after talking to these guys," Fred explained, "the team feels like we are doing a positive thing. Though we are killing, putting it plain and simple, we don't feel like we are killing humans."

"I understand," Dr. Branch didn't agree with that train of thinking, but he added, "Whatever gives you guys solace and can help you sleep at night. Just always know that we are doing what's needed. Whether our actions are wrong or right, they are sorely needed. Don't you guys ever forget that. And don't forget that our streets would not be in the peaceful state they are in if it wasn't for what you all are doing."

The men all nodded, accepting their leader's commendations. Then Dr. Branch said, "I think we all need a change of clothes and maybe a shower . . . right now. I feel like I am covered in goo, for lack of a better term."

"Yeah, me too," Anthum agreed. "I lifted one of those women on my shoulder, and now it smells like stanky cooch."

More laughter. The men made their way up the steps to the wash rooms and cleaned themselves. Their clothes would have to wait; the men would get clean items once they returned back home.

Once the cleaning was complete, they all returned to the bottom level to see what was happening with their new prisoners. Some of the prisoners were waking up and gathering their bearings. Others were still out cold but would be waking up soon.

The forty-something-year-old heroin addict woke in his cell; Eddy Crock was his name. After the sleep wore off, he was wide awake and wired. He tried to focus on where he was and how he had gotten there. The last thing he remembered was attempting to buy some tar heroin from one of the hoods, and that was as far as his memory allowed him to see. He couldn't recall anything after that. Remembering his attempted drug deal reminded him of his drug habit. By his count, he hadn't taken any heroin for more than sixteen hours. In turn, the first real pang of detox occurred – that extreme craving. His mouth went dry, and his salivary glands worked overtime. He hadn't gone half a day without heroin in ten years. This will be the first time he'd made it more than twelve hours without his drug of choice. The longing in his system was monstrous. If he had a choice of food, water, sex, love, or family, he would have chosen heroin over anything. Because he was alone in a padded room, he could think of nothing but his drug. He first noticed the metal chair in the center of the cell, then he walked to the metal door and banged. His frail, bony hands hurt after three hard raps on the door, and he refrained from hitting the metallic obstruction again. His heart beat hard, and he screamed out.

"Hey . . . Heeeeyyyyy!" Eddy screamed. "Get me out of here! Help me!"

He screamed more until his voice cracked from dryness. He really wasn't concerned about where he was. He didn't care if he would ever see freedom again. His only concern was getting some dope into his veins immediately. He was feeling a little sick. He knew the sickness would escalate, but at that moment, he just felt absolute longing. He wanted nothing more in the world than to shoot something into his veins. Only God knew how bad he ached for that sweet brown sugar to course through his corroded blood vessels. Once he saw that no one was coming, he just paced in a circle. He walked around the chair talking to himself.

The average person would have wondered what was going on and who held them prisoner. Not Eddy, he couldn't remove heroin from his mind. He would have accepted a lifetime of slavery if anyone would have walked through that metal door with some dope. He ran back to the door and screamed more.

"You at least got to get me some methadone or something" he yelled then repeated, "You got to get me something, man, don't hold out on me. Oh God." He started to feel a taste of the true sickness coming. He crouched into ball and started to whimper.

Two cells down sat Shirleen Beckman. She was once an old folk's nurse, the type that spent her work hours at her patient's home. The job wasn't that difficult, especially with the bed-ridden geriatrics. One night while sharing her living quarters with a crack head boyfriend, she gave in to his persuasion and put a crack pipe to her mouth. She inhaled the acrid smoke and was surprised that the feeling in her lungs was cool instead of warm. After exhaling the smoke, she remembered feeling better than she had ever felt in her entire life. She was happier than she had ever been, and life could not have been more perfect. Euphoria would be a serious understatement, yet no other word could describe her state of mind. She once said that it made the sun shine in her soul. She was in a blissful state of being, and nothing could touch her for all of thirteen minutes and thirty-nine seconds. Then the world dropped from underneath her, causing her to instantly feel horrible. And if asked, she would have said that someone had turned down the lights on the entire globe. As good as she felt while high instantly converted to the opposite end of the spectrum and she felt lower than low. She took another hit from the pipe, and from that moment on, she didn't look back.

She lost her job, her home, her kids, her family, and her appearance. What was once a curvaceous beautiful black woman was now a wilted, droopy body hag that once stayed unwashed for so long that she caught a level-four bacteria infection in the crevice between her breast and stomach. That area is still green to this day.

Shirleen woke in her cell with her face on the cold ground. Her eyes opened, and she looked around before pushing herself up off of the floor. She stood up and tried to recall what happened. She remembered chilling with her male companion then getting swooped up while trying to score some drugs. Seeing that she was in a padded room, she started hitting herself on the top of the head with her open hand, calling herself stupid. She believed she was in an insane asylum, perhaps at the request of her family. She figured she would wait for her doctors, but what would she do in the meantime, especially with the jitters coming?

No worries, she merely looked around to see if there were any obvious cameras, made sure no one was peeking through the door, and then sat in the metal chair. She opened her legs and stuck her right hand down her crusty panties. She proceeded to reach her fingers inside her unwashed vagina then retrieved a small balloon. She pulled it out and wiped away the juices from the knotted area. Shirleen moved frantically as she untwisted the knot to open the small blue rubber containment. She then snatched a straight shooter with a little package out, and then ever so gingerly, she opened the clear cellophane package, giving view to four little white chunks. She loaded the pipe then realized she was missing one quintessential tool needed to complete her process.

She screamed. So close but yet so far. She had the product in her lap, but no means to use it. That just made her yearning more insane. After another fifteen minutes passed, she could wait no longer and crushed the white chunks on the metallic chair with the ball of her hand and sniffed the rocky powder. She frantically inhaled only to sneeze after getting the crap up her nose. She yelled at herself and attempted to lick her snot from the ground and chair. She didn't get her fix. She merely frustrated herself more. Then it started, her skin began to crawl, and her mind started to race.

A couple of days had past, and all of the addicts were in similar states. Some were throwing up or gagging, with nothing in their bellies to regurgitate. Others were scratching at their skin, leaving horrible whelps. Others were rocking back and forth, talking to themselves, trying to stay sane. They all were a ragged bunch, and to watch them detox guaranteed a drug-free life for the spectators – the spectators being team CH.

Team CH watched the poor souls going a different kind of crazy within their cells. The team then agreed with Dr. Branch. There wasn't any type of torture they could unleash that would outdo the torment those people endured in those padded rooms. The people in the rooms continued to scream when they weren't hoarse or scratch on the door when they had strength and control of their bodies. They also did a lot of begging and pleading when the team would attempt to give them food and water. By the time their detox reached a crescendo, mostly all of the drug addicts were willing to suck a dick to get one last fix. The one amazing thing was that none attempted to fight; they were broken little dogs. When seeing their captors, no one ever fought for freedom they all only groveled. They knew they weren't worthy of a fight. They had no self-respect.

It seemed as though everyone hit their wall at the end of day three. After day three, some where able to sleep a couple of hours. After day four, everyone was able to sleep a few hours. Some people even had appetites and were capable of holding food in their stomachs. By day five, most were capable of coherent speech, and their brains began to clear. Their physical appearance couldn't have been worse, but for the first time in a long time, the fog was lifted from their brains, and clear ideas began to take form. No longer were drugs always at the forefront of their collective minds which allowed the bunch to finally think about other things. Typically, those things were family and friends, kids and cousins. That's when depression reared its ugly head, along with all of the memories and regrets, causing the recovering drug addict's mind to long for numbness again. They don't want to relive the torment they have caused their family. They don't want to remember their kids' crying faces. That's when therapy is needed. Dr. Branch knew this and was prepared. He knew they would need counseling, so he had a new form of therapy prepared for his drug addicts. Those recovering were the first to experience Dr. Branch's brand new style of drug rehabilitation therapy.

On day six the drug addicts were finally spoken to. During the entire stint, no one from team CH said a word to them. They would merely open doors and shove food in the cells, ignoring the pleads coming from the captured. This day the doors opened and the helpless victims waited for their cold cut sandwich. They were surprised by finally hearing voices. Each victim was told that they would finally find out what was going on. They were told to gather and follow one another to the large room at the end of the hall. They obliged. They exited their rooms, surprised by the number of people that shared their fate. Because they all ran in the same drug packs, they recognized each other, and smiles gleamed on some of their faces. The filthy crew whispered to each other as they slowly waddled to the larger classroom. Once there, some took seats on the metal chairs, while others were quite content sitting on the floor. After they all found seats and appeared ready for the lesson, Anthum and Deak Charleston entered the room.

Deak Charleston, the leader of team Emotional Reparation, was going to be this group's two-day drug counselor. His partner was Anthum. Deak, a handsome man walked in wearing a nice suit and clean shoes. As he entered, he caught a whiff of the subjects then gave his head a much-needed shake, attempting to clean his sinuses. Anthum, who walked right behind Deak, passed him a white tube. Then he mimed a movement showing Deak that the tube contained some type of odor destroyer. Deak squirted some of the thick goop on his finger then rubbed the stuff under his nose and proceeded to the metal chair, sitting behind the table. Anthum went to the opposite side and leaned on the table while staring out into the crowd. It was time to commence with Dr. Branch's new style of drug recovery therapy.

"Hello, all" Deak began in a soothing, calm tone. He was a stout man with a deep voice; it reverberated inside of the little room. "I know you all are lost and are all wondering what the hell is going on." He heard affirmations and continued, "Well, putting it simply, I and this man here (pointing to Anthum) are part of a coalition of black men that are cleaning up the city. If you all weren't always high, you probably would have noticed the serious change within our area." The only thing the drug addicts noticed was a sudden lack of drug suppliers in their vicinity. Deak continued, "Anyway, we have worked on the aesthetics of the neighborhood while cleaning at the same time. And when I say cleaning, I mean getting rid of the human trash. We have worked on getting rid of the thugs, gangbangers, and drug dealers, and we saw that our city was clean. Though our city was clean, we still had a pest problem. It's finally time to get rid of the roaches. You all were the roaches."

"Hey now, wait a minute, who you calling ro . . .," one brave soul started to say but was interrupted.

Anthum slammed his closed fist on the metal table with a loud bang, stopping the would-be talker in midsentence. He peered through his ski mask, letting everyone know that now wasn't the time to speak. No one else spoke out of turn.

Deak cleared his throat then continued, "As I was saying before so rudely interrupted, the roaches were infesting our clean areas and needed to be removed. There was a suggestion made." Deak, though articulate with his speech similar to Dr. Branch, was far more dramatic with pauses and a lot of hand waving. He spoke loudly at times and other times would bring things down to a whisper. It was his style; it was how he spoke to his fellow veterans when needing to get their minds off the horrors of war. He found that people with short attention spans not only focused on what is said but also how it was said. So he was sure to remain calm sounding, yet he threw in some flashes of excitement, even rising out of his seat at times.

This crowd didn't need the dramatic flare. They had been locked up for six days with absolutely no rhyme or reason. They were starved of their dependency and left to suffer the agony of withdrawals alone, afraid, and in the worse pain imaginable. Because of the aforementioned, that intimidated bunch of recoverers would have provided their undivided attention to the most boring teacher on the face of the planet. Yet their attention was held far more easily with Deak's flare. It didn't matter; they just wanted to know what the hell was going on.

Deak continued speaking with his intense style, "That one suggestion. You want to know what it was? Putting it simply, we were going to just get rid of you all like Jews during the holocaust." Gasps were heard, eyes grew wide in the crowd as Deak continued, "But that would not have been honorable . . . because each of you deserves at least one chance to show that your life is worth living. So our only option was to give you all the opportunity to get clean and stay clean." Before saying the next part, he stood and performed more hand gestures while saying, "If you all think that this is a joke . . . if any of you think that this is a game or that this is even some reality TV, then please focus your attention on those things in the back that resemble giant laundry shoots. "Deak pointed at two skinny men sitting on the floor in the back and said, "Pull those handles." They jumped to his orders and pulled hard. The giant shoots opened, and they peaked their heads in only to be quickly repelled by the intense heat. The crowd could feel the room warm as well as see the waves of shimmering heat escaping from the open hatches. For those willing to sneak a peak into the hot opening, they witnessed the final destination of the giant square shoot, which was the center of a roaring furnace. The sight resembled a fiery description from Dante's Inferno. They pushed the giant metal hatches closed, never wanting to look in there again. They got the point.

Deak continued with his spiel, "That is where we put the worthless. Before you say anything . . . we don't care how insane you think this is, just know that it is all true, it is all real. If you don't want to be a part of this new society we are starting, we are removing you from it. As previously mentioned, it was decided that instead of just killing you addicts, we figured we would show you a few days of clean living by forcing sobriety on you. Afterward, we will give you all the chance to live with us in our new society. A chance to start anew."

"Now I say all of this knowing that you drug addicts will need psychological help staying off of that crap. That is what I am here for. I am here to listen to your pain. To delve deep into your soul and hopefully aid you all in discovering what caused you to be slaves to a substance."

Deak wanted to provide clarity while saying, "Let me forewarn you, the counseling you receive here will be totally different than any clinic you have ever attended. Our therapy style is unique and quite simple. Basically, there are two aspects of this style of counseling. As I said, I am here to help you and show compassion," Deak closed.

"And I am here to remind you that if his help doesn't work, there is always option number two," Anthum said, receiving a cringe from the crowd.

Deak spoke more, "You all will get out of here soon. Your bodies will be clean, but your minds will still yearn. Your only deterrent is to know that if you ever land yourself within these walls again, we will remove you from the face of this planet. It's that simple."

Deak, reminding the crowd of one last thing, said, "Listen, you addicts, we are not your families, we are not your friends. We will not sit back and let you destroy our community because of your lack of willpower. So understand that the road you will travel now will be difficult, but you have help. You also have a hellified incentive – either you succeed or you die. Any questions?"

On the sixth day and for three days after, the addicts received constant mental therapy as well as a constant reminder of their other option. Their therapy was two sided, a lot of soul searching help provided in tandem with a stern understanding that excuses will no longer be tolerated. They were allowed to give sob stories while being reminded that life is hard for everyone, so get over it. At the end of their nine-day stint, every addict was alive and well. They all watched the history program twice and started to understand their worth. They were encouraged and reminded that everyone falls, and the next move should be to get back up. One of their important lessons was practicing to forgive themselves, which would help remove the burden of guilt. They were also made to look into mirrors constantly and to tell their reflection that it was loved and worthy of being loved. A lot of the recovering drug addicts had attended rehab before but learned nothing like they learned in Dr. Branch's speedy rehab seminar.

On the ninth night, the drug addicts were told that they would be freed. They were also reminded of the penalty of failure. They all left their cells, begging for a place to wash, but were refused. Deak told them that it was one of the most important parts of their process. To arrive at their home covered in piss, shit, and a litany of other funks, and then to witness through sober eyes how their family still loved and accepted them.

Before the recovering addicts left the facility, they were forced to clean out each of their cells thoroughly with bleach and other strong disinfectants. They were all blindfolded then led to a large vehicle. While blindfolded on the bus, the ride was quiet with every addict dwelling on their futures as a clean member of society. As they finally entered their neighborhood, they were told that the blindfolds could be removed. Even at night, the ex addicts were finally able to notice the changes in their neighborhood, and their eyes widened with wonder. Each person exited the bus but was sure to thank the driver for everything. They all were taken to their respective homes in clothes they had worn for at least ten days straight, yet none of them seemed embarrassed. They all were quite proud of themselves for doing something that a few hadn't done in ten to twenty years – kicked their long-term drug habit.

The recidivism rate was very low for that first bunch of addicts. There were only two members of that first group that chose to test the waters. Two of the men from that first group migrated to the untouched sides of St. Louis in an attempt to score drugs as well as get away from the goody two shoes. Needless to say, Dr. Branch kept his word, and the instant that he was informed of their relapse, he sent people to hunt them down. The two backsliders were soon found and returned to the HQ. Dr. Branch looked them in the eye and spoke robotically; there was absolutely no emotion in his delivery.

"Instead of letting you kill yourselves slowly," Dr. Branch informed, "I will do it for you quickly. Getting rid of people like you is what we do. You weak men were both given the opportunity to clean yourselves. You didn't take it seriously, now it is time you die."

Both men, still high from their last hit, yelled their viewpoints, one saying, "Who are you to make that decision? I'm a grown ass man. I can do whatever I want. Me using my medicine ain't hurting you."

"Sorry," Dr. Branch began, "right now, your words are meaningless. Goodbye and peace be with you on your journey to the next life."

The two men tried to speak more, but Dr. Branch left them in the cell. He would have them shot with a strong sedative, and then they would be shoved into the giant furnace. Their time was up.

Unity

After a long day of repairing one of the new members of the Twenty-Six's homes, Dr. Branch finally returned to his. He walked in ready to shower and lay his weary bones down. He was so tired he didn't even bother to notice if Christine's car was outside or not. He walked to the fridge and grabbed a jug of apple juice and tossed it up. There was no need for a cup because Dr. Branch nearly emptied the contents of the jug in one sitting. As he stood near his refrigerator, there was a knock at the front door.

Dr. Branch was quite use to unexpected guest, so he wasn't too disappointed about making his shower wait. Because his wife wasn't home, Dr. Branch returned his jug of juice to the fridge and walked to the door. He saw an old lady through the window as he approached. She wasn't anyone he recognized. He figured she was some old lady from his wife's church and proceeded to unlock his door to let her in. While unlocking the door, he could hear her debating with someone loudly. He opened the door and listened to the tail end of her argument.

The pudgy, gray-haired old lady wore an old, ankle-length colorful dress, which was covered by an even older plastic-looking red trench coat. She was telling a teenage boy behind her to shut up as Dr. Branch opened his door. Before the boy noticed Dr. Branch in the doorway, he continued talking. Dr. Branch could hear the boy pleading with the old lady. That is when Dr. Branch understood that the young man was the old lady's grandchild. He could hear the young man saying, "Leave that man alone, Grandma." The young man was about to say more, when he finally saw Dr.

Branch at the door and froze. After the lad caught a glimpse of Dr. Branch at the opened door, his mouth closed shut, and he bowed his head.

"Hello, Dr. Branch," the boy said.

Dr. Branch, generally wonderful with names, had drawn a blank with his. He certainly remembered all of the faces of his converts, but no longer could he quickly recall the names. Too much time and too many people had gone through the process.

"How's it going, young brother?" Dr. Branch responded, then he focused on the old lady, "Hello, ma'am."

"Hello, sir," the old lady said, "I am so sorry if I disturbed you, sir." The old lady talked with her purse in front of her and bowed often as words left her mouth. She spoke to Dr. Branch as though she shared her space with someone of much higher authority. She continued, "My boy Trevon there." She slowly turned, pointing at her quiet grandson, then returned her focus to Dr. Branch, saying, "Told me that you did that."

"I'm sorry, ma'am, I really don't know what you mean," Dr. Branch said.

"I am so sorry, sir," the woman apologized, "First off, my name is Mrs. Marymay Foster."

"Well, hello there, Mrs. Foster," Dr. Branch said, "Do you and your grandson want to come in and have a seat?"

"Sir, I know that you are a very busy man, and I don't wanna take up too much of your time," Mrs. Foster said, "What I gots to say I can say it out here if you don't mind."

Dr. Branch loved old black women. He always said that when his grandmother's generation dies, we as black people will lose the best of us. Old black women were the epitome of respect and ladylike demeanor. They were full of wisdom and earthly knowledge. Without any medical knowledge, they cured stomachaches, skin rashes, and other ailments. They took care of entire households while keeping everyone fed and keeping the house clean. And the respect they showed their black men was astounding. "They don't make 'em like that anymore," Dr. Branch thought.

"Sure, you may continue, Mrs. Foster," Dr. Branch said, "But know that you are welcome to come in and grab a seat."

"No thank you, sir," again, Marymay spoke kindly. "I'll just say my piece and be on my way if it's all the same to you, sir."

"Well, speak on, ma'am, you have my undivided attention," Dr. Branch told her.

"Sir, I don't want much at all. It's just well . . . well . . . I better start from the beginning," Marymay said more so to herself. "My grandson been mine to raise since he been nine years old. And since he been nine, he been a little hellion." She looked back at her grandson, and so did Dr. Branch. She continued once they both stop looking at the boy. "He used to talk to me like I wasn't nothing. He was disrespectful, didn't go to school, and disobedient. He would be gone for days at a time and wouldn't call me or nothing. But what could I do, it was just me and him, and I can barely walk sometimes."

Before Marymay continued, she raised one of her hands to the sky and said, "But thank you, Jesus, my prayers was finally answered. Just out the blue, the boy come in and is a new kid. I didn't know what happened and was waiting for him to change back to his evil self. But he is still acting like the type of boys I raised in my day . . . good and decent. I had to know what happened; I had to know what changed the boy so. I dig and dig, sir, until he finally say a name . . . Dr. Branch. I ask who is this 'Dr. Branch', and he tell me you been teaching a class to all the boys about how to be a proper man. Well I can see that you done got through to every boy in our neighborhood, and more important, you done got through to mine. I ain't got to worry about the boy being in nobody's jail cell or dead." She shook her head while thanking God once more then continued on, "Sir . . . umm . . . Dr. Branch, I just wanted to let you know how happy you done made me," Marymay said. She opened up her purse, pulled out some butterscotch candy, and popped it into her mouth.

Dr. Branch was caught off guard with the great show of appreciation. He stood tongue tied for seconds then finally formed some words, "Mrs. Foster, thank you for coming here to show me your appreciation, but I deserve none, ma'am." Dr. Branch pointed to the quiet young man behind the old woman and said, "Trevon right there deserves all of the accolades for working so hard in his effort to change his ways."

The old lady simply smiled at Dr. Branch. She believed she had never met anything like him nor would she ever again. She couldn't put her finger on this Dr. Branch character, but he had the presence of an old civil rights leader. He stood erect with steel in his backbone. He gave off a glow of power, and she believed she could see his aura radiating outwardly from his core. She was finished, but she had something more to say before she left.

"Dr. Branch, sir, I just have to let you know that it's about time," she started, "It's about time somebody stood up and took our homes back from these kids. I couldn't understand how we sat back and just let the devil come and take our babies away from us. No more, I see God working through you like he did with our strong black men of my day. You go with God, young man. And thank you again, sir." She bowed once more then sternly told her grandson, "Tell the nice man thank you!"

"Thank you, Dr. Branch," the young man said quickly.

"Mrs. Foster, you don't know what it means to hear everything that you have just said," Dr. Branch told the old lady. He continued talking to them both, "It's wonderful to hear, but I can take no credit, ma'am, really, this is a family thing, and we all have to work together to keep things running smoothly."

Marymay merely nodded, knowing that modesty was just another attribute of a truly powerful man. She showed agreement with her many nods, thanked the man once more, and left his front porch with her grandson.

Dr. Branch watched Marymay and Trevon walk away, and his heart swelled with joy. A few weeks later, something occurred that truly showed Dr. Branch the new way of thinking his neighbors possessed.

One Saturday, while out manicuring his lawn along with a few of his neighbors, Dr. Branch saw something he hadn't seen in a long time on his block. There was a young teenage boy walking around with his pants sagging. Because the works of team Twenty-Six were no longer needed in his immediate area, they had advanced into nearby neighborhoods, spreading the new law. With Dr. Branch's snipers nowhere in the vicinity, he figured he would be the one to nip this boy's sagging issue in the bud. He continued working on his lawn while the boy slowly made his way up the street. When Dr. Branch noticed that the sagging culprit was close enough to his house, he stepped out to the sidewalk. He waited in front of his property until the boy slowly walked right toward him. The boy finally reached his house, and Dr. Branch spoke to the kid.

"How's it going young brother?" Dr. Branch said.

"Whut up, cuzz?" the boy said. He wore his pants almost down to his knees, a matching shirt and jacket ensemble, with the coordinating brown boots.

"Are you from around here, young brother?" Dr. Branch asked.

The kid merely eyed Dr. Branch with a look of contempt and continued walking past without slowing. Dr. Branch saw that the kid was going to continue walking without responding to him, so he quickly grabbed the boy's jacket by the arm. The boy, feeling the tug on his jacket, turned to see Dr. Branch holding onto his new leather windbreaker and quickly snatched his arm away with some choice words.

"You better let go of me, old fuck," he said to Dr. Branch as he pulled away.

Dr. Branch typically had a mild temper; he was patient and usually hard to anger. This kid obviously pressed all the right buttons because Dr. Branch reacted reflexively with no forethought at all. After the boy spat those disrespectful words, Dr. Branch instantly saw red and cocked his right hand far behind him. Before the boy even knew it was coming, Dr. Branch slapped the boy in the face hard. The sound was similar to the ocean crashing on the seabed. The earth-shattering sound caused most of the outside neighbors to turn in Dr. Branch's direction.

The kid caught the blow fully on his left cheek. The open-hand slap from the full grown man caused the little teenage boy to fly to the pavement, landing on his butt. The kid, totally stunned by what just happened, grabbed his face and peered up at the man that smacked him. He remained on the ground for a second, looking at all the neighbors, attempting to gauge how many people saw him get struck. The boy was shocked by what he saw.

The neighbors heard the slap and looked in the direction of the commotion. The instant that they recognized it was Dr. Branch chastising a teenage boy, each neighbor diverted their attention and focused on their own chores. No one gave it a second glance.

The kid was amazed that no one gathered or even pointed. No one was calling the police nor was anyone coming to his aid. The boy, catching all of this from his seat on the ground, finally stood up cautiously. Not knowing what to do, he simply rubbed his face.

Dr. Branch attempted to explain his actions to the youngster, but the kid was already walking backward talking smack. The neighbors eyed the kid with disdain. They hadn't seen that type of behavior on their street for close to a year and hated to think that it was coming back. The kid didn't walk far. He made his way to the first house on the next block and walked inside.

Within five minutes, a light-skinned beauty came flying out of her door with the same kid right behind her. It was her son, and she looked like a mother bear about to protect her cub. She wore her relaxed weekend clothing, which was loose jogging pants and a matching top. Even in the loose clothing, one could catch sight of her tightly sculpted body. She was gorgeous and used to getting whatever she wanted.

She walked fast and hard in Dr. Branch's direction while giving him the evil eye from the end of the block. Dr. Branch knew that he would need to explain his case to the angry lady, but he wasn't about to apologize for his actions. She continued her path to Dr. Branch, almost stomping her feet on the hard pavement. Dr. Branch could see that she was livid, and he was ready for whatever was to come. She reached her target with her son close behind her. Her son's light-skinned face started to show a red handprint where he received the crushing slap. The mother and son then stood side by side as she started to fuss.

"Excuse me, did you lay your hands on my fucking son?" the lady said.

"Yes, I did," Dr. Branch answered honestly.

"Why the fuck you putting yo hands on my fucking son?" she spat.

Dr. Branch's only response was, "I can see where your son gets his exquisite vocabulary."

Dr. Branch's sarcasm only incited more anger. "What the hell's that supposed to mean?" she asked, not wanting an answer. She continued with her rant, "You ain't his daddy, you don't have no right layin' yo hands on my son. Nobody touch my son but me." She would have continued, but Dr. Branch chimed in.

"Maybe that is why he is so disrespectful," Dr. Branch told her, "because you are the only one that's allowed to chastise your boy."

"What are you talking about?" she inquired.

"Your son spoke to me using some extremely foul language," Dr. Branch informed her.

"That still don't give you no right to put yo hands on him," she shot back.

"Well, he needed to be taught how to respect his elders. That's obviously something you aren't teaching him, so I accepted the responsibility," Dr. Branch continued speaking nicely, which just infuriated the woman more.

"Listen here you proper nigga. You don't tell me how to raise my kid."

"Apparently, your kid didn't get the memo. We no longer allow our boys to look like worthless thugs in this area. I was trying to get your son to pull his pants up," Dr. Branch informed.

The woman let Dr. Branch have it after that statement. She went off in the typical ghetto fabulous fashion, a lot of finger waving and neck rolling.

"Memo . . . memo . . .," the woman said, sounding shocked. "First off, my son been with his grandma for the last year. He ain't know nothing about no memo. And ain't nobody gonna tell me how I need to raise my boy. So what, he wants to wear his pants sagging, that's what all the li'l boys doing. It ain't hurting nobody, and it ain't hurting you. I been raising my boy by myself, and I ain't never needed nobody's help, so I sure as hell don't need yours," the woman said. She continued her diatribe fussing on and on. Dr. Branch didn't say another word, he only listened as the woman complained about her life and everything else she was upset about. Apparently, Dr. Branch's actions caused every problem the woman ever had to be directed at him. She complained loudly and continued getting louder once she saw that Dr. Branch no longer said anything.

That was when the street surprised Dr. Branch, showing him that the spirit of unity was alive and well in his area. While the woman continued screaming at Dr. Branch about her many issues, most not related to their situation, the neighbors turned in their direction. Then ever so slowly, the neighbors dropped their working utensils and started walking toward the chaos. For a second, Dr. Branch thought things were going back to the old ways and that his neighbors closed in only to view the action. He was half right. The neighbors all slowly drew closer and closer to the screaming lady, and someone finally cut her in midsentence.

A man in his midfifties spoke first, "Excuse me, young lady, but that ain't no way to talk to that man right chur." The man nodded his head in Dr. Branch's direction.

"Excuse me," the loud women said. She turned to see who was talking to her and stopped talking altogether. Her eyes got wide, and her mouth seemed to pucker a little. Throughout her shouting fest, she didn't notice anyone walking toward her. To see at least fifteen people behind her caught her totally off guard.

"You excused," another woman in the crowd returned snidely.

Someone else, a younger man said, "You need to recognize who you talking to. This man is the mayor of our block. He done worked hard. He done helped us turn our street into something pretty."

"Yeah, and he ain't did nothing to hurt that boy," another lady chimed in.

As they were speaking, two white cops performing their district patrols rode past the bunch and stopped. The driver poked his head out of his car, actually surprised. The police couldn't remember the last time that they had seen any issues in that area. His partner, a little overzealous, had already exited his passenger door. The cop still in the driver seat, spoke.

"Any problems here?" the policeman asked in his best impression of Robocop.

The crowd stood firm. That same midfifty-year-old man spoke first, "We just fine, officer."

"Everything is wonderful, sir. Just having a block meeting," an older lady in the crowd said. Then she peered at the light-skinned beauty with eyes squinted and inquired, "Ain't everything just fine?"

"Everything is fine, officer sir," the fussy lady responded.

The passenger cop looked disappointed and slid back into his seat. The driver simply said, "All right, just checking everyone." Then they drove off down the street.

Dr. Branch never said a word, he didn't have to. The block started taking care of itself, and they were going to protect him whenever they saw the need. The boy and his mother saw the crowd, and the mother realized she was in a losing battle. She didn't say another word; she simply turned toward her house and stormed off.

"Thank you all for that," Dr. Branch said to the people still standing, watching the lady stomp her way home.

The crowd began to disband, and Dr. Branch heard someone say, "No . . . Thank you."

While crossing the street, the midfifty-year-old man told Dr. Branch, "It's the least we can do for you, brotha." Then he returned to his own yard, continuing with his work.

Dr. Branch watched as each of his neighbors returned to their respective homes and couldn't help but smile. He wished he could have stayed in that moment forever. His dream from years ago was actually coming to fruition before his eyes. Black folk united. The spirit had spread, and it was inside of everyone he saw. He waved once more to all of his neighbors and returned to his own yard work, whistling a happy tune.

"Sweety . . . Sweety . . .," Christine spoke softly, waking her husband during midday. Shaking him gingerly, she said again, "Sweetheart, get up."

"Huh . . ." Dr. Branch woke from a hard sleep where he was dreaming about his son. Dr. Branch slept when he could, so whenever at home, he was usually in bed. "Hey, babe," Dr. Branch said, "What's up?"

"It's some guy saying he is an FBI agent at our front door," she told her husband.

Dr. Branch heard FBI, and his testicles shot into his midsection. His stomach became queasy, and he felt sick. His wife noticed.

"What's the matter, dear?" she asked, genuinely concerned.

"Oh . . . nothing, babe," he responded, "I was just having a bad dream, and it's sticking with me. I'll be just fine." He got out of the bed speaking softly, "Is he down stairs?"

"No. He said he would wait outside," she answered.

Dr. Branch acknowledged the statement with a nod then proceeded to make himself presentable while working on his game face. He walked down the steps and opened his front door. Dr. Branch saw the back of a man wearing a plain blue suit with black leather shoes. His blond hair was cropped in a crew cut. Dr. Branch could see the muscles through the man's suit. The man turned, and his powder blue eyes peered directly into Dr. Branch's soul.

The man reached into the inside of his blazer's pocket and pulled out a golden badge while speaking, "Hello, Dr. Trenton Branch, I am Federal Agent Loggins. Do you have time to talk, sir?"

"Absolutely, Agent Loggins, please come in," Dr. Branch said without a second thought.

The agent walked in the humble yet refurbished home as Christine was going up the steps. Dr. Branch introduced his wife.

"Sweetheart, this is Agent Loggins. Agent Loggins, this is my wife, Christine," Dr. Branch said to them both.

For the briefest of moments, Christine was frozen. Not because Agent Loggins worked for the FBI, but because he had to be the most handsome white man she had ever seen. His eyes were piercing, and she almost lost herself within them. And after he smiled with a set of flawless white teeth overlayed by full pink lips, she could do nothing but smile back. She reached out her hand for a shake and spoke kindly.

"Well, hello, Agent Loggins, it's very nice to meet you," Christine said.

"The feeling is mutual, ma'am," he said with a country twang.

His southern drawl almost left Christine weak, and she could do nothing but continue to smile as she shook his hand.

"OK, sweetheart, I know that he is a beef cake. Let us get to our business, and I will have him take some pictures for you," Dr. Branch joked.

They all laughed, and Christine walked up the steps as Agent Loggins followed Dr. Branch to the living room. They walked in, and both sat down across from one and other. Dr. Branch then asked the all important question.

"OK, Agent Loggins, is there something wrong? Why would the FBI come to my house?" Dr. Branch sounded genuinely curious as he asked the questions.

"Yes, there is something very wrong here, Dr. Trenton Branch," the agent responded.

"Dr. Branch is fine," Dr. Branch interjected.

"OK, Dr. Branch," the agent said, not skipping a beat, "There seems to be a lot of missing people." The agent spoke with brevity, not attempting to play any mind games.

"The FBI came to my house to give me a report on missing people? I am lost, sir," Dr. Branch said.

"The missing people are all from a small region within the city of St. Louis," the agent informed, "They are all from this area to be exact."

"Oh, so the FBI is going around getting information regarding the missing people?" Dr. Branch inquired, with his best attempt at acting dumb.

"No, Dr. Branch, I am here to see you," again, Agent Loggins spoke succinctly.

"Agent Loggins, please speak plainly. Why are you at my house?" Dr. Branch finally asked.

Without any hesitation, Agent Loggins told Dr. Branch, "I know what you did, Dr. Branch, and I know what you are doing." After making those statements, the FBI agent peered straight into Dr. Branch's eyes.

Dr. Branch's world crumbled. That sickness came on again, and his muscles felt really weak. Dr. Branch's head spun, and his throat became really dry. Though his mind was in a state of disarray, outwardly, Dr. Branch didn't flinch. His game face was impenetrable, and he didn't give any inclination that he was extremely concerned.

"What I did . . . what I am doing . . .," Dr. Branch said, repeating the agent's points. "You really have me at a lost, Agent Loggins," he said.

"I am not here to play games with you, Dr. Branch. I only want the same respect in return," the agent said. He continued, "You are a scientist, which means you are a logical person. So I have a question for you. Did you really think you could accomplish the amazing feats you have accomplished, and no one would notice? Did you think that you could remove certain members of society? Plainly put, Dr. Branch, did you think you could kill the negative people of your neighborhood, and important policing organizations wouldn't find out?" The agent's southern drawl became more pronounced as he continued to speak.

Dr. Branch was at a loss for words. He had been found out; this man didn't leave any questions about it. If the state didn't know what he was doing, the federal government did, and this man didn't pull any punches. He didn't attempt to catch Dr. Branch in some elaborate rues, he merely brought the information to Dr. Branch's doorstep. Dr. Branch always told everyone else to be a man, so he figured this was the time he needed to practice what he preached. This man came to Dr. Branch with honesty and respect, Dr. Branch figured he would return the gesture.

"Agent Loggins," Dr. Branch said as he folded his arms in front of his chest and leaned back on his couch, "You didn't treat me as though I were dumb. I will treat you the same. I will not sit here and act as though I don't know what you are talking about. Neither will I incriminate myself. So I guess the only other question from me is do I need to get a lawyer?" Dr. Branch asked.

The agent smiled and then gave Dr. Branch the surprise of his life. "Dr. Branch, if I can be honest. I'm on your side."

After hearing that, Dr. Branch almost swallowed his tongue. He continued listening.

"I can't say I was on your side when I first stumbled onto your little, well, big operation," Agent Loggins said. He continued, "Believe it or not,

I have attended all of your sermons for the past five months. Not in person of course, but I hear them just the same. I hear your goals and your dreams for your community, and I understand that you were fed up with the city's situation. Don't get me wrong, your sermons didn't convert me, but they helped me see through your eyes. What brought me over to your side was driving through this city. While driving from one part of the city into this part, it was amazing. I thought I left the city behind. You have beautified your neighborhood greatly. The difference between the areas you have worked on and the areas that are still untouched is night and day."

Dr. Branch listened to the agent in utter awe. He couldn't believe what he was hearing. It appeared that this agent had all the information needed to end the Twenty-Six's process as well as send Dr. Branch up the river for a very long time. Yet he sat across from Dr. Branch without attempting to lock him up. Dr. Branch relaxed a little and continued to listen to the agent's points.

"I am usually not this talkative, but you will never believe how amazed I am," Agent Loggins said, "Really. To hear something, then see it come to life . . . truly amazing, Dr. Branch."

Dr. Branch finally chimed in, "Our neighborhood changing isn't enough to cause you to conclude that I have anything to do with the missing people, Agent Loggins. Help me out there, why have you drawn such a morbid conclusion without any proof?" he asked.

"Dr. Branch like I said," Agent Loggins was saying with confidence, "I didn't say I had suspicions or that I believe . . . I said I know what you did and are doing. When I say I heard your sermons, I thought you would understand that I heard a lot more than just your sermons. I hear what has been said when the crowd leaves and it is just your team of Twenty-Six, which is now what . . . a team of two hundred. You should really change that name, that's the one thing I have hated about your group. But I am getting sidetracked. Like I said, I hear what your team talks about when it's just your immediate members, but more importantly, Dr. Branch," the agent gave a long pause before saying the next part, "I have heard when you are directing your smaller team . . . what are you guys called . . . Team Cleaning House. A relevant name I might add. Yes, I have heard your nefarious plans."

Dr. Branch merely listened with a straight face; he didn't know where the agent was going with all of his information. Dr. Branch was about to say something, but the agent continued talking. Dr. Branch figured it was best to allow the man the opportunity to divulge everything before interrupting, so he sat still and listened.

"I have watched you guys in action," he explained. "I have seen you take twenty people inside your little compound, but I have only seen seventeen of those twenty leave. Nice cover by the way, using a business facility. And then I would see the immediate change of the surviving seventeen. I don't know what you guys are doing, but it appears to work wonders on your most hardened criminals. After seeing this scenario play itself out over and over, I was able to put two and two together." He paused for a minute.

Dr. Branch saw his opportunity to speak and did, "So what does all of this mean? If you have all of this indisputable information and you are not here to arrest me, what is your main purpose for being here, Agent Loggins?"

"Simply put, Dr. Branch, I came here to give you information," he said. "I know this stuff only because the agency was suspicious and put me on your tail. Don't worry, they know nothing more than you are a major part of the neighborhood revamping. They have no idea about how deeply you are involved in the other aspects of the city's cleanup. And I am not going to tell them a thing."

That last statement almost caused Dr. Branch to jump up and hug the agent. Dr. Branch had to ask, "I know I shouldn't look a gift horse in the mouth, but why not? It is your job."

"Dr. Branch, I have always felt that my job is to make America a safer place." Agent Loggins got very honest. "But after working in the protective field, I realize that our jobs are to keep certain people safe while being unconcerned about the rest. After following you for these last few months and following your progression, you have shown me that I need to remember why I got into this business. I see that you have the best idea for fixing what has always been deemed unfixable. And honestly, Dr. Branch, I really want to see the finished product."

Dr. Branch was flabbergasted. When first seeing the agent, Dr. Branch believed he would be behind bars soon. After hearing the guy, Dr. Branch realized that he may have an ally in a really high place. Dr. Branch said the only thing he could say, "Thank you, Agent Loggins."

"Don't thank me yet," the agent advised. "Like I said, I am the only agent on this case now, and I will continue to tell them that you are not involved in any dubious activities. But that is not to say that more agents won't be assigned to the case. You are known now, you are in the federal database as a figurehead. So know that and began to move like you know that. Though you have been covert, you will have to improve that process."

After that, the agent finally stood, held out his hand, and said, "Dr. Branch, I think it is time I bid you farewell."

Dr. Branch, still stunned by his miraculous fortune, hopped up after the agent and grabbed the agent's hand in both of his. He shook firmly and said one last thing to his newfound friend, "This is amazing, you could ruin this entire endeavor, but you choose to support it. You are a damn good person, Agent Loggins."

The agent simply said, "It's Tyler," and left Dr. Branch's home feeling high. He would continue to watch Dr. Branch's movements because it was his job, but he never planned on bringing any of his information to light. He drove away believing he finally followed his heart instead of his command.

Revamped Education

It was the dead of winter, and Shannon Progress made his way to Dr. Branch's house. He figured he would take a stroll through the new snow that fell throughout the night. It was a gray morning though the day was brightened by the three inches of clean snow on the ground. He walked and gave greetings to the people coming out or going in their homes, with them returning the gesture. He gave critical advice to the kids sledding down hills and provided tactical advice to the others in the midst of snowball fights. Shannon saw the change in the inner city and couldn't wait to see Dr. Branch's affect on the school system. He carried his laptop in a pouch that was strapped to his shoulders. After much work and consideration, he was finally prepared to tell Dr. Branch about his team's success. This upcoming fall, the Inner-City Private School will be fully staffed and fully functional. Now all he needed were the students. He made it to his destination and knocked on the door, which was opened almost immediately by Christine.

"Hello there, Shannon." Christine said. After hearing him huffing, sounding out of breath, and not seeing his car outside, she inquired, "You walked over here in that crap?" She pointed at the snow and then chastised him, "You could have slipped on some ice and broken your neck, boy."

"I know, Mrs. Branch, but it's a beautiful St. Louis snowy day. I figured I needed the exercise anyway. Look at me, I'm putting on my winter weight," Shannon finished and they both chuckled.

Dr. Branch joined in on the laugh as he descended the staircase, then he and Shannon walked to the kitchen. They sat at the round table and spoke about the school.

"Tell me something good, Shannon," Dr. Branch said.

"It's funny you should say that Dr. Branch," Shannon told his leader, "I actually have some really good news to give you."

"What do you have for me?" Dr. Branch asked.

"The building and all of the renovations will certainly be completed well ahead of the upcoming school year. And I have found educators for all of the classes we want, all handpicked by my team."

"That is wonderful news," Dr. Branch exclaimed. "So we will be able to start our school on time?"

"We only need to fill the classrooms with students," Shannon informed then stated, "If I remember correctly, that is your department."

"No worries, my friend. I have been preparing for this moment before your team was constructed," Dr. Branch said. He then told Shannon, "I already have things in motion, I just needed to know that your end was covered. Now I can finish my process and do what I need to do."

Shannon didn't know why he was so surprised. Dr. Branch had never been caught off guard, and he was always three steps ahead of the game. Regardless, it still amazed Shannon to see a man who was ready for everything.

"So what's the plan, Dr. Branch?" Shannon asked, "Where are the students coming from?"

"They are coming from the city schools," Dr. Branch responded.

"From the city schools?"

"Yep. I am going to travel to every inner-city public school and grab volunteers for this educational revolution we are about to embark upon," Dr. Branch answered, he continued, "I have been in constant contact with key faculty members across the city. I have told them my plan, and they are on board."

"I still don't see how you are going to get volunteers. What are you putting out? A commercial or something? What are you doing to even get the kids attention?" Shannon provided some really good questions.

"I will use my natural God-given talent, Shannon. I am giving a speech. I'm going to travel to every single inner-city public school, and while there, I will recruit the kids that are willing to step it up," Dr. Branch told Shannon.

"So you are just going to give an auditorium presentation at each school and hope to get some participants for our school. I don't know if that will work," Shannon said.

"Oh boy . . . Am I going to have to start calling you Doubting Thomas now?" They both smiled, and Dr. Branch continued, "First off, the expectations I have for the students that attend our new school are huge. The workload will be at times overbearing. And the moral fiber I will expect from them is unparalleled to anything they have witnessed in their neighborhoods. Forcing those types of expectations on a kid will cause him to fail if it's not something he has chosen to accept." Dr. Branch felt the need to explain further, "To put it simply, I don't want to draft kids for this war; I want a volunteer army for this educational battle."

"I get you a hundred percent," Shannon said. "So when does your school tour start Dr. Branch?" he asked.

"Tomorrow," Dr. Branch said, and Shannon just shook his head.

"OK, ladies and gentlemen, let me get your attention . . . Everyone please calm down." Ms. Patty Smith trying to get her students to quiet the teenage commotion spoke a little louder next time, "Ladies and gentlemen . . . Please quiet down." Ms. Patty was a short, pudgy, dark-skinned lady that spoke with a polite tone. This impeccably polite demeanor hid her darker side that had only been seen by her problem students. With a dimply smile and glasses hanging on the bottom of her nose, she raised her voice at her chaotic students that had piled in. "OK guys . . . It's time to get started." She stood behind a podium within a high school auditorium, speaking firmly into the microphone. She was the high school's principal, and she was there to introduce Dr. Branch. She continued, "All right students . . . Keshon, please have a seat . . . Get off of the phone, Rebe . . . OK . . . Now, hello students of Vashon High. I know this is a surprise auditorium session we're having now, so thank you and the teachers for taking time out of your busy schedules for this. From what I understand, it shouldn't be long at all. Please pay attention to who I present to you today, ladies and gentlemen. He is providing a rare and interesting opportunity. Well with no further ado, I bring Dr. Trenton Branch to the stage." She clapped as she backed away, with a few of the kids joining in with their own applause.

Dr. Branch entered the stage from behind the curtain. No student had seen him until that moment. Dr. Branch shook Ms. Patty Smith's hand and walked to the podium. He wore a navy blue suit with a stylish pair of Stacy Adams. The shirt was a pressed, pin-striped oxford with a tie that blended the ensemble into artistic gold. His face held a goatee trimmed to perfection with a head of hair cut with laser precision. He looked like a politician. He approached the podium with a smile and caught a couple of faces in the audience he recognized. Those faces certainly recognized him, and they instantly straightened in their seats and gave their undivided attention. Some were even elbowing their neighbors, encouraging them to do the same.

Dr. Branch stood erect, shining proud, giving an air of power without saying a word. His presence affected the youth somehow for they all silently waited on his words. Some of the teachers were already part of his pseudo-socialistic system, so they knew him. And a few of the male teachers where actually in the process of joining team Twenty-Six, so they knew of his oratory prowess.

Dr. Branch started, "Hello fine students of Vashon High. I hope you all are well and fine. I'm sure you are: young bodies and all." Only the faculty laughed. He continued by getting straight to the point, "I am here to present to you all an opportunity of a lifetime. Before I do that, I will first inform you of the change that is occurring within our beautiful city of St. Louis. Then I will speak on the opportunity, which will not only affect you and your community today, but this opportunity I bring will impact future generations as well."

Dr. Branch continued, "Young ladies and gentlemen, I know that right now your concerns are elsewhere, and education is at the bottom of that list. Listening to me right now may even be a chore for some of you." He stopped after that last sentence, looked down, and shook his head. His planned speech wasn't feeling right. His soul encouraged him to take his subject elsewhere. Dr. Branch looked at the faculty lining the walls of the auditorium, some sitting in reserved teacher seating, and asked them a question, "Is it OK if I get real for a moment. I have some things I want to tell the students, but I know the truth can hurt." Without waiting for a response, he presented the truth, "My young brothers and sisters, do you know that you are the most despised people on the face of the earth?" That caught the attention of the audience, and he continued, "Everyone calls you lazy, shifty, untrustworthy, reckless, violent, dangerous, animalistic, ignorant, and incapable of learning at an equivalent pace as everyone else on the globe. They see you and they want to run away. They see you and they want to close their doors. They see you and police are called. No one wants a group of young black teenagers anywhere around them. The reputation that follows you all is horrendous. What really compounds the issue is that we as older black folk tend to feel the same way about our youth. We look at you in disgust, we fear and loathe you. We drive past our children on the street and feel nothing but disappointment. That needs to stop."

He had the crowd's undivided attention after that bit of ranting. Dr. Branch spoke as he always did: full of power and with just the right amount of flare. He never had a problem keeping the audience's attention when they were adults; it appeared that he held teens under that same trance. He stayed on the hate subject as he said more, "If you all think I am joking regarding everyone hating you, let me say that I am not. And I just don't mean America. Please believe that nations across the globe, large and small, hate you. And they don't even know you. I am serious. You can grab a native-born African that looks exactly like you, and he will choose to live around all whites before dealing with people that share that all-important feature. Think about that for a moment. This man from another country would rather place himself among whites instead of gravitating toward people who resemble his likeness. That is insane and should help you all see my point."

Dr. Branch explained the reasoning behind international hate, "First off, whether it's the media or the movies, other nationalities get their opinions of the U.S. from watching American TV. Things are slowly improving, yet the only thing most foreigners have seen throughout America's Television history regarding black people is that we rob, sell drugs, fight, kill, and participate in loads of debauchery. Though some of us do indulge in these heinous activities, an entire ethic group should not be so blanketed. Foreigners can't understand that, so they have taken America's hate of black people and made it their own. For instance, I just read an article about how Japanese people believe that blacks are an intellectually inferior race. Conversely, they feel that whites are superior in almost all aspects."

Staying on the same point, Dr. Branch harped on, "Oh you all still don't believe that the world hates you? OK let me tell you a quick story that taught me how I was seen. This should really fortify my point too."

He provided his anecdote, "In college most foreigners shied away from me – always keeping a safe distance between us. Yet I met some people from other countries that were nicer than nice. Anyway, I reached a point of extreme curiosity. I had to know why so many foreigners ran past me. So I spoke to people from numerous countries and asked the same question. Why do your people treat me as though I have the bubonic plague? Every person I asked that was willing to answer provided the same truth. In their countries, we are seen as the most violent people on the planet. What makes matters worse is that when they enter our country and go through customs . . . you all know what customs is?" Most of the kids shook their heads no, with some saying no, so he explained, "Customs is an agency that is responsible for the people and the merchandise that come in and leave our country. So they are like the gatekeepers. You all understand?" They all nodded, and Dr. Branch enjoyed providing the little sidebar. He returned to his story, "So as I was saying, foreigners enter our country, and they have to pass through customs. And the one piece of advice that they receive while entering our fine United States is pretty straightforward and quite brutal. The customs agents would tell the foreigners that black people equal danger. If you are around a black person, you are around danger."

The end of Dr. Branch's story caused an outburst of vociferations. Dr. Branch smiled at the emotional response and was elated to have the kids so absorbed. The lure was out there, and they bit, it was time to reel them in. He spoke more, "Do you know what is worse than everything I just told you? What is worse than everything I just said is that . . . you hate yourselves . . . We hate ourselves." He had to get a little louder for there were some kids expressing their disagreement. "Yes, you do . . . yes, you do. No, don't deny it . . . OK . . . OK . . ." Because the kids began to feel the need to participate, Dr. Branch waved his hands, signaling the crowd to quiet. Eventually they did, then he continued, "All right, listen to me now. I know you think you love yourself, but loving yourself would force you all to do so much better . . . to want so much better . . . to be so much better. If you . . . scratch that . . . if we loved ourselves, we wouldn't allow people to have the ammunition to form those opinions. But you know what, we do. We do make ourselves look bad. Young ladies and gentlemen, let me share a fact with you. If we look at the top ten places in the country that have earned the title of murder capitals, they are predominantly black. We make up 12 percent of the country, yet we make up more than 60 percent of the murders. And 95 percent of the people we murder look just like the man in the mirror. So I say again, we hate ourselves. Otherwise, we all would have stood up and stopped this bullshit a long time ago." Dr. Branch cursed on purpose, and it caused the kids to sit at the edge of their seats.

Dr. Branch then spoke on the change, "This is why here, now, we have to stop this insanity. It is time to truly fix what is broken. And that is what I and a team of men have been doing. We have come together to stop all of this destruction and violence. We have also come together to beautify our neighborhoods and give our people the much needed emotional support that's lacking in our community. And most importantly, we have come to revamp the educational system and turn you all into the young black men and women you were meant to be . . . the young black men and women you are supposed to be . . . the young black men and women that we need you to be." The crowd was bubbling with rabid emotion. The excitement in the air felt like electricity coursing through everyone's nervous system. The entire auditorium felt it. Dr. Branch new it was time to let them release that energy, and he continued by starting slow then reaching a fevered crescendo unlike he'd ever done before, "By fixing all of those things . . . by giving you what you all need to be the successful shining stars that you are meant to be . . . by being better parents, teachers, and leaders . . . we will start to see that love for ourselves. That love of self will start like a small flame. But we will continue to feed that flame, and that self love will grow and grow and grow until it is a roaring inferno unable to be extinguished by anything. We will love ourselves like no other race has ever loved itself. And when that time comes, when we can look in that mirror and really love what we see. We won't care what other countries feel about us, and we won't care what America feels about us. We won't care what they write about us in the papers or over the Internet. We won't care about how we're portrayed on TV. When that time comes, we can stand proud all together and say screw you all." Dr. Branch was speaking very loudly by now, and some of the kids were on there feet, unable to contain the flow of power they felt by his words. He spoke on with a demand, "Stand up . . . raise your middle fingers to the world."

The kids stood up as soon as he said, but when he said his last bit, a lot of them froze. A few of the students happily obliged and held their hands to the sky with their middle fingers pointing upward. The teachers looked at the principal, the students looked at the teacher, and the principal looked at Dr. Branch.

Regardless of everyone's shock, the energy was too hard to deny, and when Dr. Branch said to Ms. Patty Smith and the faculty, "You too, we are all in this together. It's us against the world."

Ms. Patty Smith led the crowd with the crude gesture after she stood to her feet. Then everyone followed in suit.

Dr. Branch exclaimed, "We don't care what anyone thinks about us. It is us against the world. It is us united against everyone else. You know what I say . . . fuck the world."

The crowd raised their hands higher and roared. Some people stopped flipping the world the bird and applauded. Some of the more undisciplined students echoed Dr. Branch, yelling out the same obscenity. Because Dr. Branch didn't want to stop the celebration, the hyper commotion rang for almost two minutes. Dr. Branch watched the kids all jumping around, joined on one accord, and the scene began to play in his mind in slow motion. He thought about his favorite quote, "He alone who owns the youth gains the future," The man who provided that quote was no saint, but he spoke succinct logic. It was time to bring it home.

He spoke directly into the microphone loudly, attempting to speak over the chaos, "All right, everyone, all right, everyone . . ." He grabbed their attention then said, "OK, time to sit back down . . . down everyone." Everyone eventually obeyed, and the auditorium quieted. He continued, "You know all of that is possible. It is not a dream. It is actually taking place as we speak. The neighborhoods are changing; some of you may have already seen us in action. Some of you may have even seen our finished work. My point . . . you all can start helping us right now. How? Start doing better in school. Take your education seriously. Give your teachers your best effort. Make these standardized tests your bitch. Take pride in the way your school looks. Step it up, guys." Dr. Branch saw some distant eyes, he didn't want to lose anyone, so he said, "Look, I know what you are thinking: I came up here, got you all hype just to tell you to do better in school. Then I'm going to leave here and not think twice about you all ever again. Well that is wrong. I mean what I say, and like I said, it is our job to give you the resources you all need to be the people we need you to be." Dr. Branch finally got to his point, "One of these resources is a new school. This new school will have all of the newest and finest equipment our small supply of money can buy. Going to this school will guarantee that you reach your full potential academically and artistically. Let me warn you before you guys run to the application table. This school is not for everyone. Only the people who are ready to sacrifice their lives for the greater good of their people should apply. I say that because this school will expect a lot from you. The workload will be unbelievable. The curriculum will be on a college level. You will be required to become fluent in another language, and the only sports that are played at this school will be for exercise purposes only."

"I know it doesn't sound too enticing, and that's good. Like I said, this school is not for everyone. Now don't get me wrong, we expect big things from all of our public schools starting with you students sitting in those seats. Vashon High will receive everything it needs to create the brightest minds America can offer, but this new school is going to be on another level. We only want to populate the classrooms with our brightest and most self-sacrificing children, students who are willing to do three to four hours of homework a night. Just know that when you graduate from this school, you will leave capable of teaching your professors how to teach their classes." Dr. Branch chuckled while saying, "I'm just kidding, you won't be that smart, but you will be more prepared than 99 percent of the other kids leaving any American high school."

Dr. Branch looked out at the kids and said, "Thank you all so much for having me here today. Thank you, Vashon, for giving me your time and your attention. I see a bright future for each and every one of you. If I leave you with one thing to remember, it's this: you all have the power, never give that power to anyone else. I love you all, Vashon, be safe, and I am out of here."

Dr. Branch waved at the kids as he backed from the podium and watched as everyone gave him a standing ovation. He turned and shook Ms. Patty Smith's hand and exited behind the curtain. Ms. Patty approached the podium, gave the command to return to class, and then she joined Dr. Branch behind the curtain.

"Dr. Branch, I didn't know that you would use curse words," she told him.

Dr. Branch looked at the pudgy, dark-skinned woman with her dimpled smile and polite demeanor and thought that she was cute as a button. He then said to her, "Ms. Smith, I am so sorry. It's just that I really wanted to get and retain the kids' attention. And I know that kids tend to listen to adults more intently when a few cursed words are sparsely thrown about."

Ms. Patty Smith could do nothing but agree, "I understand. So you are giving this speech to every public school in the city."

"Yep," Dr. Branch answered, "If not this speech, I will say whatever is in my heart at that moment."

"That is astounding," she fawned, then she said, "And I have seen the neighborhoods that have been revamped. That was you?" she inquired.

"Not just me but a large group of men exactly like me," he told her.

"That is amazing. I heard something else, and if it's true, I would like to know more about it," she said.

"Oh yeah, what is it?" Dr. Branch asked.

"Um . . . I heard that you are part of some socialistic system, that if I give you half of my check, all of my bills will be paid. Is that true? If so, count me in. But that can't be real . . . Is it real?"

Dr. Branch just looked at her and smiled. They spoke for another thirty minutes, and Dr. Branch left the school only to drive directly to another one nearby. Dr. Branch did reach out to every public high school throughout the inner city, with his speech touching a lot of the kids. Before his tour was complete, Shannon Progress had already received over four hundred applications.

Sasha Miller woke up out of her bed excited. She couldn't believe her life. She thought she was in an eternal dream. Sasha was a cute, sassy fourteen-year-old girl. Her skin held a red hue, showing her Indian/ African heritage, and her curly cue rolls bounced over the top of her head. Blossoming, her breast began to perk and fill out, with her butt starting to gain some girth. For the first time in her short existence, that moment rising out of bed was the first she could ever remember truly being happy. A smile lit her face as she smelled breakfast cooking. She stretched and skipped her way to the shower. Before going under the water, she turned on the CD player, turning up the music loudly. With the great acoustics in the bathroom, "Unthinkable" by Alicia Keys reverberated throughout the small enclosed area. She stepped under the stream and allowed the hot water to roll down her young supple skin. She swayed her hips, dancing to the smooth melodic beat while rubbing soapy suds all over her body slowly. She calmed her slow belly dance and stood still, with her face directly under the spout, the water washing her clean from head to toe. She remained under the shower for what felt like hours as she flashed back to the past.

Now living with her mother, uncle, and her grandmother, she remembered when it was only her and the grandmother. During those times, she only saw her mother once every week or so. The same scenario would play itself out over and over. One night, her mother would come banging on the front door. The grandmother would slowly open it, and after a few choice words, would allow Sasha's mother entrance. Her mother would then go straight to Sasha's bed and crash. That was the routine. Her mother would stay away a week at a time on crack binges, and just when her body was about to give up, she would sleep the way of the dead. For a day and half, Sasha would sit by her mother as her mother's body caught up on required rest. This was the only time Sasha could talk to her, so Sasha would maintain hours of one-sided conversations with a living corpse. She would even read love stories to her mother as she snored aloud, hoping the comatose lady would retain some of the positive points. Sasha would do anything just to spend some time with the woman that birthed her. Even though her mother was a major burden, she wasn't the only hardship in Sasha's life.

Being a very bright girl, she yearned for intelligence, yet the school she attended wasn't conducive to her mental gift. Her classes were overrun with kids wanting to be cool. The teachers spent most of their time with these problem children, leaving her to learn for herself. With no guidance, no encouragement, nor any real mentors, she was destined to lose her affinity for learning.

She hated having to walk home from school. There was a group of much older boys that would always grab her and pinch her butt or touch her in other uncomfortable ways. There was also a giant vacant house that terrified her on the way home. She could always see herself getting raped and murdered in that abandoned building. Every day was a battle for young Sasha, and merely attempting to get a meager education forced her to traverse a ruthless route. Her one best friend was already pregnant at the age of fifteen, and her only other friend's main concern was fighting. Sasha hated her life . . . then . . . Now was a different story.

Now her mother worked downstairs cooking breakfast for Sasha and her grandmother. She thought about that – how one night there was a knock at the door. Sasha knew who it was and expected a replay of the typical scene. Except that night, things were very different. They started the same, with the grandmother slowly opening the door and throwing out some few choice words. Then something different happened. The grandmother stopped talking and stepped back with a worried look on her face. Her mother slowly entered the house, and Sasha got a strong whiff of something that she could only compare to the horrible smell of a dumpster on a hot day. Her mother looked the worse she had ever seen. Her mother wore clothes that were tattered, torn, and covered in filth. Incapable of processing the picture she saw, she cried. That was the only response her body could perform. Then Sasha looked into her mother's eyes and saw something she hadn't since she was a child – clarity. Her mother's soul belonged to the owner for the time being, and Sasha could see that fact staring into those clear eyes. Her mother only looked down sadly then made her way to the bathroom. Sasha could hear the tub filling with water. She waited by the bathroom door until she was sure her mother was in the water then knocked. She entered after receiving permission with a trash bag and gathered the disgusting rags lying on the floor. Her grandmother told her to throw them in the dumpster.

After her return from the alley, she made her way back into the bathroom with her mother. Her mother lay in the tub with the water to the top. She was covered in bubbles and looked comfortable with her eyes closed and her head tilted back. Sasha turned on the little radio hanging on the wall, and Alicia Keys's "Unthinkable" played softly. Sasha grabbed some shampoo and moved to the edge of the tub. She began lathering her mother's hair, helping the older woman cleanse the old dirt from her body completely. Her mother didn't look at Sasha in the eyes any that night nor did she say one word to her daughter. The mother only glared at the ceiling, with tears running down her cheeks into the bath water as Sasha massaged and cleaned her head. There is a part of Alicia Keys' song where she screams, "I'm ready". Though the song is about forbidden love, Sasha's mother continued to cry while repeating those lyrics over and over, "I'm ready . . . I'm ready."

From that moment on, her mother instantly became a serious part in her life. She had gotten a job and did all the motherly things Sasha had only witnessed on TV shows. Now her mother would drop her off at school every now and then. She would attend parents-teachers conferences. She had even played a role in getting Sasha into the new school she attended. Looking at the past and the present was a delight in Sasha's eyes, and she counted her blessings: her mother was present, the groping boys were no longer on the corner, and that creepy, vacant house was now remodeled and occupied. She now attended the new Inner-City Private School where her fellow classmates shared her fervor for learning, and the curriculum matched her IQ. Eventually, her uncle moved in for a short time to remodel their house, so the aesthetics of her living arrangements gradually improved. Everything in her life was wonderful. She had nothing to worry about, nothing to focus on but her grades and future, which allowed her to indulge in the childish things life had to offer.

She thanked God as she stepped out of the shower and replayed the song that reminded her of the day her mother returned to her life. The CD blasted Alicia Keys once more, and she continued her morning rituals until she joined her family for breakfast. Pancakes . . . today was going to be a good day for little Ms. Sasha Miller.

Sasha's story was not unusual. Team Twenty-Six's slow grind and the piece-mealed goal accomplishments brought an actual change to St. Louis neighborhoods street by street. Though everyone in the clean part of the city appreciated this spectacular difference, the people that benefitted the most were the children. Those same poor, angry, unfocused, black children began to exhibit signs of peace. Their stony hearts began to soften, giving rise to kids that longed for the freedom to enjoy their childhoods. No longer concerned with gang violence or a drug infestation, they began to show a readiness to learn and a respect for life. With a constant undertone of "them against the world," they all united under one flag. This change didn't only occur with the kids that attended the new Inner-City Private School. This change affected every other kid under the protection of the Twenty-Six.

Nearing the end of the first year of being in charge, Shannon Progress was astounded by how well the school had performed. He didn't know that the city held so many bright kids. He felt bad thinking about all of the intelligent boys and girls lost to streets in the past. Well, no longer.

Dr. Branch had not only provided a class A educational opportunity to the youth, but also safe streets to use while traveling to their respective schools. Shannon saw what these kids were capable of when able to focus on learning and not survival, and what he saw impressed him.

The beginning was a bit of a trial. As the applications poured in, Shannon realized far more children than expected wanted to attend the new school. After much consideration and deliberating with his team, he finally gave Dr. Branch his opinion. He felt the school should start with a large freshmen and sophomore pool, with no juniors or seniors. He explained that he felt uncomfortable graduating seniors from a supposed prestigious school without showing the correct aptitude, and that juniors wouldn't have the time to adapt to the curriculum. He encouraged Dr. Branch to fill the school with the underclass and train them. Dr. Branch agreed, and that's what they did.

The Inner-City Private School opened with five hundred students – two hundred fifty freshmen and two hundred fifty sophomores. The kids started with standardized test to give the faculty a bearing on what level of intelligence they were working with. The results were disappointing. The kids all scored well below what was expected.

With a speed course in the basics and a lot of really hard work by a lot of kids, they caught up and caught on fast. The curriculum Shannon's Inner-City Private School presented was top notch, and only top notch learners could keep up. A few of the kids could not handle the work load and opted to return to their old schools. After weeding out the incapable and removing the beginner's jitters, his first students accepted the challenging curriculum and excelled. With the elite faculty along with an exquisite facility, the kids quickly realized that they were receiving the best resources possible. Appreciating that fact, the kids spent tireless hours at the school and at home studying constantly. Shannon told the kids that their goal was to improve their scores on the standardized test by 10 percent.

At the end of year one for the Inner-City Private School, an auditorium session was held. The faculty and the kids waited in their seats for an important announcement coming from Shannon Progress. He told them that before the summer started and the school ended, he just wanted to let them know that they did very well on their standardized test. He told them that not only did they far exceed every city school in all of St. Louis in their first year of existence, but their test results had improved by 35 percent. The crowd was emphatic. He let them know that he expected better the next year. The school year ended with much fan fare and even a news story.

By the end of year two, the standardized test showed interesting results. Though the scores were still high, some of the kids were showing serious growth in some areas while staying somewhat stagnant in others. That is when Shannon's teaching style came to light. The St. Louis board of education was then informed about his new way of teaching high school students.

This new teaching style was built on strength finding. That is what the first year was all about. The faculty studied their students more than the students studied their homework. The teachers then provided a detailed list of information on each student. This information provided the strength of each and every kid. Soon it was understood that every student wasn't going to be good at history, but if he had a propensity for math, then focus his learning in that direction. Some students had really hard times grasping mathematical concepts, but they were able to write well above their grade level. Those students would get a basic math education while perfecting their reading and writing skills.

A kid once had geometry, algebra, and trigonometry all in one semester, with his friend taking multiple English classes because that is where he showed promise. At the end of that second school year, the standardized test showed that while some students scores were average in certain areas, their scores in other areas were above most of Missouri's high school seniors. A basic level of all classes was necessary for each student to learn, but the advanced, specialized classes were only given to the kids that showed a natural ability in that respective discipline.

By the end of year two, the Inner-City Private High School contained some of the smartest kids in Missouri. Because fluency in another language was required before graduation, every kid held a duel focus. They had their primary major, being in a core study area such as math, English, history, or science. On top of their major, they were required to choose a foreign language to study. So after two years of the rigorous course load, kids were capable of speaking to one another in a language other than their native tongue. Some of the kids spoke rough Spanish to their classmates, while others spoke bad French, some spoke a little Swahili, and a few ventured off into Italian, German, Chinese, and even Arabic. As Shannon canvassed his school, he would here a plethora of languages spoken while passing his students. If he closed his eyes and walked around the building, he would have believed that he worked in an international center. His kids constantly impressed him. He could only tell himself that Dr. Branch was right.

The teachers all submitted to the new socialistic economic system and lived within the city. A lot of the teachers were very apprehensive about moving to St. Louis when first recruited. Most of them were well aware of the negative stigma attached to the city: number one crime rate in the country, number one murder capital in the country, as well as a city with a high STD infection rate. Numerous members of the teacher influx had children, and they did not want to subject their progeny to the dangerous inner-city lifestyle. The teachers were then given tours of the new school, which coincided with a neighborhood tour, and they saw and understood the change that had taken place. Teachers new to the area couldn't believe that the north side of the city was ever a bad place for it looked so peaceful and pristine. The teachers quickly understood the goal accomplished by Dr. Branch and his team. They also appreciated and loved the opportunity to be a part of something so monumental.

With the news of the new school's extreme success traveling across the entire city, everyone began to feel responsible. The parents of these hard working kids were amazed to hear their kids now speaking far more properly than they had ever heard before (at times even correcting their parents' broken English). The parents were also shocked when hearing their children speaking their new languages with slight skill. The black adults throughout the city began to look at the kids with hope instead of dread. Adults no longer shied away from the inner-city youth and instead began taking pride in their community's youth while claiming responsibility for their profound change.

With a strong anti-litter rule in effect, the city stayed clean. Everyone worked to keep their neighborhoods trash free. Adults did there part and were amazed to see the kids discard all of their waste in the proper containers as well. What cemented the change in the youth's attitude was a video captured of a random teenager walking down the street. This teen saw a peace of paper floating past him, and he took the time to catch the paper, ball it up, and put it in his pocket. Putting the trash in his pocket was such a small thing, but it had never been done before by a black teen voluntarily. That video went viral, truly showing the change in a mind-set that existed throughout the city. Young and old, black American's began to unite. Change occurred slowly throughout the city, but the success of the Inner-City Private High School became a catalyst that sped the process up substantially.

Once the news of the school's success reached the philanthropist that volunteered money to get the school started, they wanted to give more. Some even wanted to talk to Dr. Branch about opening similar schools in other cities. Dr. Branch certainly accepted all donations from anyone willing to give, but he informed the hopefuls that his school was a success for numerous reasons. He explained that his students not only received a high-priced building, but they also received a good environment in which to learn. He explained further that his kids had been united with family; they now had clean, safe streets to walk through, and that they no longer had adult-level stresses clouding their immature brains. And most importantly, his children had a new mind-set. Only with all of these things working together could any other city ever expect to affect their black children living in the ghetto. Regardless of Dr. Branch's refusal to move his school idea across state lines, the philanthropist continued to support the Inner-City Private School within St. Louis with more large donations. After a newscast brought the school's many instant successes into light, wealthy white people for the first time wanted to also provide monetary support. Dr. Branch happily accepted their money as well. He took care of his school, but he spread the money to the poorer school districts within the city as well.

Dr. Branch was elated at the results of his schooling system. Revamping the educational system for the young black kids was the most important endeavor in his eyes, and finally seeing some results in that area filled his heart with joy. When Dr. Branch thought back about the inception of his team, he remembered it was all about the kids. The ultimate reason for all of their hard work was to ensure that no other kids would lose their life to senseless violence. He knew education was the key. He put plans in motion, and it all was coming to fruition. What truly amazed Dr. Branch was to see that once the school opened, the cleaning of the city became easier. Things moved faster: more people were willing to help beautify their areas without coercion, more kids stopped banging or selling drugs without being touched by team CH, and the positivity slowly trickled throughout the city. It was something about the youth. Once they joined in a united front, the idea of uplifting the city spread like a virus from one street to the next. Dr. Branch didn't really understand how the school's success charged everyone throughout the city, but it did. He wouldn't complain; he was happy things turned out the way they did.

New City

Four years after team Twenty-Six moved into the city and began their endeavor, Dr. Branch stopped giving his weekly sermons. He only gave a speech once a month. This Thursday, he sat at one of the largest churches in all of St. Louis and gathered himself for one of the most important presentations he would ever give. The audience was in the thousands, and the church was beyond its maximum occupancy. No one cared. Because Dr. Branch only spoke once a month, people couldn't wait to hear their leader recharge them as he always did. His candid opinions and his sage advice seemed to come from some higher power, and the people reveled in his aura.

Dr. Branch sat in an office within the church with his two body guards at the ready.

"I never thought you guys would ever see me in a Catholic church," Dr. Branch said jokingly. Anthum and Mathew chuckled slightly, as he continued, "But this is the biggest church in the city. The only place that could possibly support the mass of people I am expecting today." He then said, "They wanted to charge me for the night, but when I told them who I was and what was going on, they quickly recanted."

"Of course they didn't charge you," Anthum said, then he finished with, "You just don't know the power you now possess, Dr. Branch."

"The power we possess," Dr. Branch corrected, "I would be nothing without having the backing of an entire city."

The men agreed. They rarely debated with Dr. Branch, and as of the last year, after seeing the city's process almost complete, they totally ceased altogether. It was understood from the beginning that Dr. Branch had the final say, but his team would still offer other options. As of late, whenever Dr. Branch offered an idea, there was no opposition at all. Even Shannon Progress and Doubting Thomas rode the wave that was Dr. Branch.

"You know that all of this is amazing, don't you, Dr. Branch?" Mathew asked

"Yeah," Anthum said, backing his partner, "Did you really think things would get better? Did you really think that you would make such a huge impact?"

"I tell you guys what, if I hear 'you' one more time, you two will bring out the beast in me," Dr. Branch said still joking.

"OK, Dr. Branch, you are right . . . we," Anthum said, looking at Mathew and smiling. He wouldn't dare debate with the man that constantly impressed him, so he corrected himself, "Did you really think we would make such a huge impact? Did you ever see this happening, Dr. Branch?"

Because the questions they asked coincided with the subject of his presentation, he leaned back and smiled. He thought deeply then answered, "Honestly, I truly didn't see results occurring the way they did. Though things have been very difficult and the road has been full of divots. I did expect a lot more opposition and hardship. Watching our people readily join this revolution amazed me immensely. But it just showed us all something. It showed us that our people were tired. They are tired. For a long time, our people have been drinking from the fountain of pain and destruction. We brought them clean water, and in the past they would have continued drinking the tainted solution with clean water as an obvious alternative. I believe that right here, right now, our people were finally fed up. And I believe that they were ready to dive headfirst into the crystal clear fountain spring that we have provided, my friends." He thought more then said, "So to answer you guys' question, I have to admit I didn't see us having success. But I was going to die trying, my friends."

"So were we, Dr. Branch," Mathew said, and Anthum nodded in agreement.

"OK, Dr. Branch, I guess we better not keep your fans waiting. The crowd can get a little restless if their star ain't out there to perform on time," Anthum said sarcastically.

Dr. Branch gave Anthum a cold stare, and everyone in the office broke out into a good hearty laugh. Just what Dr. Branch needed to relax his soul. Mathew opened the door, and Anthum walked out first followed by Dr. Branch. Dr. Branch walked down the hall of the huge ornate church sandwiched between his protectors, listening to the roar of the crowd through the walls. Nothing about his process had changed in his four years of speaking. He never used an introducer nor did he include music when coming out. He would simply enter the stage from the back door, surprising the audience.

Dr. Branch walked out to the pulpit followed by his centurions, and the crowd erupted. Mathew and Anthum quickly grabbed the nearest seats to the podium and watched the crowd intently. Dr. Branch wouldn't dare sit in the gaudy seats. They represented everything he hated about religion . . . a bunch of money spent on unimportant things . . . a bunch of contradictions.

Dr. Branch stood there, hands atop the podium, waiting on the crowd to quiet. They did eventually and those that could, sat down. Newer members of the Twenty-Six all stood. The team was enormous and the entire lower wall was covered with the neophytes. The new members all stood shoulder to shoulder with their backs against the wall. They were so close together that one couldn't tell where one shoulder began and the other ended. Dr. Branch looked out into the audience and waited to hear absolute silence. Soon he did. That is when he began.

"How is everyone doing tonight?" Dr. Branch started with his typical greeting. The crowd quickly responded, and he continued with his speech, "It sounds like everyone is doing well. That is what I like to hear. Me . . . I am doing wonderful. Why, you may ask? Well today I sat back and thought about where my team and I started, and then I thought about where we are. When I think about that, it just makes me happy. Let me explain to everyone in here why it makes me so happy and just maybe it will make you all happy too."

"I will start with my memories. Whenever I ventured to the city in the past, I remember seeing gangbangers and drug dealers on every street I passed. There was a time I drove by a low-budget apartment complex and saw enough trash sprawled about to fill three, five-gallon trash bags. I remember hearing these kids out here showing no respect to adults. Even worse, I could see that the adults didn't deserve their respect. I remember seeing vacant homes, transients lying about, and people with no values. I can recall a vast array of problematic situations plaguing our city. I know you all can easily remember those horrible things too. Then a few men decided to become superheroes and save our city."

After the cheers, he then said, "My team and I started with one goal in mind. It was to make the streets safe for our kids. Well I look out at our city, and I think it is far safer than it has ever been. Yet I must confess that accomplishment isn't what makes me happy. It's this right here." Dr. Branch held his hands out to the crowd and continued, "It's looking out into an audience of black men that love themselves. For the first time in my life I can honestly say that most of the black men in St. Louis are on one accord; we are united in our cause. What is our cause? It is to continue to greatly improve the lifestyle of every black American living in this city and soon the country. It is to show that we can keep our money in house. It is to remind everyone of priorities. It is to remove that innate love of that all mighty dollar."

"Let me ask, do you all still love money?" The crowd answered "No". He continued, "Do you all need that new 500 Benz?" The crowd answered "No". He asked another question, "Do you need to spend 400 dollars on a pair of pants?" The crowd said, "No" again, he asked one more question, "So what is the most important thing out here?" The crowd answered, "We are." He then said, "Exactly . . . We are."

Dr. Branch then jumped subjects. "These improvements and this change in mind-set didn't come overnight nor did it happen by sitting back praying for a change. No . . . The many blessings bestowed upon us came from hard work and a united front. I think you all need to hear some examples of the mini-miracles we have going on right now. Sit back and listen."

Dr. Branch spoke about the many blessings, "Guys, do you know that we now have our own little thriving economy? Really, our part of the city is bringing in money. Let me tell you how we have caused our neighborhood's economy to grow. From the beginning, we encouraged our people to start buying all of their needs from their neighbors. We said: go get your groceries from Pop's Sursave, go get your clothes from the small black-owned clothing stores, go get your food from the black-owned soul food restaurants, go get your car repaired at Old Jake's Auto repair, go get your home repairs done by our carpenters, and so on and so forth. Well, you all listened and you all complied. Now let's look at the thriving businesses within our city because of that one sacrifice."

Dr. Branch went down the list of successful black-owned businesses. "You all remember how Pop's Sursave was a little, dimly lit, hole in the wall, imitating a grocery store." The owner was actually in attendance and yelled out, "Aww come on, it wasn't that bad." And the crowd roared with laughter. Dr. Branch heard him too and joined in the laughter. Knowing the owner personally, Dr. Branch then said, "It wasn't that bad, but you got to admit, Pop, your store did need some serious improvements." The old, gray-haired man nodded, and Dr. Branch continued, "With everyone supporting his store, he was able to improve it, hire a lot more people, and now that store rivals any Shnuck's or Dierberg's. Something you guy's probably didn't know is that Pop receives 85 percent of his supplies from black-owned farms, being shipped by black-owned truckers. Now Pop is making more money than he ever made." Dr. Branch made eye contact with Pop and said, "Let me borrow a dollar, Pop." The crowd laughed aloud again.

Dr. Branch stayed on topic, "All right, you all may not know the Francis brothers. They're out in the crowd somewhere being incognito. I really like their style because they have always been some really nice, low-key type of fellows. They had the right idea. They wanted to encourage people to wear nice clothes that didn't carry someone's name on it, so they opened a store called 'No Names'. It was a very thoughtful idea, but you all know we needed to see a Polo logo or a Tommy Hilfiger crest on our shirts. Well, once we all stopped caring about that and started keeping the money in house, their store grew faster than what they were ready for. They bought out the other two neighboring stores, and now, they own that entire plaza. And you know what's even better? They get most of their clothes from people in our neighborhood. Yeah, you are wearing jeans actually made by Ms. Selma Johnson. The demand grew so great for her clothing line that she needed to hire five of her girlfriends to keep up. Those bad dresses that we all like to see our wives in, those are coming from my little cousin Roseanne. That was always her dream. Now she makes dresses day and night and is happy as a clam. She actually had to hire people as well."

Dr. Branch continued, making the explanations shorter, "Luke Chodi, my dear friend and one of the first on team Twenty-Six, has a carpentry business with over fifty men under him. There isn't one day that all of his men aren't working. Business is doing well for Luke."

"I already mentioned Old Jake's Auto repair. So many of us frequented his shop that he had to hire ten new men. Those new hires come from our neighborhood. His store grew, and he is doing quite well. Wouldn't you say so Mr. Jake?" Mr. Jake Salone nodded.

"We stopped eating McDonald's every night and started only eating at the few black-owned restaurants in our neighborhood. Those restaurants have thrived, hiring more and adding our people to the workforce, lowering our unemployment rate."

Dr. Branch then said, "Now this is the thing that delights me. I love to show the connection. It's quite simple. Just listen and follow. The owners of each of the businesses I named are all a part of our system. So no matter how much money they make, they give half of it back to us. There are no loopholes for them, and there is no dirty accounting they can perform. They willingly give half of their profits back to us. They are doing damn well financially, and it is because of us that they are doing so well. Yet we are all secure because of them. It's because of them that your kids will get a college education. It's because of them that we all never have to worry about our essential bills. Do you all see the connection? They do good . . . we do good . . . It's that simple."

He went to another topic, "Let's talk about education. It was obvious that our kids had no interest in the curriculum the system provided, so we made our own. We used this new curriculum as a foundation for the new school we built. I am sure you heard about it or even read it in the *Post Dispatch*. Our new school, dubbed the first of its kind, is the one and only Inner-City Private School. If you haven't seen the kids that attend this school, you are in for the shock of your life. These kids are excelling unlike any group of kids you have seen in your lifetime. What we have always known is finally coming to sight. We knew . . . Well, I certainly knew that our young brothers and sisters are capable of exceptional feats. I am sure you all saw the talent of each and everyone, covered by the cool. Their gifts stifled by decades of negative brainwashing. Things are different now, visit our school and see children that belong to us. See a young brain that only has room for education and true growth."

He then said, "These are the kids that have accepted the task of changing the face of black America. They have opted to carry this heavy load and be the first to step up. They work hard in school while accepting many of our lifestyle challenges."

Seeing some confused faces, he explained his point further, "A good example of one of our challenges to the children is to abstain from all forms of media for a month. The only form of entertainment they are allowed is book reading or listening to music, yet the piece of music must come from a Classical or Jazz selection. Once a year, our children and faculty – the entire school – unplugs all of its devices and turn off all electronics. For a complete month, they study their lessons, they read good books, they listen to great music, they have wonderful conversations, and they learn. It's amazing to see our kids a month later no longer inundated with media's mental garbage. Their eyes truly brighten, their shackles are removed, and they relax. Unrestrained by a need to do what the TV tells them, you begin to see individuals. And they are awesome.

"I can talk about that school forever, but I won't. I will only bore you with the facts. Three years after the school began, our kids have already outdone 80 percent of their peers throughout the state of Missouri. With standardized testing being the only form of comparison, it's the primary bases in which our students are judged. Our students have shown an average increase of thirty-five points on those tests gaining great attention from the board of education. And you all want to know what's funny? They want to contribute money to the school now. They want to take credit for this vast improvement. Well like I said from the beginning, no one will have the right to say they changed black America but black America. When we needed their money, they refused. What makes them think we want it now.

"Our school and our kids have greatly affected the community. Now other public schools have adapted their curriculum style to somewhat mock ours, and their scores have vastly improved as well. Their improved scores have granted them their much needed financial support."

Dr. Branch went to another subject, "There is no longer a need to leave the city. Isn't that great? If you start doing well, you don't feel the need to leave your people. See, that's the love I am talking about. You love your brothers and sisters now. No need to venture out to an area with people that don't want you around them in the first place. You are comfortable where you are, and you are around like-minded people. It's a wonderful thing. Our neighborhoods are spotless, homes are looking new, and the trend is still spreading.

"I don't know if you guys have noticed the results of a new project initiated by our kids. During their month-long electronic hiatus, they banded together and formulated a plan. They came to their teachers who then went to their principal, who then came to me. We all then discussed the idea and agreed that it was great. The idea was agriculture. They wanted to begin planting in the large lots within our neighborhoods. We have tested the idea out, and if you go past Ms. Palmer's house on Cook Ave., you will see our first experiment, which I think was a roaring success.

"If you have never driven down Cook Ave., I will explain what it looked like then and what it looks like now. Cook Ave., like most streets on the North side of the city, contained beautiful homes worn and torn from years of neglect. In between a large volume of these homes sat vacant lots covered in broken glass, used condoms, contaminated needles, and other trash. After the neighborhood change, the homes were restored to their former beauty, and the vacant lots were cleared of all debris. Yet we all knew that those vacant lots would eventually have to be filled because they were the latest eyesore. Without any prompting, the kids approached their teacher with an idea of replacing the empty space with some form of crop. I was thinking of building homes in the empty spots. I actually liked their idea better."

He explained his lack of vision, "And I want you all to see where young untainted minds can at times see more clearly than our old ones. I thought about the money, more homes meant more money, right? The kids thought about the beauty. I would have never contemplated filling those empty spaces with agriculture. They brought a fresh new idea to the table, and it was actually better. When I realized I had to choose between money and beauty; you guys know beauty will win every time. Before I could ask, the kids said they would be the ones to tend to the large gardens, so we did it."

He then said, "Like I was saying, if you go pass Ms. Palmer's house on the 5200 block, you all will see a completed sample of their project. There was an empty space five houses wide between her and the neighbor. The kids toiled, and now there is a flower garden between the two houses. When spring comes, the flowers erupt, and the multicolored picture is breathtaking. A large garden filled with roses, tulips, orchids, and many other colorful flowers all between two large, old English homes." The crowd was stunned by the idea and the pictures in their head.

He continued with the same subject, "They gave me more ideas, so picture this, gentlemen: most of the empty lots in our neighborhood covered with sunflowers, peppers, fruits, vegetables, and other items. It will not only improve the aesthetics, but it will benefit our environment greatly. Sorry I am harping in one area, I just like to show how impressive our young minds are. They are our future, and it is now starting to look very bright."

Dr. Branch left the kid subject and spoke on the money aspect, "The vacant houses are being remedied. Either they are sound enough to be remodeled or they will be demolished. That has been in process, and it will spread. Look around the neighborhood, and you will see the change there. But because the accumulation of this property is the most expensive aspect of this endeavor, it has been moving the slowest – well, no longer. We now have the funds to really attack the vacant house crisis, and with every man's help, we will see each and every vacant home destroyed or rebuilt. There will be no eyesores in our beautiful city."

Dr. Branch continued, "Though the physical labor that we all are providing is vital to the change that has swept this city, I want you all to know that the money is crucial too. I think it's time that all of you know where it came from and where it will come from. The amount of money it has taken to achieve these goals has been immense. Though I hate to admit it, we could have done none of this without capital, so I want to credit the people that really donated to the cause. I solicited almost every black multimillionaire in the country. Many of them contributed to the school idea, but after seeing the change across the city, many more joined. I want you all to know that many of your ball players, your entertainers, and your elite businessmen supported our cause. I know this man doesn't want me to say his name, but we all know Melly, the rap sensation from right around the corner. Well, I was just informed that this brother has donated over 70 percent of his funds to this cause. He had already given us money for the schools when this endeavor was initiated, but after driving past his old neighborhood and seeing the huge difference, he wanted to give more. So he is on stage busting his ass because he knows that an entire neighborhood is living comfortably because of him. He epitomizes the attitude I encourage us all to have. He has a longing to help his fellow man more than anything in the world.

"We will continue to receive support from our millionaires, but something else has happened that greatly added to our stockpile of wealth. We began a business about four years ago, Satelite Sciences. I am sure you all have heard of it; a few of you work there. Our company has hired people throughout St. Louis City as the car industry kept the city of Detroit working. To accommodate for the newly acquired massive workforce increase, we have expanded and reopened factories in the city. Industry, my brothers. We have also implemented a new work strategy, which allows us to triple our workforce. We only require our workers to work five hour days."

The audience gasped; he continued, "Yep, studies have shown that throughout an eight-hour workday, the average person only works five of those eight. So we use that to make our workplace more efficient while spreading employment opportunity to more people from our neighborhoods. We get three five-hour shifts from our crew a day. The first crew comes in at six. They work until eleven. The second crew comes in at ten to overlap the first crew, and they stay until four. Finally the third crew comes in at three, and they work until eight o'clock. Our workers love the idea. They love their environment. And they love their jobs. But there is one contingency, you have to donate fifteen hours a week to assist in the city's improvement.

"For example, I know Jesse. He comes in Monday at six, he works until eleven, and then he donates fifteen hours straight to the volunteering program. And though he is exhausted by the end of that Monday, for the rest of the week, the man leaves work at eleven, and the rest of the day is his. The rest of the week is his." Dr. Branch then asked, "Jesse, what do you do with the rest of your time?"

Jesse screamed from the audience, "Spend it with my kids, Dr. Branch."

"Exactly. Spend it with his kids. See, gentlemen, that is another philosophy that we need to take on. We work to live. We don't live to work. And there shouldn't be a select few of us who get to lie around enjoying what life has to offer, while the rest of us work our souls to death. If we all work together, if we all unite, that's less work per individual, that's just logical. That gives us individuals more time to do the things we enjoy. Indulge in the fruits that life has to offer. No man should work himself to death, unless that job is his passion, and unless that is what he truly wants to do."

He said again, "So Satelite Sciences is doing wonderful, and we have officially been included in the NY stock exchange for we are a part of the Fortune 100 club." The crowd roared with applause, he continued, "A portion of those profits will of course go to our workers and keep our business going, but we finally have the type of funds necessary to truly rebuild our city. That is where a large portion of our profits will go – right back to the city, right back to you all. We are one, and we all will celebrate this victory as one." The crowd erupted again.

Dr. Branch was getting ready to close, "All right, let's settle down, gentlemen, for I have one more very important subject to touch on. It's the effect that our change has on the rest of the city. I don't know if any of you thought about this, but with this change in attitude and environment comes a change in our governmental needs. We no longer need this huge police force. We no longer need all of these correctional facilities. We no longer need all of the judges and lawyers, especially now that we handle most of our own affairs. Really, we do, if I can get off subject for one second, I want to tell you about Mickey. She is a young lady living on Maffit with her two little girls. Well, she heard a crazy noise one night while sleeping, and instead of calling the police, she called her neighbors. The men in the area quickly gathered at two in the morning at her door and searched her surroundings. It turned out that the noise came from a falling branch that damaged her roof. Do you guys see my point? We no longer need the system; we rely on each other. No longer do we need to be policed by people that don't like us and truly don't care about us. We now keep ourselves in check."

He then made his point, "Because of this change, a lot of people have lost jobs and more are being removed every week. My sources from the downtown judicial system told me that a lot of the lawyers and judges had to move to other cities where the crime rates are still outlandish. The people that have made themselves rich off of institutionalizing our boys and girls are now being displaced, and the prison system changed its style as well. With so few of our boys feeding themselves to that beast, they are keeping their cells filled with prisoners from overpopulated penitentiaries from other states. Did you watch the news a few weeks ago regarding the layoffs that will hit the St. Louis City Police Department? The captain stood on camera and said, and I quote, 'In the current climate of the city, with the lack of crime and the potential for crime to be at an all-time low, I am sorry to say we will have to lay off half of the police force.' The captain spoke as though he hated to see the Negroes behaving themselves. Isn't that what police should hope for? That they successfully vanquish the crime, that their area is restored to a safe place, and that they are never needed because the people have learned the error of their ways? It should be the goal of every policeman. But it isn't. They need crime, violence, and fear to sustain their living. So why have a goal of success if your mortgage payments depend on failure. Well, no longer will that way of thinking affect our community. A huge police force is no longer needed, and our black police officers aren't worried . . . are you guys?"

There were "No's" shouted out from the crowd, including Mathew.

"Of course you aren't. Because 80 percent of the black police force is part of our economic system. Even if they were to be laid off, they will be taken care of. They don't have to worry about how their bills will be paid. Money is no longer a concern. No longer is it the reason behind everything we do. For the rest of America, it continues to be the sole purpose for every move made by man, and it's that reason that I say be on alert, my brothers. Our lack of hate has touched their pocket books, and I know that they are unhappy about that."

Dr. Branch was ready to close out, "All right, guys, like I said when I started this, I am happy. Hopefully, after everything I have told you all, you can leave here happy as well." The crowd erupted once more, and he finished, "Everyone please continue the work. Please continue the respect and love, and this city will one day rival New York and Los Angeles. We are getting more and more people wanting to move up here, Atlanta is no longer the black Mecca. Our city is getting more attractive, and it's because of each and every one of you out there."

"In closing, I just want to remind you guys that there is nothing more important than our people. Money is no longer our God, so don't worship it. And our children are once more ours. If we continue this righteous path that we are on, it will only get better from here. Good night, everybody, drive home safely."

The men jumped up instantly and gave their leader a standing ovation. Dr. Branch waved and offered a humble look that told the crowd that he didn't deserve their adoration. It just incited more applause and cheers. After it died down, as usual, Dr. Branch told members of team Twenty-Six to remain at the church, and he sent the others on their way. Another aspect of his speeches that hadn't changed was the energy he instilled in his audience, for the men that left as well as his team members that remained could barely sit. They all were so charged. The guys outside of the church remained a while longer, putting their own helpful plans together, and the men inside conferred about the latest achievements and their future aspirations.

The night concluded, and Dr. Branch walked out of the church with his two protectors at his side.

"Dr. Branch, great speech as usual," Mathew told his leader as the three men approached his truck.

Dr. Branch forbad the guys to open the door for him, so as he opened the backdoor himself, he said, "Thank you very much, my friend. I thought so myself." He hopped on the backseat, and the truck roared to life. He then finished his point, "I actually listened as I spoke, and hearing our accomplishments did make me happy."

The guys all laughed, and Dr. Branch said, "I'm hungry, guys. You guys hungry? Let's go get something to eat – my treat."

"Hell yeah I'm hungry," Anthum said, "You know I got to feed these," he finished by kissing one of his biceps, which brought on more laughter. He then said, "Have you guys heard about the new, nice steak restaurant on the corner of Kossuth?" Mathew and Dr. Branch shook their heads, and Anthum continued, "Well, it was just a regular house. Y'all remember that big house on the corner? Anyway, the owner of the house fixed it up and turned it into a dine-in restaurant. It's really nice too. He turned the rooms into little eating areas with like two or three tables in each. He has his kids waiting so each room has its own personal server at all times. The first time I went, I had a room and a server to myself. I damn near made the little dude cut my steak and feed it to me. If it was legal, he would have wiped my ass after I took a dump too." His audience was cracking up by now. Dr. Branch had gotten use to Anthum's crude humor and actually started to like it. Anthum completed his point, "Seriously, it is a really nice place and the steak is great. It is pricey though."

"It sounds like a plan," Mathew said.

"From the way it sounds, maybe I should go with my wife first," Dr. Branch thought aloud.

"Why don't we go pick her up now?" Mathew offered.

"Now why didn't I think of that? I can make it seem like you guys are chauffeuring us . . . hey it's a plan," Dr. Branch finished and then called his wife.

She accepted his offer, and the guys picked Christine up from the house. She sashayed down the steps looking Leena Horne elegant in her flowing beige, silk dress and hopped in the truck. Mathew drove through the city and made his way to their destination. Anthum was right, it was a nice place. The house was an original, yet it had a lot of work performed to restore it to its old glory.

The crew left the truck, with the protectors walking in front of the happy couple. They made their way to the front door and knocked. The door instantly opened, and a young girl dressed in a tight black dress let them in. They all stepped in and a cacophony of spices cooking tickled their olfactory nerves. Their mouths slightly salivated with anticipation. The girl announced herself as the hostess then told them that there was an hour wait. With disappointment apparent on their faces, Dr. Branch and his wife meandered over to the waiting area, which was nothing more than bench style seats within the foyer of the house.

"Where is the owner, li'l Mama?" Anthum whispered to the young girl.

"He's in the kitchen cooking, sir," she answered.

"Tell him Dr. Branch is out here and needs a place to sit," Anthum said.

The girl gave the supersized, dark-skinned man a contemptuous look then walked toward the kitchen. Within a minute, the owner busted out of the kitchen in a large apron and a chef's hat. He was a man that held all of his fat in his stomach. It poked out like he was pregnant.

"Dr. Branch . . . Dr. Branch. Welcome to my restaurant," the portly cook said as he walked over to Dr. Branch and his wife. He continued talking while grabbing Dr. Branch's hand and shaking, "Please forgive my daughter. She didn't recognize you." He looked at his girl and said, "What you doing making this man wait? He gets an instant table. Take him to the third floor. Sit him at the back window. Hurry now, girl." The older gentlemen slightly bowed with a smile and waited until Dr. Branch and his crew ascended the steps before saying, "I am going to make you all something very special. Don't worry about the menus." After that statement, the old man walked back into the kitchen.

The young girl led the crew up two flights of stairs to the small eastward room on the top floor. There was no door, and the room was comfortably decorated, with the chairs and small tables having a wooden, African motif.

The window was open, providing a slight breeze of fresh air as well as offering a view of downtown St. Louis. Anthum and Mathew sat at the table closest to the doorway, allowing Dr. Branch and Christine the window view. The married couple sat and stared at the lights given off by the many cars and buildings in the night scene. During the quiet, late-night dinner, Dr. Branch's phone rang, and he turned it to silent. Right after his rang, Mathew's and Anthum's smart phones buzzed to life, so he then advised his guards to do the same. The crew had their own waiter throughout the night, and they were fed the finest food the five star establishment had to offer.

After a great dessert and a couple of drinks, Dr. Branch, his wife, and the two bodyguards made their way down the steps of the house/restaurant. The owner met them at the bottom. They all showered the owner with compliments regarding his business and promised to return soon. They exited the fine establishment, and after getting inside of the truck, all of the men turned their phones back on. Each man looked at their phones with awed expressions then listened to their many messages.

"I have ten missed calls," Anthum said, "With ten messages."

"I got fourteen." Mathew said.

Dr. Branch looked up from his phone and said, "I have thirty missed calls and twenty-four messages. What the hell did we just miss?" Dr. Branch asked. "Well, hurry and get us home, guys, and listen to these messages on the way."

The men listened to their messages with every one saying something similar.

"Everybody's telling me to go listen to the news," Anthum said.

"Yeah I am getting that one along with a few others," Mathew offered.

Dr. Branch then said, "Yeah, I am getting those as well. But I am also getting the reason we should run to our TV sets. Apparently, there has been a murder within my district, and it is getting a lot of attention." Before Dr. Branch could say more, Mathew was pulling up to his house.

"Really?" Mathew asked. "You guys wanna roll to the scene and see if it's still active?"

Anthum quickly replied with an "Of course."

Dr. Branch looked into his wife's eyes and said, "No, guys, I am going to end my day right now. Whatever is going on is already done, so I am going to watch the news and call it a night, my friends."

"OK, Dr. Branch, you all have a safe night and call us if you need anything," Anthum said.

The couple slid out of the large SUV and held hands as they walked up the steps to their house. Upon entering, Dr. Branch attempted to make his way to the TV room when his wife grabbed his arm.

"Babe, come on up to the bed. We can watch the news together," Christine coaxed.

"Absolutely," Dr. Branch agreed and followed his wife to the bedroom.

They removed their clothes and rolled under the covers. Not wanting to seem too anxious, Dr. Branch allowed his wife to grab the remote and turn on the TV. She found the eleven o'clock news and increased the volume.

On the TV screen was a bald anchorman explaining the days return to chaos. The bald man informed the viewing audience of three young black boys shot to death on the north side of the city. Each murder appeared to happen in the same manner. Drive-bys were suspected, and each victim was left with a colored rag over the body insinuating gang violence. The anchorman went on to remind everyone that he had predicted that the city would return to its past violent ways.

The anchorman then passed the rest of the story to the reporters on scene. Each reporter shouted into the microphone with police cars behind them and CSI trucks in their camera shot. They sounded excited to finally have more deadly news to report. The reports provided the names of each of the recently deceased boys. And all three were known by Dr. Branch. They were old gang members changed by their time at CH HQ. The reporters said though the ex gang members were changed men, their past apparently came back, and their cocks came home to roost.

Dr. Branch watched it all in absolute anger. How could this happen? Right after such a great speech . . . such a great night with his family. Those boys all belonged to him, and now they were dead. Some one came to his protected land and slaughtered his soldiers. Who would have the audacity? The emotion welling in him left a blank expression on his face. His wife noticed and started to massage his scalp while reaching for the remote. Christine hit the power button, shutting down the TV, and continued massaging her husbands head. Dr. Branch slowly allowed the tension to leave his head, and he closed his eyes. He drifted into a dark sleep and dreamed the dreams of the tormented.

The next morning, he and his wife were both awakened by the door bell. When he turned over to his little digital clock, he saw the red 6:07 a.m. staring him in the face. He wondered who could be bothering him during his established down time. His wife turned over and groggily spoke.

"I will get it dear," she said more so out of habit than anything else because her legs didn't move.

"No worries, babe, stay in the bed. I will curse out whoever it is," he told his wife as he kissed her forehead.

"Yeah, you do that, sweetie," she said and turned over almost instantly returning to her REM state.

Dr. Branch put his legs into his brown khakis that lay crumbled on the side of the bed. He slid his feet into his fluffy house shoes and then staggered down the steps like a drunken man. He walked to the door and opened it without even looking out the window. What he saw woke him up instantly.

The sun barely peaked its edge over the horizon, and its rays offered little light, yet it was enough to show the wispy clouds in their slow dance across the open space. The soft cirrus clouds flowed across every color in the spectrum as the sky received its first bit of sunshine. The scene was picturesque, but Dr. Branch saw none of it. He only saw bright lights twinkling and large objects pointing at him. After a shake of the head to help wake his brain, he realized he was being attacked.

The attackers were reporters. He knew not why, but it appeared as though every reporter in St. Louis was at his doorstep that morning. Before he could open the screen door or say a word, he was hit with a bunch of people yammering at once. All he could hear was his name being yelled multiple times by different people wanting his attention.

"Dr. Trenton Branch . . . Dr. Trenton Branch . . ."

A few of the closest reporters stepped back, allowing Dr. Branch just enough space to open his screen door. He did, and without stepping out, he spoke softly.

"Excuse me, guys, what is going on here?" he said as the crowd quieted. He then asked, "Why am I a main attraction all of sudden?"

The reporter nearest to Dr. Branch, a biracial lady with her white features being the dominant phenotype, spoke directly to the man.

"Dr. Branch, this is Marcy Pennerman with Action Five Morning News. I am sure you've heard of me," she spoke flamboyantly. "Do you mind answering a few questions for me and the rest of St. Louis?" she fired off rapidly.

"Uhh . . .," Dr. Branch, so rarely caught off guard, was out of place. He was still half sleep, and his eyes were unfocused because of all the bright lights and camera flashes. He still didn't know why he was so popular all of a sudden. Never wanting to shy away from answering questions, he answered in the affirmative, "Yes, Ms. Marcy Pennerman."

"Do you know about the three boys murdered last night?"

"Yes, ma'am," he responded.

"How do you feel about that considering you are the honorary mayor of this city?" she said.

"Well, I don't know where you get your information, but I'm no politician, and it's a shame tha . . ."

She interrupted, "Everyone tells us that you are the reason for this new safe city, how do you feel now that it is falling back into its old ways?"

"Well, I don't think it's . . ."

"Do you feel like a failure? Like all of your work was for nothing?" she spat, interrupting again.

"A failure? Why would I . . ."

"Do you know the evidence that was found with the boys, Dr. Branch?" she asked, interrupting yet again.

"No, I just woke up, Ms . . . .," Dr. Branch growled, getting a tad perturbed.

"Two of the kids had books on sniper rifles and how to use them." She never allowed Dr. Branch to complete one statement as she continued, "The last kid had a book on bomb building. And if that isn't bad enough, they all had the same tattoo on their left shoulder blade. At first, the police thought it was a new gang starting, but it might be something else. The tattoo is three letters, DTB. After consideration, I've surmised that it stands for Dr. Trenton Branch. These young boys are your henchmen, and they were gunned down by an enemy faction. Is that true Dr. Trenton Branch?" The woman spoke with passion and with speed at the same time – getting her points across quickly without allowing Dr. Branch a second to tell his side.

All was quiet then, except for the clicks of the flashing lights. Dr. Branch, completely dumbfounded by her line of questioning, swallowed hard and spoke without his usual authority, "Um . . . I have no idea about anything you are talking about. I umm . . ."

"Well, maybe you will know about what is going on at your multimillion-dollar company, Dr. Trenton Branch," Marcy Pennerman was a conservative capitalist, and she knew about Dr. Branch's socialistic society. She also knew that one day, she would have the opportunity to destroy this man's faulty dreams, so she sat back and waited. Last night, not only did the police call her with the story of the decade, but the numbers came back regarding Dr. Branch's company. She was in hog heaven with a bunch of information she was sure he hadn't yet received. She continued antagonizing the man, speaking into the microphone then shoving it directly under the man's bottom lip.

She harped on his company, "As owner of Satelite Sciences, you should know its affairs. I would hope you know that much, Dr. Branch." She spoke to the man as though he were some type of dumb criminal. She kept on, "Your company has officially entered the one-hundred-million dollar territory, and as a man that promotes socialistic ideas, I understand your bonus cleared a whopping 4.5 million. How do you explain that, Dr. Branch? How do you tell all of your cohorts to give all of their money to the cause while you pocket it all for yourself?" She bombarded Dr. Branch with her own crazy interpretation of the facts, "So you have boys reading books on bomb building and sniping, you're stashing millions in the bank, do you have something you want to explain to your city, Dr. Branch? Are you uniting these kids in a fight against their country? Are you involved in terrorist activity?"

Marcy had him right were she wanted him. She looked at this so-called powerful leader in his night shirt, hair a mess, crust in his eyes, barely awake, and gloated inside. He couldn't put two words together to form a sentence. Being the cause of this great man's downfall would surely get her that new anchor position. She glowered at the man with the microphone under his chin, while she fantasized about her rocketing stardom.

Dr. Branch's brain was about to shut down. He didn't know what to say. He could only attempt to process all of the data that he just received from the witch with the long hair. With lights in his eyes and a cat stealing his tongue, he looked at the camera frozen. He was unable to even close the door and leave the scene; he was caught like a dear in headlights. That's when Mathew showed up out of nowhere and began breaking up the scene, walking up the steps with his partner. Mathew walked right up the steps mashing faces and cameras out of his way. He then grabbed Dr. Branch and shoved him in the house. They walked inside, while Mathew's partner remained outside dispersing the reporter crowd. Both of the men were on duty that morning and happened to pass the street. They stopped after seeing the commotion and all of the flashing lights.

"What was that all about, Dr. Branch?" Mathew asked his leader politely.

"They are making me out to be some type of terrorist leader, Mathew," Dr. Branch quickly said. "Did you hear about the boys being killed? They were ours, but they are saying that they had my initials tattooed on their bodies. They are also saying I got a 4.5-million-dollar bonus from the company," Dr. Branch explained frantically. By this time, his wife finally showed up at the top of the steps with her robe on. "Go back to the bedroom, dear," he demanded.

She complied without question, hearing the anger in his voice.

"Well, if you did get that bonus, you deserve it, Dr. Branch," Mathew said, trying to sooth his leader.

Dr. Branch picked up a small porcelain sculpture of a little black boy on a skateboard and slung it against the wall. It exploded as he yelled, "That isn't the point, Mathew. I can't sit here telling people to give their money like it's no big deal while I am off hording millions for myself. Gimme your phone."

Dr. Branch quickly called Malcolm Banks. Malcolm answered the phone after two rings.

"Why are you calling me so early, Mathew," Malcolm asked, answering his phone.

"This is Dr. Branch."

Malcolm jumped out of bed and stood as though Dr. Branch was in his presence. "Um yes, sir. Is something wrong, Dr. Branch?" he stammered.

"How the hell did you allow me to get four million dollars and not tell me about it?" Dr. Branch yelled.

Malcolm had never heard his boss so angry.

"Only because I didn't know, Dr. Branch. Give me thirty minutes to do some research, and I will call you back, sir," Malcolm said.

"Malcolm . . ."

"Yes, sir?"

"You got fifteen minutes. I'll be sitting here waiting."

"Yes, sir," Malcolm responded.

Dr. Branch pressed the end button on the cellular phone and handed it back to Mathew.

"Wait down here. I will be back in less than five minutes," Dr. Branch said as he stormed up the steps.

Dr. Branch entered his bedroom. His wife sat on the edge of the bed, obviously eavesdropping the entire time.

"What's going on, dear? Why are you so upset?" Christine asked gingerly.

"Christine, that bitch came to my door and got me good," he crudely explained as he put on socks and the rest of his day's attire. He continued explaining, "She caught me in midsleep and attacked me with a bunch of questions against information I wasn't privy to." Dr. Branch punched the wall and said, "And I just stood there looking like I couldn't put one fucking sentence together. She wouldn't let me get a word in anyway." He spoke frantically as he explained more. "Do you know she said that I received one bonus check worth over four million dollars?" Christine's mouth dropped as he continued, "Think about that, dear, I'm out here preaching an idea of giving and I'm hoarding the money for myself. That makes me look like every phony cult leader that ever existed. Babe, something like that could instantly turn people's hearts." He told his wife, "And could quell this entire revolution."

"Dear, you are not yourself. Calm down and take a breather before you go anywhere . . . Trust me, babe," his wife advised.

He wouldn't listen. Dr. Branch had too much negative energy coursing through his veins, and it needed releasing.

"I'm sorry, babe, I don't have time to calm down. All of this needs to be handled one way or the other," he said and walked out of the bedroom. He finished his morning rituals and joined Mathew down the stairs. "Tell Anthum to come to my house now, Mathew," he told his friend. Mathew instantly picked up the phone and called his friend.

"Hello," Anthum answered, sounding completely awake. He was in the middle of his morning stretches, ensuring his body was ever ready.

"Ant," Mathew said, "Dr. Branch needs you at his house now."

"I'm there," Anthum said and hung up.

Exactly seven minutes later Anthum pulled up to the house and leaped up Dr. Branch's outside steps, missing most of them. He saw the police car, and worry entered his heart for a second. Before he could bang on the door, it opened and Mathew welcomed him in.

"Where is Dr. Branch?" Anthum said, and he saw his leader coming around the corner from the kitchen.

Dr. Branch was pacing, waiting on the return call from Malcolm. "I am right here," he answered and began telling Anthum everything that had transpired within the hour. While explaining, Mathew's phone rang, and he handed it right to Dr. Branch.

"Yes. What's the deal?"

"It appears that your company did very well this year, and all of your board members received some pretty hefty bonus checks from the profits." Malcolm then told Dr. Branch something that left him seething, "Mitchell truly is a Wall Street savvy brother. Because he labeled the funds as bonus money . . . completely separate from the typical salary funds, the money bypassed my security checks and went directly into banking accounts unseen by our system. He is a very smart man."

"Too damn smart if you ask me," Dr. Branch said. "Thank you, Malcolm, I have all the information I need." He hung up the phone and said, "Let's go."

He stormed out of the house, with the men following him. Dr. Branch walked to the police cruiser and hopped in the back. The two cops looked at one another and shrugged. They were both on duty, but they would gladly assist their leader with this apparent critical matter. Anthum joined Dr. Branch in the backseat, and the policemen sat in the front.

"Let's go to HQ, Mathew," Dr. Branch said.

"But there is no one there but the actual workforce right now, Dr. Branch," Mathew reminded his leader.

"Exactly," Dr. Branch said.

The police cruiser pulled up to the building and parked directly in front of the doors. The two officers hopped out and opened the doors for their backseat occupants. Then all four men high-stepped their way to the building's main entrance. Dr. Branch pulled the large mechanically assisted doors and briskly walked through the hallway. Though some people were casually performing their duties, they all were working. After catching a glimpse of Dr. Branch, everyone straightened and made their best attempt to look superbusy. Dr. Branch was unconcerned with them. He made his way to his friend's office. Manno Gully's secretary held her finger up trying to get Dr. Branch's attention, but he stormed past her and walked inside the nice-sized room. No one was there.

"Where is everyone?" Dr. Branch demanded.

The secretary quickly answered softly, "Dr. Branch, I was trying to tell you that they are in the main board room. You have to go through that door."

"Thank you, Susie, you are doing a great job," Dr. Branch said absently.

Dr. Branch turned and walked toward the board room with his entourage. The many employees in view mimed some type of work, but they were all watching their boss's boss storm pass them toward the board room. Dr. Branch paid no attention to his underlings and busted into the board room.

There he saw his best friend sitting with the rest of the board members. They were in the middle of laughing until they noticed Dr. Branch standing at the door. Once Dr. Branch saw Mitchell, he made a B-line directly for the man. Dr. Branch heard Manno say some words, but his focus was on Mitchell alone. He walked up to Mitchell's leather chair and kicked the seat on the arm hard. The chair flipped back with Mitchell falling backward with it. The board room sat too stunned to move or say a word. Finally Manno spoke loudly.

"Trent!" Manno said, "What the fuck man?" he exclaimed.

Mitchell stayed where he was on the ground, looking up at a very angry Dr. Branch.

"What the fuck is your problem? What am I doing with four million dollars in my account?" Dr. Branch demanded to know.

"Is that what you are mad about?" Mitchell asked, believing it had to be something else. "How are you upset about that?"

"Do you not get it? Do you not understand what all of this is about?" Dr. Branch asked. Then he told him, "I am building a society of sharing. We cannot behave greedily." He then exclaimed, "I certainly can't be the one hoarding money!"

"Well, I don't understand. We built this company. I made the right moves. We profited over 30 million last year alone. That came from my ideas, from our ideas. The people who make the decisions are compensated for those ideas, Dr. Branch. We deserve to be rewarded. I certainly deserve to be rewarded. It's the American way, man." Mitchell clearly made his point while placing his chair in its rightful situation.

As soon as Mitchell sat back down, Dr. Branch kicked it over again. "You haven't done a thing. They did it." Dr. Branch pointed out the door toward the workers. He then screamed, "Without them, none of this would be possible. It's their hard work that sustains this place. Your wand waving and slight of hand merely inflates our stock prices, Mitchell. Listen, we are not America. I will not see my leaders making hundreds times their employees; that *is* America's way, but it is not ours, my brother," Dr. Branch said to him and the rest of the board members.

He then said, "I said it before and I will say it only once more. You all are the thinkers and the leaders; more responsibility is on your shoulders. So your compensation should be more, I understand and agree with that. But there is a point when the difference becomes disparaging and downright evil. Our company works under the constraints of the American system, but we will not follow their wicked ways. Put those millions back in the pot. You all deserve and will get a damn good bonus, but you share some of that wealth with your workers and put the rest back into the business. You understand me Mitchell . . . CFO?"

Mitchell had fixed his chair again and sat back down. "Yes, sir. It will be done, Dr. Branch."

"Thank you," Dr. Branch said and stormed out of the board room with Manno failing to get his attention.

He was returned home, and for the rest of the day, reporters harassed Dr. Branch. Because he refused to ignore his phone, he ended up on numerous radio shows explaining his case. The day was horrendous and immensely tiring.

Anthum cancelled his self-defense classes for the day and stayed with his leader. He had never seen Dr. Branch so distraught. Anthum finally saw the major conundrum. Though Dr. Branch had constantly told everyone that the power was in the united front, people still placed the load on their leader, causing the man to feel that without him, the entire revolution would crumble. Maybe Dr. Branch was right. Maybe without him, the neighborhood would instantly revert back to the hood. Regardless, Anthum would no longer place that burden on Dr. Branch's shoulders. He would show Dr. Branch that he now understood that the power lie with the people.

Anthum resided in the TV room, relaxing on the couch listening to Dr. Branch rant and rave on the phone upstairs. He watched his leader's attempt to salvage the day by getting through to just one person. It didn't seem to be working. Everything Dr. Branch said was turned around on him. Though Dr. Branch had always seemed to be in total control and three steps ahead of any situation, he couldn't seem to out debate any of his opponents that day. Anthum stopped listening after a while and kept his eyes on the window. He peered out the window and let his mind drift, meditating. He began whispering some mantra, which he repeated under his breath over and over as peace overtook him.

By day's end, Christine had turned off her husband's phone and locked him in the bedroom with her. She would not let him get riled any further. She sat with her husband and watched him as he brewed in his own anger. She hadn't seen him this upset since their son was murdered. She could only do the things she knew he couldn't resist. She began to rub his back with her knowledge of physical therapy and slowly relieved some of his tension.

"Please relax, babe," she told her husband.

"I'm trying, babe. It has been a day and a half," Dr. Branch said to his wife.

Dr. Branch lay on his stomach, and his wife sat on his bottom. She began to give his back a deep tissue massage. The firmer the better. She rubbed and rubbed while speaking softly into his right ear. She worked rapidly and whispered sweet nothings to him as he drifted off into slumber land. She raised herself up and tucked her husband in for the night. She wasn't sleepy, so she went to her study, being sure to stay upstairs with company downstairs.

Dr. Branch found himself at CH HQ. The place was packed to its hilt with vile men of all ages. He was in the hall and could hear the screams and pleads of some while hearing the disobedience of others. The lights were dimmer than usual, and the hall had a funny sway to it, almost as though MC Escher had drawn the blueprints. One of the doors opened slowly, and a very tall man wearing SWAT gear exited in slow motion.

"This way, Dr. Branch," the tall man said in slow motion, making his deep voice even deeper.

Dr. Branch didn't want to follow, but he had no control over his feet. He couldn't help but to follow the tall man. That is when Dr. Branch had a realization. He was dreaming. It was a reoccurring dream. Nothing ever changed; the same thing happened over and over. This dream was a culmination of all the atrocities he'd participated in while at CH HQ. This current replay was of one of his most horrible acts while trying to convert the wicked.

Dr. Branch walked past the doors of each room in slow motion, giving him the ability to see each crack in the wall, every striation in the metal doors, and every little bug scampering about usually too small to see in the dimly lit facility. His subconscious had recorded the scenario in super high definition and would replay it in a speed with a tad more lag than actual life, which allowed his eyes the perfect amount of time to consume every aspect of that night.

The tall man, being Anthum of course, spoke more with that super deep voice, "We did like you said, Dr. Branch. We put the three hard heads in the dungeon chains."

Dr. Branch watched himself speak, "That's good. If they refuse to listen to reason, it's time we free them."

"Yeah, but we have no proof that they ever killed anyone. And I know how strict you are about that," Anthum said, being the voice of reason.

On an ever-vigilante rampage Dr. Branch then said, "Either they join us or they die, Anthum," he said as his mind begged him to quit the insanity.

They walked into the room made like a classroom, and it was full. Each metal seat had a filthy occupant. There was something different about the room. The difference was three boys chained to the side wall.

Before Dr. Branch showed up at the HQ that night, he'd received a call from the team. They informed him that they were working with some really tough guys. Dr. Branch was told that these were some of the last guys needing to come to the light, yet they were the most nonresponsive. It seemed as though they all got power from three knuckle heads. When Dr. Branch heard all of the information he needed about the three roughnecks, he told his team to do something a little different. He told them to chain the guys up in the classroom but not in the metal seats. Dr. Branch described the way he wanted them chained and it matched the dungeon dwellers of old. He wanted the culprits to hang above ground by their wrists, mimicking what has been seen in old comics for ever.

His team did what he requested, and when the dreamy Dr. Branch saw them, he felt like he was back in ancient Rome exacting some type of cruel torture on the wicked. The three tough guys hung by their wrist with their feet dangling a few inches above the ground. Though the lower level was typically cool, all three of the hanging victims sweated profusely. It appeared as though the awkward positioning left them exhausted and overworked. Dr. Branch walked to the one in the middle, which was the head troublemaker and spoke.

"Cleon, why are you fighting this?" Dr. Branch asked the hanging fool.

"I know who the fuck you are," Cleon quickly retorted, he continued with vitriol, "You ain't stopping my cash flow fool. I been hustling for ten years, I ain't never been caught, you think you gonna stop me now? Fuck that." Cleon, a naturally muscular, brown-skinned fellow with a slick bald head spoke with conviction. His voice was raspy, gritty, and held power in its own way, "I don't give a fuck about no safe neighborhood. I don't give a fuck about black power. Fuck all y'all. I know who y'all are, the Black Boogie Men. Oooooh," he said mockingly like a scared child then continued his rant, "Man, I don't give a fuck. Soon as I get out, I'm going back to hustling. Too much money in it, cuzz."

With the slow motion dream state occurring while Cleon spoke, Dr. Branch could see every harsh facial expression clearly. He could see the white foam forming on the corners of Cleon's mouth, and he could certainly see the spit cloud that erupted after every harsh consonant was pronounced (especially his *P's* and *T's*). Dr. Branch then noticed every male in the classroom and could sense them getting energy from the strong, boisterous drug dealer. He looked at the young man and figured in another life, he probably was a great leader.

"Cleon, I am not going to say this more than once. Either you are with us or against us," Dr. Branch said ("No," his mind shouted, "Don't do it").

Dr. Branch got close enough to make great eye contact, and Cleon let Dr. Branch have it.

"You think I don't know what y'all doing. Man, I ain't no chump, you caint break me, might as well just let me out now. Fuck all y'all," Cleon said, and in a fit of emotion, blew a big wad of spit onto Dr. Branch's face. It landed right on the corner of his mouth. Again, the slow motion effect caused the scene to look even grosser than it did when first happening in real life. The crowd inside the room roared with cheers and laughter until each of the detained idiots joined together chanting Cleon's name.

Dr. Branch knew what had to be done. Cut off the head, and the body will flounder. He wiped his face of the spit hanging from his own mouth and yelled at Anthum.

"Go to room two and bring me *The Emergency*," Dr. Branch ordered.

Anthum eyes widened beneath his ski mask, and he darted out the door leaving Dr. Branch alone in a room full of rough vagabonds. They all continued to chant until Dr. Branch spoke over them all.

("Please don't do this," his mind yelled.) "You all think this man is cool," Dr. Branch said. "You all want to follow him. That's fine. I am trying to present you guys with an option, but if you think this is a joke, if you want to follow this man, I will show you were he is going before you make your decisions final."

Right as Dr. Branch finished that statement, Anthum walked in with a giant object. It was an ax, but not just any ax. It was huge – the type used by lumberjacks before chainsaws replaced the old-fashioned lumbering tools. Its handle was three feet long, which allowed a long arc when swung correctly. The blade was at least a foot-and-a-half wide, and its edge glimmered, showing its insane sharpness. The entire ax was stainless silver and glistened in Dr. Branch's hand once Anthum handed it over.

"What the hell you gonna do with that?" Cleon mocked, "You gonna cut my leg off like you hard are something. I know you . . . you a nerd. You ain't gangsta." Cleon continued, antagonizing the man with the giant ax, "You might as well use that muthafucka to cut these damn chains and let me out this bitch. 'Cause when I do get down I'm gonna kick . . . Ahhhhhhh." Cleon's rant was interrupted by searing pain.

In the midst of Cleon's tantrum, Dr. Branch's brain shut down, and he swung the ax like it was a baseball bat right at Cleon's side. The blade struck home with a gushing sound that would be unpleasant to any man's ear. The forceful swing caused the blade to slice right through the skin and flesh. Somehow, the arc caused the path of the blade to go between his lower floating ribs and right above his hip. This allowed the blade to basically travel unimpeded to his spinal cord. The ax slid through his flesh, organs, and intestines until it lodged itself within Cleon's spine. What came next was a bloodcurdling scream, unlike any the captive audience had ever heard. They watched while the tough guy's eyes almost bulged out of their sockets as he screamed in a pitch that should have been unattainable for a man. The bulk of the ax's blade resided within Cleon's nerve bundle, so Dr. Branch had to wiggle the blade in order to free it from the body's clutches. Each wiggle of the ax sent packages of pain to Cleon's head that sent his brain into overload, and shock was imminent.

"Oh no you don't, I want you to feel all of this, tough guy," Dr. Branch said as he pulled the ax free. With his superslow, matrix-style motion, he could see the bone fragments fly from the gaping wound as the ax was pulled free, along with a spray of thick blood. The crimson fluid dripped from the ax as well as poured down Cleon's legs like thick red syrup. The boy finally started to plea. Not knowing that he was already dead, he pleaded with what little faculties remained.

"Pppplease," Cleon stuttered as though he was instantly placed under ice water. "Dddddon't kkkkkkill mmmmmeeeeee," he pushed out with blood trickling down his lips.

"Too late," Dr. Branch said coldly.

Dr. Branch swung the ax again as hard as he could, and it finished the job. It sliced right through Cleon's spinal cord and the rest of his flesh. The lower half dropped to the ground followed by a bucket load of intestines. The innards splashed to the floor in a messy heap. Cleon's head looked down at his missing waist then at Dr. Branch. He looked down at his missing section then at Dr. Branch again. He looked down at his missing section once more, and his head stayed there that time.

The crowd all instantly quieted and pleaded for their lives. The other two hanging troublemakers instantly changed their tune as well. The rest of the prisoners complied to team CH, and when the time came, they learned what was provided on the movie. That large group turned out to be a set of the best converts Dr. Branch and his team touched.

All of that happened in real life, but in his dream, things took a scary turn for the worse. Cleon did look up one more time. And with incredible strength, he released his arms from his shackles. His upper body then dropped into the disgusting pool of bloody organs lying beneath him. Dr. Branch looked around for Anthum, but he was alone. The door was locked, and Cleon's undead top half was sliding his way toward Dr. Branch's direction. Because Dr. Branch was unable to run, Cleon's long bloody fingers gripped his pant leg and drug him to the floor. Dr. Branch was face to face with the pile of flesh covering the ground. Just as Cleon's zombie attempted to smother Dr. Branch in intestines, Dr. Branch woke up.

His heart beat hard and fast, and he was drenched in sweat. It was five in the morning, and that dream woke him up completely. He turned his head over and saw his wife sleeping sound. He wished his mind was as clear as hers. She slept easily and without disturbance. His sleep was hard and wrought with turmoil. He stayed in bed, not wanting to get out. His body told him to stay in, while his mind said something totally different. What, he didn't know. He was exhausted, and his soul carried a heavy load that morning. He felt really bogged down, tired, and weary. His body didn't feel bad, but his insides dragged as though he hadn't slept in years. He also sensed something really strange, he couldn't put his finger on it, but his spirit was warning him that morning. It was like his spider sense was tingling and something was telling him that today just wasn't going to be a good day.

Before he knew it, he hummed a song to himself quietly, not wanting to wake his wife beside him. At first he couldn't remember the words; he could only recall the tune. Even without the words, the song was persistent, and it continued to ring inside of Dr. Branch's head. Not wanting to wake his wife, he hummed the melody over and over deep in his throat. He hummed the song and dozed off for a few minutes here and there, really not noticing his sleep. Eventually, his wife finally got out of bed, and he got up with her.

"Hey babe, good morning to you," Christine yawned to her husband.

"Good morning, sweetheart," Dr. Branch replied.

"How did you sleep?", she asked, it was one of her typical morning questions.

"I slept just fine," he said not wanting to divulge the truth.

"That's good. You got big plans today, sweetie?" she inquired.

"Um . . . naw, I was going to go handle some business, but something is telling me to stay my ass at home, and that's what I am going to do," Dr. Branch told his wife.

"Well, that sounds smart to me. What's wrong, babe? Something you want to talk about?" she asked, always ready to be a support for her busy husband.

"Naw, I just don't feel right today." Dr. Branch tried to explain the best he could. "And like I said, something is telling me to stay my tail in this house and relax today. That is what I think I am going to do," he told his wife.

"Well, good for you, a spontaneous day of rest," she said. "When was the last time you did that? I sure can't remember. Enjoy it, babe."

He tried, he couldn't. The only thing he could do was get out his electronic keyboard and release the song that had played in his head over and over. He pressed away on the keyboard as he sang the song, "Oh when I come . . . to the end of my journey . . . weary of life . . . the battle is won . . . carry my staff . . . the cross of redemption . . . we'll understand it . . . better by and by . . ."

As he sang, the rest of the song slowly took form, and he was able to put all of the lyrics together. He didn't know why, but he had to continue playing the keyboard and singing that song. He dinked away on the electric piano until his fingers hurt, until his wife drug him away for lunch, and until his eyes caused him to take a nap right there on the couch with the keyboard stationed in front of him. The song reverberated in his head so loudly that he would get a migraine if he didn't let it escape. So he did. He sang the song over and over, not paying attention to his wife when she expressed her lack of interest in hearing the song played again. He sang it while the TV played and while his phone rang. He could focus on nothing else but the song.

Late that night, while Dr. Branch stepped away from the keyboard, his wife approached him with the house phone in her hands.

"You got a call, babe. I think it's important," Christine told her husband.

"Who's calling me on the house phone, babe?" Dr. Branch asked then said, "I never give the house number out."

"Um I think that's why this is an important call. This is the FBI agent." she informed her husband, "He told me he'd been calling your cellular phone all day, but you didn't answer so he called our house. I think you know it would be pretty easy for him to get our number, dear." She smiled and gave him the cordless phone.

"Hello," Dr. Branch started.

"Dr. Branch."

"Yes," Dr. Branch answered.

"This is Agent Loggins, and I have some extremely valuable items to give you," he said bypassing the small talk, "I can't say much over the phone, but I will say I have some very important information for you. You have to meet me now," the agent said.

"Why now, and what is this information, Agent Loggins?" Dr. Branch asked.

"Because you need it now, and the information is in regards to the recent string of murders happening in your safety zone." The FBI agent spoke quickly, "I have proof that the police department is committing the acts in an attempt to encourage the city to keep them on the payroll. They are trying to incite violence in your city once more, Dr. Branch. And it isn't right. So don't worry about how I got the information or the proof, just know that it is irrefutable. I can't come out with it, but you can."

"Yeah, OK Agent Loggins, I understand. Just tell me where to meet you," Dr. Branch said.

"Come to the hotdog stand down the street from the dancing school," the agent instructed.

"I'm on my way," Dr. Branch told the agent.

"What's going on?" Christine asked after she heard her husband hang up the phone.

"Babe, we are getting set up by the police." The spring returned to Dr. Branch's step, and his energy was back. He told her, "Agent Loggins has something for me, I am going to step out to meet him real quick, and I will be right back."

"But I thought you said you weren't going anywhere today, babe," She said then asked, "Why can't you do it tomorrow?"

"This is too important to wait until tomorrow, Christine. I will run there and be right back," he said.

"Are you calling Anthum or Mathew to go with you?" she asked, sounding concerned.

"Not necessary, babe, it's just around the corner," he comforted his wife, "I am driving there and driving back, I won't even get out of the car . . . OK, dear?" He said, hopefully soothing his wife's sudden fears.

To handle his own fears, Dr. Branch pocketed his .38 caliber pistol without his wife's knowledge and exited the house. Before he left, he gave his wife a hearty kiss and walked down the steps. The street appeared darker than normal and eerily quiet. Dr. Branch slowly made his way down the steps of his front porch and walked to his car, which he hadn't driven in a few days. His paranoia was on high alert, and he looked around the area while taking each step toward his vehicle. He walked around the back to the drivers side door and was about to open it, when he saw two headlights slowly heading his way.

His senses screamed, and his internal alarms went off. He acted as though he was entering his car until the van pulled on the side of him. Before the passenger could utter a word, Dr. Branch had already pulled out his pistol, and it was pointed at the person's nose.

Once Dr. Branch caught the passenger's face, he relaxed and apologized.

"I am so sorry, Artist." Dr. Branch said, "My mind is on high alert for some reason.

The driver yelled over Artist, "Are you OK, Dr. Branch? You don't look like yourself, hon," Artist's wife said to the man.

"Yeah, Dr. Branch, you OK? That don't seem like something you'd do. And where are your bodyguards?" Artist inquired with concern.

"I am fine, and I am sorry again for that. I am going to take care of something, and I am bringing these weary bones back home because I am seriously under the weather," he explained.

"Well, you make sure you take care of yourself, Dr. Branch. We need you to be around for a long, long time," the wife said, and she and Artist laughed together as they drove away.

Dr. Branch just grabbed his heart and told himself to calm down.

"You almost shot a couple of members of your team. Relax yourself," he said aloud.

He was about to open his car door, when he saw more headlights coming down his side of the street. Though his system was on high alert and told him to beware, he didn't take any heed. He reached for his door handle and pulled as someone called his name. Dr. Branch then made a complete 180-degree turn toward the vehicle's passenger. He was about to respond when his eye quickly registered two large barrels directed at his chest. He smiled to himself as a bright light flashed from both barrels simultaneously.

The shotgun blast threw Dr. Branch through his window, back first. He ended up lying face up, looking at the roof of his car, with his legs dangling outside of the window. Broken glass was everywhere, and he smelled gunpowder. Dr. Branch's brain sent signals to his appendages, but nothing responded. He wanted to turn his head, he wanted to rise up, but nothing worked.

After a minute, he could hear people talking as they approached the car. He heard the passenger side door of his car open, followed by an brain splitting scream. He recognized it instantly as his wife. She begged him not to die and screamed for someone to call an ambulance. He could hear his wife pleading to God, saying, "No, not again, dear Lord, please not again." He continued focusing on his wife, unable to respond to anything she said or did. As he continued listening to his wife's frantic pleads, he noticed that her voice slowly faded as it was smoothly replaced by the song he had sung all day . . . Oh when I come, to the end of my journey . . . Weary of life, the battle is won . . . Carry my staff, the cross of redemption . . . We'll understand it, together by and by. As the song faded from his mind, so did the lights.

Edwards Brothers, Inc.
Thorofare, NJ USA
October 13, 2011